Bath
Thoughts
from Berkeley

Em Randolph

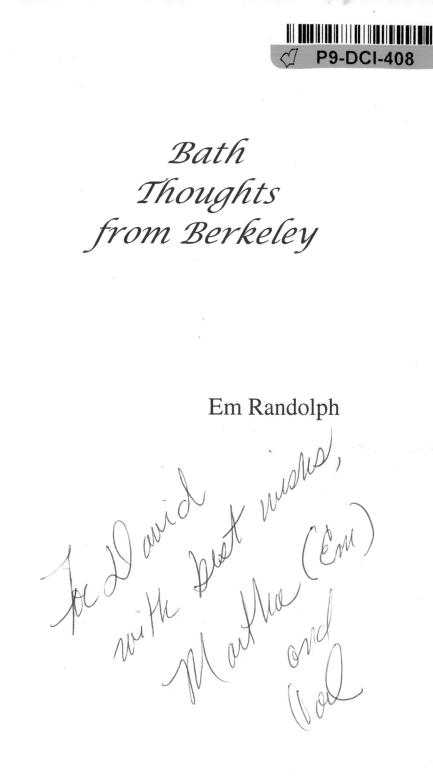

For David
with best wishes,
Martha (Em)
and
Val

Dedication

To family and friends, far and near,
whose spirits enliven this adventure

Acknowledgments

Heartfelt thanks to the many friends who devoted time
and energy to this tale. Special thanks to Janet
Batchelder whose patience and amazing eagle eye
turned dreary tasks into pleasing adventures. The love
and support of Nick Pfeiffer and Carl Austin were
ever-present and cherished. Special gratitude to
Megan Clark Turner, whose lyrical pen guided us so
magically in developing Catilin's voice.

PROLOGUE

The bath bubbles rose magically and invited
Mattie to lower her chubby, young body into the warm
water. She hurried, understanding that the bubbles would
soon disappear like the snowflakes she'd seen once in the
foothills of the Sierra. Her toes investigated the nature of
bubbles as unruly thoughts surfaced, burst, and reformed
in her mind, insisting on her attention.

Mattie's Bath

Father loves his tenors, calls them "exuberant." I
like that word. I'm going to use it when I grow
up. . . . I hope I get to grow up and listen to the
tenors. It's nice the way they make the Victrola
shake, nice how Father stacks his records six deep
so he'll have plenty of time to doze off. . . . He
was going to turn off the radio news and stack up
his records. That would have been so much
better . . . just music . . . no radio stories. . . .
Where is Pearl Harbor, anyway? . . . Mother said
to hush-up, she'd tell me later. I still don't know.
I think I need to know where it is . . . how close
to our house. . . . She gasped so loud, and Peter
stiffened, white stiff and scared, like when he and
Father cornered that prowler out at the barn.
Father called the prowler an "Oakie.". . . I don't
know if prowlers and Oakies and invaders are the
same. Peter says they're different. I don't know if
he's right. He says the Japanese can't invade our
house because we have a hundred acres of prime
soil, and it's fenced. He says we have a lot of
guns. Father uses them to hunt ducks and
pheasants, but he took a gun to look for the
prowler. Does Father have to shoot invaders?

1

Can't he just scare them away, like the prowler? . . . Father shouted so hard at Mother . . . "Calm down!" . . . because there's a new baby in her stomach. And pains. Maybe those were her pains in my stomach. . . . How does she do that, make everyone share her pains? . . . Maybe Mother's new baby won't have anything to eat or any place to grow up if the Japanese come. Maybe the new baby can eat ducks and pheasants. Maybe Gabriel Heater and President Roosevelt made a mistake on the radio. Maybe the new baby will be a sister. . . . We can read stories together, better stories than the radio tells.

———

"You remember how stories begin, don't you, Mattie?" Josie asked as she tucked the hairbrush into the folds of her nightgown.

"Of course I remember, Josie. Now hold still." Mattie struggled with the rubber bands that held Josie's pigtails and finally reached for the hairbrush where strands of Mattie's straight brown hair and Josie's towhead curls were matted into the history of their evening ritual. Mattie brushed quickly, removing tiny, crushed pieces of dry alfalfa from her sister's hair as she worked toward a mass of tangles at the tender neckline.

"I don't know how you get so many tanglewitches in one day, Josie. Now hold still, or I'll pull."

"You are pulling, Mattie. You always pull."

When Josie had as much untangling as she could tolerate, she wiped her tears on the sleeve of her nightie and tore out of the steamy bathroom. "And I want you to open the window so I can smell the horses," she demanded from the safety of the hallway.

"I always open the window. What do you mean about smelling the horses? Come back here a minute and tell me."

Josie returned only as far as the bathroom doorway. "I like their breath. If you open the window, I can smell their breath, and then I get good night pictures."

"Night pictures are called 'dreams,' Josie. . . . Here, hold the brush. Two more pin curls, and then we're ready."

"Do you have night pictures, too, Mattie?"

"Well, yes . . . some dreams . . . probably not as good as yours. I imagine more horse breath would help."

Mattie poked the final bobby pin into a wisp of her hair. She grasped Josie by the shoulders and duck-walked her into their shared bedroom where they would settle into a cat-crowded, double bed for what had become their necessary link to each other and their imagined future. She pushed up the wood-framed window, listening for the thud of the heavy counterweight to assure her the task was done properly. The open window that delivered the odor of horses to her sister carried little more than worry to Mattie. She wasn't sure her plan would work. If the war brought invaders to her valley home, could she lower Josie to the ground through this window, jump to the ground herself, and then slide with Josie under the barbed-wire fence? Could they do it in time? Josie was already good at avoiding the sharp barbs, as Mattie had taught her. If they got past the barbs, Mattie imagined, they would catch their breath behind the big shattuck tree until they were ready to make a run across the pasture to the corn field, a superior hiding place. A searching, foreign eye would encounter only broad, scratchy leaves and the weeds beneath them. From the far side of the corn field, it was an easy sprint to the old oak tree where Mattie had many times practiced

3

boosting her sister to the lower branches. Mattie knew Peter also had an escape plan, but he would seldom talk about it, and Mattie wondered if the siblings might all three meet in the majestic, old tree. Peter agreed with Grandpa R that the war would soon be over, but it remained unsettling to Mattie that wars had numbers. When WWII war was over, would there be more numbers, more wars?

Mattie brushed away her worries as she nudged a calico cat off her pillow and noted that Josie's side of the bed had more room in it for animal orphans than her side. She smiled as she remembered the time Josie invited their sixty-pound collie to join them, suggesting he could sleep at the foot on the bed so the cats wouldn't be nervous.

"What story shall we have tonight?"

"Whatever you like, Mattie, as long as you tell it right."

Josie's formula for bedtime stories was precise, and if the author failed to meet her requirements, Mattie would create a suitable modification. Josie specified "no bushes," and Mattie came to understand that lengthy descriptions of the landscape were not welcome. "Forest" or "beach" or "meadow" were sufficient to stir her sister's vision of where a princess might live, where the dragons and ogres could be found. "No clothes" was soon added to Josie's list; she wanted Mattie to understand that she was quite capable of creating suitable gowns, gem-encrusted sandals, and silky satin capes for her favorite characters.

Josie settled in amid her menagerie, smoothing her flannel nightie and pulling the cotton quilt up to her chin. "I'm ready now, Mattie. Can we begin?"

"Once upon a time there was a storyteller who wrote this tale just for you, Josie."

Part I --Fertile Soil

CHAPTER 1

> *It ain't so much the boredom*
> *But the fire in her soul*
> Arlo Guthrie
> "All This Stuff Takes Time"

The sisters were valley girls — not the San Fernando Valley, they were quick to say, but California's rich Sacramento Valley where, they believed, any seed that found its way into the soil would thrive, some plants growing more lazily than others, but each finding its way into the golden sunlight. The bittersweet aromas rising from the valley floor penetrated their psyches and lingered in the mist of their memories so that no amount of their mother's *Chanel No. 5* could obscure their rural beginnings.

Josie was born into the family during the troubled times of the second world war, but Mattie imagined that once the war was over, life would return to normal. "Normal" was little pockets of memory, not in the least the norm, but they formed a pattern in her thoughts, and she liked to reweave the threads that made up her childhood, snaring joyful moments and proclaiming them reality.

A good omen for Mattie was the birth of her little brother on the Fourth of July, only a month after D-Day — June 6, 1944. He was easy and agreeable, and she knew his arrival signaled good times. He was called "Beau," a name that meant beautiful brother to Mattie, but with no French ancestry Father's Southern heritage prevailed, and the name became Bo. Because the war was ending, Bo would never have to be a soldier, nor would Peter.

Mattie hoped the war-counting was over, and she prayed that she and her siblings would soon be able to play Beckons Wanted, Grey Willie, Annie Annie Over, and Kick-the-Can on long summer nights without the shadows of war darkening their pleasures. She felt uneasy and then betrayed when Father and Grandpa R soon began to bring new words to the dinner table. Mattie once tasted an olive right off the tree, uncured and too bitter for her mouth to hold. The same bitterness spewed from Grandpa R's mouth when he spoke of "McCarthyism." Most any threat to his country, he insisted, came from inside now -- from Congress and from the witch-hunters who were able to find Communist infiltrators lurking behind every curtain from the State Department to the Hollywood stage. When her father introduced "thermonuclear war" and "cold war" into the dinnertime dialogue, Mattie wondered if "peace" was a real word.

The men were still enjoying oatmeal and oratory when Mattie left home to begin college at UC Berkeley, tucking into her suitcase a small Mason jar of soil from her father's garden. Abandoned by her sister, Josie raced through her adolescence, soothing bumps and bruises with dreams of a brighter story in the days to come.

Mattie scrutinized her tiny Berkeley apartment and determined that somehow there would be room for her little sister; they could share a lumpy double bed again and adventure together in Berkeley where Peter was already setting a swift pace, establishing milestones of success. For Mattie, success was more elusive. She had hoped to find certainties at college – facts more reliable than the slippery information acquired in adolescence, perhaps even a sense of purpose. But it was neither certainty nor purpose that captivated her; her passion was for discovery itself. She could imagine herself engaged forever in some meaningful research project, spending the rest of her life on her beloved campus, energized each day by another colorful page to turn.

A friend in the English Department referred to journalists as the stepchildren of the intelligentsia, but Mattie was happy in the Journalism Department and eager to support her Berkeley addiction as long as possible. The sisters would settle in and find a way to manage together as they had before – their father's black moods, Peter's "No Visitors" sign on his bedroom door, the haze surrounding their mother's presence, even the scoldings they got from hired hands who arrived at harvest time and had no patience for the help the sisters would give them on the hay wagons. The hay wagons and harvest time were among Mattie's fondest memories. She stacked the odor of new-mown hay along with the musty-sweet scent of the campus libraries into her cache of good moments, much as her Grandmother R must have added embroidered linens to her hope chest with the notion that life would soon be happening.

"I hope you've thrown away the crayons," Josie had said when she called to tell her sister she was running away.

"What crayons? Why throw them away?"

"Don't you remember the time you sneaked into Peter's room, stole a black crayon from his treasure chest, and then drew a line down the center of our bed sheet? You said, 'This side is mine. The other half is for you, your dogs, your cats, your horse – whatever you want. But don't even think of crossing over the line, not one little toe over the line!'"

Josie's sun sign was Gemini, and Mattie was certain that at least two Josies had shared her bed.

"Josie, please don't bring any animals. They're not allowed here. I'm sorry."

"Don't worry, Mattie. I'll just bring some clothes, some lipstick and stuff. Maybe some new bubble bath if I can go shopping."

"How's Mom taking this?"

"It doesn't matter, Mattie. She's horrid, and she hates me. I'll explain later."

"Have you talked to Father?"

"Nope. He and Marge are on a cruise or something. Sort of a delayed honeymoon, I guess. But I think he'll understand. He couldn't live with Mother, either."

"Josie, I really don't want to talk about the divorce right now. Not ever. I'm going to run now and make some room for you. Just get here."

Mattie spent the afternoon cramming old clothes into boxes and sorting through treasures, discarding one, saving another with little regard for why one crumpled party invitation had more value than the next. She was tired and anxious but managed to laugh aloud when she found Black Mariah on the closet floor — Black Mariah, queen of girdles, twenty hooks and eyes, eight bone stays, breast to thigh, garter straps almost to the knees. She giggled as she placed the wicked witch into the dresser drawer she had just cleaned for Josie.

"Enough," she scolded herself. "I've got to study before Josie gets here, got to finish my paper. Nice if I could write my master's thesis before she arrives. Now there's a challenge. Stuff a year's work into an afternoon."

Mattie was a good student, quick and reliable, but reluctant to learn that some of her notions of a good life collided harshly with events beyond campus. She hadn't gone to San Francisco to protest a House Un-American Activities Committee hearing, but when student protesters were hosed down the steps by riot police, Mattie could see herself being washed out of childhood, sliding out of the silent generation. Her certainty that her age of innocence was over had come one autumn day when her still-married parents visited the campus, not for a football game or alumni event, but for a meeting with Peter and her — a breakfast meeting at Berkeley's tiredly elegant Claremont Hotel, surreal in Mattie's mind, but perfect for her mother who would appreciate the double rows of cold silver at every fine plate and the crystal stemware that crowded the hard-starched table linens. A table to make a dishwasher cry, Mattie remembered.

She remembered, too, how attentive her father had been to the siblings' breakfast wishes, but it wasn't until the eggs Benedict were served that Mattie and Peter discovered what the breakfast was about. After a twenty-two-year experiment with "the good life" in the Sacramento Valley, Will and Nora Randall planned to divorce. Nora would move to Sunnyvale and go back into teaching. Will had purchased an interest in a small, daily newspaper and would now pick up a career that had been set aside during the Depression years when Grandpa R issued a "come home" call. The ranch would be sold. Josie and Bo would be ferried back and forth between parents. Grandpa R had already moved into a little house on the edge of town where he had his own garden. A "splendid" plan, overall, the parents said.

How tidy, Mattie thought. *Whose reality is this? Where are the parents who stayed up half the night to nurse an orphaned calf, gave festive dinner parties, and made holidays so magical . . . the ones who were supposed to see me through college, supposed to tell happy family stories to future generations? Were those parents stolen away by the ever-so-proper waiter, replaced along with the crystal by these cardboard cutouts who stored their emotions beneath the linens, starched and folded?*

9

"Will Bo be coming to Berkeley?" Peter offered to the silent table.

"And perhaps Josie, as well, if . . ." Will began to explain.

"We have learned to accept Josie's vicissitudes," Nora interrupted, "and she is learning to control her whimsical nature. She will live with me; Bo with your father."

Mattie's mind was stuck for a moment in questions about why a whimsical nature needed to be controlled. "Grotesque," she finally whispered as she nudged her thoughts away from the hateful breakfast table to begin a random search for a better place. She saw herself seated in the large auditorium of UC Berkeley's Wheeler Hall where a tall, grey-haired professor would have her grasp some of the incongruities of her nation's history. The year was 1898, February. The American battleship *Maine* had exploded in Havana Harbor, and the Spanish-American War would soon commence. Secretary of State John Hay would call it "a splendid little war." Mattie took the phrase apart to try to understand it. Yes, it was a war. What makes a war big or little? How does a war, large or small, become splendid? Was it Teddy Roosevelt charging up San Juan Hill with the Rough Riders? Was that splendid? Was it the length of the war — only four months? Was that splendid? Was it the number of casualties? Could there ever be something splendid about casualties, few or numerous?

The war spilled over into Manila Bay as Mattie watched from the hotel dining room. She heard Admiral Dewey call out "You may fire when you are ready, Gridley," but the thick, red tomato juice from her glass bled onto the white linens carrying her back to the breakfast table and the news her parents had delivered.

"Splendid," Mattie said. "I thought war was obsolete. Not yours, I guess. I'm not going to be a casualty of this war."

As Will began to speak soothing words to his eldest daughter, Mattie returned each piece of her silverware to its original position, folded her napkin into a tight square, and stood to leave the table, the dining room, the hotel, and the childhood she wondered if she ever really had. Peter stayed at the breakfast table a little longer, pushing eggs around his plate and trying to be fair, understanding, adult, trying not to let his parents down, and trying hard not to cry.

———

Josie's war with her mother had started in the fall of 1960, her last year in high school. Nora was convinced that her offspring would pull through the turmoil of divorce, no doubt be better off for it. Josie's hostility was natural, she thought, rather like a normal childhood phase, growing pains. And so the gap between Nora and Josie grew spacious and quiet. Their war was not a cold war, or a hot one. It was silent. Josie simply closed her ears and eyes and let images of other women — mothers, helpers, friends — replace the elusive presence that was her real mother. One of Josie's other women was Marilyn Monroe, the beautiful actress whose daring and unabashed ripeness made her a timely model. Another was an unlikely visitor who came into Josie's mind uninvited and unexpected. In her last high school semester, Josie had written a brief and careless report on Rosa Parks, a simple paper to meet the requirements of her U.S. history teacher. Josie didn't know why she had chosen a black woman from Montgomery, Alabama as the subject of her paper, nor did she now note any serious contradictions in the Marilyn-Rosa team who shared their peculiar surrogate mother roles in her imagination. Rosa

Parks sat herself down in Josie's mind, just as she had sat down in that Montgomery bus. Rosa heard the driver say, "Niggers to the back," but she just sat, forty-three years old, tired, full of dignity and determination. She was arrested and lost her job, but she became a mother to the civil rights movement. And now she sat in Josie's young mind, waiting.

Josie wished she knew what Rosa was waiting for; she wished that she, like Rosa, had a young pastor to champion her cause, a young Martin Luther King, Jr. who would enter her life with his sorrowful eyes, bless her, and set her free. Free for what? she often wondered. Josie had mastered neither the Marilyn walk nor the Rosa-inspired sit-in against her mother when she graduated from high school and moved in with Mattie.

"Why is Black Mariah in my dresser drawer, Mattie?" Josie's attempt to squeeze her ample wardrobe into Mattie's crowded closet was a challenge, and she had already tossed a number of items into a heap in the corner of the bedroom — by silent agreement between the sisters, a neutral territory.

"I'm giving her to you, Josie. All yours. You'll have to wear her for job interviews."

"Black Maria is a body cage. Why do I have to wear her?" Josie plucked the black satin garment from the drawer and threw it onto the discard heap. "Here, Mattie, I brought you some bubble bath."

"Great. Thanks, Josie. Great about the bubble bath, sorry about Black Mariah. I don't know why we have to wear a girdle to have a job interview. You certainly don't need one to take restaurant orders, but maybe the customers need to know your body is caged. Maybe that's it. We have to tell the world that our bodies are caged so no one will get nervous."

"Nervous about what?"

"I'm not sure, Josie, but here's an idea. The old witch fits very nicely in the glove compartment of the Ford, if you scrunch her up a little. So, get an interview, get a job, and stuff her in the glovebox."

"Why don't we shred her and toss her in the trash can?"

"Better yet, let's wrap her up in antique lace and hide her in the back of the closet until . . . . Let's see . . . until . . . I know . . . the first daughter born to one of us gets Black Mariah."

"That's fine, Mattie, as long as you have the first daughter."

Mattie retrieved Black Mariah from the discard heap and stuffed her into the back of the bathroom linen closet while Josie ran a hot bath. The bubble bath she had purchased for her sister was now a shared belonging, and Josie added the creamy liquid to her bath water – enough, she hoped, to soothe the fatigue in her spirit.

Josie's Bath

This is a nice tub . . . deep and shiny. . . . Mattie's so orderly. I wonder if I have to be orderly . . . probably do, in this tiny apartment . . . hardly any place to stand. . . . I need a place to stand. . . . Well, it's better than Sunnyvale . . . better to share a room with Mattie than live in that stupid, French Provincial mother-decorated box. . . . Mother is not my mother! She hates me! The fairies brought me just like Mattie used to say. . . . I hated that room; there was no me in it. . . . I don't remember if I ever had a real room. I was supposed to have one at the ranch, but after Bo came, my room kind of got lost. . . . Peter had one, with windows on three sides, sunlight coming in, a big room, looking out on the fields, a really good room where sometimes he would let me listen to the radio with him. . . . "The Lone Ranger"

13

and "Green Hornet". . . . I was the only one he ever let in his room. . . . She would make it beautiful for me, she said, so I wouldn't hate coming to live with her, but she didn't ask what I wanted. It was her room, not mine. Why give me the master bedroom with the shower? Parents are supposed to have that room, two parents, not just one. . . . Showers always have spiders in them. . . . I hate spiders and showers! . . . Mother is a spider, a black widow. . . . Mattie said the old green car was full of black widows. . . . I always remember it as the old green car, but I guess it had to be new sometime. It just sat under the big oak tree and got full of spiders after the war. . . . I'd climb up on the running board and peek in, but not get in, too scared with all the black widows. . . . I squashed the egg of a black widow spider once. . . . My egg is squashed, too, squashed and down the drain with the blood. . . Kurt was all I had. . . . He wasn't really a cousin, Black Widow just said he was so he could stay with us . . . and then the black-widow mother took him. . . . He couldn't help it. She said she would have him arrested. Statutory rape? There was no rape between Kurt and me. She raped us both, inviting Kurt to live with us all winter after he finished pouring the patio, then leaving us alone all day. . . . "You two be good, don't do anything wrong. I know you won't". . . left us in our beds, Kurt in the spare room, me in that stupid room with the shower. . . . I showered the blood down the drain . . . gone just like Kurt. . . . I'll never shower again, I will have baths so I won't go down the drain with the blood. . . . Maybe I wasn't pregnant, but the doctor said so. . . . Black Widow sent Kurt away, and my insides split open. . . . The egg couldn't live there anymore.

Mattie's Bath

How nice of Josie to bring bubble bath. Maybe I can wash off some worries, soak out some of these aches. . . . So many boxes, so many clothes. . . . We can trade clothes this summer . . . nice to have such an elegant wardrobe. . . . What an ordeal moving is. It didn't help having Mother call every half hour, trying to explain away Josie's flight from the nest — a nasty nest, Mom, not the lovely ranch house, but a shoe-box house in Sunnyvale — Anywhere USA. . . . I wish you were still in the kitchen on the ranch, canning apricots and peaches. If you were canning apricots and peaches, you would still be Father's wife. . . . One thing I want you to know, Mom. I can't be Josie's mother. I'm her sister. You never really got that straight, did you? I was only seven when you assigned Josie to me: "Look after your sister!" you'd say, as you closed the door and headed down the walk. Of course I looked after her, but a seven-year-old is not a mother. You are the mother! Why is that so hard? Why always so irritable? . . . Why were you so irritable about Father's victory garden? It was one of his good places during the war . . . out there after dinner to tend the tomatoes, pick some giant zucchini, water here and there. Even Grandpa R didn't intrude; he knew the victory garden was a good place for Father. . . . He'd finally come in, arms full of tasty garden things, but you would sigh and slump . . . one more chore. . . . I had chores with Father; I helped him in the victory garden, but then you'd get irritable with me, too. I wasn't a conspirator; I was a kid playing in the garden with Father. . . . I asked you one evening if victory and peace were the same thing, and you got irritable. How hard is it to answer a child? How hard is it to be a mother?

―――――

15

Josie's move to Berkeley coincided with Mattie's move into the volunteer ranks of a close presidential campaign with John Kennedy and Richard Nixon standing toe-to-toe at the door to the White House. The black-and-white television that bombarded the sisters' little apartment told them the nation was astir with curiosity about JFK. What about his Catholicism? Was he old enough to be president? Was dirty money the basis of his wealth, and would old Joe Kennedy orchestrate the administration as he was choreographing the election? Could JFK rewrite the Vietnam scenario? Was he really a strong civil rights champion? Could he win? Mattie worried little about the questions surrounding JFK, and she had no idea that Richard Nixon would be her *bête noire* for years to come, but she knew that Nixon's presence in the White House as Eisenhower's vice president was a personal affront. She could not forgive General Eisenhower for dragging Tricky Dick into the nation's capitol for eight long years, and she must see him evicted. Mattie had fallen in love with Adlai Stevenson in the previous national election and had eagerly volunteered to work in his California campaign. She went to class, studied, and volunteered to wear out her shoes in the ill-fated effort to put the witty, avuncular man in the White House. Now four years later, it was not adoration for the Democratic candidate that pushed her to volunteer again; it was simply necessary. Grandpa R would insist. Although he was not presiding at her Berkeley dinner table, Mattie knew what he wanted of her, and of Josie, too. Mattie hoped it wasn't her task to acquaint Josie with the family's political dogma, but she thought Josie might like to help with the campaign. She could meet some nice people, get acquainted, go to some of the parties.

Mrs. Kennedy's sophisticated, designer attire had not yet impressed Josie, who chose to wear the provocative, body-tight sheath dress as often as occasions

16

called for it and frequently when they didn't. Sexily overdressed, Josie figured that if she didn't know who she was, she surely knew who she wanted to become. She spent the summer studying French and mastering the Marilyn Monroe look more than verb conjugations. It was a wonderful summer, sharing Mattie's apartment, sharing clothes, and making new stories.

Saturday mornings often took the sisters from their apartment on Channing Way, just below Piedmont Avenue, uphill to International House, where they whispered and giggled about the qualities of various male residents, had some breakfast, and sorted out schedules and shopping chores. Josie said the food at I House was wretched, not nearly as good as the breakfasts that Mattie made, but it was cheap, coffee refills were free, and eating out together was a treat, an opportunity to unravel the twisted threads of work, late-night studies, and dates.

Peter joined his sisters on occasion, but he was now in high-energy success mode, planning to leave in the fall, grant in hand, for a year-long field study that would add meaningful footnotes to his Ph.D. in archaeology.

"I've only got a few minutes, gals. Why do you like to meet here? The food's terrible. Have you heard anything from Father? How are your studies? When . . ."

"Peter," Mattie interrupted. "Do you remember that sing-song thing we learned together about the swift-flying blue-pit palluli bird who flies in concentric circles of ever increasing velocity, ever-decreasing magnitude, and goes up in a puff of blue smoke?"

"No time for childhood rhymes, Mattie." Peter took a deep breath and deftly steered their talk toward his academic work and toward some of the campaign issues — equality in housing and education, Cuban communism, the space race, and the supposed missile gap between the United States and the Soviet Union. He was animated about the campaign debates that would take place in

17

September — the first televised debates in the history of presidential campaigns. The initial debate would focus on domestic issues, and Peter was certain that JFK would have the advantage, Nixon being more experienced in international affairs, JFK's vigor and charm recommending him as a champion on the home front. Mattie was insulted and Josie was amused when Peter found a subject he thought would interest the girls: The FDA had approved Enovid, the country's first birth-control pill.

"We do read the papers," Mattie said, as she pondered the eldest sibling's self-selected obligation to keep the clan informed and struggled with her irritation at being so frequently discounted by her one-time playmate.

"Great," Peter responded. "And I suppose you're writing a few papers. You going to get your master's pretty soon? You were all excited last month about freedom of speech and all that. Hey, I've got to run. You kids be good."

After breakfast, the sisters often wandered down College Avenue and onto the campus, directly to Faculty Glade — their favorite place. If they were feeling brave, they would walk through the Faculty Club, pretending to be looking for their host and hoping no one would expose them as intruders. The sortie through the club, usually brief and uneventful, was always punctuated by stifled giggles and hurried steps. Mattie loved Bernard Maybeck's design for the Faculty Club and dreamed that she would one day find his reincarnation to build her a home and let the same soft, filtered light into her soul. Josie was enchanted by the redwoods and rhododendrons along Strawberry Creek, and both girls looked forward to sitting on the moist lawn where they could engage in their favorite sport: faculty-watching.

Josie said she could always tell the Math Department faculty because their socks never matched;

Mattie could spot the English Department men by their Harris-tweed, leather-elbowed jackets. Philosophy was more difficult, but the awkward haircuts gave a clue. Josie wondered about the engineering students. Did the size and position of the slide rule on the belt announce more interesting attributes?

"Don't girls ever become professors?"

"Of course they do," Mattie responded, hesitating to locate the source of her information.

"Well then, where are they?" Josie asked.

Mattie recalled a rather dowdy, fiftyish woman parking her car in the faculty lot behind Dwinelle Hall. Her walk was a march, and Mattie was sure she was faculty. There was also a friend in the English Department who had written her thesis on the Bronte sisters and taken a job at Yuba Junior College. Another woman Mattie remembered had refused to sign the loyalty oath a few years earlier and had disappeared from grad school. Clouds drifted between the women and the sun, and Mattie draped Josie's pearl-buttoned sweater back over her sister's shoulders.

CHAPTER 2

So let's tell the world about it now
Happy days are here again . . .
Milton Ager / Jack Yellen
"Happy Days"

"It's kind of like working at the cannery," Josie said when she joined Mattie in the hot little office where volunteers stuffed envelopes and licked stamps. "And how come only the men have offices and telephones," she continued as she surveyed a group of women working at long tables in the center of a dreary, uncarpeted room. She said Jack Kennedy was classy; his Bostonian accent was cute and so was his wife, but it would be "kind of disgusting" if JFK's running mate ever became president. "Lyndon B. Johnson reminds me of some of Father's horse-thief ancestors," she said and lamented that California's governor Pat Brown wasn't on the ticket. "Why would two Catholics be any worse than one? Neither one is the Pope, is he?"

"Dicky Madhouse Nixon" was Josie's name for the Republican presidential candidate, and she named his running mate "Hari Kari Lodge." Naïvete and wisdom were both welcome contributions to the campaign office where Josie soon found that laughter among friends gave her strong medicine to drug the dragons of her brief past. The past was over. Josie would be an adventurer in Mr. Kennedy's new frontier. The '60s would be her very own decade – a time to blossom.

By the end of summer, Josie and Mattie's hectic work-study-volunteer pace took an unexpected turn when Howard entered Josie's life as more than her French-language instructor. The soft, flowing rhythm of the sisters' Saturday mornings together was gone. The

21

days now became hurried because Josie and Howard were taking a picnic lunch to Tilden Park, going hiking in the redwoods above the campus, taking in San Francisco's nightlife — Lupo's in North Beach for good Italian food, the Jazz Workshop and the hungry i for entertainment, City Lights Bookstore for enlightenment and more entertainment. Several years would pass before San Francisco's flower children would sprout in San Francisco's Haight-Ashbury District, but the seeds of change were in the Bay Area's rich soil, and Josie sensed the euphoric vapors of flux. Lawrence Ferlinghetti had been found innocent of obscenity charges when he published Allen Ginsberg's "Howl," but Lenny Bruce was yet to be arrested at the hungry i for saying "cocksucker."

"Rabelaisian" was Howard's comment on the North Beach scene, but Josie's delight in diversity soon drew the couple into a gentle Bohemia — not a psychedelic paradise/ghetto, but a glorious adventure for Josie.

"I especially like the late-night sounds, Howard, and the smells . . . . You can tell when San Francisco is wide awake."

"Your enthusiasm is fun, Josie, but we must be careful."

"Why do you always get worried, Howard, when we're just starting to have fun?"

Howard guided Josie past a topless bar and hurried up the street to the Bocce Ball where the couple would have a glass of wine and a taste of operatic entertainment before heading back across the bay.

"When we're through here, let's go hear some Dixieland. Mattie says Bob Scobey and Clancy Hayes used to play just down the street . . . The Frisco Jazz Band. . . . I've got their records. . . . I love 'Wang, Wang Blues' and 'The Saints Go . . .

22

"Settle down, Josie," Howard interrupted. "I don't understand jazz, but we'll have lots of fun, just like you said. I know this is all new to you, but just remember, that there is no instant path to enlightenment."

"Enlightenment" was a clumsy word, not entirely new to Josie, but awkward and uninviting. "Settle down" had a heavy, familiar drone. It was a Father admonishment, the first warning, one that used to come well before being spanked and sent to bed if Josie didn't control whatever it was she was supposed to control. "Settle down" had a nasty taste, like horehound candy disguised in an inviting dish of Christmas sweets. Josie spit the disgusting taste from her mouth and washed it away with red wine and the notion that Howard cared for her, would hold her hand as she adventured, and would be an anchor if she drifted into dangerous seas.

When Josie announced she wanted to marry Howard, Mattie could only think to ask, "Are you pregnant?"

"Of course not," Josie answered. "I'm just in love." She was sure it was love; nothing else in her eighteen years on the planet had been so compelling, so needful of her complete attention. "November," she said. "We're going to be married in November, right after the election."

As if managed by a master puppeteer, Mattie turned abruptly from her sister and took a clumsy step toward the kitchen, toward the Kleenex box she knew she would need.

"What it is, Mattie? What's the matter? I thought you would be happy."

"I'm sure I'll be happy for you, Josie, whenever my grotesque memory sets me free."

"Whatever are you talking about, Mattie? I want to know. Now."

23

"Josie, I never told you because . . . because you were so young, and you were living with Mom, and . . . That's not why, Josie. The reason I never told you about Steve is that I don't know how to tell about torment and despair."

Mattie stuffed a wad of tissues into the pocket of her denim skirt and lowered herself onto a kitchen stool. "It was only a year ago, Josie. Steve, my friend Steve, was seated next to the window. I'm sure he was. He liked to look out at the lush growth along Strawberry Creek. They were discussing California poets. Probably Robinson Jeffers. They must have been. That's how I imagine it. Steve was leaning forward toward the wide desk of his professor. Both men were intense, and the conversation was pleasing. It was always like that for Steve."

"What happened, Mattie?"

Mattie stared into the past, searching every inch for something that would make sense. "The office door opened," she blurted, ". . . a man walked in and fired a shotgun."

"Why?" Josie shrieked.

"He just said he was hunting Communists," Mattie whispered. She never knew when the frozen moment would rewind and play itself again in her sorrow. And she would never know if Steve had been a target in the demented man's mind or just somehow in the line of fire. Steve's mentor lived through the attack and continued to teach, lumbering to campus with a scarred body and a depth of sorrow that reduced his physical stature and sat heavily in his soul.

It was an especially bitter fact for Mattie that Steve had come to campus as a veteran on the GI Bill, having survived General MacArthur's UN invasion of North Korea and the massive counteroffensive by the Communist government of China. That particular war had ended where it began, on the 38th parallel that marked the border between North and South Korea. Thermonuclear weapons had not been used; Steve was not one of the 54,000 Americans who died in Korea, and he would bring his tall, handsome, unwounded body and his eloquent poetry to the Berkeley campus, where a paranoid posse-of-one, riding high on drugs and self-righteousness, would kill him.

Steve and Mattie had shared a love of places — California's rugged North Coast that infused Steve's poetry and the Sierra that whispered tranquil songs to Mattie. On a long weekend, the couple could take-in a bit of both, tossing sleeping bags on the beach, wandering the next morning along the fog-laden coast, and then heading east into the morning sunlight, across the Great Valley, into the gold country and finally to the mountains where Mattie had a favorite place on the Rubicon River. Sunday mornings often took them into the high country of the Sierra whereupon they would rediscover they needed another day before they could return to Berkeley, to classes, jobs — the other world that claimed their allegiance. Mattie and Steve agreed they were not soul mates, but they were kindred spirits who had the freedom to adventure together. Their love-making was not without passion or the urgency of youth, and Mattie enjoyed the predictability of Steve's occasional gifts — never a negligee, perfume, or jewelry; always a book, sometimes poetry, often a field guide to the birds, trees, seashells, mammals, wild flowers, mushrooms . . . of their favorite places.

Steve was a scholar by habit, a poet by nature, and it was his curiosity and intensity that drew the couple to the edges of the Beat movement, just as Josie would later be captivated. Six Gallery in San Francisco's North Beach had become the gathering place for Bohemian spirits from across the country. Steve was particularly attracted to Gary Snyder's poetry and the integration of Zen philosophy into his timely, very American, work. Mattie savored what she called the "calm silences" in Snyder's poems, comparing his spiritual confidence to the harsh lamentations of his friends and fellow poets. And yet it was the opening line of Allen Ginsberg's "Howl" that lingered in Mattie's mind long after Steve's death: "I saw the best minds of my generation destroyed by madness."

Steve's mother, widowed and reclusive, had swept her son's torn body away to a remote, arid piece of the California landscape, his childhood home. She would bury him alone, offering her own private service to her only child. Mattie's heart often investigated the mother's anguish, coming to know that it was relentless, never-ending. Her own grief was lessened only when she carried a bare-root dogwood into the Sierra and planted it alongside the Rubicon where the couple had so often shared the quite night sky and carefree sips of wine. She returned to the ocean some seashells they had gathered and waited for her pain to subside.

"Would you like me to help with the wedding?" Mattie asked. She dried her tears and rose to give her sister a hug, welcoming Josie's spontaneity and hunger for life. Who, she wondered, could know what a wise path looked like – mapped and thoughtful, or uncharted, unrehearsed, open, and vulnerable?

———

Peter declined Josie's request to call their father with news of her wedding plans, and the task fell to Mattie. Josie promised to follow up in a day or two, just wanting someone else to bear the glad tidings first. She was relieved when she heard laughter coming from the bedroom where Mattie's trembling hands clutched the telephone as her tongue searched for words to avert a storm. Their laughter was part of a father-daughter ritual that had evolved since the divorce. They would first talk politics, then health and weather; difficult subjects would be tucked into the end of their conversation and pondered over time. They were laughing about President Eisenhower's statement that if he had a week, he might think of a major decision Nixon had participated in during his eight years as vice president. Her father offered some information about local and state issues. Mattie reported on the sisters' campaign work. Next came Bo's good grades in high school and the fall football schedule. Mattie responded with pleasing news of good weather, good health, hard work. Finally . . .

Josie heard a new variation of detachment in her father's words when she made the promised call a few days later. Yes, he agreed, this must be very exciting. No, very sorry, he wouldn't be able to attend the wedding. Her mother could handle that. He would send Josie a gift to wish her a good life; sorry, but he couldn't continue to support her if she weren't in school. His mask sat firmly in place, his voice betrayed little, and Josie was grateful the black mood hadn't erupted.

Josie's mother, on the other hand, found relief from her worries in Josie's announcement. Nora chained herself to the telephone and set about making plans for a grand event. With only a few months to plan the wedding of her youngest daughter, Nora managed to keep their conversations focused on the details of hospitality, carefully avoiding any dark pockets of their relationship.

With three siblings who were all over-achievers in her mind, Josie had not often enjoyed the limelight, but now she glowed on center-stage. She shared the spotlight for an evening in late September with Jack Kennedy and Richard Nixon as she and Mattie joined seventy million others to watch the candidates' first debate. Josie concluded that Nixon looked unhealthy and sinister, while her handsome guide to the new frontier was vigorous and enchanting. She was pleased because the radio that had brought politics into her life as a child had been replaced by television. She could vaguely remember President Roosevelt's voice on the radio. Truman, too, had an interesting, feisty sound; Eisenhower's speeches, although he was the current president, were beginning to fade into the grey dust of olden days. Now she could actually watch as Kennedy wove his charm through facts and figures that pushed Nixon into an unbecoming posture. Commentators couldn't decide who had won the debate, but Josie could, and she celebrated the victory with Mattie, staying up late into the night to hear, again and again, the voice of her gallant knight. Rosa Parks offered a brief and tentative smile as Josie drifted into sleep in the early-morning hours.

By mid October, with the election and her wedding only a few weeks away, Josie packed her bags for a honeymoon trip to Carmel, and Martin Luther King announced he had a suitcase full of votes for Mr. Kennedy. King's son, along with thirty-five others, had been arrested after staging a nonviolent sit-in at an Atlanta snack bar where service had been refused. When Robert Kennedy helped secure bail for the young minister, Josie took both families into her heart as she readied herself for the big events of November.

Mattie's Bath

Dear little sister, maybe you really are in love, maybe that is why you are only eighteen years old and getting married. Are you in love? What is that like? I've never been in love; I have tried and failed. . . . Twenty-four years old, and never in love. . . . Steve and I loved each other, but we weren't in love in that misty way I imagine . . . . You were only six years old when Father bought Misty for you. You'd get up with the bird songs, find someone to help you saddle and bridle Misty . . . and then you were off. I can't believe

Mother let you ride out there in the fields all alone for so many hours. You weren't even around for breakfast. The rest of us would sit down . . . so much talk at breakfast, so many worries . . . Hiroshima, the Hollywood Ten, House Un-American Activities, and hot oatmeal. . . . Grandpa R was heartsick about the HUAC hearings, and you were riding Misty in the wind. You especially liked to ride in the wind. You told me you *were* the wind. I think maybe you were. Maybe it's my fault. I read your favorite stories about prince charmings rescuing fair princesses. Didn't you notice that those stories ended when the fair maiden was rescued? Are you rescued now? Rescued from what? For what? Where is Misty? . . .The year before you got Misty, you were required to come to breakfast. Father and Grandpa R filled the room with their debates about free speech, and you couldn't get a word in edgewise. I saw you tuning out, picking only a few words and moods out of the morning air. That was the year you named one of your fairies Enola Gay. You said Enola Gay lived under our bed in a pile of dust. No one was allowed to sweep there. Are there any fairies under the bed in Howard's apartment? Is there even any dust? Did you feel terribly betrayed when you learned that the other Enola Gay carried an atomic bomb to Hiroshima? . . . You were about eight when you announced your were going to marry Roy Rogers. Are you going to feel betrayed if Howard isn't Roy Rogers?. . . I wanted to marry someone who sounded like Orson Welles, or maybe Jussi Bjorling. . . . I wanted to wear Grandmother's wedding gown, the one in that tired old box in Grandpa R's closet. . . . Don't know what to wear tomorrow to your wedding . . . maybe that smart silk dress you borrow so often, you know, the black one. The old maid of honor will wear black to your wedding.

Josie's Bath

Oh, good! Mattie didn't take all the hot water, and she left me lots of bubble bath. . . . She was so quiet at our rehearsal dinner. . . . Maybe she's jealous of me. . . . This is so exciting! It feels so good to just soak up all this warmth and soak my thoughts into one giant bubble. What a perfect life I will have. Howard, so wonderful, so handsome and smart. . . . I'll be a professor's wife! . . . won't be long either, the way Howard works all the time, so good about sticking to his study rules. Wish I could be that organized. . . . It'll be neat to have a nice house, have his colleagues and their wives over for dinner. Fun if he had some colleagues with husbands. . . . I'll have to ask Mattie to help me learn to cook better. I know I can do it. I just need a chance to learn. Well, Howard's thesis won't be finished for a few years yet, plenty of time for me to learn stuff I need. . . . I agree with Howard about the baby. I'm too young, and he needs to do his work. . . . The baby and I can walk down to meet Howard on his way home. . . . I can bathe the baby while Howard practices his flute. . . . Howard will play with the baby while I cook dinner. . . . Howard will go study while I put the baby to bed and do the dishes. . . . Howard says someday I can maybe go back to college . . . after he's finished, of course. . . . Howard can look after the baby while I go to a class or two. I think I'll be a zoologist. Howard and I can both have our work. . . . Professors make really good money so maybe someday I can have a horse, keep it at Grizzly Stables and ride a few times a week. Howard doesn't like horses, but that's okay. I don't mind really, I like to ride alone. . . . I think Father is proud of me. I wish he could come to my wedding. I guess I understand. It might be hard to see somebody after you divorced them, but I wish he could come anyway. He could leave Marge home; Father and Mother could sit on different sides of the room. Well, Peter will give me away to Howard; that's fine. . . . Peter was so nice about getting us the Faculty Club for my reception. . . . I don't know a lot of the people Mother's invited. I guess that's what happens at weddings, I don't know. . . . I think Howard's parents really like me even though I got sick when I met them. I don't think they would drive all that way for our wedding if they didn't like me. It's going to be nice to have them for my baby's grandparents. I bet they will spoil her. . . . Howard teases me when I say "her" about the baby. I know it will be a girl because Rosa told me in my dream. She changed a white butterfly to a silky kitten, then into a beautiful baby girl asleep in a white, satin bassinet. . . . I wish Howard would let me get pregnant soon. He just doesn't realize how nice it would be. . . . I guess I'll have to get a job to help Howard while he's in grad school. Lots of wives do it. I won't have much to do anyway if I can't go to school and can't have a baby. It will be fun to have a real job, a job on campus; Howard and I can have lunch together. We can go for walks in Faculty Glade. . . . Mattie says I shouldn't wear Black Mariah tomorrow. She says I don't have to cage my body up in a girdle while I'm getting married. Mother says I should wear a lightweight panty girdle, though. She's probably right, I'll look better. . . . Marilyn Monroe wears a panty girdle, I know she does.

———

Rosa Parks didn't visit Josie again until the fall of 1961 when Josie gave birth to Caitlin, a seven-pound baby girl who, properly, looked like both parents, more

31

beautiful, more nearly perfect than either. Rosa sat in a gauzy corner of Josie's mind and stitched intricate flowers on a baby dress. There were tears in her eyes, and Josie was sure they were tears of joy. She was glad no one else could see Rosa because she didn't know how to explain why a black seamstress from Montgomery, Alabama was the midwife at her daughter's birth. She just was. Sitting there with Josie, not wanting to be explained. Rosa looked a bit grandmotherly, Josie thought.

"Just in time," Josie said. "Caitlin needs you, and so do I."

Peter was back in Berkeley for a brief visit with colleagues so he and Mattie arrived at the hospital together, meeting Howard not in Josie's room but in the reception area where he paced and pondered. Mattie knew Howard was so absorbed in his work that he frequently got lost as he left his French Department office in Dwinelle Hall. Not lost, perhaps, but disoriented, not remembering where he had parked. He often wandered the Bancroft and Telegraph area until some accidental collision of information jogged his memory and he found his car and his way home to the sunny apartment the couple had taken south of campus near the Berkeley-Oakland border. Mattie told Josie Howard should take the College Avenue bus since buses are hard to lose, but Josie had decided to see charm in Howard's wanderings. She had decided to see him as charming and loving, and her determination spilled out into every corner of her daily routines, perhaps, though, not into every corner of her mind.

Peter, too, was out of touch that morning, Mattie thought, not pacing as Howard did, but traipsing off with words to peculiar sites of information and returning with equally peculiar tidbits, facts more useful in creating space between the siblings than in uniting them. Mattie's hand-me-down Ford had guzzled its final tank of gas, and she announced she was giving up cars — too expensive; she liked walking and taking the bus. Peter responded he would give her his Simca when he left for Mexico, but she must be mindful of the insurance and registration; tires would soon need to be replaced; the engine was leaking a little oil; the seat covers were worn through on the driver's side, but it was all he could do for her right now.

Howard found his way to Josie's room in time to receive a hand-shake from Peter and a warm hug from Mattie. The new family member was perfect, they agreed, after Peter had checked for the proper number of toes and fingers. He cautioned Josie to take it easy and announced he had to rush for an appointment on campus. As they left the hospital, Peter moved the conversation onto a family favorite, politics, and used up several blocks of Ashby Avenue enlightening Mattie about the political fallout from the Bay of Pigs incident that was so humiliating to the Kennedy administration. Peter was full of information, but he was not full of joy about Caitlin's arrival, not enjoying time with his sisters, and not really a part of things close to Mattie's heart. Rather like the Berlin Wall that had been constructed during the summer, Peter's thick, multilayered wall was strong and divisive, separating friends and families as it was intended to do. Being the eldest in the family was a burden for Peter, but Mattie hoped the wall would one day come down. She regretted she had ever envied Peter's first-born status.

Mattie hesitated to tell Peter her part-time clerical job in the campus information office had turned into a full-time position with a minor promotion to editorial assistant. It was a glorified proofreader's job, Mattie said, but a good step for now, and she had decided to drop out of school for a semester or two. Peter warned that she would never go back if she dropped out, but Mattie had decided she could live with the status of "graduate student on leave." She continued to use that description of herself for a number of years, as if the current events in her life were a mere time-out from her proper reality.

Josie's Bath

I don't understand why Howard's so angry. Things were so different before Caitlin was born. . . . He wouldn't even hold her in the hospital . . . sent a note saying she's beautiful. . . . Why a note instead of telling me? . . . Why won't he talk to me about things? . . . Doesn't even sleep with me. . . . What am I being punished for? I'm only nineteen. I can't be expected to do everything right, can I? I'm a good mother and try to be a good wife. It isn't easy with Howard closeting himself in his little cubbyhole, studying all the time. I read whatever he's reading so he'll talk to me about something. He interprets those stories so differently than I do, says I'm missing the point. Well, maybe he's missing the point. Why do I have to be the wrong one all the time? I'm not stupid. . . . Says if I would read them in French, I would understand them better. If I'm missing the point by reading translations, then it's the fault of the translators, not me. . . . The party was a mistake, Howard and his friends sitting sedately in the living room, sipping their red wine, and for God's sake, only speaking French and talking about Camus and Sartre. The rest of us were having a good time, I think. It was fun dancing again. I haven't danced in so long. . . . Well, I can sort of understand why Howard might be a little miffed this morning, but he doesn't have to be. After all, I was with my big brother . . . and Carlos . . . He's so sexy. . . . I just didn't feel like having the party be over so soon, only eleven when Howard's friends left and he went to bed. . . . We just went out for a little while. I just had a couple of puffs. I mean everybody else does it; Carlos and Peter were doing it, and I just wanted to see what it was like. It's not like I'm hooked or anything. Just made me real hungry. . . . I wonder how long I dare to stay in here. Howard doesn't like me to use too much hot water. Ha! There's no such thing as too much hot water. I really don't want to face Howard. Let him look after Caitlin this morning; it'll be good for him and better for me if I stay in here. . . . Howard says we can't get a kitten, but I can't let Caitlin grow up without pets. . . . Howard's mad at me about the piano, too. We couldn't really afford it. I know teaching assistants don't make a lot of money, but it was only fifty dollars. It wasn't my fault his friend broke his foot trying to get the piano up the stairs. I told them we should pay a little extra and get piano movers. Now Howard's mad because I don't practice three hours a day, says I will never get any good if I don't practice at least three hours a day. Does he imagine I have three hours a day to practice, Caitlin just sitting quietly in the corner? Why three hours, why not four or six or two, whatever? Just because he plays the flute for three hours doesn't mean I have to practice for three hours. I haven't noticed him getting all that much better with his three hours, anyway. . . . Howard doesn't want me to take the genetics class either, says I should take more French. I don't want to take more French. I'm still mad at him for giving me a B+ instead of an A. He knows I deserved an A . . . said the other students would think an A was just because we were dating. He doesn't think a genetics class will get me anywhere. Why do I have to get somewhere, some place besides where I am? Do I have to be someone else, too? It's true, I want to be a zoologist someday, but Howard says it's unlikely I would ever go back to school now that I'm married and have a baby. He's married and has a baby. What's the difference?

———

Mattie's finger retreated from the doorbell when she heard Howard's loud "No!" coming from the other side of the door. She would wait in the car until Josie and Howard settled their disagreement. It wasn't their first argument, but Mattie trusted that Josie could hold her own, and the sisters would soon be on their way to the university's Charter Day ceremony. The spring of 1962 had been lovely, and this particular day was bright and breezy, a perfect day to hear President Kennedy address the dignified university faculty and a crowd of welcoming students in Memorial Stadium. Mattie had packed some pillows to buffer the cold concrete seats, and she had tossed in some new toys for Caitlin.

Howard had explained to Mattie on the telephone that he saw the event as a splendid opportunity to get some work done in his office – all the faculty gone, all the students gone – so Mattie had trouble imagining what the trouble was.

"The trouble is, Howard, I don't understand your worry."

"You seldom do, Josie, but you must change your plans. I won't allow Caitlin in Memorial Stadium. It sits squarely atop the Hayward fault. There were tremors last month. A major earthquake could happen any moment."

"That's certainly true, Howard, and we are going to have major problems if you don't accept the fact that my grandfather, my father, my aunts and uncles, and my brothers and sister have enjoyed years of events in Memorial Stadium. Caitlin is the first in the new generation. I can't leave her home just because you've decided Mother Nature has a private grudge against you.

36

She will be kind today, I'm sure — no earthquakes — and I will be home in time to make dinner. It's a little strange to me that you're okay with my going, but you won't let Caitlin go.

"I'm not responsible for your foolishness, Josie, but I must protect Caitlin."

"Very well, Howard. I'm going to Charter Day. Caitlin can spend a few hours with you in your office since you're determined to keep her away from the stadium."

"Josie, you really don't understand about my work, do you? Take Caitlin with you if you must go."

———

"I know more about earthquakes than he does," Josie said. She related the argument to her sister as they edged their way north toward the campus on crowded College Avenue. They would be three of the 90,000 who would attend this year's colorful ceremony. Caitlin would have wonderful stories to tell as she grew up, "I-was-there" stories that would unite her with her family and with her country.

"This is an important day for Caitlin," Mattie insisted. "President Kennedy will certainly win a second term in office, and Caitlin will come to know who he is. Maybe she'll join his Peace Corps, maybe she'll come back here as a professor of history and teach our grandchildren. Isn't this a super day, Josie?"

"It could have been," Josie responded.

"Does Howard really think Dwinelle Hall is any safer than the stadium?" Mattie asked. "I mean, if there were an earthquake, a big one, does he think he knows where the safe places are?"

"Mattie, I don't think this is about earthquakes. It's about control. Let's just enjoy the day."

During the ceremony, Caitlin's thoughtful attention was granted to the ants crawling along the edge of the bleachers, but the sisters felt blessed that day by her presence, by the sunshine, by the long, dignified faculty procession, and by President Kennedy's spirited words. They returned home slightly sunburned but refreshed in spirit. It *had* been a super day, and the sisters eased back into their routines with vigor and enthusiasm.

When Richard Nixon resurfaced that same year to run for governor against California's Pat Brown, Mattie again threw herself into campaign work. She couldn't imagine how her very own state would provide a political refuge for her personal ogre so she worked hard to ensure Governor Brown's reelection. With several months to go before the votes were cast and before Nixon announced "You won't have Dick Nixon to kick around anymore," Mattie invited Josie for a drink – another pre-election victory celebration – at the Claremont Hotel.

Josie was fascinated by the thin, suntanned women who played tennis on the courts below the hotel, and she dubbed them "the Claremont wives." The hotel itself was "the old lady of the hills." Josie was searching for a word that would combine decadent and opulent as she settled into a window seat in the dimly lit lounge overlooking Berkeley and Oakland. San Francisco was a sparkling jewel far across the bay. The restaurant where Mattie and Peter had dined with parents several years before was across the hall and a considerable distance from the refurbished lounge that had recently become a secret hideout for the sisters.

Mattie and Josie sat side-by-side so they could whisper and share little packets of private thought that had accumulated over the weeks since they had been together. With conversation dancing around the outer rim of more serious matters, the sisters frequently began with enthusiastic comments on what they were reading.

John Steinbeck, one of their favorite native sons, had won a Nobel Prize, and both sisters were rereading their favorite stories. For Josie it was *In Dubious Battle.* She was on her third read-through, and by now Jim, Mac, and Doc were like distant kinfolk, seldom seen but always welcome. Josie could imagine Pete Seeger's double-time banjo thumping out the heart-beat of the story, easing her through the tears that flowed more freely each time she read the scene where Joy was killed. And she could relate the scene of Jim's death with amazing accuracy, nearly certain she was there, among the masses of men, shivering with Mac as he called out to the crowd: "This guy didn't want nothing for himself."

"There are those kinds of people, aren't there, Mattie?" Josie asked. "I think Martin Luther King, Jr. is one, probably. . . . I keep wondering about what Jim said before he died: 'All great things have violent beginnings.' Do you think that's true? Howard said . . . well, it doesn't matter what Howard said. . . . Did I tell you I made Howard take me to the Salinas Valley on our honeymoon? He didn't understand how the valley was so important to Steinbeck, but, you know, Howard's never gotten around to American literature. He's stuck in Paris, might never get out."

Mattie could remember being in grade school with some of the "Okie kids" whose families had found their way to the rich Sacramento Valley. Mattie and Peter had picked prunes one year – for pocket money – along side dustbowl families who picked prunes for survival. It was sad for Mattie that her dusty, orchard friends moved on so quickly to another town, another valley, where something else wanted harvesting. *Grapes of Wrath* was thus Mattie's favorite, although she didn't like having to choose.

Josie had little to say about the French novelists Howard wanted her to read, but she had finished *Catch 22* and handed it on to Mattie.

"You may not like this book, Mattie. It's kind of a satire about war, but it's pretty funny, a protest against stuff that chews up your spirit."

Mattie was trying to find her way through the concept of a funny war, when Josie snatched the book back saying "Here, let me read you one line. 'Maybe a long life does have to be filled with many unpleasant conditions if it's to seem long,' Is Heller just trying to be funny, Mattie? I wonder if a long life is really important. It can't be very important unless you're doing something, can it?"

The broken laughter surrounding Josie's question was harsh, more distressed than amused.

"Is everything okay, Josie?"

Josie delicately tucked the remains of her shredded cocktail napkin into her purse and cycled through a cache of responses until she settled on an answer that would ease the sisters out of uncomfortable places.

"I haven't read any fairy tales lately, but Caitlin has grown a lot since you saw her. When was that? Three weeks ago? Yes, the night Howard had an evening seminar. You came for dinner. I made Spanish rice, and you really liked it. Caitlin fell asleep in your lap. Well, Caitlin is fine. Her hair is getting thicker. It's turning to auburn, just like Mother's hair, and her eyes are sparkly."

Caitlin's bright blue eyes, her new teeth, her efforts to crawl, and her first few words that were so clear to Josie saw the sisters through a second gin and tonic before Josie excused herself to make a phone call. She returned to the table with tears in her eyes but few words to describe the sour blend of anger and sorrow churning in her stomach and surging toward her heart.

"Howard says I have to come home. Caitlin woke up from her nap and needs her diaper changed. You know, Mattie, a diaper is a square you can learn to fold into a triangle, if you want to."

The sisters left the hotel together, enjoying a cool breeze that blew in from the Bay, carrying a sweet, salty taste to the place where Josie's old lady of the hills squatted and oversaw the comings and goings of Berkeley folk. Mattie honored her sister's silent farewell and looked up at a *Chronicle* delivery truck as its driver thumped another edition onto the sidewalk beside the hotel entrance. She glanced at the headlines and made a promise to buy herself a good atlas. President Kennedy had sent more troops to Vietnam, and it was time she figured out, for sure, where Vietnam was – Cambodia, Laos, and Thailand as well.

––––

Josie's Bath

What a wretched day. . . . I've got to get some sleep. I didn't know cutting teeth would keep Caitlin up all night, fussing, fussing, fussing, needing something. What?. . . Don't know what to do, and Howard's so irritable, not just with me, but Caitlin, too. She's only an infant, Howard. She can't jump whenever you want her to, the way I do. . . . It's not right the way I try to make you happy and pleased with us, with Caitlin and me, but you go on finding fault everywhere. I'm tired of jumping, Howard. I'm tired of cleaning the kitchen windows so you will enjoy the morning light. I can enjoy the light whether the windows are clean or not, so maybe you should clean your own damn windows, do your own laundry, prepare your own dinner, walk the floor half the night with Caitlin. No, actually, you can't walk the floor with Caitlin. She won't be here. She goes with

41

me, Howard. I'm not jumping for you anymore; I'm jumping ship this time, for me and Caitlin. . . . Wonder if Mattie remembers the time she told me to jump the sewer ditch. . . . She called it a drain ditch, but I'm the one who should know what it really was. . . . We were sneaking across the pasture to Thompson's house to get a peek at Junior Thompson's new bride from England. . . . Mother called her a war bride, and I didn't understand what that meant. Do men get brides to go to war with? I think that's what Howard did. . . . Mattie said "Jump, you can make it!" I jumped hard, but I can still feel myself slipping down into the sewer ditch, my brand new shoes sliding down the bank, with me in them. . . . We didn't need ration stamps for those shoes. The war was over. The radio said the war was over, President Truman said so. . . . It's not over here, Howard. Well, actually it is. We don't need a war, Howard, I'll just be a deserter. No war. . . . Mattie snuck me in the back door, helped me climb into the laundry tub, and she washed me down real fast. We didn't want to be in trouble for falling in the sewer ditch. . . . Mattie, I need you to wash me off again, wash this Howard person off of me. He's all over me, and he's nasty, and he makes me hate the way I smell, the way I walk, the way I talk, the way I am. . . . The lawyer said I need a witness. Mattie can be a witness, tell the judge how I don't want to be in trouble, but I can't live in the sewer ditch.

CHAPTER 3

And you feel the reins from yer pony are slippin'
And yer rope is a-slidin' 'cause your hands are a-drippin'
        Bob Dylan
       Last Thoughts on Woodie Guthrie

"It's only a visit," Mattie lied. She couldn't bring herself to look oily old Beelzebub in the eye, not because of the lie, but because her landlord had destroyed any hope of a comfortable relationship the day she moved into her precious one-bedroom apartment. Mr. Florintini had grinned sideways and assured Mattie they could find her requested curtain rods. She must accompany him to the basement to make her choice. The swarthy, strutting little man led her to a spidery corner of his workshop and pulled several curtain rods from a tired cardboard carton. They didn't fit together. He tried again, inserting one rod into another, pulling them apart, and inserting them again. "The male part must fit into the female," he whispered.

Mattie didn't get it at first; she trusted easily and was ashamed of herself when she discovered her trust was misplaced. But when Mr. Florentini's left arm brushed roughly against Mattie's breast — he was reaching for another curtain rod — Mattie's alarm bell went off. Without forethought, she pushed aside the hairy arm, reached across Mr. Florintini, and grabbed a fistful of rods. "These will do just fine," she said. Her heavy footsteps echoed throughout the cold basement as she strode across the concrete floor, up the rickety stairs, and into the light of the tiny garden area that crowded the basement door. "I'm going to plant tomatoes here," Mattie challenged. "I'll keep the apartment if I can plant tomatoes." She didn't wait for a response, and she planted tomatoes the following spring. She mailed rather than delivered her rent check, and she used her new-found, strong, resolute walk whenever she encountered the nasty little fallen angel. The encounter with Mr. Florintini hadn't been the descent into hell that it might have been, but the incident continued to gall Mattie, and she planted tomatoes with a vengeance. Some years they produced fruit; mostly they grew tall and rangy, reaching for the light.

Mattie faced Mr. Florintini about Josie and Caitlin with a hard knot of anxiety and disgust pounding in her forehead. His "no children–no pets" policy had bothered her from the first day, and although she had managed without pets, she was looking forward to time with her eleven-month-old niece, the first of the new generation and, indeed, the inheritor of Black Mariah. Mattie and Josie had surreptitiously moved most of Josie's belongings into the apartment throughout the previous week, then the bulky baby gear – stroller, playpen, high chair, diaper bags, boxes of noisy toys, books. At last, they plopped themselves down into their puddle of chaos to read e.e. cummings poetry and some familiar fairy tales. When Caitlin finally fell asleep amidst the boxes and debris of new beginnings, Josie asked about Mr. Florintini's conditional approval for a "visit."

"First, Caitlin mustn't cry. How's that, Josie? Think we can manage that? Then, he's going to inspect the apartment. Frequently. He says he'll do it while we're gone so he won't bother us. And, finally, he says he has the right to change his mind – anytime."

"We'll be fine, Mattie. We'll just have to check under the bed again for ogres. Every night we'll do ogre patrol like we used to." Josie laughed as she pulled herself up from the floor to turn on the little black-and-white TV for late-night news. Mattie headed straight for bed when she saw the images of Marilyn Monroe and heard the announcement of her death. Josie didn't want to hear the troublesome story alone and was comforted when Rosa Parks materialized in her mind to cushion the shock that ricocheted through her body. Josie felt sorrow, too, and someplace in her being was a soothing pocket of relief that she hesitated to investigate, finally recognizing that her adventure into motherhood had made burdensome the task of emulating the dazzling, Hollywood star. Caitlin's awakening to join the late-night mourning party provided an additional buffer. A new tooth was causing pain, so Josie, Rosa, and Caitlin sat together for several hours, sharing baby aspirin, wine, and tears.

The next morning, Josie asked Mattie to watch over Caitlin as she hurried out to the market for rice cereal and a new teething ring. A cursory search through the still-unpacked boxes had left Josie feeling bombarded by the tasks in front of her; fresh air and a few minutes to herself might help. She was gone only twenty minutes, and Mattie hurried to open the apartment door when she heard Josie fumbling with the lock.

"Someone just left him there," Josie announced.

"Where? Who?"

"He was in the parking lot. He's an orphan, Mattie," Josie announced as she pulled an eight-week-old black kitten from her shopping bag.

"Josie," Mattie sighed, "Mr. Florintini will have a fit. We're already pushing things to the limit. We could be evicted. Mr. Florintini is such a demon, a nasty little gargoyle perched and ready to attack."

"Well, then, we'll name this little guy 'Nemesis,'" Josie responded as she handed the kitten over to Mattie and busied herself unpacking a box and searching for one of Caitlin's old blankets to make a bed for the newest family member.

"Mattie, we'll find a home for him, okay?"

"I imagine we just did," Mattie responded, as her eyes scanned the disarray of her home in search of a box

45

of crayons she was sure she had left on the desktop. Mattie mumbled something about needing to draw a dividing line, but Josie's enthusiasm for a new life in the crowded little apartment soon drew the sisters into whispered schemes to deal with Mr. Florintini, and to find a job for Josie; get a sitter, vaccinations, shoes and diapers for Caitlin; make the Simca run; see the attorney; find a veterinarian; and bring family members up-to-date on events at the Channing Way shelter for drifting souls and orphaned pets.

Both sisters were pleased when Bo arrived late in the summer to start his freshman year at Berkeley. Mattie worried about her little brother and tried to fuss over him, but Bo rather quickly set his own course. Mattie was strangely ashamed when he joined a fraternity; she wasn't sure fraternities were part of the family script. Peter hadn't joined one, and she couldn't remember about her father, but it didn't seem likely. She settled her thoughts with a notion that at least Bo wouldn't be on a picket line, protesting some social injustice, getting himself arrested. He could spend his spare time drinking beer on the fraternity lawn where he was safe, and Mattie could stop worrying.

Not really. Mattie couldn't really stop worrying. She wondered if there were huge holes in Bo's soul because he had been so easily overlooked in his childhood. He just seemed to grow up in the middle of it all – easy, agreeable, and seldom noticed, seldom appreciated. Years later when Mattie had a proper garden, she would never pull out the chickweed plants that were so delicate and endearing, so pervasive, and so determined to have a place in the sun. They reminded her of Bo, and she gave them lots of room in her garden.

It was Mattie's opinion that if there were a true intellectual in her family, it was Bo. Unlike Peter who was so accomplished at accomplishing things, Bo

46

wandered through his ever-present books, absorbing information into his entire being, not categorizing and storing it, but letting it become part of him, wallowing in questions, trying new information out in unlikely places. Learning was not a procedure he set out to complete; it was a process as familiar to him as taking in air to maintain his well-being. Bo had more questions than he had answers, but that was the nature of things, and he moved about comfortably in his particular domain. In contrast, Josie's style of knowing was swift, acute, intuitive. Mattie knew Josie suffered the self-doubts that plague those who are blessed by the fairies, but she wondered, too, if Josie's inheritance might someday be wisdom.

Mattie gave little thought to where she fit into the grid she had constructed to keep track of her siblings. Self-appraisal was not one of her strengths; a huge critic loomed in her mind, threatening to emerge at the mere hint of an invitation, correcting and shaming her for the slightest transgression. Mattie assumed that her critic was some peculiar knotting of genetic threads that had found their way into her being, accepted but never invited.

Josie found it strange to introduce Bo to Caitlin as "Uncle Bo," but she liked the new appellation. It suited him, and she hoped that she and her little brother would now have an opportunity to become acquainted as would-be adults. Josie felt some shame about their early years together, about how she had been jealous of Bo, his charm and his ease, about how he got to live with Father and Marge, while she lived with her mother. But now they could start afresh. It was a special delight to Josie when Bo invited her to a fraternity party. He was required to have a date, and his sexy sister would do if she promised not to tell anyone who she was.

Josie's Bath

What a fun party. I didn't know Bo could dance like that . . . fun to be a sorority girl for one night, wonder if I missed anything important not being a sorority girl, getting dressed up every morning, going to classes, flirting with my teachers. . . . Nobody at the party knew that I'm really a mother. . . . When Caitlin grows up, I'll tell her about being a student at Berkeley. Well, I was, really, I took Howard's French class, didn't I? . . . Don't want to think about Howard. . . . Nice getting to know Bo again, a little bit, so long since we were close. . . . Were we ever really close? How old was I? Mother says I couldn't possibly remember that day, but I do. I was so excited, Mother and Father bringing home a new brother. I'd been waiting ever so long . . . can't remember who was looking after me. Mrs. Thompson, maybe. I know it wasn't Aunt Minnie because I didn't feel bad about anything I'd done. Where were Mattie and Peter? Must have been at school. Nope, it was July. No school. Maybe they were picking prunes or something. They sometimes did that. Glad I never picked prunes. . . .Yeah, it must have been Mrs. Thompson. I liked her, never knew her first name, just Mrs. Thompson. Mr. Thompson was scary, but he did help Father . . . milked the cows, pitched hay. . . . Mrs. Thompson would read *Little Black Sambo* to me. Must have read it to me a zillion times. Funny, but I can't remember the story . . . must be a reason for that. Are there any copies left in the world? I could read that story to Caitlin. I could read it to myself so I could remember why I forgot it. . . . Mrs. Thompson ironed when she wasn't reading to me, ironed Father's dress shirts for him so he could go to weddings and funerals and

Rotary Club, and she ironed the sheets. . . . Mattie and I don't iron our sheets. No way! . . . It would be nice to sleep in ironed sheets again, if we had Mrs. Thompson to iron them, standing so long in the hot kitchen. It was always hot in the summer, especially in the kitchen, especially just standing . . . Standing at the back door looking through the screen, waiting for "Bo" . . . couldn't say brother . . . waiting forever for Bo. . . . Forever takes so long when you're little, so long to wait for the old green Ford coming up the lane between the palms, stopping under the big oak tree, Mother looked so thin walking up the little dirt path between the yuccas. . . . Mattie made us hula skirts from the fronds. We'd giggle as we wiggled our hips. . . . Mother's so thin! . . . scared me . . . she had always been fat, always "on a diet" . . . always eating – "tasting" she called it – "making it right" for the family. . . . I'd never seen Mother from so far away, bringing home a Bo after she had been gone so long. First time I remember seeing her look beautiful, didn't know who she was for sure, carrying a Bo to our house, looking radiant. . . . Joe Magpie was making his "here kitty, kitty" sounds, and the cats came running. . . . Why did they do that? They were never fed at the house, just the barn, but Joe Magpie would call them, and they would come. . . It was a perfect summer, the cows in the pasture to the south of the house just kind of lazy-dazing, finding the four-leafs I never could find. One, I think, in all those years, though I didn't spend a lot of time looking. Mattie used to spit-glue the fourth leaf, and I always believed her. . . . How much more can I remember before I face going out the screen door to see a Bo? . . Tadpoles plopping in the pond, chickens scratching, horses neighing, tractors throbbing in the distance? Funny how much of a picture my brain can hold.

Okay, here I go, out the screen door, down the path, running, running to see what a Bo would mean.

"Can I hold him?"

"Of course, Josie, just be careful," says Mother.

"Don't!" says Father.

"Why not?"says Mother.

"She will drop him" says Father.

Joe Magpie was still calling the cats, and they were coming.

———

Bo wondered if anyone in the family knew him. Having escaped the new home of his father and Marge, Bo had wandered throughout the summer, his freedom ride more an inward journey than a purposeful protest. Had he been born earlier in the twentieth century, he knew he would be riding the rails with Loren Eiseley or William O. Douglas, sharing hobo stew and grand thoughts. He would have joined up with Ed Ricketts and shared with him the pleasure of punctuating John Steinbeck's novels. Ed would be Doc, and Bo would be . . . . Who would Bo be? It was not strange to him that his wanderings took him more into the past than into the future. The present was elusive for him; the future, a lonely place. With a copy of *On the Road* and an acceptance letter in his backpack, Bo had managed to find his way to Berkeley in the late summer of 1962. The only certainty he had acquired in his eighteen-year trek from infancy was that the western edge of the North American continent was his proper place on the planet. He sensed that it might be many years before his spirit could find a home.

Most of Mattie's concerns about Bo dissolved later that year when he began talking about the Peace Corps. That was it! Bo would join up with Sargent Shriver and march off to the Peace Corps. He would never have to be a soldier, and Mattie could stop worrying about what she had failed to do.

"Bless you, President Kennedy, for making a proper place for Bo. You will be proud of him."

And so the three siblings eased into early fall with ample opportunity for Saturday morning coffee, occasional lunches, and breezy walks on campus with Caitlin. Mattie wondered which ancestral threads were showing their colors in her niece – adaptable and comfortable wherever she was plunked down, knowing precisely when to cast an adorable smile at Mr. Florintini and, all by herself, stretching the forbidden "visit" at Mattie's apartment into the winter months. Her smile, though, didn't suffice when I-House had to be stricken from the siblings' list of favorite meeting places. Josie had arrived a little late for lunch, parked Caitlin and her stroller at the end of the table, and slid into her chair to join Mattie and Bo in a discussion of *Fail Safe*. Josie hadn't yet read the book, but she joined in the argument as to whether or not accidental war was possible. Josie said she knew it was, Bo pondered the question from as many angles as the quick lunchtime get-together allowed, and Mattie declared the subject bizarre, turning the conversation to how it was possible for Burdick and Wheeler to work together on a novel. The prose was a bit academic, she said, but not jagged the way some collaborations seemed. Caitlin's only opinion was that she was bored, her only view from stroller-level being six legs and a table post, and she began to fuss. Perhaps the I-House powers-that-be took sympathy on impoverished students or perhaps felt the need for an additional condiment to make the food more palatable; whatever the reason, small packets of soda crackers were tucked in with the mustard, catsup, salt, pepper, and sugar at each table.

51

At Caitlin's first sign of distress, Josie, by course of habit, unwrapped one of the packets and handed a cracker down to Caitlin who immediately ceased mewling. Seeming to work, this pacifying technique was repeated in turn by Auntie Mattie and Josie, whoever wasn't engaged in conversation at the moment. Caitlin caught onto the game and disposed of each cracker as quickly as her tiny hands could crunch them up and throw them on the floor. By altering the decibel level of her lamentations, Caitlin soon found she could get two of the treasures at once, one to chew on, one to crunch.

Bo was advancing the notion that computers might eventually penetrate businesses, even homes. You might actually be able to send mail by computers, pay bills, even order groceries – "everything from soup to nuts," he said, as he crunched one of the remaining crackers into what the menu said was split-pea soup. Mattie signaled for more coffee, and the waitress made a reluctant move to meet the request. As she approached the table, she let out a bellow followed by an angry diatribe on the disgusting, saliva-saturated mess her shoes were grinding into the carpet. Recovering from the near-tears brought on by the waitress's tantrum, Caitlin looked up and gave her a radiant smile, seeming to say, "Isn't this a truly wondrous thing I did?" Mattie informed the waitress she would clean up the mess if provided with a broom and dust pan. Josie tried to explain that babies sometimes make messes and no real harm was done, and Bo remarked he was meeting a friend at the library.

"Must be the wrong time of the month for her," Josie said huffily, pushing Caitlin out the door after the manager joined the ruckus and asked them to leave and never show their faces again. Mattie thought the situation called for a wounded, dignified exit, but she was giggling too hard to develop the appropriate walk and decided to

52

work on it at home. It would be a useful addition to her repertoire.

The power walk that had sprung from Mattie's encounter with Mr. Florintini turned out to be useful to both sisters. Josie adopted it for job interviews, adding an aura of self-assurance. She set about making things right for herself and Caitlin, and although she was seldom certain what "right" was, she knew that if determination counted, she would find the path.

Josie and Mattie looked through the classifieds and discussed what Josie might do about employment and babysitting. Her ninety-words-per-minute typing skill was impressive, but Josie didn't actually see herself as a typist. She could, if she stretched, see herself as somebody's private secretary, tending professionally to her employer's every need, graciously greeting clients, and, of course, dressing elegantly. Mattie worked diligently to produce a resume for her sister, who would soon come to recognize the far-away glaze that appeared in the eyes of would-be employers when she mentioned a small child at home. She was actually grateful when Miss Werner, assuming that a single mother would be diligent and determined to keep a good job, offered her a position in a small print shop on Telegraph not far from Ashby.

"Sensible shoes! Miss Werner says I need to buy some sensible shoes. No more three inch heels. And I have to make friends with a diabolical mimeograph machine that spews ink all over my clothes."

"What's she like, Josie?"

"Well, she's right out of a storybook – crippled by polio, all bent over and old. She lives with her two sisters and a mess of cats in an apartment above the shop. She's a spinster and a crone."

"That's not a very nice word, is it, Josie?"

"Which word? 'Spinster' or 'crone'?"

"Both, I guess. Crones have some appeal, but 'spinster' is sounding a little scary to me."

"'Divorced' seems a little shabby, too," Josie responded, "but 'married' didn't take, did it?. . . Can't imagine how you see yourself as a spinster at twenty-five. You just need to get out more often."

"Right, Josie. In my spare time?"

"Please don't get snitty, Mattie. We'll survive our labels, maybe create some new ones. I kind of like 'stable.' You know, 'stable' as opposed to 'emotionally crippled.' Not a bad idea, a stable label, attached to the forehead so everyone can see, worn with sensible shoes. Do they still make sensible shoes?"

Josie soon began to wear clothes that could be washed out at home, not sent out for dry-cleaning, and she scarcely noticed that *Miss Dior* never got replaced on the dresser-top. She proudly contributed her paycheck to her babysitter, the disgusting landlord, and the nearest grocer, hoping each month that her effort would somehow give her a toehold in the world she could scarcely perceive.

The car that Peter had left with Mattie was too expensive to maintain, so the sisters were immensely relieved when a neighbor agreed to look after Caitlin along with her own infant and five-year-old. Josie would not be loading Caitlin into a cold car every morning or buying gasoline to deliver her to a sitter. Caitlin would be right next door to the only home she knew, cared for by Brenda, a proper mother and a friend of Mattie. Josie struggled to remember that Brenda was not named Rosa. She looked just like Rosa would have looked at twenty-seven, and Josie felt blessed to have her on the Channing Way survival team.

Mattie's path took an unexpected turn when her campus editorial job put her in touch with a small publishing house looking for a trainee knowledgeable

54

about the space race. Sputnik's little beep-beeping trek around the planet had scarcely captured Mattie's attention in 1957. For her, it had been 183 pounds of Soviet muscle, interesting but not worrisome. She had been focused that year on Little Rock, Arkansas where Governor Orville Faubus and his state troopers had provoked more fear than any intercontinental ballistic missiles the Russians might develop. Nine black children had entered Little Rock Central High School, and President Eisenhower eventually sent Federal paratroopers to Little Rock to defend the court's sovereignty and the children's safety. Mattie could quote passages of the *Brown v. Board of Education* Supreme Court decision. Separate was *not* equal, and she agonized over her nation's struggle to let schoolchildren go to school. The weight of the second Sputnik lofted by the Russians was 1,100 pounds, and it carried a little dog, but it didn't carry for Mattie the weight of the 1,100 federal troops in Little Rock.

The following years added little to her understanding of the politics and paraphernalia of either the arms race or the space race. She hadn't asked Mr. Florintini to install a bomb shelter in the basement as so many were doing. The notion was absurd, she thought. But Mattie's attention was finally directed to the stars when President Kennedy, during his first few months in office, responded to Soviet cosmonaut Yuri Gagarin's orbit of the earth on April 12, 1961. President Kennedy strengthened the space program with a NASA budget that was $125 million more than Eisenhower's recommended $1.11 billion. NASA responded on May 5 of that same year when Alan Shepard became the first American in space. His suborbital flight aboard Freedom 7 lasted fifteen minutes, twenty-eight seconds, not too impressive when measured against Gagarin's earth orbit, nonetheless impressive enough to capture the nation's attention.

Within a few weeks of the successful flight, President Kennedy vowed to send men to the moon by the end of the decade. NASA hadn't even achieved earth orbit, let alone lunar orbit, lunar landing, and return to earth, but the vow had been made, and the space race now had all the qualities of a masterful drama.

It wasn't until February of 1962 that John Glenn became the first American to orbit the earth, nearly a year behind Russia's Gagarin. Encapsulated in Friendship 7, and existing in about thirty cubic feet of space, Glenn circled the planet three times in a flight that lasted nearly five hours. Within that same year, Scott Carpenter orbited the earth in Aurora 7, and Walter Schirra completed a six-orbit flight in Sigma. Surely lunar orbit would soon follow, and projects Mercury, Gemini, and Apollo began working their way into the nation's vocabulary as grant money earmarked for science and math education began filtering down into even the smallest space-race endeavors.

Among the beneficiaries were Frank and Emily Feldman and their fledgling publishing house, where Mattie sought an editorial position that would require her to make understandable the dumbfounding notion of a man on the moon. It was amazing to her when she was offered the job she so dearly wanted. It must be the power walk, she decided, as well as the many hours she had spent cramming for the interview as she had never crammed for a class. The astronomy textbooks she picked up at Sather Gate Books gave her a headache, and she was a neophyte with the technology, equipment, and special language of NASA. But she had the job, two roommates, a Nemesis, determination, and not enough sleep.

On Friday nights, the sisters allowed themselves a long quiet evening as they shared food and wine and shed the cares of the work week. Josie added the seductress walk to their repertoire, Mattie demonstrated the

Monday morning frump-slump, and both worked hard on the career-woman look. By the end of summer, Josie was practicing a princess posture. Mattie would play the dowager queen, and Josie would present herself with regal dignity. Josie had offered Marilyn's place to a new mentor after the sisters had seen *To Catch a Thief* at the nearby arts cinema, donning the cool, elegant charm, the dignity and smoldering sensuality of Grace Kelly as easily as she pulled on Mattie's cashmere sweaters.

But dignity got harder and harder to come by as weeks turned into months, and one crisp Saturday morning in mid autumn, Mattie invited Josie to one of her secret places — the Morrison Room in the main library. For Mattie, the sedate reading room exuded wisdom, and she often used it as a place to think through problems and make plans. Today she would take her sister and her niece to her secret hideout, and they would all be the better for it. Things turned sour for the sisters when Josie found a quiet corner to change her not-so-quiet daughter; they were asked to leave when some of the visitors complained. Josie was embarrassed, and Mattie was angry. But the day was fresh, and Mattie decided to share her second-most-treasured place. They would walk up to the Botanical Gardens, taking turns pushing Caitlin's stroller up the long, steep incline of Strawberry Canyon.

Sunshine had managed to find its way into the morning fog by the time the threesome approached the upper edge of the campus proper, and Mattie traded her rancorous mood for the role of tour guide. She pointed out Stern Hall where she had lived her first year at Berkeley and then Bowles Hall. Josie glanced quickly at Peter's undergraduate province and declared that "It looks like a castle. Not where the wizards live, though. They're at the top of this road, aren't they? 'We're off to see the wizard,'" she sang as she bent toward the stroller to make sure Caitlin acquiesced to her rendition of adventures promised.

"Tell me about the wizard," Mattie prompted.

"Well, there's a whole bunch of them — a whole congregation of wizards — who live at the top of this hill. This is the cyclotron hill, isn't it, where the radiation lab is?"

Mattie paused to catch her breath and consider where the conversation was heading. "Yes, Josie, but we're only going as far as the Botanical Gardens. I don't know much about the rad lab."

"Do you think it might blow up?" Josie asked. "Isn't that where they make bombs?"

"Of course not," Mattie snapped. "It's a research facility. The university is very proud of these particular wizards — Oppenheimer, Teller, Lawrence, even Seaborg. He used to be our chancellor, you know, but President Kennedy appointed him to be the head of the Atomic Energy Commission."

"Well, Ginsberg called them 'scholars of war,'" Josie responded.

"I don't think that's fair! They have all won Nobel Prizes, you know."

"Peace prizes?" Josie asked.

The sunshine had finally won its skirmish with the morning fog, and it was time to shed a layer of clothing, make adjustments for Caitlin's comfort, and, Mattie hoped, redirect the conversation. She was aware that over half of the University's research budget was provided by the federal government and that powerful economic interests in the state were represented by members of the Board of Regents. It was information she didn't want to share with Josie because it was unsettling — not a part of Mattie's plan for the morning. As they approached the trailhead to the redwood grove, Mattie offered to push the stroller for a while so Josie could catch her breath and perhaps wander more freely.

Mattie thought her sister would enjoy the light and fresh air that now filled the canyon, but the next stretch of road was the steepest, and she soon suggested it was Josie's turn to push. The sisters traded places, and Mattie walked on ahead until she heard Josie's muffled sob, then a cry, and finally a top-of-the-lungs scream that moved quickly from anger to despair.

'I can't go on. Can't you see how tired I am? . . . You didn't answer me, Mattie, about the wizards!"

Both sisters knew it was more than the steep hill that sent them home to their crowded apartment. Fatigue had settled into their muscles and their imagination, and they agreed to drug themselves with whatever television offered that night. Caitlin's bath was overlooked and her dinner was hurried, while popcorn and left-over red wine would make up their own meal. As they settled into their all-purpose living-dining-studying-TV room, Josie said a monster movie would be fine; Mattie preferred a spy thriller, and they both got their way. Nikita Kruschchev, the newscaster said, had ceased banging his shoe on the table at the United Nations and was now rattling swords. American spy planes had discovered Soviet missile sites in Cuba. Russia and the U.S. were on the threshold of war.

Josie had just finished reading *Fail-Safe* – Moscow had been obliterated, and New York City was next. Events in the novel, prolonged TV coverage of the Cuban missile crisis, and fatigue were the vital ingredients for Josie's hysteria that ended the evening.

"Turn it off," she sobbed. "I don't want Caitlin to know about this."

Caitlin was, in fact, too young to take in more than the noise of TV. She was sleeping soundly, and she remained an agreeable child throughout the thirteen days her country waited to see if President Kennedy could conjure up some magic elixir to sooth the war dragon. This was the big dragon, the master dragon who could toss thermonuclear warheads with reckless abandon, or with acute precision, as his moods determined.

President Kennedy and the nation were still suffering loss of prestige throughout the world after the Soviet launch of *Vostok I* and the Bay of Pigs fiasco, both in April of the previous year during Kennedy's first months in office. Kruschchev had not missed his cue and had begun heavily arming Cuba. Kennedy now demanded removal of missile sites; Kruschchev blew dark smoke in the air. Kennedy ordered a naval blockade to quarantine Cuba; Kruschchev huffed and puffed, blustered and threatened. Kennedy prepared to invade Cuba. Mattie and Josie, their parents, their siblings, their grandfather, their friends, and their unknown kin who inhabited the planet waited. Finally, on Sunday, October 28, 1962, Radio Moscow carried an announcement that crates of arms would be returned from Cuba to Moscow.

Hope for a good life returned sluggishly to the Channing Way apartment as the sisters began to adapt to the adrenaline rushes that invaded their sensitized bodies whenever a neighborhood car backfired. Bitter-sweet thoughts of holiday time began to replace their fear of obliteration, and the sisters allowed some tentative plans for Thanksgiving. Mattie had collected a number of cookbooks and was certain they could roast their own turkey. Gravy was not yet on her list of kitchen accomplishments, but she would try. Bo was studying for midterm exams but said he would enjoy a break and would join his sisters for dinner. None spoke of going home for the holiday because they weren't sure where home was. They would try not to notice that the nuclear arms race and their new view of Caitlin's questionable future on the planet limited their holiday joy.

Mattie was apologetic about the stuffing for the turkey — too moist — but she enjoyed her role as the kitchen witch. Josie had found candles and a holiday dress for Caitlin at a thrift shop on College Avenue. Bo brought along a nice wine and a fraternity brother who said it was too expensive to return to his home in New York for a Thanksgiving feast. All in all, the holiday was a pleasing one, and each of the siblings returned to Monday-morning tasks with renewed vigor.

Josie talked to her attorney about Howard's lapsed child-support payments, but he offered little encouragement. She wondered about the child-support laws that were so easily ignored and wondered if her lawyer really cared about her situation. Robert did seem to care when he asked her out to dinner just after the Thanksgiving weekend. Still feeling sullied by her day in court, Josie looked forward to sorting out why Robert felt it necessary to present her to the judge as a crafty blond whose seductive chicanery had entrapped a struggling academician. Josie and Mattie probably made matters worse by appearing in court dressed to the nines and adopting Hollywood personas, Josie in her Grace Kelly mode and Mattie trying on a Lauren Bacal look. The sisters had decided to try to make light of the otherwise dehumanizing procedure, but there remained in Josie an anger about it. Robert had explained that incompatibility was the only suitable grounds for her divorce; he hadn't explained why Josie had to play the villain.

Dinner with Robert was nice, and so were the martinis. Josie felt quite elegant dining with a successful, young lawyer on the terrace of the Rusty Scupper, listening to the waves lapping against the pylons at Oakland's Jack London Square. Robert seemed only vaguely interested in Josie's attempts at conversation, but he enjoyed talking to her about his political aspirations. By the time dessert and brandy were served, Josie's questions about the divorce were only faint background noise in an otherwise pleasing evening.

Robert was helping Josie into his vintage Jaguar when he suggested they stop by his place in Alameda for a nightcap. He needed to make a phone call, and he wanted to show Josie the Victorian he had restored. Josie was feeling light-headed and a bit queasy, but Robert assured her that a little more brandy would fix her right up.

The restored Victorian was beautiful, and Josie was impressed by the smart entry hall where simplicity, brass, and oriental rugs conveyed that this was the place of someone important. Robert's living room was all it should be in Josie's opinion, right out of a movie. She headed straight for the leather chaise and positioned herself in a cool, sophisticated pose while Robert opened an antique cabinet and drew out a bottle of Remy Martin with two brandy snifters.

Something wasn't quite right for Josie when vaporous images of the house tour Robert had directed — brandy in hand — began to merge with a growing awareness that she felt sick to her stomach and was uncertain where she was. Struggling to focus beyond her throbbing head to the sensation that she was being roughly disrobed, Josie managed to cover herself, Robert, and Robert's bed with a reeking brew of martinis, lobster tails, chocolate mousse, and Remy Martin.

As Josie stumbled into what she thought might be a bathroom, Robert mumbled something that might have been "I'm sorry." She threw up again and didn't care that she missed the toilet. Removing the rest of her clothes, she wadded them up and wrapped them in one of the two plush, burgundy towels. She used the other after showering, left it on the floor, and walked nude back into the bedroom. Robert was sitting on the side of the bed with his head in his hands, and Josie ignored him except to say, "I will be ready to go in five minutes." There may have been a faint smile when she remembered the mess Robert would find wrapped in his monogram.

While Robert was dealing with the bathroom scene, Josie rummaged in his closet and pulled out what she hoped was his best shirt, a new pair of Levis, and a belt. She dressed quickly and found her way to the kitchen where she drank two large glasses of water, paused to consider throwing up again, then went to retrieve her purse and the car keys from the hallway desk. As she unlocked the Jaguar, Josie gulped in the fresh, sea-tinged air and eased herself onto the cold leather.

Nothing was said during the twenty-five minutes it took to drive her home. Nothing was ever said about the clothing exchange that took place in Robert's Victorian. Josie did call his office to ask about a bill for five hours of legal advice, and Robert mumbled something about a secretarial mistake, said he'd take care of it, not sure what he could do about the child-support problem. Josie never offered to return the Levis, shirt, and belt. Nor did she wear them again. They collected dust on top of Black Mariah in the back of the linen closet.

CHAPTER 4

*You put your whole body in/ You put your
whole body out/Your whole body in
Now shake it all about.Do the Hokey Pokey
Turn yourself around,That's what it's all
about.*

LaPrise-Macak-Baker
"The Hokey Pokey"

Josie's Bath

Jeremy. Do I like that name? I like the way he says it
— JAR-a-me. Not quite, but close. Do the British
always make that stuffy sound? JAR-a-me sure
wanted that job in a hurry . . . . Nice of him to invite
me to the reading, probably thought he had to since I
worked so late on his program. I didn't want to work
late today, promised Mattie I'd cook dinner. Don't
know why she wants me to cook when she's so good
at it. Well, my spaghetti's getting better. Caitlin likes
it, anyway. . . . Wonder what JAR-a-me eats. Is there
a British cuisine? Never heard of it. What is a
"reading?" JAR-a-me says he dresses up like Charles
Dickens and reads a Dickens story. . . . I read *David
Copperfield* in high school. Hated it, and I remember
seeing *Oliver Twist* in San Francisco. Mother took
me. It was real scary. Maybe I was too young to see
it. JAR-a-me's program didn't say anything about
Oliver Twist, so maybe it'll be okay. It'll be fun, I
guess. . . . Mattie and I can dress up . . . hope Brenda
will keep Caitlin . . . . We haven't dressed up in so
long. What shall I wear? What do you wear to a
reading? God, I don't have any clothes I like
anymore. Maybe Mattie has something. Nope. She's
wearing mostly career stuff these days, navy blue and
boring. Why are clothes so expensive, especially baby

65

clothes? They grow out of clothes so fast. I guess I could just wear my Levis. No, I'd like to look really nice for a change. I wonder what Princess Grace would wear to a reading. . . . I know, a camelhair skirt. Simple. Camelhair skirt, black cashmere sweater, and pearls. Well, Mattie has the skirt and sweater, and I have the pearls. Kurt was so excited when he gave them to me. . . . God, that seems so long ago. I wonder how he is. Who was it told me he married a woman with three kids, the "town whore?" Why do people have to do that? Why are we so quick to label? Wonder what my label is. I wonder if JAR-a-me has put a label on me yet. "Hello, my name is JAR-a-me, and I am going to label you." Oh, well, doesn't matter. I'll probably never see him again after the reading.

But Josie did see Jeremy again, and again, and again, all throughout the holidays. It was a difficult time for the sisters. Sorrowful thoughts insisted on popping into their memories of "Christmas past," as Josie took to saying. Jeremy was introducing her to Dickens, and she was trying hard to get beyond the dreariness of his Victorian England; trying hard to separate Dickens's misty, grey fog from that which swirled throughout some of her own memories. "Bless the sunshine," Josie mused. "At least we have nice, winter light shining on our follies. Don't think I could live anyplace without a lot of light."

Josie let the wax drip into the holder, inserted the last candle, and waited for it to set. "I hope Jeremy appreciates all the work we're putting into this dinner. He told me his family has lavish holiday celebrations. Somehow I don't think we're going to come close to lavish."

"I hope you're not getting nervous, Josie. Look at the positive side. You made one trip to Goodwill, got the place mats and a dozen candles for just a dollar. You were lucky to find green candles this time of year. They look great."

"Yeah, they're okay, Mattie, but I'm disappointed about Howard's mother's mother's tablecloth. God, what a mouthful! . . . Wonder why she gave it to me, anyway."

"It was a wedding gift, wasn't it?"

"Right. Kind of a challenging wedding gift, don't you think? What went wrong, Mattie? With the tablecloth, I mean, not the marriage. I thought your idea to use spaghetti water for starch was brilliant, saved us a buck or two. I sprinkled it, rolled it up, put a sheet under the ironing board, just like Mrs. Thompson used to do, but the more I ironed, the wrinklier it got. What magic did Mrs. Thompson put in the cloth?"

"Josie, please don't worry about it. We're not going to add 'ironer' to your resume. We get to fail at some things. Where'd you put it, anyway?"

"Mattie, don't you dare ever tell Howard, but I put it in a plastic bag and stuck it in the back of the closet with Black Mariah. I'll pass it along to Caitlin if she's out-of-favor when I'm old."

"Can't imagine Caitlin ever being out-of-favor with you, Josie."

"True, but I guess mother-daughter stuff gets kind of complicated. . . . Wonder why Mom wouldn't come up for dinner. . . . Maybe she's got a boyfriend or something."

"That's a fairly disgusting notion, Josie. . . Wonder if this turkey's done yet."

"It smells wonderful. You're getting good at turkey, and the pies look fantastic."

"Thanks, Josie. I hope so. Only the salad left to do. Then we'll declare this dinner 'lavish' and press on to the new year."

Josie's Bath

So many candles on our table. Mother setting the table so carefully . . . white linen napkins . . . water and wine crystal just so above the knife . . . white linen table cloth ironed so neatly. Our Christmas dinner was nice, too. . . . not like on the ranch, though. Probably just as well. . . . It was never what it pretended to be, no matter how beautiful the table. . . . always my fault. I could just never do it right, didn't really quite know what "right" was, but knew I wasn't doing it. I would start out okay, napkin placed on my lap, hands folded, water already poured in the beautiful, long-stemmed crystal, Father carving, Mother serving lots of special things. But pretty soon Peter would do something wicked that no one but me could see, and it wasn't long before Father would send me from the table for acting up. "Get to your room and stay there!" He always said it like that. Sometimes the acting up caused my milk to spill, and that was really, really bad because the "get to your room and stay there" was punctuated by a fairly strong swat. Mrs. Thompson would have to iron that tablecloth again. . . . Why is it that the painful memories always get first billing? I know there were happy Christmases, lots of them. . . . It was what happened to Father that made things so sad. Mother worked so hard without much help from the aunts. . . . always Father's family who came, never Mother's. His mother, his sisters, his brothers, all the cousins . . . . . Father bought and wrapped the presents for them and a special present for each of us kids. . . . I never knew what I wanted from Father until he gave me my special gift, and then I knew for sure. . . . It was such a small box . . . had to be jewelry. I unwrapped it slowly to let myself get really excited, opened the

68

box, and took out a rhinestone sweater pin. . . . I'm holding it up for everyone to see . . . Father jumps from his chair and storms out the front door. . . . Slam! End of Christmas! . . . I don't know what I did wrong, nobody knows. . . . Mother is saying something to Uncle John . . . everybody leaving . . . we children going to bed . . . Mattie crying. . . . Don't remember when Father came in or where he had gone. . . . It was the worst of times. . . . I'm even sounding like Jeremy. . . . It wasn't until the next day that Mother told me Father had mixed up my present with one for cousin Julia. She got the gold locket he had bought especially for me . . . but I loved the rhinestone pin, so grown-up . . . never understood what Father wanted from Christmas, what he wanted from me that he didn't get. . . . Nice of Peter to call on Christmas Eve, said he was sending a new album of Harry Belafonte music, a little late. . . . Didn't know what to say to Father, really, and Marge was so syrupy, talking about babies as if they never cried, just sat like China dolls . . . no runny nose, no earaches . . . never a fever that worries you to death all night long. Wonder why Mother sent that huge *Better Homes and Gardens Cookbook* when she knows I hate to cook. . . . haven't got much of a home, either, no garden at all except for Mattie's scraggly tomatoes . . . dead now that it's winter. . . . I caught her down there once, talking to the tomatoes. . . . She said she was talking to Grandmother R . . . dead so many years . . . hardly remember her . . . scared me, so stern and strict. . . . Don't think Mattie really appreciated getting *Sex and the Single Girl from Mother* . . . Jeremy thought it was kind of a funny present, too, but he read quite a few chapters . . . funny how we never talk about those things, only read them . . . interesting present I got from Bo, the *Feminine Mystique* . . . says everybody is reading it . . . not sure I want to. . . . Mattie got me *Travels with Charley* though, and a Robert Frost collection, I'll read those first. . . . "Two roads diverged in a yellow wood / And sorry I could not travel both". . . . can't remember the next line. . . . I really miss Robert Frost, never met him, just miss him . . . kind of like you miss a parent if you're an orphan.

———

New Year's Eve was a mixed bag, "mixed-up bag" Josie let slip, referring to her mother as she and Mattie were discussing what to wear. Peter was back in Berkeley after a dig in the Yucatan, and Nora had decided the family would see in the new year together at Oakland's Lake Merritt Hotel — on her, of course. It was more a summons than an invitation, but there was a hint of gleeful mystery in Nora's voice, and goodwill seemed intended. Jeremy had previously invited both sisters to spend the evening at Big Bear, a roadhouse in the Berkeley Hills, where a group of his friends were getting together, but when Josie mentioned her mother's invitation, Jeremy graciously agreed to accompany her, commenting that he would be pleased to get acquainted with other members of her family.

Josie warned Jeremy that the family gathering might seem more like an encounter group than a New Year's celebration, but he was eager to get his feet tangled in an American version of ballroom dancing, and Josie was eager to impress her mother with her distinguished, British friend. It was irritating to Josie that she still sought her mother's approval — one of those slippery wishes that might never be granted. Nora had occasionally suggested that Josie and Caitlin might be better off if Josie had matured a bit and stayed in the marriage with Howard, whereupon Mattie countered that

70

Josie and Caitlin would be better off if Caitlin had a grandmother who was more than a worried voice on the phone, someone who would appear from time to time to babysit.

Howard agreed to take his daughter for the night as long as she was fed and dressed for bed before being delivered to his apartment. To spare Josie any unpleasantness on this special evening, Mattie dropped Caitlin at Howard's and hurried home to dress. She chose a long, fawn-colored velvet gown she had made with her mother's old Singer sewing machine, no longer a part of Nora's necessary equipment. By the time the sisters were ready for the evening, Mattie had achieved a rather pleasing elegance. Josie thought her sister looked beautiful, beautiful and solidly reliable.

"Mattie, I really wish you were going tonight with someone special. I think you're carrying this mourning thing about Steve a bit far. Don't you get kind of frustrated and lonely?" Josie knew she was on dangerous ground because the sisters normally bowed to the taboos of the time, allowing only knowing glances and raised eyebrows to acknowledge their sexual behavior. They would not have believed that within a decade or two, female orgasms would be the subject of television talk shows and female body parts would be discussed with as much detached authority as were the stock market fluctuations.

"If there were someone special," Mattie snapped back, "why in the world would I invite him to this event?" She was quick to apologize for her outburst, agreeing with Josie that they didn't need to start the evening with an argument nor should they start the new year with ruffled feathers. She promised herself that, tonight, she would be charming, cheerful, agreeable, open, mindful of everyone else's feelings.

71

"Peter called this afternoon to make sure we were coming . . . said he was bringing a colleague. Her name is Melanie."

"'Colleague,'" Josie laughed. "Now there's a great euphemism, a new label. Wonder if I should introduce Jeremy as my colleague? Or how about my associate? I wonder who would correct me first — Peter or Mother — if I just said, 'I want you all to meet my lover, Jeremy.' Maybe it's Jeremy who would correct me . . . can't quite figure him out."

"Well, you've got plenty of time to figure him out. He's not returning to England until spring, is he? . . . I've got to run," Mattie said as she searched for the car keys amidst the clutter of makeup on the dresser top. "I'm picking up Bo. He said there's no one special in his life, so he's my date for New Years. See you at the gala."

Carefully following her Grace Kelly formula, Josie had dressed with the hope of impressing her family when she and Jeremy, fashionably late, made their entrance into the festive dining room overlooking Lake Merritt. She was sure she could at least hold her own if things got difficult.

"Best laid plans of mice and men," she muttered to herself after she introduced Jeremy — as her friend — around the table. Having exchanged hellos and handshakes with Jeremy, the entire party quickly returned their attention to the distinguished looking gentleman seated next to Nora. Josie and Jeremy took their seats and joined in the listening as Bertram continued his discourse on the latest trends in psychotherapy. Peter interrupted occasionally with comments. Having already read Eric Berne's book, he was aware of how its special terminology was beginning to permeate common language.

Mattie was attentive to Bertram's oration, but she was suspicious of anyone who turned "method" into

72

"methodologies" with such alacrity. She turned slightly to survey the dance floor and the hotel orchestra, observing that there was no one under fifty in the musical group. She leaned across Bo to get her sister's attention and whispered, "Looks like a Guy Lombardo night."

Josie giggled with glee and offered that it certainly didn't look like a Rolling Stones concert, whereupon Nora leaned toward her daughters and, shaking her head a bit sternly, suggested that this was not the time for secret conversations or raucous behavior.

"Mother," Mattie returned, "I'm twenty-six years old; Josie is twenty, and maybe this is not the time for you to monitor our behavior. Let's just celebrate the new year. . . . You look lovely tonight; things must be going well for you."

Nora returned a smile that was playful, immediate, and genuine, creating for Mattie a sudden longing to simply hold on her lap the little child-like mother who sat expectantly on the far side of the solid dining table. Mattie would bundle her mother in a soft woolen blanket and rock her in the old rocking chair, the one that got disposed of along with a hundred acres of prime soil and a life that probably never was. Her image of Nora-the-child both surprised and disgusted Mattie, who brushed away a tear and turned to the dance floor where Josie and Jeremy were having no trouble finding the beat to "Moonlight Serenade."

"I love Glenn Miller music, Mom, but I wonder if this orchestra is going to find its way out of the '40s." Dancing had been a strong glue in their family, and Mattie was hoping a new rhythm would guide her into a festive mood.

"You girls are so beautiful tonight," Nora said.

Alarm bells! Mattie could hear the alarm bells ringing. Since Josie was still on the dance floor, Mattie wondered why she was addressed as "you girls," why she couldn't be an individual with a name in her mother's life, not a litter-mate of her siblings, nor a functionary in Nora's realm.

"Are you really twenty-six years old? . . . It seems like only yesterday . . . . Do you think you will ever marry?" Nora asked, reaching across the table to give Mattie's hand a soft pat. Mattie could remember this particular pat, the mechanical one Nora had used so often when Mattie was allowed to sit-in on the pre-school reading lessons her mother conducted for Peter. Pat-pat. "Not now, Dear, your time will come." Pat-pat.

It was fortunate that the beat of the music picked up suddenly, and Mattie excused herself to find her favorite dance partner. She and Peter had shared high school years, going to Friday-night dances after football games and developing a hoe-down version of the jitter-bug that energized them both and gave them close ties and fond memories. Melanie was dancing with Bo, and Mattie had no difficulty tearing her brother away from Bertram. Peter was already on his feet when Mattie arrived beside him, and she responded with energy to the firm arm that guided her to the dance floor.

"I don't know what's the matter with me," Mattie said. "I'm having a tough time tonight."

Peter glanced down into her eyes, recognizing a familiar blend of anger and sorrow. "Let's just dance," he muttered. Grateful for a good suggestion, Mattie poured her energy into the near frantic steps of the jitterbug until, finally, fatigued and cleansed, she returned with her brother to the family gathering.

It was fortunate that the beat of the music picked up suddenly, and Mattie excused herself to find her favorite dance partner. She and Peter had shared high school years, going to Friday-night dances after football games and developing a hoe-down version of the jitter-bug that energized them both and gave them close ties and fond memories. Melanie was dancing with Bo, and Mattie had no difficulty tearing her brother away from Bertram. Peter was already on his feet when Mattie arrived beside him, and she responded with energy to the firm arm that guided her to the dance floor.

"I don't know what's the matter with me," Mattie said. "I'm having a tough time tonight."

Peter glanced down into her eyes, recognizing a familiar blend of anger and sorrow. "Let's just dance," he muttered. Grateful for a good suggestion, Mattie poured her energy into the near frantic steps of the jitterbug until, finally, fatigued and cleansed, she returned with her brother to the family gathering.

After Josie made the amazing discovery that "Bo can waltz!," Nora and Bertram strutted onto the dance Nora and Bertram strutted onto the dance floor. Melanie and Mattie found a few moments to take up their would-be sister-in-law dance, not a ballroom dance-step but an intricate sorting out of likes and dislikes, a kind of pecking-order ritual that both engaged in but neither enjoyed. Mattie offered that it wasn't easy to fit into the family, and Melanie responded that she wasn't really a member of the family. Feathers were smoothed during a quick trip to the restroom, and the two women returned to the table where Peter and Bo were engaged in brotherly duck-hunting stories. That looked like safe territory, and Mattie eagerly became an enraptured audience for the all-male dialogue until Bertram invited her to dance to a suitable set of generation-spanning melodies.

An awkward stillness settled over the dinner table when Peter, having run out of hunting tales, glanced at the dance floor and explained to his little brother that one of the Beat poets referred to dancing as "dry fucking."

"What?" Josie shrieked, as she sought to control the gin-induced giggles that surely were not a suitable part of her evening's costume. Jeremy coughed as he leaned forward to better hear Peter's discourse, which had now shifted to the relationship between religious fervor and sexual energy: "All the same," Peter announced.

To Josie's delight and amazement, and to the entire party's relief, the orchestra she had dubbed "The Geriatric Gents" decided to "do the twist." Chubby Checker would have been proud to see the entire family loosening frozen hip joints by joining together in the newest dance craze.

Just before the New Year was rung in, a waiter arrived at the table to pour champagne all around, whereupon Nora rose to her feet and announced that she and Bertram were to be married. She would be moving to Kansas City, she explained, where Bertram had his practice; she would be studying to become a transactional analysis therapist. Bertram rose to toast his soon-to-be bride and her remarkable family.

If Alfred Hitchcock had been directing the celebration, the orchestra would segue into something heavy and foreboding when Nora leaned across the table and patted Josie's hand, offering "I'm sure Bertram could help you, Dear."

Mattie saw the deep pain in Josie's eyes, but remembering her earlier promise to herself, struggled to rein in the words that would bring the evening to an abrupt close. Mattie took a deep breath and began a ritual that sometimes worked for her. Mattie was the only one of the siblings who had been blessed by Mrs. Fowler's seventh-grade English class where the amazing teacher had managed to make English grammar an exciting subject for anyone who would listen. Mattie had listened, and she knew she could take her mother's sentence apart, break it into little pieces, glue it back together, and come to understand its meaning. "I'm sure Bertram could help

76

you, Dear." Direct address, simple declarative sentence, nothing difficult there. Bertram *could* help if *what?* There were implied conditions, and Mattie was sure they were insulting to Josie. And even if Josie were willing to declare herself emotionally handicapped, how would Bertram help? Would he send Josie money once a month for rent and groceries? That would certainly help. Would he drop in from time to time to babysit? That would help . . . difficult, though, from Kansas City. Maybe Bertram would stir up a tornado and whisk Josie away to Kansas, where he would endow her with magical, ruby-red shoes that would carry her home. Did Josie want to go home? Where was home?

"Mother, you started that the day Josie was born. You said you would give her to the gypsies because she was a 'problem child.' Do you mean for your definition to stick to her forever?"

"I hear your anger, Dear, " Nora responded. "Your father had an anger issue, too."

Mattie didn't know that anger was an issue; she had seen it more as a momentary band-aid for sorrow or pain. Faced now with fight-or-flight options, Mattie gathered up her satin stole and purse, agreeing with the family that it was time to depart. She wished her mother and Bertram a happy life together and wished she had not put herself through another gathering of folks who would love each other if only they could find a way.

Josie didn't come home at all that night, and when fatigue brought an end to Mattie's worries, she drifted into a fitful dream-filled sleep. The house – the ranch house – was on fire, and Mattie was alone and frightened, calling out for her mother. The long hallway separating Mattie from her parents' room was thick with smoke; not smoke, it was a dense, gummy, translucent slime. Mattie couldn't tell who was struggling to push through the muck to reach her.

Mattie's alarm clock announced the first day of 1963 at 6:00 a.m., forcing its nasty, insistent ring through the haze of her unpleasant dreams. She found a rumpled sweater on the closet floor, added a heavy tweed skirt, shoes, and a coat, and rushed into the cold winter morning, wishing the Simca's heater had self-repaired during the night. She hurried along the empty streets of Berkeley to get to Howard's on time, having agreed to pick up Caitlin before 7:00 a.m., Howard's work schedule still a powerful enigma to her. At best, he would have had a two-hour visit with his daughter on New Year's Eve, and Caitlin would be awakened this morning to meet her father's expectations of what New Year's Day should be.

And what should it be, Mattie wondered. What would the entire new year look like? Once the cold, rainy season was over, would California's spring of 1963 bring fresh energy and excitement into the sisters' lives? And would the nation make some New Year's resolutions? Put some teeth into a nuclear arms treaty? End the messy involvement in Vietnam? Find room in its heart for racial equality? Put a man in orbit around the earth? Mattie hoped so, and she hoped Josie would find a way to settle her thoughts about Jeremy's departure. His American sojourn was ending after Spring semester, and he would be returning to England. Jeremy avoided discussing the departure and would respond with "quite" when Josie lamented how difficult it would be for them to part and how awful for Caitlin who had made such a strong bond with him.

The traffic lights Mattie encountered were already set for commuter traffic, and Mattie smiled at how nice it would be to be so well-prepared for the future. Commuter traffic wouldn't inundate Berkeley for another twenty-four hours, but the engineers were ready. Caitlin was ready, too, dressed, sleepy-eyed and ready for the trip home and breakfast with Mattie. Howard handed over his daughter along with a note addressed to Josie. Mattie hoped a long-overdue check might be included in the envelope as she bundled up her niece and wished Howard a happy new year, whatever that might look like.

Mattie avoided the major thoroughfares on her way home, concerned about New Year's revelers who might be careening home before sunrise. She turned off of Ashy Avenue onto Piedmont where she encountered two of Berkeley's ubiquitous raccoons – urban dwellers *par excellence* – making their way across the street and into the neighborhood underbrush.

"Those creatures are survivors!" Mattie announced to her niece. "Clever and adaptable, a little like your mom."

———

Josie's Bath

I did it! We're going to England! Oh, Jeremy, how I love you! You won't regret it, not for a minute. What a pretty, little ring, a moonstone. . . . but, you see, Jeremy, we can't get married in England. We have to get married before we go. I'll just feel better that way, don't you see? It would just be too scary to go that far away only as your fiancee. I have to think of Caitlin, too. Too much could happen if we waited. . . . You'll see, I'll plan it all, and you'll like it. . . . Mother will help when I explain how good you are for me and Caitlin, how happy I am. No more struggling and juggling the money around. . . . Just like Princess Grace, I'll go abroad and become a princess, too.

Howard's New Year's note to Josie troubled her very little. He had taken a position at Duke

University and would soon be leaving the Berkeley campus. He would miss Caitlin, but he would make every effort to tend to her financial well-being. Brief, to-the-point, no doubt well-meant. "It's written in English," Josie announced. "That means he's focused and trying hard."

CHAPTER 5

The tune goes flat from time to time,
The lyrics sometimes fails to rhyme . . .
   Tom Paxton
   "Annie's Going to Sing Her Song"

"Somewhere, over the rainbow," Josie hummed as she tightened Caitlin's seat belt and then reached for Jeremy's hand. Pleasant weather at La Guardia had been announced, and the flight attendant was proceeding with instructions for a safe landing in New York, her imperious monotone scarcely penetrating the young bride's thoughts. *Will my heart strings break, or can they stretch over the ocean? . . . Will I ever see my family again? . . . Am I doing the right thing?*

The send-off at San Francisco airport had been exciting for Josie – the first leg of her new journey – but something peremptory in the mood of the day nagged at her like a musical refrain insisting on her attention.

"I can hear the melody . . . just not sure of the lyrics," Josie mumbled.

"What's that?" Jeremy asked. "What are you saying, Josie? Are you excited? I certainly am. Let's get settled in quickly. I want to see your biggest, busiest city."

"I'm not sure I want to claim ownership of this city, Jeremy, but yes, I'm excited. I've never been to New York . . . never been very many places."

Josie made an effort to capture some energy from Jeremy's enthusiasm, but she struggled, too, with fear and sadness that were knotted tightly in her chest, straining her breathing. She confessed to herself that what she wanted to do in New York was get to the hotel, feed

81

Caitlin and put her to bed, and then have a long, hot bath — a chance to look back over her wedding and her farewells to her family. Nora had been especially agreeable and easy to work with on wedding plans, and she had not balked at the expense. On the contrary, she had paid for the wedding and the honeymoon.

"Uncle George, the judge" — one of Josie's favorites — performed the marriage ceremony at his enormous Tudor-style home in Hollywood. Bo had agreed to give the bride away, allowing that he rather enjoyed playing grown-up, and Mattie had agreed, once again, to be Josie's "old-maid bridesmaid." Josie's Aunt Thelma, Nora's youngest sister, had provided refreshments with a refined touch she described as understated elegance, all wonderfully suitable for Josie and Jeremy. The groom had insisted their honeymoon be a Disneyland pilgrimage. He had been collecting jewels of Americana since his arrival in the States, and Disneyland was a major treasure-trove. Nora had paid for the plane fare to New York, as well, and for the hotel there. She paid for the cabin on the extravagant *S. S. France*, and she had paid for Caitlin and Josie's wardrobes. She paid and paid and paid, while Josie tried hard not to let all the paying drag her into dark pockets of her mind. *Rosa, you can worry about what the paying is all about. I'm still on my honeymoon!*

Settling herself and Caitlin into the taxi, Josie began trying to see the Big Apple with Jeremy, starring out the window of the cab as she kneaded anxious thoughts into the rim of a brand-new bonnet Caitlin had refused to wear. Several times she had asked Jeremy why his family would not help with the wedding and travel expenses. He had explained that although they were wealthy in some sense, they didn't have much fluidity. *A useful word?* Josie wondered. *Another very British euphemism?* She had read the letter from Jeremy's father,

82

warning Jeremy of the difficulty of having a ready-made family when he was just starting his new job at university. Jeremy's mother had not written anything, but the family, according to Jeremy, had agreed to host a reception at the Dorchester to introduce Josie to her new family. Josie thought about the reception, wondering what she would wear and decided to ask Jeremy's mother to help her shop for something appropriate.

That's something we can do together to get acquainted. It will be okay; we come from a good family, with lots of British ancestors. They will like us. How could they not like Caitlin? They will like me, too, after a while. They'll see how good I am for Jeremy, how I help free him from his British stuffiness, how he is learning to express his feelings.

Having arrived at such a positive solution, Josie took a deep breath to relax just as the cab pulled up to the hotel entrance. She turned to Jeremy and said, " 'I'm an optimist. I don't know where I'm going, but I'm on my way.' Grandpa R used to say that."

"Actually, Josie, that's a Carl Sandburg quotation, you know," Jeremy responded.

Josie's nod to Jeremy quietly acknowledged that she may have allowed Sandburg and Grandpa R to merge into a single figure — someone wise and gentle and loving who appeared to see her off on her new adventures. It was difficult being on the other edge of the continent, heading across a vast ocean, east into Dickens country. Mattie had promised to send lots of books, books by American authors, American authors who were still alive. Josie had decided English authors had to be dead for a long time before anyone noticed them; scholarship was safer that way. Josie would share her American friends — Frost, Whitman, Eugene O'Neill, F. Scott Fitzgerald, Hemingway, all of them dead — with her new family, and things would be just fine. Mattie would keep her up-to-date with writers who were still alive.

———

No longer absorbed by heaps of baby gear, the noise of Mattie's television now reverberated throughout her apartment, creating cacophonous drifts of loneliness that lingered long after the off button was pushed, long after Josie and Caitlin's farewell hugs. For several months, Mattie continued to listen for Caitlin's voice from across the breakfast table and for Josie's giggles that made light of minor misadventures or a difficult work day. She even welcomed her mother's phone calls from Kansas City, neutralizing Nora's worried voice with the suggestion that the fairy queen had whisked Josie away to England to become a princess. And maybe Josie's journey was a fairy tale; maybe Josie and Caitlin were having a picture-book adventure. Jeremy was certainly a caring man, thoughtful and attentive, mindful of Caitlin's needs and besotted by his young, American bride.

Restless and disorganized, Mattie wandered through the spring. "Plodding," she said. "I'm plodding through my life now. This is one walk Josie won't have to learn. The plod. Not very appealing."

It was her employers, Frank and Emily Feldman, who gave Mattie an opportunity for new directions when President Kennedy announced that the country would soon send a man to the moon and bring him home safely. Mattie was sent to Florida, to Cocoa Beach and Cape Canaveral in the summer of 1963. Frank and Emily were pleased with Mattie's work, and her trip was to be a kind of paid vacation: Attend the NASA seminar, take notes, bring home buckets of material, lie in the sun, eat, drink, and go looking for pink flamingos.

Mattie discovered a flock of roseate spoonbills preening in the tall trees along the Indian River, and she had an amazing sunburn by the time the conference began. "Nobody knows me here, so the sunburn doesn't matter," Mattie assured herself as she stepped out of the bright sunlight into the huge conference room. She apologized for bumping into a hurried NASA engineer, although the bumping had a rather pleasing quality. The man smelled good, and he looked more like a gardener than an engineer, earthy and genuine, focused.

"Are you a tenor?" Mattie blurted.

The man answered Mattie's question with a puzzled smile, taking in the tight, rosy glow of her sunburn with an amused smile. "If I could sing, I would probably be a tenor, but right now I have to be a speaker. I'm sure singing would be more fun."

Raymond Robbins was one of the reluctant panelists in a morning conference session. His brief, clear, a-b-c answers left many of the conference participants puzzling about his clarity and precision, each wanting time-out to scrutinize the simplicity of his comments. Raymond frequently deferred to other panelists while he doodled on his yellow notepad, drawing boxes upon boxes until they crowded themselves off the page whereupon he began a fresh page. He occasionally glanced at the agenda to reminded himself that the session was about whether or not the Apollo program could serve as both an earth-orbiting laboratory and as a program for circumlunar flights that would lead to a landing on the moon. A man on the moon?

"Yes," Raymond said.

"That's it?" Mattie asked herself. "Just 'yes'? I've come a long way for one word."

When Raymond realized the group wanted more than a one-word answer, he rose to his feet and approached the blackboard.

"The equation is really simple," he said. "T+M+C = S."

"Time plus money plus commitment equals success," Mattie bellowed. She thought it was a bellow because far too many eyes were on her, and she quickly sought to calm her enthusiasm — enthusiasm for her clever answer, for the conference, and for the NASA engineer she found so captivating. It was his hands Mattie couldn't ignore, hands very much like Grandpa R's — tough, used, functional hands. They might be scratchy to the touch, but Mattie was sure there would be a gentleness beneath the rough, suntanned flesh.

Mattie hoped her question to Raymond about the Saturn S-1C rocket would disguise the jellied weakness in her knees; she hoped he would notice her, invite her for a cocktail before lunch. But lunch was delivered to the conference room in stacks of sterile, white boxes, and Mattie got caught up in a conversation with several East Coast science writers.

The afternoon session was strangely flat and boring to Mattie, full of figures and charts, not melodious speakers. She did her best to take some meaningful notes as her eyes searched the room for a pleasing, rugged face, a face that seemed, now, quite familiar to her.

"What's happening to me?" Mattie wondered. She questioned herself, and argued with herself, throughout much of the afternoon until she finally spotted Raymond Robbins easing his way through the room, moving straight toward her.

"Yes," Mattie said. "I'd like to have dinner with you."

"How did you know I was going to ask?"

"It had to be," Mattie responded.

Mattie's Bath

Hey, Raymond. I want you to listen hard. . . . Take off that narrow tie, toss the slide rule, and listen. I can't sit in that seminar any longer. I am leaving little

86

heat puddles on every chair I use. Everyone else knows that. Do you know that? Are you listening? Why is this happening to me? . . . You said you're an engineer working at the Cape, sending rockets to the moon. A rocket scientist, no less! Well, Raymond, how about shooting one of those rockets my way? Who would miss one little rocket tucked away inside of me? . . . How very sad you already have a wife. You told me that, rather like you were telling me the time of day. I was drinking dry vermouth with a twist of lemon, you were drinking in my body, telling me about a wife you already have, your big wet eyes made wetter by the tears. So, Engineer, where's your blueprint now? . . . One thing you could do for me, Raymond: keep your lovely hands in your pockets. Just stick them in your pockets, hide them from me. . . . I want those hands all over me all of the time. Your hands look just like the hands of my soul mate. . . . Raymond, listen to me. I only have one soul mate. In the whole cosmos, I have only one soul mate. Why didn't you wait for me? I waited for you. All my life I waited for you. No, actually, I waited for you forever, since I was a little glob of protoplasm waiting for evolution to happen so I could be here, now, with you.

———

"You're love sick, Mattie," Brenda Darcy said. As the first to recognize the symptoms of Mattie's affliction, Brenda hoped she had won Mattie's confidence and would get to hear titillating details of her adventures. The neighbors-who-would-be friends were huddled in Mattie's kitchen while Brenda's son fiddled with the TV knobs and her toddler daughter cooed to her teddy bear in the living room.

Mattie was unaccustomed to sharing private thoughts with anyone but Josie, but she appreciated her neighbor's interest and little-by-little began to reveal the circumstances that accounted for the lilt in her voice and the hazy dreaminess in her eyes. When the flood gates opened, there was little about Raymond Robbins that Brenda didn't learn: ten years older than Mattie, five-eleven, pleasingly curly hair, a voice to call the angels, hands "you wouldn't believe," an only child but thoughtful, sensitive, direct, playful . . . married.

"Married?" Brenda blurted, her voice tinged by what Mattie thought was disapproval.

"Brenda, please don't judge me. I'm doing enough of that myself. I just can't help how I feel. Please understand. If he can get a damned rocket to the moon, he can get his life together," Mattie argued. "Getting his life together" of course meant taking Mattie into his soul.

Brenda's tall, handsome body relaxed as she extended inviting arms toward Mattie. "Honey, I do understand. . . . You are headed for a shitpile of grief."

Mattie was trying to imagine how grief might intrude into her euphoria when young James Darcy raced into the kitchen, announcing that Dr. King was on the TV. A quarter of a million people had flocked to the Lincoln Memorial. They were singing "We Shall Overcome," the unofficial anthem of the civil rights movement, and Dr. Martin Luther King, Jr. was describing his vivid, eloquent dream, challenging the nation to make and fulfill a promise that "all God's children" would be judged by the "content of their character" not the color of their skin.

Dr. King's rhetorical masterpiece stirred Brenda to divulge that her husband was going to run for a city council seat in Berkeley, and Mattie eagerly offered to work in his campaign. Brenda's hesitation was only momentary, and she graciously welcomed her neighbor's heartfelt offer.

"You know, Mattie, Willy is a bit of a radical. Let's see how things go."

Indeed, "let's see how things go" was the mode that governed Mattie's thoughts, and she was relieved to have the challenge of another campaign before her.

Josie's Bath

It could have been wonderful except for her. Trouble started with the shopping and went downhill from there. I wanted that long, plum velvet gown, so beautiful and elegant. It would have been perfect, but, no, Catherine said it wasn't proper for the occasion . . . made me feel stupid, like I didn't know anything about clothes. I hated the one she made me buy, looked like something from the '20s, something a flapper would wear, a Great Gatsby dress. . . . The reception wasn't fun, no dancing, I didn't know anybody . . . all so polite, but I could tell they didn't like me . . . except maybe Jeremy's two old-maid aunts. I kind of liked them, but they live off in the sticks somewhere, and I'll probably never see them again. Jeremy's grandmother reminds me of Queen Victoria . . . must have really bad vision from looking down her nose all the time. "My Dear" she kept calling me. Never used my name once. Patted my hand just like Mother does, poison pats I can feel through my skin . . . asked me all kinds of questions about my family, and then interrupted with "quite" before I could quite finish what I was saying. . . . Catherine said I couldn't have another drink, said it wouldn't be proper. Jeremy and Clifford drank all evening, but I could only have two. . . . I don't understand these people. . . . Why don't they ever laugh? When did laughing, telling a few jokes, become improper. . . . Nothing I want to do is proper. I'm beginning to hate that word. Jeremy uses it all the time, too. . . . It's cruel to be proper all the time. What are they afraid of? I think Bertrand Russell talks about that, about how fear makes people cruel. . . . It was cruel for Catherine and Clifford to find us a flat so close to them, so close we can walk to their house . . . every single Sunday. . . . I have to be proper every Sunday for the rest of my life! Caitlin has to be proper, too. Jeremy keeps insisting . . . and then goes up to London, leaving us with nothing to do. . . not much fun for us in London, either, with Jeremy just dragging us around to Dickens places. "What the dickens are you doing?" Father used to say. Well, what the dickens is Jeremy doing, dragging us all over to look at crumbly old buildings? "Little Dorrit slept here, Oliver Twist slept there, Mr. Pickwick slept here." Well, he didn't exactly say they slept there, but he might as well have. He acts like they're real or something. They're just characters in books. That's all he ever talks about, characters out of books or the people who wrote them. I hate Dickens, I hate Little Dorrit, I hate Mr. Pickwick. Why can't we do fun things . . . with real people?

CHAPTER 6

I can't remember if I cried
When I read about his widowed bride
But something touched me deep inside
The day the music died.

Don McLean
"American Pie"

The bullet that pierced John F. Kennedy's skull on November 22, 1963, lodged in the heart of the nation, where it would fester for decades, invading the minds of unborn generations and shattering the myth of hope that had enlivened so many for such a brief time. The people had elected a president, but they had created a prince, a prince whose senseless death had no power of redemption.

The young president had been elected by 49.7 percent of the popular vote. After the assassination, two thirds of Americans voters swore they had voted for John Kennedy. Even those who had not agreed with his policies, who had not shared in the glow of his torch, believed they had lost someone close and dear; they had lost, in fact, a part of themselves, the part that was self-aware, vigorous, and idealistic.

Nearly all who were asked could relate in infinite detail where they were, whom they were with, what they were doing when the kingdom crumbled, when Dallas, Texas became the final resting place of the New Frontier. When parents heard the news, they instinctively needed to know that their children were safe, and they rushed off to schools in fifty states to gather up their progeny, the inheritors of a gossamer future.

The only future Mattie could imagine when she heard the news was a cold terror that drove her rushing from her office, frantic to get home to Nemesis and her telephone. She must hear Raymond's voice, and Josie's . . . Caitlin's bright, British accent, her father, her mother, her brothers. "Are you safe?"

There had been no cataclysmic earthquake, but there was nevertheless a crack in the nation's psyche, and toxic fumes might soon follow. Television coverage of the assassination implanted images that would not soon dissolve, images gleaned from jumbled bits of information about a motorcade in Dallas; about shots that had been fired — one shot, no three, maybe two; about a cheap mail-order gun found in a book depository; about a Dallas police officer who had been shot; about a sudden arrest; about a young president's body whisked away to a hospital; about Air Force One and the swearing-in of a new president; about a widow, her children, a nation, a world in shock.

"Never," Mattie cried, as she opened her apartment door for Bo. "Never will we recover." Recovery, for Mattie, meant returning to a felicitous condition as if the fatal wound had never torn open the flesh. "It's not possible," she sobbed, cradled in her brother's arms and rhythmically swaying to share some solace that words couldn't bestow.

Bo and Mattie stayed in the apartment for days; she couldn't remember how long it took before Mrs. Kennedy led the world to her husband's burial place. Deliverymen who brought pizza or fried chicken to so many doorways throughout the country bowed their heads and excused themselves promptly, apologizing for intruding on families' grief.

Brenda brought her children to Mattie's uninvited but welcome, and in time Bo, Brenda, and Mattie found themselves beginning to investigate the tangible remains of their existence. There would be classes for Bo; work for Mattie; mothering and an election for Brenda; little-by-little, ghosts of the future began to take form, imposing themselves as interlopers in a frozen time. It was Bo's words that jerked Mattie into her new present.

"Mattie, I'll be dropping out of school for a while. I'll finish this semester, then I'm going to Mississippi. . . . I need to do something, something useful."

Brenda gasped even before Mattie had absorbed Bo's announcement, and she found a gentle way to warn Bo that not all blacks welcomed "whitey" in the freedom rides and freedom marches. "Bless you, Bo. Be careful."

For Mattie, fear for her brother's well-being battled ferociously with her pride in his commitment. When she finally found a voice, she offered Bo Peter's still-running Simca, provided directions to their mother's house in Kansas City just in case he wanted to stop by "along the way," gave him Raymond's telephone number just in case he needed a friend who could give him a hand, and she gave him a trembling hug.

"Father will be really worried, Bo," Mattie suggested, perhaps hoping that a worried father might deter Bo when Mattie couldn't find a way in her own heart to dissuade him.

"Maybe Father should worry less and do more," Bo responded. Mattie and Bo exchanged knowing glances, each acknowledging that Father still spoke of "niggers" – perhaps in his mind a separate, lower branch on the tree of evolution. It pained Mattie to remember her childhood pride in tales of her ancestral family – a Southern family, statesmen, plantation owners . . . slave owners.

"You know, Bo, you're not responsible for the past," Mattie offered.

"Perhaps not," Bo responded. "But I'm trying to get a glimpse of the future. Maybe there's a place for me in the future."

There was a big place in Mattie's heart for Bo, and she wept as she watched him put his political science degree on hold and, late that fall, rev the faltering engine of Peter's Simca. Mattie was sure the road to Mississippi was not a smooth one.

"Please, dear Lord, whoever you might be, keep my brother safe."

Mattie stayed up late that night to forestall the nightmares that were gathering like warlocks in her lonely bedroom. She tried to reach Josie, but the broken, noise-infested line to the international operator prevented even a sister talk that night. Soon enough she would learn that Josie's life in England was not yet that of a princess.

Josie wasn't quite sure how to describe her life in England, one grey, orderly day much like the last. But as Christmas approached she found renewed energy and suspected she was pregnant. With the excitement of the wedding, the flight to New York, the Atlantic crossing, the reception at the Dorchester, and settling into their flat in Richmond-on-Thames, she had occasionally forgotten her pill. She was enthusiastic about the pregnancy and hoped it would give her some kind of acceptable status in Jeremy's family, knew it would if the baby happened to be a boy. She decided that not celebrating Thanksgiving was barbaric, and she was determined to make her first Christmas in England a warm and cozy time until Jeremy's mother called with one of her "you will attend" invitations to a gala event and a splendid feast at Briarwood, the family's country home.

"Whose family?" Josie wept as she tried to explain to Jeremy what Christmas was all about in her far-distant family, forcing her memories into bright, well-lighted places.

"I'm so alone in your family," she told Jeremy.

Mattie, too, was alone during the holidays – Josie in England, Peter who-knew-where, and Bo on the road again, heading into the deepest, bleakest South Mattie could imagine. She called both parents, wishing them good cheer and expressing pleasure in the gifts they had sent, carefully avoiding conversations about Bo's departure. Having declined a half-hearted holiday invitation from her father and Marge, she spent Christmas Eve talking to Josie who had taken the telephone into a cloak room at Briarwood in order to diminish the background sounds of a would-be festive holiday at the in-laws. On New Year's Eve, Mattie baby-sat for Brenda and Willy. Their children were her daily source of comfort and joy, and the telephone was her lifeline to Raymond and Josie. The New Year – 1964 – would be the year of the monumental telephone bill. And it would be the year of overload for Mattie and Josie.

Sometime within the next 365 days, Josie would give birth to a handsome baby boy who would have the name of Gareth and would look like an English child from the moment he entered his parents' hearts. In turn, the British Isles would send The Beatles to the United States where their irreverent lyrics and exceptional musical know-how would broadcast to the nation still-in-mourning that its values were in question; established authority, politics, and hypocrisy were lustful bed partners; and affluence was not necessarily a virtue. Insisting that complex stereo equipment, cranked to its highest volume, was a necessity of life, not a luxury, American youth would race off by the millions to purchase 33-rpm albums that wrapped cynicism and disillusion in sophisticated, appealing, and affordable packages.

During the same 365 days, Martin Luther King, Jr. would receive the Nobel Prize for Peace, and

Congress would pass the Gulf of Tonkin Resolution, unveiling the truth that the Vietnam War was indeed a war. And Congress would pass the long-awaited Civil Rights Act that didn't ensure equality but confirmed the undeniable injustices that pock-marked the body of the nation. A Ranger-7 lunar probe would be sent to crash into the moon as NASA struggled to race from earth orbit to lunar orbit to lunar landing; discotheques throughout the country would launch the watusi into the feverish, dancing bodies of American youth. Cassius Clay would claim the heavyweight boxing championship and a new name, Muhammad Al; Lyndon Johnson would defeat Barry Goldwater to begin towing the country into the Great Society. Pantyhose and the National Organization of Women would invite women to rejoice in new freedoms. Joan Baez would offer her honeyed voice and stirring protest songs to the Free Speech Movement that would cast college students as culprits and would bring the National Guard to campus.

_____

Josie's Bath

This is the worst of times! God, I hate England! Well, not hate it exactly. There are actually a lot of things I do like . . . quaint little cottages . . . not supposed to say "quaint" . . . quaint little cottages with thatched roofs in the countryside, steak and kidney pie, and the beer. That's all I can think of right now because I'm tired, tired of the dreary color of the days, tried of walking to the greengrocer, the fishmonger, the chemist . . . tired of what passes for a washing machine . . . roll it over to the kitchen sink, hook up the hoses . . . don't quite fit on the taps, and the damn thing always leaks, and it never wrings the clothes enough so you have to do it by hand anyway. Mostly, I'm tired of the damp. The clothes are damp. They all have to go into the airing cupboard before

96

you can wear them. The bed is damp . . . . Remember to put a warming pan in about an hour before bed, and if you forget, it's god-awful. But right now, this minute, it's okay. At least I'm warm . . . the only time I'm ever warm, and it won't last long. The hot water won't last very long – goddamn night-storage heater full of bricks. For Christ's sake, this is the twentieth century. Do these people really like to live this way? . . . Feeling guilty for turning on the space heater. How can electricity cost so much? You can't see it, you can't touch it, you can't eat it, wear it, or drive it. You'd think being warm would be some kind of right. Part of the Bill of Rights or something. Maybe that's the problem. Maybe these people never thought of a Bill of Rights. Maybe that's why everything is always damp and I'm always cold. Probably why my ancestors went to the good ol' US of A and made a revolution. They just got tired of being cold. . . . What am I doing here? How did this happen? . . . . Mattie says there is a revolution going on in the States, a new organization of women . . . . I read about that. . . . Wonder what you wear to a revolution. . . . Wonder what I can do with myself with a three-year-old and a baby on the way?

Bo called Mattie that summer with a colorful inside story about how gender got included in the civil rights legislation. Speaking in a crude Southern accent, Bo told her that one of the South's good-old-boy congressmen was determined to kill the legislation, so he offered an amendment adding "sex" to the list of qualities that needed special protection. He was certain his colleagues would not vote to ensure equality of the sexes, never imagining that women would soon file more discrimination complaints than any other single group.

"Take that!" Mattie shouted as she feigned a tight-fisted blow at the image in her bathroom mirror. Maybe Mattie saw some of her Southern ancestors in the misty mirror; maybe she simply wanted some way to share in the courage of Bo's odyssey. His phone calls were precious to her, and when he called in early September, Mattie silently celebrated her relief that Bo had escaped from the South. Offering little information about his trek, Bo said he and a friend were now putzing around in Washington, D.C., looking for work.

"Mattie, I met your friend Raymond in Huntsville," Bo tossed into a momentary silence.

"He didn't tell me! How did you meet him? What fun!" Mattie shrieked.

"Well, it wasn't exactly fun, but he's a gentle person. I can see why you like him."

"Bo, it's not that I like him. I love him. . . . Can't help it. . . . Tell me how you met. What was he doing in Huntsville? What were you doing in Huntsville?"

"Huntsville is one of their space-flight centers, Mattie, you know that. . . . Actually he bailed me out of jail. I don't want to talk about this right now, don't want Father upset, either. You know, Mattie, when Martin Luther King, Jr. was in jail in Birmingham he wrote that anyone who breaks an unjust law must do it openly, lovingly. Civil disobedience is a pretty delicate thing. The charges against me were finally dropped, Mattie, and things are fine. I'm fine. Raymond's a good person . . . his wife is . . ."

"Bo, stop! I don't want to know." Mattie hated being "the other woman," and now her mind raced over the hundreds of times she had vowed to stop thinking about Raymond, stop taking his late-night phone calls, stop calling his office, stop planning secret get-aways. The couple had managed to arrange a few stolen weekends together, and Mattie knew she would fail if she made another vow of forbearance. She knew that her image of Raymond's wife as a Cape wind-up Barbie doll was a shoddy evasion, and she knew she had no idea what she must do.

"Exciting times at the Cape, Mattie," Bo offered as a way of easing his sister out of her prolonged silence.

"Why didn't he tell me you had met?"

"Mattie, he worries about you, doesn't want to make things worse. . . . It's hard for him, too. But he's fine, you're fine, I'm fine, and I've got to run. Hope to see Raymond again if he gets to Washington. I'll let you know, but right now Gerald is waiting. . . . I'm signing off now . . . your jailbird brother. . . . One more thing: the Simca died in Birmingham. Just as well. Hope Peter won't mind."

"Peter won't even remember," Mattie mumbled as she hung up the phone. She wasn't sure she was fine at all. She couldn't imagine Bo in a Southern jailhouse, any jailhouse. She ached with longing for her far-away lover, but a phone call to Raymond was cut short by interruptions in his office. Mattie's yearning grew as she paced through her apartment, picking up and petting Nemesis, putting him down, seeking him out again. Nemesis quickly became accustomed to Mattie's pacing ritual, and by the end of September he had learned that he could get additional strokes if he made the edge of the telephone table his napping, waiting place.

———

"He's back, Josie. He's back," Mattie yelled into the phone. England was an unknown, remote place for Mattie, and she imagined she had to yell to reach her sister, so far away.

"Bo? Bo's back?"

"No, no, he's in Washington. He's got a job there, maybe he'll go back to school. No, I mean Nixon.

99

He's back . . . nominated Barry Goldwater to run against Johnson. Can you imagine? Won't he ever disappear?" Mattie imagined a puff of blue smoke that would carry her other nemesis into an infinite black hole, finally, forever.

Josie had never shared Mattie's fascination with the cast and the drama of politics so she eased the conversation into more familiar ground, allowing that there were plenty of evil spirits to go around.

"I guess I've got my own ogre now, Mattie. Catherine is the wicked witch of Richmond-on-Thames. She actually corrected me last week, in public, about the fork I chose to eat my goddamn salad with. That's what they called it, a salad, but the English haven't ever figured out salads, you know, so it shouldn't matter so much which fork, should it? I used the small, outside fork just like we were taught at home, but no, the waiter had snuck in a special fork with the disgusting dish they called a salad. And the veggies, Mattie, they're all overcooked. Nothing crunchy . . . might make too much noise, I guess. Can't have a lot of noise, nobody make noise, shhh . . .and you should see how they feel about the student riots you're having. They make it sound like a big, brawling, disgusting panty raid, so very American. Catherine calls it boorish. What's it really like, Mattie?"

"Oh, Josie, it's not really a riot, and certainly not a panty raid, although I guess some of the reporters are talking that way. It's strange that the whole thing got started at the *Tribune.* You remember the Oakland *Tribune?* Some students were picketing there because of racial discrimination so one of the executives called the university to the university to complain. He said the students were organizing on campus. . . . True, I guess, but not a very serious charge . . . and the next thing you know the university says students can't use that area at

Bancroft and Telegraph, you know, the place Jeremy liked so much? . . . He called it Berkeley's 'Hyde Park.'"

"Yes, Jeremy loved that place. Used to wait for me there while I finished up at work. He'd listen to every word, even the religious fanatics. Oh, Mattie, I miss it!"

"I'm sure you do, Josie . . . Do you remember that young poet, Michael, the one who wanted to date you, but you were already seeing Jeremy. He was at one of Jeremy's readings. Do you remember?"

"Remember?" Josie shouted. "He was so adorable. . . . His father worked for a socialist newspaper, didn't he? I really wanted to know him better. He was so . . . "

"'Sexy,' Josie, I think that's the word you're looking for. I agree. . . . Well, he's mixed up in this movement. They call it the Free Speech Movement. He's a friend of Mario Savio, that philosophy student who's so eloquent about civil rights . . . and civil disobedience. He quotes Thoreau a lot. Michael says Savio's actually kind of shy, but his speeches are magical . . . really pulls the students together. . . and some of the faculty."

"Are you dating Michael? That would be great. . . . Is the riot settled yet."

"No, I'm not dating Michael; we have coffee together. . . . I thought you understood about Raymond . . . . Please don't call it a riot."

"I don't understand a thing about Raymond, Mattie. He seems unreal to me, and kind of scary. . . . What shall I call the riot? What can I tell Catherine?"

"I don't know, Josie. . . . What do you call it when a lot of people get disillusioned, kind of like rebels looking for a cause and finding lots of them. . . . that wretched war in Vietnam . . . the civil rights problems. . . . Josie, a bunch of students got suspended, and one of the kids, Weinberg – his name is Jack Weinberg – actually got arrested. He was handing out material about

CORE . . . you know, Congress on Racial Equality . . . but they couldn't take him off to jail because hundreds of students sat down around the police car. They stayed there for thirty-two hours, and then Kerr . . . remember, he's the university president . . . Kerr said he wouldn't give in to mob action, and before you knew it, there were Oakland police, county police, and state troopers on campus, right there by Ludwig's fountain where we used to take Caitlin?"

"She loved to watch that dog playing in the fountain," Josie returned, as her thoughts poured back over cheerful, sun-laden days on campus. "Where do things stand now?"

"Pretty much in limbo, right now. There were some compromises to avoid mass arrests, but the movement is pretty strong. Even Youth for Goldwater kids are involved. . . . LBJ is going to win the election, I'm sure, but these are strange times, strange that a liberal university is having a free speech movement, strange that the 'peace' president is sending so many troops to war."

Mattie paused as she confronted the dilemmas she had just uttered and was relieved when baby sounds were interjected from Josie's side of the conversation.

"How is my new nephew, my one and only nephew?" Mattie asked. "Can't wait to see him. Josie, when will I ever see my new nephew, you, Caitlin, Jeremy?"

"Don't know," Josie responded. "Seems like the only travel I do is down the road to the greengrocer. I'd better go, Mattie, this is costing you a fortune, and Gareth is fussing for dinner. Love you. Bye."

Josie's Bath

Thank you, oh, thank you, Jeremy, for taking the children out for a bit so I can enjoy my bath! So good to hear from Mattie! She was so excited about this

Raymond person that I just couldn't tell her all my big, little problems. I'm afraid she's terribly smitten. . . . It's about time! The wife part bothers me, but Mattie can quite take care of herself; she always has. . . . Can I take care of myself? The therapist is making me angry. "If he's comfortable with it, then it seems to be your problem, not his." I hate it when therapists say that. How could she look at it that way? I told her how shocked I was when all those "membership" cards fell out of Jeremy's wallet: *The Moulin Rouge, The Gentlemen's Club, The Naughty Nighty*. In that split second I understood so much about Jeremy: why he comes home from London acting so lecherous, wanting sex, not love-making; why he goes for long times without wanting me at all. . . . I tried to understand by going with him once. It made me sick to my stomach, seeing all those dirty old men ogling tired women bumping and grinding their clothes off. . . . Jeremy says he only goes a few times a month. That's why we only have sex a few times a month, and when we do, it's as if Jeremy isn't really there. . . . Of course he's not there, he's at the club, and I don't exist. Then, afterwards, he's angry with me. . . . Jeremy says it's because wives are supposed to be pure. They're the mothers of men's children. Two kinds of women, he says, those you marry and those you screw. He even used that word! He said he only wants me when he can forget I'm his wife, and then he gets angry with me for falling off the pedestal. . . . Catherine embarrasses me when she talks about sex as something nasty, puts me and Jeremy in separate bedrooms at Briarwood! And Jeremy does nothing. He never does. Jeremy did nothing when I announced I was pregnant with Gareth, and Catherine whispered to Jeremy, "There's still time to push her down the stairs." . . . She meant it! . . . Jeremy did nothing when Catherine took him and Caitlin to Briarwood, and I was alone in the hospital for six days with our new baby. Catherine said they would be more comfortable in the country where she could look after them . . . and Jeremy went.

___

Mattie's Bath

Wow, what an evening! . . . . Brenda was so beautiful, calm and regal . . . and Willy so serious, little James so proud of his papa. Said his dad was going to be president of Berkeley. . . . So glad Brenda let the kids share in the victory glow, didn't put them to bed early . . . James does glow. That's it exactly. He glows. . . . Why is it little black kids, especially boys, are so incredibly adorable? . . . Do I have to stop thinking like that? Is that some kind of racial bias? I just want to bundle-up James and hold him, let his gorgeous glow get all over me. . . . I could use that! I could use an Afro haircut, too. Wonder if that would be okay. Brenda is so stunning! Wonder if Raymond would like me in an Afro. . . . Here's the deal, Raymond. I'll get a new haircut and then I'll need a little something from you. See, Raymond, my uterus is in a tizzy because there's no adorable little boy-child in it. . . . Mattie, stop torturing yourself. . . . Raymond isn't going to drop his rockets on the floor and appear, unmarried, at your doorstep, all handsome and ready for life with Mattie . . . . Talk about handsome! Ron Dellums was absolutely regal. . . . Nice of him to come by. . . . He's right about the Vietnam mess. . . . People say he's too radical, but actually, his is the voice I want to hear. . . . And Raymond. I want to hear Raymond . . . You do sing, don't you, Raymond, soft, gentle songs of love? . . . Who was that loud guy from Oakland? So angry! . . . Wish he hadn't come to the party. . . crouching just

104

like the panther he said he was, leaning all over Willy to take a stand on something that doesn't even have to do with Berkeley. . . . Mattie, you are so naïve. . . . Well, naïvete isn't a character flaw, is it? . . . Could be, if it's willful. Willful naïvete might be a character flaw, Mattie. . . . What should I do? . . . Well, you could start by admitting that not every black politician is a carbon copy of Martin Luther King, Jr., so strong and determined, so gentle. . . the gentle warrior. You really like that notion, don't you? But that guy from Oakland was not so gentle, was he? That handshake with Willy was kind of scary, wasn't it, Mattie? . . . Anger is always scary, isn't it? . . . How about Malcolm X, how do you feel about him? His home was burned down and his father was lynched! Lynched, Mattie! Do you think he might be a little angry? . . . Listen, I got in this tub to relax. Couldn't I have a little time-out? You're so rancorous tonight, whoever you are. . . . I'm you, Mattie, and you can do whatever you want. You forget that. Go to bed, Mattie, but just one thing. Why is it that all your heroes are men; aren't there any women you admire? . . . Well, I like Maya Angelou, so strong, so determined . . . that beautiful voice . . . . Go to bed, Mattie! But just remember, I'm not through with you yet.

———

The rain had turned to occasional sprinkles, and Mattie decided to walk home from work. She would pick up a few groceries and hurry home, maybe call Raymond. She glanced toward the Darcy house as she scurried home, turned up her steps and encountered an immense purple umbrella, suspended on the top step. No, actually, there was an adorable child under there.

"James," Mattie cried. "How nice to see you. Are you waiting for someone or just waiting for more rain?"

"Waiting for you," James responded. "Mama says I can come up to your place and see Nemesis. If that's okay."

"It's not just okay, James. It's magical. Let's tiptoe in and see what Nemesis does when I'm not home."

James stood patiently while Mattie inserted her key and turned the doorknob, slowly easing the door open.

"Something's wrong, James," Mattie whispered. The bathroom door was closed. Mattie never closed that door; the litter box for Nemesis was in the bathroom. But now the door was closed, and Mattie could hear faint scratching sounds. And something else. From down the hall, in her bedroom, there was something else.

"James, please run home and ask your mama to call the police. Please, James, we'll play with Nemesis a little later."

James stood firmly for an instant, disappointed, and then raced off to get his mother. Mattie forced her body to creep up to the bathroom door. She opened it quietly and bent down for Nemesis. Before she could straighten up she was assaulted, not by a hatchet or a knife, or even a heavy fist, but by a loud, vicious scream from red-faced Florintini.

"You've got a cat in here."

"And you've got my panties in your hand," Mattie yelled. "Get out of my apartment!"

"No, Mattie, you get out of *my* apartment. No pets!
Give me that cat!"

"No way! Give me my panties, and get out!"

As Mr. Florintini reached for Nemesis, the frazzled cat reached for Florintini, finding the side of his face a suitable home for outstretched claws. Blood was flowing from Beelzebub's cheeks when the police arrived, and Mattie was ordered to sit down and breathe deeply while things got sorted out.

The Berkeley police were better known for their diplomacy than for their muscle, and once Florintini had been sent to his apartment to cool off and tend to his scratches, one of the officers sat with Mattie and listened thoughtfully to her version of the altercation. There probably wouldn't be any charges, from either side. Landlords had the right to enter apartments as long as they paid some of the utilities; Mattie had the right to feel invaded.

"I'm not spending one more minute in this nightmare," she sobbed.

James was delighted when his mother invited Mattie and Nemesis to spend the night at the Darcy's. He petted Nemesis while Mattie read a bedtime story. Mattie was asleep before the child was, and he gave her a soft, goodnight kiss that worked its way into her dreams about a home in the mountains, a home with Raymond and children, lots of children.

CHAPTER 7

And what did you hear, my darling young one?
I heard the sound of a thunder, it roared out a warnin',
Heard the roar of a wave that could drown the whole
world,
Heard one hundred drummers whose hands were a-
blazin', . . And it's a hard rain's a-gonna fall . . .
           Bob Dylan -- "Hard Rain"

"I just can't make it this Christmas, Mom. I'll try to get away in the spring. Hope you understand. I'm just settling into my new place. It's wonderful! A whole cottage – two bedrooms, just in case Peter or Bo or Josie and the kids come back. . . . Lots of sunlight, further over on the south side, just below the Claremont Hotel. I had to move in the rain, but my bosses loaned me their car, even gave me a hand with big boxes. Oh, and I bought a new bed, a big bed. I've saved a little money since I gave up nursing old cars."

"You don't have a car, Dear? I thought Peter took care of that for you."

"And, Mom, I even decorated my bedroom. First time I've ever decorated a room, really. It's beautiful, soft and snugly . . . even found some all-cotton sheets. . . . A friend of mine is going to be here during the Christmas time." *Here it comes. I guess I'm going to tell my mother that there's a Raymond in my life. I'm going to do that . . . right now.*

Is she someone I know?" Nora asked.

". . . I guess not," Mattie murmured. "But it would be nice if someday you could meet my friend."

"Well, you have a good holiday, my dear eldest daughter," Nora recited. "Bertram will be very disappointed you aren't coming for Christmas. He says he wants to get better acquainted with my family."

"Have a wonderful holiday, Mother," Mattie responded as she slowly traded the phone for Nemesis. *And what about Nora? Will she be disappointed? Would she like to get better acquainted with her family? Guess not. Ah, well, soon enough I'll tell her about Raymond. . . . Please hurry, Raymond. Get on the plane and get here!*

Raymond agreed that Mattie's all-cotton sheets were lovely, and for several days the couple found little reason to get out from between them. Mattie had spent hours preparing for Raymond's visit, so there was a wreath on the door, a little Christmas tree in the casual, hand-me-downs living room, food in the twice-cleaned refrigerator, and love in her heart. Time was irrelevant for Mattie as she lost herself in the rapture of Raymond's presence, his voice, his touch, his scent, his love-making.

"My best Christmas ever!" she announced.

Mattie didn't ask why it was that Raymond had the holiday to himself, didn't ask about his wife, didn't ask why they couldn't just stay bundled up forever in her new bedroom, snuggled away from the cold, winter winds.

"There's so much we don't talk about, Raymond. Is that okay?"

"Well, Mattie, we can talk about anything you want. Talk is pretty easy; doing is sometimes a challenge. But, I'll start. I've got a gnarly problem at the Cape. It demands my time because that's what I allow. I've got a wife because I made a mistake; and I've got you in bed with me because that's what I want. Your turn. What do you want to talk about?"

110

Mattie confessed she actually didn't want to *talk* about anything, she wanted to *do* something, something besides wear out the new sheets.

"I want to take you to a secret place," she announced.

Raymond's Florida clothes were amusing in Berkeley's wintertime, but the couple got put together enough for a quick stroll up the hill to the Claremont Hotel — bright, festive, and lavishly over-decorated. Christmas carols oozed from every corner of the massive building.

" . . . *a beautiful sight, we're happy tonight, walking in a winter wonderland.*"

"I knew you were a tenor, Raymond. It had to be," Mattie laughed, as a young waitress, dressed in little besides a fuzzy Santa hat, directed the couple to a table in the center of the lounge.

"We need to be by the window," Mattie whispered to Raymond, and arrangements were soon made for Mattie and Raymond to enjoy their last holiday night overlooking the glistening cities of San Francisco Bay.

"This is where my sister and I hide out . . . used to hide out before she moved to England. We never let anyone else come here with us, but she won't mind if you're here with me."

"Tell me more about her, Mattie."

"Well, she's very beautiful . . . a great mom. . . . She has two children now, Caitlin and Gareth. She reads to them a lot. . . . Raymond, she's actually rather like the wind. You know? . . . She flows with the energy that's around her. And she adds energy to whatever is going on. Don't know how wind works, really, but that's what she's like."

"Few people know how the wind works, Mattie . . . . You miss your niece, too, don't you?"

111

"Oh, my, yes. She was so adorable when she left, and now I only have pictures."

Mattie's eyes were a little misty now as she thought of her family, so far away, scattered about the world like snowflakes that might melt and disappear before she could truly appreciate them.

"Raymond, you never, ever mention your family. You said we could talk about anything. How about your family?" Mattie questioned.

Raymond shook his shoulders as if to clear away any dusty debris that might have settled there when he wasn't looking and hesitated long enough to take in a good supply of air.

"If you don't know your childhood is strange, then maybe it's not strange at all," Raymond began. "I had a little sister. Her name was Sarah. . . . I was five. . . .We were staying with my uncle in Maine. . . . My folks went into town for groceries . . . took Sarah with them. . . . I didn't want to go. . . . They didn't ever come back . . . . There was an accident . .

Mattie's heartbeat must have drowned out the Christmas carols, the busy holiday sounds of the lounge, for now there was only a cold stillness surrounding her, invading her spirit and forcing her to investigate what it would mean to lose her entire family, in an instant.

"This is too much, Raymond. Too much for me to take in."

"Then, let me tell you the rest. It will brighten things a bit. I just stayed on with Uncle George, my father's oldest brother. He was a surgeon — busy, kind, but detached. There were women in his life, but no mate. It might have been a truly peculiar childhood, but he had the wisdom to hire a nanny for me. And a tutor. Together, they forced me into a tolerable childhood, made me get acquainted, play with other kids. I was a good student . . . lost myself in studies . . . astronomy,

112

mostly. One strange thing, Mattie, my high school physics teacher gave me a present when I graduated. He gave me books – complete works of Shakespeare – said it would be easy for me to learn about the heavens, harder to understand the soul. He was right, of course, but don't give up on me, Mattie."

Mattie could remember Grandpa R's determination to make even little Bo sit quietly while he read passages from Shakespeare. During the winter months, he'd build a fire and gather the family together after dinner for a reading. Josie often complained that it took too long to hear his stories, but Grandpa R insisted. "Some families read the Bible together," he stated. "We read Shakespeare."

"And did you read those books, Raymond?" Mattie smiled at the idea of an aeronautical engineer reading all of Shakespeare, of *anyone* reading all of Shakespeare.

"Well, I'm not through yet. Here, I have one for you: 'The wounds invisible that love's keen arrows make.' That's from *As You Like It,* isn't it Mattie?"

Mattie was struggling to remember if she had ever read *As You Like It* when Raymond offered another line: "'Down on your knees, and thank heaven, fasting, for a good man's love.' We can skip the fasting, Mattie. I'm pretty hungry. Let's go home and eat, and then we'll make some children. At least one."

"Home?" Mattie said. "Make children?"

"Mattie, home for me is pretty much wherever you are. We can put off the children for a while if you want to. But let's go practice." The sheets had cooled during the couple's adventure to the hotel, so Mattie and Raymond warmed them together and drifted into a blissful sleep. Raymond's early morning flight back to Florida seemed in the far-distant future.

Mattie cursed the 5:00 a.m. alarm as Raymond fumbled with the sheets and reached for her one last time. Her tears dampened the pillow as she tried to imagine the new year without Raymond beside her, inside her, part of her.

For Josie, 1965 held both promise and sorrow. Early in the spring Jeremy's father discovered he had throat cancer. After his surgery, Clifford sold their house in Richmond and retired to Briarwood, leaving his younger brother, Jeremy's Uncle Sedgwick, to run the family business in London. The absence of in-laws in her daily life gave Josie new resolve to make her marriage work, and she continued her weekly sessions with Joan, her twenty-seven-year-old counselor. Jeremy reluctantly agreed to accompany Josie whenever Joan thought it might be valuable for the couple to work on common issues. Those sessions usually left Josie feeling rather adrift — anxious and depressed and lonely — but she poured her energy into trying to adapt.

———

"No more Sundays with the witch!" Josie gleefully announced to Mattie on the telephone. "We only have to do the holidays now. Isn't that great! I guess Clifford will be all right, although he can't talk very well. Of course, he never said much anyway. What's happening over there? I'm so homesick!"

"I am, too, Josie, and that's pretty strange since I'm living where I want to live. . . . It's not all good news here . . . kind of like a big storm is coming. When Malcolm X was killed in February, the black militant movement really took off. There's a lot of anger, everyplace you look, and, you know, lots and lots of drugs. Telegraph Avenue is beginning to look like a slum — groggy, lonesome people sitting around in doorways — and the Vietnam thing seems like a bad movie that just

114

won't end. Johnson's war on poverty is all tangled up with the war in Vietnam. I wish presidents would declare peace on things instead of war. It kind of messes up your mind when everything is a war. . . . . Strange, though, we're not really at war; we didn't actually declare a war this time. Thousands of people being shot in this non-war. It's a nightmare."

"Speaking of nightmares, Mattie, I got a really nice call from Peter when he was in Israel, but that night I dreamed that you and Peter and Bo came to visit me here in England. I was super excited, but when you arrived, Peter had gotten lost in the tube, Bo was dressed in a military outfit, and you were just crying and crying."

"No! That couldn't happen. Bo wouldn't go into the military! He's fine. He and a friend share an apartment. Bo's going to school at night, almost through with his degree, and he's doing some neat research. Congress is working on a bill for universal medical coverage. They call it Medicare, and Bo's working on some of the drafts. . . . Just like him, in the thick of things.. . . .What did Peter have to say? I never hear from him . . . well, a quick note now and again. He talks to Mother a lot, of course, and I guess he sends a dutiful letter to Father about every six months, but I really would like my very own letter from my very own big brother."

"Well, tell him! That's what my therapist says. You've got to tell people what you want. I don't know, Mattie, it's kind of like telling people what you want for your birthday and then there's no surprise. Maybe I'll get it right one of these days. . . . How about you and Raymond?"

"Oh, Josie, we had a super time at Christmas. Isn't it wonderful what she did?

"Who, Mattie? Mother? What did Mother do?"

"No, no," Josie. "Wrong mother. I mean Mother Nature. Thank God she gave us these bodies that feel so good when the right man comes along. . . . Raymond will be out

115

again this summer, whenever he decides to look up from his equations and formulas. . . . You remember Steinbeck's comment? 'Look from the tidepools to the stars and back again.' Well, Raymond's in there someplace, looking and looking. . . . He wants me to visit him in Florida, but I don't know how I feel about going into his territory, his wife's territory, I mean. . . . And I'd have to go on a telephone diet to afford the trip. . . . Guess I need to do that anyway, but we'll stay in touch, Josie. Are you fine? Having fun in merry old England? What's it really like?"

"Mattie, we're having such a good time now that we don't have to do the Catherine-Clifford dance all the time. Now we spend most Sunday afternoons walking in Richmond Park. Jeremy even insists we go when the weather's horrible. 'Just bundle up,' he says, 'must take our exercise.' I love the park, Mattie. I wish you could see it . . . lots of deer and birds, sheep, too . . . . We stop at this marvelous, old home in the park they've made into a tea room. It's called Pembroke Lodge, and Jeremy says Bertrand Russell lived there once. . . . Don't know why it's so important to the English to keep track of where everyone lived. . . . And guess what. There's a place called Thatched House Lodge right in the park. It was built in the 18th century, and guess who lives there? Princess Alexandra! And do you know, well, of course you don't, but she's six feet tall and so beautiful. Mattie, when we walk past there, I try so hard to imagine what it would be like to be a princess living in such a magnificent place. We still go for walks along the Thames, but now I enjoy it because we're not walking to Catherine and Clifford's for roast duck ala Catherine. Well, I'm rambling, but we're starting to have fun again, Mattie. Jeremy's so different when he's not around his mother, more like when we were in Berkeley. I think everything's going to be fine. Well, I better let you go, didn't mean to go on so long, it's your dime. Actually, it's your $25. Love you, Mattie, bye."

Jeremy and Josie would often get away to London for an Indian meal, sometimes a play, or sightseeing. Josie refused to see any more Dickens places, so Jeremy would plan the usual tourist attractions, Buckingham Palace, Madame Tussaud's, St. Paul's, Big Ben, The Tower of London, and, of course, Hyde Park Corner. They occasionally met friends at a local pub on Saturday afternoons, ending a pleasant day with a tour of Kew Gardens. The children were doing quite well, although both suffered from catarrh, brought on, according to the doctor, by the Thames Valley weather.

"Why did he say the Thames Valley weather?" Josie complained. "It's the weather in the whole damned country!"

"Bundle up, Josie. We can't change the weather."

Josie often wondered what she *could* change; certainly not the weather, perhaps her spirit. Perhaps she could find a way to actually enjoy the grey, uneventful days while Jeremy was teaching in London and working on his book at the British Museum Library. "Sir Robert Smirke!" Josie shrieked when Jeremy told her the name of the museum's architect. "Now there is something I would have changed. I would have changed my name!"

An unwelcome change in family routines came about as Clifford's health declined and Josie, Jeremy, and the children began spending more and more time at Briarwood. Catherine and Jeremy would argue about "what to do with him," Catherine opting for a home, and Jeremy pushing for a home nurse. Jeremy didn't push very hard, and Catherine's plan was adopted as Josie knew it would be.

———

God, we're right back where we started. . . . Not
quite. Now we spend every Sunday at the nursing
home! Down to Briarwood on Saturday, spend the
night, drive two hours with Catherine, visit Clifford
who can't talk — so hard to visit with someone who
can't talk — drive back, farewells to Catherine, drive
home. Not exactly a pleasant family outing in the
country. . . . She says the children give her a
headache in the car. Then Jeremy tells me to make
them be quiet . . . She's the one who gives headaches.
Why can't she bring Clifford home to die like he
wants? That's what he wants. His eyes can talk. He
feels so caged up in that old, dying body, lying there
in a strange bed, in a strange place. Why can't a
person just die at home? Why doesn't Jeremy insist?
The nursing home is awful! It's damp and dreary,
right out of *Oliver Twist*. . . . "You smell bad." She
actually told Clifford he smells bad! Can't believe
Catherine said that! Well, he does smell bad. Maybe
dying makes you smell bad. She makes him feel bad.
Jeremy pretends not to notice. It probably makes him
sad and angry, but how would I ever know?

———

Sadness and anger, like a disease, oozed into the
lives of both sisters that day. Mattie had slept poorly and
tried to sweep away the debris of her nightmares with an
early-morning call to Raymond. An efficient southern
drawl, remote and uninterested, informed her that Dr.
Robbins was in conference — by now a term on Mattie's
list of most-hated euphemisms. She arrived late for work
where she encountered a grumpy co-worker chewing out
the receptionist. Frank and Emily were having a spat
about budgets, and their behind-closed-doors argument
soon spilled over into Mattie's office when they stomped

in, insisting that the printing estimates in one of Mattie's projects couldn't possibly be correct. Frank was red-faced and rude, Emily straight-backed and rigid when Mattie agreed that the estimates couldn't be right; they were estimates, and not much could be right today. When Emily proclaimed that she didn't appreciate Mattie's being sassy, Mattie announced that she would be leaving work early that day.

Although it was mid summer, the bay fog hung heavy and moist over the city as Mattie wandered along Telegraph Avenue toward her favorite coffee house where she would sit quietly and read Herb Caen and then maybe turn to her fresh, new copy of *Saturday Review*. Summer session students normally seemed relaxed and carefree, but today there was tension and worry in many of the faces Mattie encountered. Even the ever-present posters that so often amused her offered little reprieve from the gloom. Timothy Leary's latest directive, "Tune in, turn on, drop out," seemed more of a requiem refrain than an invitation to an acid paradise, and when Mattie heard a chant emanating from a crowd on the corner of Telegraph and Haste, she decided to forego the coffee. "Hey, hey, LBJ, how many kids did you kill today" continued to reverberate in her mind as she made a quick right turn and headed up hill to the Darcy's. She was looking forward to a visit with Brenda and, of course, James, who always had a smile for Mattie. Josie had sent a new book for Mattie's birthday, a delightful story about furry-footed hobbits, elves, and dwarves, terrifying orcs, and a magical wizard. James would love the wizard. Mattie and James could read Tolkien together, and Gandalf, the powerful wizard, would lift the heavy gloom from Mattie's spirit.

Her first view of James didn't mesh with her Tolkien fantasy, and Mattie stood for a moment, frozen in place, as she watched her young friend – not an adorable

119

hobbit, nor an endearing elfin child, but a very angry, tight-fisted, young, black male — reaching for another rock to hurl at the window of Mr. Florintini's apartment building.

"James, what are you doing?" Mattie called out as she began to run toward the child. "James, stop! You could get arrested for that."

"No more police!" James responded, scarcely noticing Mattie and certainly not pausing to offer his usual welcoming kiss.

"James, please stop. You mustn't do this, no matter what the problem is."

"You don't know about problems, Mattie. You're white!"

Mattie's body stiffened as she tried to absorb the blow from James, to understand that "white" was an accusation, not a skin color.

Little made sense to Mattie, but a mother-bear instinct forced itself into her muscles, and she grabbed James by the arm and tugged him toward the house.

"Yes," she said. "I'm white, and I'm your friend, and I'm not going to see you arrested."

Brenda greeted Mattie with a hug and tears in her eyes, a tumbler of red wine in her hand. The disorder of the normally tidy and peaceful home shocked Mattie's senses as she moved toward the kitchen table where Brenda's daughter fussed with an unwanted snack. The Darcy apartment was filled with screams and raging fires, police and national guard, gun shots and death, as a detached TV newscaster called it the worst riot in the country since the Detroit race riot of 1943. The Watts riot claimed thirty-four lives, all Afro-Americans, many of them angry arsonists and looters, blacks who were killed by white men in uniforms.

"Willy and I celebrated the Voting Rights Bill just last week," Brenda sobbed. "Now we will mourn. Maybe there will be no end to mourning."

Years later, when Mattie looked back over the months, even the years following the Watts riots, she found little that had clarity, purpose, or meaning. It was as if the entire country were treading water; no, not water, but slime, gooey slime that refused to wash away. Nor would the slurry mess allow motion; it simply held the nation in its stagnant grip. There were, of course, personal events – birthdays, weddings, funerals – and national events – campaigns, elections, legislation. But the many studies and conversations about what was wrong in America were like dialogues between the deaf and the blind. Comfortably polarized issues were blown into fragments, peppered with fearful, strident gestures and little understanding, no direction.

The one voice Mattie was able to discern in the cacophonous tides that flowed into the coffee houses and homes of Berkeley folk was that of Martin Luther King, Jr. He held the line on domestic non-violence, and on New Year's Day of 1966, he published a paper that established a strong position against the war in Vietnam. Historians would argue for years about his comments; not so much about the moral issues – he would later remind the nation that "morality is indivisible" – but about political and economic myths and realities. Some realities were rudely obvious. Relatively few young Afro-American men were college-bound; deferment from the draft, not an option. In relation to population, twice as many Afro-American soldiers were coming home from Vietnam in body bags than were white servicemen. The nation's experience of slavery, racism, and segregation had clearly hurtled itself into the battlefields of Vietnam, where the theory of equality fought deadly battles with the reality of privilege. In Washington D.C., the budget for the Office of Economic Opportunity dropped from $750 million in 1964 to $1.5 million in 1965. As of January 1966, the White House expected to commit over 400,000 more men to the war in Vietnam. Five billion dollars had already been added to the federal budget; an additional $10 billion would be needed the following year. Commenting on congressional deliberations, one government official said, "With the Vietnam buildup, they just had to drop this other thing."

"This other thing" was the nation's commitment to achieve racial equality. Rioting in the nation's ghettos would capture newspaper headlines for another four years, while at home, next to San Francisco's sprawling, graceful Golden Gate Park, colorful flower-children, rock stars, and drug gurus would gather in the Haight-Ashbury to proclaim a new consciousness and a new slogan: "Make love, not war."

CHAPTER 8

Ain't there no one here that knows where I'm at
Ain't there no one here that knows how I feel
Good God Almighty, that stuff ain't real . . .
Bob Dylan -"Last Thoughts on Woody Guthrie"

Shortly after Clifford's death, Catherine announced she was letting Briarwood and taking a flat in Richmond. Jeremy could be so helpful to her now that she was alone, and she would be able to spend more time with the children, she said.

"I won't do it Jeremy! I'll divorce you! I'll go back home! I'll take the children and go back to the States. I'm as serious about this as I've ever been about anything. If you care anything at all about me and the children, you'll do something about Catherine. I won't live near her ever again. You have to do something."

Jeremy didn't do anything, and Catherine did take a spacious flat four blocks from Josie's small one. Catherine would arrive just before tea, on foot if the weather was nice, by cab if not. Josie would serve her, and when Jeremy arrived home, he would drive Catherine home and return for his dinner.

"What are you doing, Josie?" Jeremy stood stiffly at the bedroom door, the only sign of distress an uncharacteristic tightness around his mouth.

"What does it look like I'm doing?" Josie replied, turning toward one of the suitcases lying open on the bed. "What in the hell does it look like I'm doing, you son-of-a-bitch! I told you, and now I'm doing it," Josie cried as she stuffed in more of the children's belongings. "I'm leaving! You can move in with Catherine for all I care! I'm not living like this anymore, damn you!"

"Josie, you know how I feel about swearing. Please stop."

"Damn! Is that all you can say? Is that all you have to say? I can't believe you, you know. I can't believe that's all you have to say. I'm leaving tomorrow. We're going! I took the money we were saving for the house. I've got the tickets, and we're going! Do you understand?"

"Josie, please don't do this. Please, we'll work something out. I don't like the situation any better than you do, you know I don't, but she's my mother after all."

"You have to choose, right now, Jeremy. It's me and the children or her. Right now, this minute, choose."

"All right, Josie, just let me think about it for awhile."

"One hour! I'm going to the pub! You have one hour!"

———

One hour was how long Mattie had been waiting for Raymond's delayed flight from Florida. She had rented a car in Berkeley and arrived at San Francisco International airport with plenty of time to redo her makeup and calm her excitement. Now, with insistent announcements of delayed flights, she became restless, trying to ignore the fetid breath of imaginary fortune-tellers who might, in an instant, pierce her bubble of joy. *I wonder how they announce a flight that doesn't make it, one that just doesn't arrive . . . one that simply falls . . . thud! . . . out of the sky and lands on your heart, ripping your life into pieces and scattering it as garbage around the countryside. . . . I need something to read, something to settle my nerves.*

124

There was little in the newspapers and magazines strewn about the waiting area that interested Mattie. Escalation of the Vietnam War was the ever-present theme, one heart-rending photograph replacing another, and she eventually turned to the NASA materials Raymond had sent her. She would focus on his world, and soon he would arrive in hers. She could easily understand Raymond's excitement the previous night when he telephoned to give her his flight schedule and to explain events at the Cape. Three astronauts had been chosen earlier in the year for Mission AS-204 — the first Apollo manned earth-orbit. Gus Grissom, Edward White, and Roger Chaffee were scheduled to make a voyage around the earth for up to fourteen days before the end of 1966. A second Apollo team — Walter Schirra, Don Eisele, and Walter Cunningham — had just been announced, with Frank Borman, Thomas Stafford, and Michael Collins as backups. The design certification committee had completed its review and declared the space vehicle flight-worthy, recommending correction in several deficiencies. There had been complaints that the crew was not getting enough time in the new simulation and checkout facilities, and there were still concerns about a leak in the service propulsion system, problems with the reaction control system, troubles in the environmental control unit. A new unit would soon be shipped from its California assembly site to the Cape, the circumstance that permitted Raymond a brief California holiday with Mattie. Apollo's pathway to the moon was becoming perceptible.

Mattie had made dinner reservations at the Awahnee and had reserved a cabin in Yosemite Valley. They would have three days together "in heaven," Mattie said, then drive over Tioga Pass and up the back shoulder of the Sierra to Lake Tahoe and D.L. Bliss State Park, where Mattie had a favorite rock to sit on, just beside the water. Raymond would finally have an opportunity to see the jewels of her beloved state at one of her favorite times of the year – after the summer crowds had hurried down the mountain and before the snow and skiers arrived, a bitter-sweet time of change.

They had played together in San Francisco on Raymond's previous late-summer visit, and now Mattie wanted Raymond to discover, share with her, the grandeur and the peace of the Sierra. Raymond's flight to San Francisco had been delayed by several hours, but eventually the couple arrived at Yosemite, just at dusk, slowing down only briefly to catch a glimpse of Bridal Veil Falls and El Capitan through the misty blue-grey of evening that had settled into the valley. Raymond could sense the excitement in Mattie, and he promised to get up very early to hike with her.

Dinner at the Awahnee was not at all as Mattie had imagined it would be. The setting was as grand as Mattie remembered, the service pleasant, the food attractive and tasty. It was the conversation that seemed out of phase with Mattie's notion of a lovers' romantic rendezvous. A tall, suntanned waiter had served a first-course soup and was exchanging pleasantries with Mattie when Raymond's voice – the one that offered straight information, no embellishments – penetrated the dialogue.

"My wife left me, Mattie, two weeks ago. I've been wanting to tell you. She returned to her parent's home in Michigan."

Mattie exchanged the soup spoon in her right hand for her linen napkin to wipe away the tears forming so quickly in her eyes. The young waiter dissolved into the mist of her tears and the noises of the crowded dining room, and Mattie wondered if her entire body might slip away from her.

126

"Are you alright?" her voice finally managed to utter.

"Well, my pride's a bit wounded. She was a good friend, Mattie, and I didn't realize how troubled she was. She's thirty-seven . . . said she just wanted a chance to fall in love before it was too late. . . . But my heart isn't broken, Mattie. It belongs to you."

Raymond removed the parsley from the side of his shrimp bisque, and Mattie wondered if his commentary was complete. He had given her the important information; did he imagine the conversation was over? Questions surged to the tip of her tongue, but with a clarity that would see them through many years together, Mattie assumed a posture similar to Raymond's, found a firm, quiet voice and said, "I'm pregnant, Raymond. I've been wanting to tell you. I hope it's a boy."

Mattie calculated that, allowing for deep breaths, their conversation had taken maybe 15-18 seconds, about as long as it takes to lift off a Saturn rocket.

"Mattie," he said. "We need a plan. We'll hike tomorrow and make a plan. . . . A girl would be okay, wouldn't it?"

Mattie found Raymond outside their cabin the next morning. She watched him trying to take in Yosemite for the

first time, trying to absorb its power and beauty, waiting to be absorbed in return. Sunlight had reached the very tip of Half Dome, starting its perceptible, magical slide into the valley, setting the pace for the tears that streamed down Raymond's face. "There is so much to do, Mattie. Your mountains are a good place to begin."

By the time the couple reached Mattie's piece of granite on the edge of Lake Tahoe, a plan had been formed. Mattie and Raymond held each other in the sand beside the lake until well after dark when a park ranger politely hustled them off the beach and wished them a good life.

———

The one hour deadline Josie had allowed Jeremy was extended through the Christmas season, and by early 1967 Jeremy had accepted a lectureship at the University of Kent at Canterbury. Josie was excited to be going to a more rural setting not far from the ocean. She missed the Pacific Coast and the mountains. Jeremy had promised her mountains when he took the family on holiday to Wales, and Josie thought the Brecon Beacons were lovely, but "they are not mountains," she teased.

The couple found a pleasing mock-Tudor home, and Nora sent them the down payment, along with a copy of Eric Berne's *Games People Play*. Both gifts, Josie thought, were laden with messages she didn't care to receive.

Josie's Bath

Well, I guess I did it again . . . . Those pompous asses. . . . Dinner at the high table, how exciting. How absurd! . . . I didn't think Jeremy really meant the table would be raised up above the students' tables. . . . lowly students, I guess, need to be reminded of their proper place. . . . So do I, apparently. . . . Port, cigars, and jokes about how the men were allowing the ladies to join them in the lounge. Ha ha, really funny. How was I supposed to know that "ladies" don't drink port? Nobody told me. I just prefer port to sherry so I took port when it was passed. God, the looks on their faces. Another crass American, I bet they were thinking. Jeremy was really embarrassed. Crime of the century, I guess. . . . Didn't much like any of them. They use a lot of words but don't actually talk about much. I mean there is so much going on in the world right now. . . . What's wrong with a good argument? All I wanted to do was liven things up a bit. I was excited! . . . Mattie had been so excited on the phone, and so was Bo. . . . Thurgood Marshall to the Supreme Court! That's pretty spectacular. . . . I just kind of wanted to bring my family and my country to the party . . . not really a party! . . . Jeremy should have given me the script: "Ten Things Not to Do When Meeting the Higher-ups for the First Time." Subtitle: "How to Fit in When You Don't Really Want to" . . . or how about this: "How to Pretend that Racial Inequality Was Invented in America." It's a good thing Jeremy already got this job. I expect they wouldn't have offered him the position if they'd met me first. . . . Well, it wasn't difficult to help them all feel superior. . . . Oh, Mattie, I wish you were here. There's a walk that goes with the looking-down-your nose posture. Sort of stiff, but floaty, too, so your feet don't really touch the ground. . . . Don't think I'll ever get it right. Makes your back hurt, and your heart ache.

Josie gave the dinner parties she was expected to give, dreading each formal event. The *Larousse Gastronomic* Mattie had sent the previous Christmas guided her through the ordeal of menu planning while Jeremy guided her about expectations and behavior.

"I get it, Jeremy. Entertaining colleagues at Canterbury isn't the same as having a party. It's an initiation ritual, and I doubt that I'll make it into the club. . . . Why can't we have a real party? Dance, laugh, get drunk and play strip poker? Don't you think this is boring? Boring and hard work. Aren't there real people inside those, those . . . I can't stand this!" Josie shoved an onion quiche into the oven and slammed the door.

"Josie, grow up! Aren't you ever going to grow up? I've done everything I can to make you happy, and nothing seems to work. Why don't you try a little harder? I don't know, just try to fit in. You might like it."

"I'll never like it," Josie shouted. "I can't stop being me just because you want me to. What's wrong with the way I am? You say you love me, then want me to change. What in the hell does love mean to you anyway?"

"I want you for my companion, Josie. As people get older they want companionship more than the other."

"The other what?" Josie spat. "What are we talking about here?"

Well, you want excitement in everything you do. You can't always have excitement, and you must realize that, Josie. Can't we just settle into a nice, comfortable life? Just get on with it?"

After an argument with Jeremy, Josie frequently had a sleepless night and then allowed fatigue to direct her through the next day's household routines. *Let's just get on with it*, she would recite, as she set about her chores. For the family, Josie cooked steak-and-kidney pie, bangers-and-beans, bubble-and-squeak, trifle, and scones. "I may be limited," she would admit, "but so is English cuisine." She never stopped aching for cheeseburgers, and Jeremy hardly noticed what he ate. He was working on the final revision of his book, something to do with Dickens, of course, but Josie had given up interest in Jeremy's work, and Jeremy had given up interest in sharing it with her. The two lived a very British, usually polite existence as did most of their acquaintances. Josie mastered the art of responding to almost anything with "quite," and it seemed to suffice in most situations. Sex for the couple normally left Josie stranded somewhere between arousal and frustration, between tears and anger.

Caitlin began school in the fall, and although Josie didn't like uniforms, she thought Caitlin looked adorable

130

dressed in the grey pinny, white blouse, red tie, red knee socks, red beret, and black plimsolls. Josie didn't get off on the right foot with the headmistress, when, on the third day, Caitlin was sent home for arriving at school tieless. The relationship deteriorated further when Josie became aware that the school day started with prayer. She informed the headmistress that she didn't believe in prayer at school; the headmistress in turn informed Josie that the only option was for Caitlin to leave the class during prayer time and sit in the hall with the little Jewish girl who quickly became Caitlin's best friend. They shared whispers in the hallway while their classmates said prayers and while Josie struggled to understand her alien status in England. Something to do with the war, she remembered the fishmonger telling her. "The bloody blokes came just in time to claim they saved us. We didn't need 'um, didn't want 'um neither."

By the time Gareth was three, he and Josie enjoyed meandering down the high street for the daily shopping and hurrying home for an early tea. Josie joined a group of other mothers who took turns hosting coffee klatches so the young children could play together. The conversations of the women centered around entertaining, child rearing, recipes, and occasional light and guarded talk of husbands' follies. Josie often left the gatherings with the thought that she must have some parts missing, some essential ingredients omitted when she was born.

———

Mattie's Bath

I guess a hospital sponge bath will have to do. But we will soon go home, you and I. . . . How amazing you are, already the center of the universe, a proper place for you. I had no idea how much power you would have. First you took over my belly, kicked and

131

pushed to announce your presence, and now here you are, taking over my soul. Some people might think we are two separate entities — you and I — but we know that is only an illusion. We are one. I delight in us. . . . Tonight I will read you a story. Too young for a story, you say? No, my dear one, there are so many stories; we must start now. Tonight I will read to you a letter from your father. Yes, he's the other half of you, the handsome part, the beautiful hands, the tender eyes, the strong back bone. . . . Please don't be angry because he is not here right now. I am angry; that's enough for us. You must have known I was angry when you were floating about in my belly, a beautiful boy-child about to become a magical person. Let's try not to be angry. We will read stories together, and we won't be angry with your father. We will wait for him together, and he will be along. He will tell you fine tales about sending a man to the moon. Really! Yes, it sounds a bit silly, but perhaps we will come to understand about silly things together. We will be fine, you and I. . . . Your name is David Randall. It's a fine name for the fairest of children. In time, you will have another name, the one your father will bring along with him. I should probably tell you right now that your father wasn't listening very well when Dr. Freud said that man needs love and work. Maybe he only heard the last part . . . so busy doing and providing. We must work hard together to show him how lovely it is to just be, be in love, be loved. We can do that, you and I together can do that. In time we will; now we will have a bedtime story.

———

Mattie reached across the hospital nightstand for her purse and removed a much-read letter from the side pocket. She was elated that the newborn infant in her

132

arms appeared to be listening to the first words he would hear from his father.

"Dear Child of Mine,

I hope you are a boy because that is what your mother wants. I'm sure you are a boy because she has a way of making things happen when they are important to her. That's what I am trying to do, too. I'm helping to make things happen that are important to me. I hope they will seem important to you one day. Maybe they will only seem like small steps when you look back on our struggles. But however they appear in the future, I want you to know what is happening right now for me.

Early this year some of my good friends, some brave people, were killed here at Cape Kennedy. I would like you to know their names: Virgil Grissom, Edward White, and Roger Chaffee. Each of us here at the Cape is finding a way to mourn, and at the same time we are trying to keep the fires of life from going out in the Apollo program. Your mother will tell you more about Apollo, the first one. He was a Greek god, the son of Zeus, as I remember. He represented order and civilization. The sun was the chariot he rode in across the sky so we are using his name to describe our program. We are building a chariot that men can ride in. They can ride around the earth, and if we are very good at what we do, they can ride all the way to the moon and back."

Mattie refolded Raymond's letter, re-examined every inch of her son, and whispered "perfect" as she and the child drifted into peaceful sleep.

———

"Hi, Honey, this is your mommy."

"Oh, hello, Mother," Mattie drowsily replied as she shifted slowly on the firm mattress of the hospital bed.

"How is the wee one, Dear? And how are you? What does it feel like to be a new mother? It must have been difficult at your age."

"No, it wasn't bad, Mother, actually pretty exciting, and I'm fine. David is beautiful. He looks so much like his father," Mattie replied gazing down at the small bundle nestled in her arms.

"That's lovely, Dear, and what does your man think of his new son?"

"His name is Raymond, Mother, and I told you he couldn't be here. There is too much going on at the Cape. You remember that terrible flash fire in January? . . . But, yes, he's very excited. I spoke to him right after David was born."

"Well, Honey, I have exciting news! I'm going to be able to come out there to help you. Isn't that wonderful! Bertram is part of a little men's group, and they're going off on a week's retreat. I told him I wasn't going to be left with the hind tit. His clients go into separation anxiety when he's gone, and their neuroses escalate. I'm not going to be left fielding all his calls and taking care of his *kids*. I'd much rather take care of my own child."

Mattie vaguely remembered her mother telling her that Bertram's work involved something called reparenting. It had sounded strange to Mattie at the time. Something to do with clients reprogramming their lives, sucking on baby bottles, getting hugs from the therapist whom they call "Daddy." There was even a client living with Nora and Bertram now who referred to herself as their daughter.

"You don't have to come all that way, Mother," Mattie said. "I can manage fine, really. Brenda is planning to help out, and James said he would run errands for me."

"Is Brenda that black friend of yours?" Nora asked.

134

"Yes, Mother, Brenda is my friend, and yes, she is Afro-American."

"Well, that's nice, Dear. I used to think how nice it would be to have an old, black mammy around when I had you kids. But I think you need your own mommy at a time like this, especially since there's no father on the scene."

"When are you coming, Mother? How are you going to get from the airport?"

"Well, I haven't thought that one through yet," Nora replied. "Maybe your friend could pick me up. Do you think you could ask her? Does she have a husband? Maybe he would like to earn a few extra dollars. I don't mind paying. I'll be there Wednesday about two."

"Brenda has a husband, Mother. His name is Willie. He's an attorney, and he's on the Berkeley City Council. I'm certain he doesn't want to play chauffeur. He's black, too, Mom, and he celebrates his skin color. . . . Please don't worry about the transportation; Frank and Emily are coming by this afternoon to see me and to meet David. They'll arrange something. . . . You don't have to pay anything, Mother."

"That's fine then, Dear. I can't remember right now where my ticket is, but I'll call you back with the information. I'm going to call you twice a day until I get there, just to check on you and give you moral support. Would you like that, Honey?"

"You don't have to do that, Mother, I'm fine. I'll be pretty busy with David, and I want to try to get as much sleep as possible."

"Well, we don't have to talk long, but it's important for you to feel cared for at a time like this. It's not a good time to be alone."

"I'm not alone. I have friends, and I have Raymond."

"Well, you know what I mean. So, I'll phone you this afternoon or this evening. Better go now, so much to do. Do you remember when we'd try to get away from the ranch for a little vacation, how hard it was to bed down the cows? Well, it's kind of like that here, you know, with all these needy people in and out all the time. I love you, Sissy. Kiss the little one for me, and tell him Grandma's coming."

Mattie replaced the receiver in its cradle and shifted David to her other arm. She was a mother now, and she wanted quiet time to ponder the amazing sensations that coursed through her entire being.

———

Mattie was sleeping when the door bell of her cottage rang. Pulling herself slowly out of her exhaustion, she tried to remember her dream and tried to remember why she felt so much tension throughout her body. She had been up most of the night with David, and she woke up wishing there was someone to help her out, someone to turn down the bed, fluff the pillows, bring cottage cheese and applesauce, ice cream, chicken soup, macaroni and cheese — her comfort foods. Running her fingers through her tousled hair and moving slowly toward the door, Mattie let herself believe the helper she had wished for was on the other side of the door, bringing gifts of care.

Nora's energy preceded her into the cottage; Mattie felt it like the quiet that happens just before a summertime wind, and she perceived its color as muddy-yellow.

"Hello, My Darling, I'm finally here! It was a terrible flight. I'm exhausted. It's so good to be here with my dear ones."

Frank followed Nora into the cottage, set down her bags, and went to give Mattie a hug. "Your mother is a remarkable woman," he said. "I can't stay right now, but give us a call if you need anything, will you? Emily said to tell you she's cooking up a fantastic meal. She'll drop things by later this afternoon."

Nora caught Frank's sleeve and drew him toward her. "Thank you so much, Frank Feldman!" She paused, thought for a moment and repeated slowly, "Feldman, that's a Jewish name, isn't it? I didn't realize my daughter was working for Jews. You people have such difficult scripts to deal with. But I'm so glad you came to get me. It was nice we had a little chance to get acquainted."

Frank was gone before Mattie could find a way into the conversation, and Nora was surveying the little house. "You've done quite well for yourself. It's a little love nest. No wonder you got pregnant."

"It's nice to see you, Mother. I planned to let you have my room upstairs. I'll be in with David, just across the hall."

"Oh, Sweetheart, you'll have to take my bags up for me. I have problems with my knees and can't carry much weight, especially up a flight of stairs. . . . Do be careful. We don't want you hemorrhaging or something nasty like that. Be careful, Dear. . . . Oh, Sissy, I'd love a cup of coffee when you get back. I've got a little headache, traveling so far, you know. Do you have any coffee made?"

"No, Mother, but you can certainly make some. The coffee's in the cannister on the counter. It's Peet's coffee. . . . really nice new coffee house here. . . . There's a grinder next to the brewer. . . . I'd like a cup, too."

"A grinder? You'd better do it, Dear. I'm not good with coffee makers. Bertram always does that little chore."

Leaving Nora's luggage at the foot of the stairs, Mattie moved toward the kitchen. "How is Bertram, by the way? Did he get away for his trip?"

"Oh, yes," Nora replied, shaking her head. "You know how boys are. It took me hours to get him ready. He's so particular about his wardrobe. He's got tons of clothes, but he spent a whole day shopping while I stayed home washing his dirty underwear."

"Well, I hope he enjoys his time away," Mattie responded. "You haven't seen David yet, Mother. I can hear him beginning to fuss. Would you get him please? I don't like to let him cry," Mattie called from the kitchen.

"Oh, dear," Nora replied. "I'm afraid I'd drop him coming down those narrow, steep stairs. You'd better do that, Sissy. I just can't wait to hold him."

Mattie placed David in Nora's arms, delivered the coffee, and eased herself down onto the couch.

Nora gazed at her grandson's face with a troubled look. "I certainly hope the little guy won't be hebephrenic," she said, glancing quickly at Mattie.

"Hebe-what?" Mattie asked. "What are you talking about? He's perfect. He's fine. The doctor said he's fine."

"Hebephrenia is a form of schizophrenia, Dear, and we suspect that it's caused by babies not bonding with their parents."

"David is bonding with me, Mother. Why wouldn't he be? I'm with him all the time. I'm not going back to work for months. I'll be doing some work here at home."

"I know, Darling, and I'm sure you're a wonderful mother. I'm just concerned about your man not being here, that's all. Children need to bond with both parents to become fully integrated. He may have to do some reparenting when he's older. But let's not worry about that now. He's a beautiful baby . . . quite a bit like Peter was. . . . By the way, Sissy, I didn't eat much on the plane, such wretched food. Could you get me a little something to nibble on. I don't think I can wait 'til

138

dinner. What are we having for dinner, my dear eldest daughter? You're such a wonderful cook. I know it will be yummy."

"Emily's bringing dinner for us, Mother, so I can get some rest."

"Yes, you need to get plenty of rest. Have you talked to your sister lately? Shall we give her a call? She was so happy about your baby last time we talked."

———

Josie's Bath

Men, mistress, myth, *merde*! Fuck you, Raymond, fuck you, and the flying phallus you fire into the heavens to rape the beautiful Diana! . . . The myth – the wife and the mistress – Oh, you had a wife alright, but it wasn't Mattie! You have a mistress, but it isn't Mattie! You and Jeremy are so alike. Are you all that way? I think so . . . . This is how I see it, Raymond, you shit. Beware. We are wising up. You call it "your work." You all call it "your work!" Makes you feel valiant, doesn't it? "I have to go to work." "I have so much work to do." "I am so overworked." What a great euphemism for your mistress. No man prepares for his soul mate the way he prepares for his "work." . . . . You begin young, hammering a little peg into a little hole with your little hammer, little league, your car, high school A team if you're good enough. . . . Wise up, Raymond, you're missing it, you are all missing it. . . . You go through the dance with us, saying the right words – love, devotion, commitment, they come easily to your serpent tongues. You are the predator, we the prey. Of course we are captured, we want back inside you, want to be swallowed and taken into your souls . . . . What was that bit I read? Something about a human male being genetically less than one percent different

139

than a male chimpanzee, three percent different than a human female. Right! Good stuff, Raymond, we're learning who you are when we are "let" to learn!. . . Mattie says you will come, and I expect you will when you tire of your mistress, when you find her lacking, when the empty place inside you grows, as your child grew in Mattie. . . . When you boys tire of your toys, you come home to momma to be suckled, nourished . . . . Mattie will be fine, she told me, I believe her. The child will be fine, too, Mattie will make it so . . . . Raymond, if I could meet you, I would ask you this question only, "How is it you panic when you're ten minutes late for work, and you don't panic when you're months late for Mattie and your son?"

CHAPTER 9

I see a bad moon rising
I see trouble on the way
I see earthquakes and lightning
I see bad times today . . .
John Fogerty / Creedence Clearwater Revival
"Bad Moon Rising"

The widows of the three astronauts who were killed by fire on January 12, 1967, requested that "Apollo 1" become the name of the flight their husbands had hoped to make. The nation joined in mourning its heroes while NASA persevered. By November 9 of that same year, the five engines of the Saturn V first-stage ignited and lifted the unmanned Apollo 4 into earth orbit from the Florida Wildlife Game Refuge, now known as the Kennedy Space Center. It was the first launch of the complete Saturn V and the first flight of a simulated lunar module. A record 124 tons of technology, vision, and hard work would circle the earth for over eight hours at a distance of 10,700 miles. After two orbits of the earth, its rockets would successfully fire to cast the craft back into the atmosphere. Seamen of the *U.S.S. Bennington* would recover the spacecraft and join the nation in celebrating the belief that Apollo was destined to rendezvous with the moon goddess.

Another first that captivated the country in 1967 was Super Bowl I, played in Los Angeles Memorial Coliseum, with quarterback Bart Starr leading the Green Bay Packers to a 35-10 victory over the Kansas City Chiefs. If Bo hadn't mentioned the game in a call to Mattie, she clearly would have ignored it, certain there was more cultural significance in Dr. Martin Luther King, Jr.'s comment at Riverside Church in New York: "The great Society has been shot down on the battlefields of Vietnam."

Josie's attention was captured by Arlo Guthrie's anti-Establishment hit tune, "Alice's Restaurant," and the death that same year of Woodie Guthrie, Arlo's father and the nation's most beloved folk-singer. Josie felt the ties to her homeland dissolving, and she and Caitlin played "Alice's Restaurant" and Woodie Guthrie's "This Land Is Your Land" incessantly until Jeremy offered to introduce them to some charming British folk songs, whereupon Josie developed the habit of humming " . . . from California to the New York island" throughout the private part of her day. She added to their meager record collection the music of Pete Seeger, Cisco Houston, Tom Paxton, and the Weavers.

When Mattie called with news of Carl Sandburg's death, Josie slipped into silent despair that was only slightly relieved when one of the mums from the coffee klatch began stopping by after dropping her husband at the station to catch his London train. Portia had sensed Josie's depression, and she offered the friendship of a self-defined "white witch" – gentle, caring, and peculiar. As the friendship developed, Portia informed Josie there was a ghost in the house. She said she felt it at the top of the stairs when she went to the loo, but didn't feel it was a problem to Josie's family, didn't sense any bad vibrations. Jeremy wouldn't allow any talk of ghosts, but Josie thought the idea of a ghost and a friend named Portia rather intriguing, "quite proper, in this foggy land," and especially welcome since Rosa Parks had not chosen to relocate to England with Josie. The other mums found Portia a bit odd, and she was not included in their wider social circle. Neither was Josie, for that matter, so it was not surprising that the friendship grew.

"You should join me for badminton, Josie. Exercise is good for the body and the spirit. You need to get out now and again."

"What would I wear?" Josie asked, feeling excitement for the first time in months. She remembered movies portraying women who played badminton at country homes, women from a different era who wore long, white dresses to trip about manicured, grass courts.

"A tennis dress will be fine," Portia said. "That's what women wear at the club."

Josie loved the game and was very good at it. She knew she looked good, too, in the short, white tennis outfit. At twenty-five, Josie had a ripeness in her figure and an awareness of her body that only seemed enhanced by her having borne two children. She enjoyed the people she met and played with in matches, and she managed to convince Jeremy to accompany her occasionally. Jeremy had played at Oxford and could hold his own with some of the better players.

Josie became optimistic again about her life in England and was sure the tide was turning. All would be well. She was genuinely disappointed the day Jeremy told her he couldn't play as they had arranged. He had a tutorial, he said, with a student who was having difficulty in one of his classes.

"Oh, oim sorry you can't come, but there'll be next week, luv," Josie replied, trying to imitate the cockney accent of a man who had recently shown up at the club, winning most of the singles matches and whatever doubles he played. Josie wasn't in his league but sat on the sidelines and watched him when she wasn't playing. They sometimes exchanged a few pleasantries, and Josie soon learned that Tom was a carpenter who played at the club on a schedule that corresponded agreeably with hers.

There was a good deal about Tom that was agreeable. He was healthy, high-spirited, and, in Josie's eyes, ruggedly handsome – a Marlboro man who seemed a temporary visitor to this badminton club in a misty, foreign land. Josie sometimes daydreamed about where this man, Tom, might be more at home: Wyoming, maybe, or the Badlands of Dakota. And she enjoyed remembering the first time she had spoken to him. It wasn't the words she remembered, but the smell of him.

Tom had come off the court laughing after a difficult match with Nigel, who had been the unchallenged champion until Tom came on the scene. The two men approached their ongoing rivalry with good humor as they attempted to push each other beyond their limits. Nigel had taken the match when Tom attempted to return an impossible shot, lost his balance, and fell. He assured everyone he wasn't hurt and left the court to retrieve his towel from the chair next to where Josie was sitting, watching.

Yes, it was his odor that preceded him, his odor and the laughter that came from deep in his chest, a broad, muscular, hairy chest that Josie could easily imagine supporting and directing his tawny arms as he lifted and manipulated the tools of his carpentry trade.

Josie liked man smell, not the acrid odor of an unwashed body, but the pungent, earthy, duff-molding-on-the-forest-floor odor that men sometimes exude. Josie remembered the first time she and Jeremy had made love in Berkeley, and she playfully sniffed his entire body, rooting around like a dog for the perfect place to mark. Jeremy laughed, embarrassed, and Josie was puzzled that he didn't have the odors she could remember some of the hired hands brought with them when they came to help her father at harvest time. Kurt had had the good smell . . . . *I can't remember about Howard . . . .*

144

When Josie's senses registered this almost-forgotten aroma given off by Tom's sweaty body, she inhaled deeply, privately taking in Tom's essence with an intensity that both excited and frightened her.

"I guess you wouldn't be laughing if you'd been hurt."

"Naw, not really. Maybe a bruise or two, weren't nothing. Thought I could get that one, but Nigel's a clever bloke and knocked me on my Khyber Pass," Tom mumbled through the towel he was rubbing over his face.

"Khyber Pass?" Josie queried, watching the towel slide over Tom's chest, down his arms, and over his legs.

"Kingdom come, bum, backside. You're American, aren't you? You got a bit of limey, but I can tell. I've seen your sort in the flicks. You're a right comely twist and twirl, you are." Tom tossed the damp towel aside and smiled at Josie. "I've noticed you once or twice, I 'ave."

Before Josie could ask for a translation, Portia approached with her car keys jangling. Josie relied on Portia for transportation to the club, having given up her efforts to learn to drive Jeremy's Austin on the "wrong" side of the road. She thought maybe being left-handed had something to do with her failure. As Portia grabbed her arm and pulled her toward the door, Josie looked back over her shoulder and softly said, "I'll play again on Thursday."

"Until Thursday, then," Tom responded.

Josie thought alot about Tom during the next few days. She liked the way he played, not only badminton, but the other game, the flirting game. "It's just fun," she told herself, "makes me feel good, no harm done, is there." It was not a question but a reassurance to herself that flirtation was a normal thing as long as you kept it in check.

Josie and Tom managed to exchange a lot of information during the minutes they increasingly found to talk together at the club. Some eyebrows were raised by other members, but Josie ignored them, had no time for them. She recognized few of her emotions except an increasing urgency to know as much about Tom as she could in the short time he had left in England.

"I'll be going down under," he had told her one evening between matches, and the already existing knot in Josie's lower abdomen tightened. "I'm off to Australia. There's nothing here for me, leaving in a fortnight, just thought you ought to know."

Josie didn't want to know. She only wanted to follow this intriguing road whose end she couldn't fathom. She knew she should leave it alone, but she knew, too, that she wouldn't.

————

The phone call for Portia came a few minutes after she and Josie arrived at the club. Lief, Portia's four-year-old, had a fall on the ice, her husband said, nothing too serious, but he thought Portia should come home. Josie had gone to get her things when she saw Tom step from the cold wind into the clubhouse.

"If you don't mind, Portia, I'll just stay. You must feel hurried. You won't have to go out of your way to drop me off. I'm sure I can get a ride with someone. If not, I'll call a cab."

"Of course, Luv," Tom replied when Josie explained that she needed a lift at the end of the evening. "But I don't feel much like the game tonight. Let's go now and stop at the near and far for a pig's ear. I fancy having a tot with someone else's trouble and strife."

Josie thought Tom was laying on the Cockney thing a bit thick, but it amused her, and she didn't bother asking for a translation. She could only focus on the fact

146

that he was asking her to go somewhere with him, and she was ready. Josie grabbed the massive fur coat Jeremy's mother had passed on to her, an old heavy thing that came nearly to the floor. Josie couldn't remember what kind of fur it was, but it was the only thing that kept her almost warm in the harsh English winters, and she had taken to wearing it wherever she went.

As she settled into Tom's beat up, old Jaguar sedan, she had a fleeting *deja vu* of the other Jaguar she had entered so long ago, innocent then. What she was doing now wasn't innocent, but it was compelling, and Josie was unwilling to see beyond the urgent sensations that claimed her body.

The pub – down a narrow alley off the high street – was not one Josie and Jeremy frequented. Josie responded quickly to the ambience of this out-of-the-way place, pleased when Tom ushered her not into the saloon bar, the more sedate part of the establishment, but to the public bar, the working man's bar where a smokey haze drifted in and out of a spirited dart game, in and out of the raucous laughter and the many dialects of a rough clientele. Josie felt a bit silly in her long, fur coat, but she was reassured when a bulldog curled under a back table greeted her with nearly total disregard, as did most of the clientele. Tom welcomed a few knowing glances as he worked his way from their table to the bar to get himself a pint of lager, a half-a-bitter for Josie.

They didn't talk much; they looked and sensed, each inviting then retreating, delaying and savoring unasked questions.

"Do you want another, luv?" Tom asked, rising from his chair and looking at his watch.

"No," Josie said softly as she rose and pulled the heavy coat tightly around her. "I'll just be a minute." She glanced at the pub clock as she wound her way among the crowded tables and headed for the loo. *I have to be home in an hour, but I could stretch it a little, say I had to wait 'round for a ride.* Josie stared at herself in the ladies room mirror for a few minutes and wasn't sure who was reflected back at her. She entered the cramped stall, relieved the pressure on her bladder, and relieved herself of her coat, her tennis dress, her bra, her panties. She slipped the coat back on and tossed the other items into the rubbish bin on her way out the door.

Some distance from town was a golf course with a short utility road leading to the 14th hole. Tom stopped the car, set the brake, and turned to Josie in a fluid, slow-motion movement as she opened the coat and took him to her. From Tom's first touch, Josie allowed a part of herself, only vaguely remembered, to return from neglected haunts. Certain that her body, mind, and soul had been separated at some time in the past, Josie now welcomed the entirety of herself struggling to fuse isolated facets into a single, smooth, plane like a pane of sunlit, shimmering glass.

Sensing Josie's journey, Tom began to help mend, slowly caressing her surface as she tended to her inner self. He smelled and stroked her hair, whispering "angel hair" in her ear. He ran his tongue behind her ears and breathed "pixie ears" into her mouth. He relaxed her lips with his finger and said she had forgotten how to kiss; he would teach her anew.

Josie was dizzy when Tom abruptly opened the car door, took her hand and motioned her out onto the crunchy snow illuminated by a rising moon. He opened the rear door, removed her coat, and spread it on the leather back seat. Josie was embarrassed and freezing standing naked on the 14th hole.

"You won't be cold long, Luv, I promise you," Tom whispered as he drew her into the warmth of the car and gently spread her out full length on the coziness of the fur. He placed himself over and next to her and began

148

vigorous warmth-giving massages to her legs and thighs. He knelt on the floor of the car, removed her tennis shoes and socks, and sucked her toes, then rubbed her feet.

Josie wondered about the time, but had lost all sense of it. They could have been there for minutes or hours, and Josie didn't care. She let her body indulge in her mounting heat as Tom's hands found her stomach and then her breasts.

"Nice Bristol cities," Tom teased as he explored the heaviness of Josie breasts. She giggled and unbuttoned his shirt.

"It's not fair," she complained. "I'm lying here starkers, and you're fully dressed."

"Someone has to be ready for the coppers when they come," Tom said, trying to be serious as Josie pretended to be frightened.

"Take it all off," Josie demanded..

Tom wrestled with his clothes in the cramped back seat of the old Jaguar but finally did manage to meet Josie's demands, all of them.

I'm finally warm! Naked on a snow-covered golf course in mid winter, and I'm finally warm in Merry Olde England.

Josie's Bath

Did he believe me? Seemed to. Just rolled over and went back to sleep. Didn't even wait up for me or anything. . . . Car trouble? Flimsy, but that's all I could think of. Wasn't he worried about me? I can never tell what Jeremy's thinking. How can you live with a man for so long and not know who he is? . . . Children were okay when I peeked in, peaceful. It's like nobody even knew I was gone. Maybe they don't even know when I'm here. Am I invisible? . . . Don't want to wash these smells off. . . . Would Jeremy notice if I didn't? Probably not. I want those smells all over me, so I won't ever forget . . . . How did he do that? How did I do that? Never knew women could respond like that, the books never said. Why didn't somebody tell me? Maybe I'm the only woman in the world who ever did it that way, without intercourse or clitoral stimulation. What a stupid word, clitoral. Some man made that one up! Why can't we have a pretty word? Why don't women make up their own word, a perfect word. Women don't even talk about it, nobody I know, anyway. . . . He just kept touching me, my face, my breasts, my belly, my legs, didn't even go there, not 'til later, not 'til after, then I did it again, the other way, with the man so alive inside of me. . . . What am I going to do? He's leaving soon. No, no, he can't. I can't stand that. Please, God, please don't let him leave me. . . . Maybe he won't go now, maybe I can get him to stay, maybe I can go with him. How could I do that? Would Jeremy let me take Gareth to Australia. Would his family? Hell with his family. They don't get to decide, do they? . . . He wants to see me tomorrow, said to meet him at the beach. I could take the bus. . . . Would Portia keep Gareth for a few hours? What would I tell her? I could tell her I have a doctor's appointment. Jeremy's going to London, isn't he? I'll think of something, I have to go. . . . God, I can't stand this, not with Mother coming for Christmas, not with Tom leaving, I can't do this, I can't. . . . Why is Mother coming now? How can I pretend to her that my life is what she wants it to be? Is she coming to see if it's the way she wants it? Is she coming to fix it? I can't stand her trying to fix me again. If she was any good at fixing, I'd be fixed, wouldn't I? She doesn't listen, just uses those stupid words: "Do you see how I'm reflecting back your pain?" when I tried to tell her about Jeremy. "The

150

playful child in you is looking for a playmate; Jeremy just needs to get in touch with his inner child. Maybe I can help him." God, I hate her. She's so proud of somebody tell me? Maybe I'm the only woman in the world who ever did it that way, without intercourse or clitoral stimulation. What a stupid word, clitoral. Some man made that one up! Why can't we have a pretty word? Why don't women make up their own word, a perfect word. Women don't even talk about it, nobody I know, anyway. . . . He just kept touching me, my face, my breasts, my belly, my legs, didn't even go there, not 'til later, not 'til after, then I did it again, the other way, with the man so alive inside of me. . . . What am I going to do? He's leaving soon. No, no, he can't. I can't stand that. Please, God, please don't let him leave me. . . . Maybe he won't go now, maybe I can get him to stay, maybe I can go with him. How could I do that? Would Jeremy let me take Gareth to Australia. Would his family? Hell with his family somebody tell me? Maybe I'm the only woman in the world who ever did it that way, without intercourse or clitoral stimulation. What a stupid word, clitoral. Some man made that one up! Why can't we have a pretty word? Why don't women make up their own word, a perfect word. Women don't even talk about it, nobody I know, anyway. . . . He just kept touching me, my face, my breasts, my belly, my legs, didn't even go there, not 'til later, not 'til after, then I did it again, the other way, with the man so alive inside of me. . . . What am I going to do? He's leaving soon. No, no, he can't. I can't stand that. Please, God, please don't let him leave me. . . . Maybe he won't go now, maybe I can get him to stay, maybe I can go with him. How could I do that? Would Jeremy let me take Gareth to Australia. Would his family? Hell with

151

his family. They don't get to decide, do they? . . . He wants to see me tomorrow, said to meet him at the beach. I could take the bus. . . . Would Portia keep Gareth for a few hours? What would I tell her? I could tell her I have a doctor's appointment. Jeremy's going to London, isn't he? I'll think of something, I have to go. . . . God, I can't stand this, not with Mother coming for Christmas, not with Tom leaving, I can't do this, I can't. . . . Why is Mother coming now? How can I pretend to her that my life is what she wants it to be? Is she coming to see if it's the way she wants it? Is she coming to fix it? I can't stand her trying to fix me again. If she was any good at fixing, I'd be fixed, wouldn't I? She doesn't listen, just uses those stupid words: "Do you see how I'm reflecting back your pain?" when I tried to tell her about Jeremy. "The playful child in you is looking for a playmate; Jeremy just needs to get in touch with his inner child. Maybe I can help him." God, I hate her. She's so proud of all those words and never really listens to me. Why can't I have a normal mother? . . . . And we're going to Catherine's, taking my mother to meet Catherine! Oh, God, I can't do this. Mother will try to fix Catherine with her talk about universal consciousness, unconditional love, warm fuzzies? Catherine will think she's bonkers, and Mother won't even know Catherine's laughing at her . . . so polite, so very very . . . laughing and hurting. . . . Tom's different, the people in the pub were different. I guess they were in touch with their inner, playful child . . . . How can I see Tom when she's here? How can I get away? I want to go home . . . or to Australia . . . . I want to go to Mattie's . . . like it used to be.

———

But time moved forward as Josie knew it would, and she made her choices. She frantically found ways to

152

meet Tom, using whatever excuse she could dream up. Jeremy either didn't notice or didn't care, and Josie didn't care which. Her times with Tom consumed her. She had to have more. The phone would ring once, their signal, and she was out the door.

"I have to go for a walk, I need some air. Back in a few. Gareth's napping and shouldn't bother you," she would say to Jeremy as she set out to meet Tom around the corner for a few brief minutes of frustrated groping in his car. They found occasional opportunities for longer times together and managed one entire night in a local hotel. Josie was clever in her fabrications. Years later she couldn't imagine how she had managed the duplicity in her life and the anguish in her soul. But she had managed.

———

Caitlin was upstairs listening to her tape recorder. It was one of her favorite pastimes, ever since Howard had sent her the portable reel-to-reel machine and a tape of himself talking about his life, playing flute for her, and reading her James Thurber's *Many Moons*. She knew the tape by heart now, and frequently recited the Thurber tale to Gareth at bedtime.

"Cait," Josie called up the stairs, "you have a telephone call."

"Could it be Daddy?" Caitlin responded as she took the stairs down in three big leaps, the shaking staircase echoing her excitement.

Once she had the phone to her ear, Caitlin recognized the white noise sound that meant an overseas call, and her heart did a little dance. It was a wonderful occasion when anyone in the world rang her up, and if it was long-distance it had to be either Daddy or Mona, Caitlin's baby name for her grandmother. Either one would be welcome. Calls from Mattie were usually directed to Josie, and Caitlin's image of "Auntie Mattie" was still vague, as were the voices of Peter and Bo. They

153

were people who belonged to her in some pleasing way she thought she would probably understand when she was a grown up.

"Hello? Who's speaking?" Caitlin queried in her perfect British princess voice.

"Well, now," she heard on the other end, "and how's my rollin' sugar donut?"

"Hiya, Mona," Caitlin cried out in girlish joy. It wasn't Daddy, but it was her next-best telephone voice.

Since Josie and Caitlin had moved to England, Nora had called every month or so. Caitlin was too young when she left the States to really remember Nora, but Josie had been careful to help engender a closeness between the girl and her grandmother. Through photographs, telephone calls, and Josie's stories — stories edited for neutrality, somehow even becoming jolly in the retelling — Caitlin had acquired a surprisingly rich relationship with Nora. And now, the little girl learned, "Mona" was coming to see her.

"Did you get the pajamas I sent to you, Honey? I thought they were awful cute, with the little bunny tail on the back."

"Oh yes, Mona, I did. Did you get my picture I sent to you?"

Josie listened from the kitchen and smiled to hear her daughter's obvious glee. These conversations between her mother and her daughter were a bit of a mystery to Josie. The financial assistance Josie had received from Nora both eased her life in England and complicated things between them. Though Josie's irritation at her mother was an ever-present layer beneath their superficial relationship, having Caitlin to talk about gave Josie and her mother some tamer waters.

"Just don't dive too deep," Josie cautioned herself. "At least Mother isn't as bad as Catherine."

Josie's thoughts now carried her back to her arrival in England. Throughout the long sea voyage she had practiced with Caitlin, showing her the photo of Jeremy's mother and saying "This is Grandma, Sweetheart. Can you say 'Grandma?'" So when little Cait debarked from the *SS France*, shy and shaky, and still a bit seasick, she looked into the English grande dame's cold face and said "Gra Gra." Josie glanced at Jeremy through glassy eyes of relief and pleasure. She fully expected that no one on earth could deny such childish sweetness, but the tears quickly drew back, like juice into dried fruit, when Catherine merely replied, "Oh for heaven's sake, child, don't call me Grandmother. It makes me feel so old!"

Sometimes, lying in bed at night and watching the traffic lights traverse her bedroom ceiling, Josie sought to shake the voice in her head that told her this marriage to Jeremy was all wrong if Catherine was her daughter's best chance for a grandmother.

"Mona wants to speak to you, now, Mummy" she heard young Caitlin call to her through her ragged thoughts about Catherine. "She's coming to see us here, in England! Mona's coming! Mona's coming!"

And Nora did come. Bertram couldn't join her on this trip because he had too many patients in crisis, he said. Nora said that was fine because "there's no such thing as time or space. Bertram and I have a relationship that transcends all that," she explained on the long drive back from Heathrow: "Our inner adults can handle the separation. Our inner parents will take care of our inner child."

Josie felt what remained of her sanity fragmenting into shards of glass as she listened from the back seat of the car. She wondered what kind of therapist Bertram could be if he had so many clients in crisis. She listened as Nora proudly explained, more to Jeremy than to her, that

Bertram had many clients he had been seeing for over ten years.

"How can Mother be proud of that, how can Bertram?" Josie asked herself, and then she asked Nora, "How can you and Bertram be proud of that? How can you see longevity of illness as a feather in your cap? I would have thought you would be prouder if you had made them well."

Nora didn't reply, and Josie assumed she hadn't been heard because Nora went on talking about re-parenting, anger work, positive and negative strokes. Josie quickly recognized that Nora was peacocking, strutting her stuff. She even looks like a peacock, Josie thought, scrutinizing Nora's choice of travel apparel, remembering her amazement when Nora came through the door from airport customs wearing a silk, paisley dress with a low-cut neckline that revealed her ample, matronly, bosom. She wore a large medallion of multicolored rhinestones suspended from a chain just long enough to allow the gaudy piece to occasionally embed itself in her cleavage. The matching earrings hung just short of Nora's shoulders, and she had topped off the outfit with a rhinestone belt, healed sandals with rhinestone straps, and a handbag with a large, rhinestone clasp.

Josie sat isolated in the back seat of the car. She didn't know these people, her husband and her mother, and she couldn't find a tether that would lash to this surreal world. There was pressure in her head, and she was finding it hard to breathe, as if something else were consuming the air around her. Afraid she was getting car sick, Josie put her head against the cold window and dozed off, dulled by the droning of the car and of the woman.

Tom had quit his job and was now wrapping up his life in England, preparing for his next journey. He tried to make Josie understand that he couldn't take her, and, no, he wouldn't change his plans. Maybe he could send for her when he got settled, depending on what she decided to do about her marriage. She needed to give it a lot of thought, he said, and she needed time to do that, to clean things up a bit and then think about it.

"It's not easy as all that," he told her. "You need a sponsor; you have to apply. They screen you pretty well, they do. They won't let just anyone in. They want certain types of people, certain professions."

For the duration of Nora's visit, Josie tried to make things appear normal, even festive. It was Christmas, after all, and Josie knew all the things she must do to set a proper stage. The family made a lively trip to choose the tree, and Josie asked Jeremy to retrieve the ornaments from the attic. Nora spent hours with Caitlin, cutting out snowflakes, stringing popcorn, and giving her warm fuzzies. She read Christmas stories to Gareth so Josie could cook the proper English fare, including Christmas pudding with the traditional sixpence hidden within.

I was supposed to make this pudding weeks ago, but nobody will care. Does anyone care? Nope. *I'm invisible. How can someone invisible be so frantic? So obsessed? Hurting so badly?*

It wasn't difficult for Josie to get away for moments with Tom – another trip to the shops, something she forgot, Nora looking after the children. Josie kept up the badminton pretense although neither she nor Tom had actually attended the club since the night on the 14th hole. Nora and Jeremy didn't appear to miss Josie; Nora was helping Jeremy get in touch with his inner child, and Jeremy enjoyed the attention, applying some of Nora's concepts to some of Dickens' characters while Nora, without doubt, enjoyed fixing Jeremy.

Josie was cautiously impressed by Nora's energy, enthusiasm, and gaiety. She looked back to the last months she had spent living with her mother, back to her senior year in high school when Nora was either crying or studying for her master's degree from Stanford. Josie didn't like the constant studying and hated the crying. It frightened her. Now this different Nora also frightened her. *Was this mother real? What dreadful thing would happen if the layers of verbiage and the layers of rhinestones were removed?*

"What a lovely home, you have, My Darling. You and Jeremy are so creative," Nora would smile and say as she looked around this or that room, but never quite at Josie. "The children are so well mannered. Jeremy has been so good for you; he has helped you rein in your anger. His internalized parent is good for your inner child."

"Mother, I think my inner child needs a walk; will you look after Cait and Gareth?"

Josie's walks soon became more frequent as she sought relief from the contradictions besieging her. She was especially relieved when Jeremy's mother rang up to beg off the Christmas celebration at the flat. A touch of the flu, she lamented. Caitlin was also relieved about the canceled visit to Catherine's, pleased to have Christmastime with just her Mona grandmother.

Christmas Present came and went with Josie barely noticing that the date for Nora's departure was a mere two days away. Tom's departure for Australia was four days away, four days into the new year and terrifying to Josie who found an abundance of kitchen chores to separate her from Jeremy and Nora's chatter.

"Is there a nice hotel where we could see in the new year, something like the Lake Merritt where we could dance? Wasn't that a delightful evening we all spent? Wouldn't it be nice if Mattie, Peter, and Bo could be here? If only I had a dance partner."

"I know someone who might be available," Josie ventured from the kitchen doorway. "You remember Tom from the club, don't you, Jeremy? I know he's at loose ends for New Year's Eve, maybe he would like to come."

"Well," Jeremy replied, deferring to Nora, "what do you think?"

"If he can dance, that's fine with me. That's all I want."

Jeremy invited Tom, as Nora requested, and a festive mood eventually captured the household. Even Josie was excited as she dressed carefully in a beautiful gown Nora had encouraged her to buy as her Christmas present. Tom had said, yes, it would be nice to have a special time together before he left the country.

Nora brought her makeup kit to Josie's room, and the two were soon like school girls laughing, primping, anticipating the evening that lay ahead.

"Tell me about this man I'll be dancing with," Nora said as she tossed her lipstick into a tiny evening bag and snapped it closed.

Josie couldn't decide if it was Nora's sexual energy or her make-up that were unsettling, but she brushed away her shadow thoughts and took over the dressing table, sorting through the make-up kit her mother had left open — a treasure chest of choices that might transform the young mother into whatever she wanted to be on this special evening. She chose a sparkly mauve eye shadow and was carefully applying it when the mirror reflected a different sparkle in the corner of her eye, tears that finally flowed as Josie told her mother about Tom.

Josie told Nora she was in love with Tom, wanted to go away with him, couldn't stand England or

159

Jeremy anymore. She told Nora about the sex, about the completeness she felt when she was with Tom. She couldn't stop telling, and Nora didn't interrupt, didn't chastize, didn't question. It wasn't until Jeremy called from the stairwell, announcing departure time, that Josie closed the make-up kit and turned to her mother for guidance.

"I'm excited about meeting your new man," Nora said. "I'm sure we'll have a wonderful evening."

Initially they did have a wonderful evening. Jeremy actually liked Tom. Tom actually liked Jeremy. The two talked about golf, and Tom invited Jeremy to play a round if weather permitted before his departure. Nora danced with Jeremy and with Tom, exchanging playful comments and playful gestures. She remarked to Josie that both were lovely men.

Josie knew she was losing it when she overheard her mother explain to Tom that Josie needed stability, hadn't had it from the father, wasn't that a shame. Josie got very drunk in a hurry and soon went to the ladies room to throw up, returning to the ballroom to dance alone – wildly, candidly with a clear "fuck you all" gesture embedded in each gyration of her hips. Nora explained to both men that Josie was letting out her playful child

Josie never saw Tom again. Their telephone signal did not occur once during the next four days, and Josie didn't care. Josie didn't care New Year's Day when she noticed Jeremy wasn't speaking to her. Nora seemed rested and cheerful as she began to gather up her various piles of belongings in anticipation of the next day's departure. She commented several times that Josie looked pale and despondent, "terrible, really," and enquired if there was anything she could do for her daughter. Josie said she didn't care how she looked, didn't know of anything anyone could do. She didn't feel anything,

160

wasn't thinking much about anything. She didn't want to eat, and she couldn't sleep.

Someone made food. It might have been Josie. Someone took care of the children. It might have been Josie. Jeremy discovered something urgent to do in his study for most of the day. Josie didn't remember if she slept that night, and in the morning she begged off on the trip to the airport, sending Caitlin in her place. Nora didn't seem to mind and said it would be fun to have Jeremy and Caitlin to herself for a few hours. She hoped Josie felt better soon, was sure she would.

"Holidays are very trying," Nora said while waiting for Jeremy to warm up the car. "They kick off all kinds of things. We call it 'rubberbanding'. It would help if you would work on your issues."

Josie didn't know what Nora was talking about and didn't care. She minimally attended to Gareth's needs throughout the day, sometimes wandering through the house and sometimes just staring into the far distance.

The date of Tom's departure came and went. Josie was aware of it on some level, but couldn't find the agonizing pain she had been sure she would feel. Josie and Jeremy resumed their polite interaction, and Josie wondered what he had done with his anger about her New Year's Eve behavior. Perhaps she had only dreamed the previous weeks.

Portia resumed dropping by in the mornings once the holidays were past, but Josie would meet her at the door, telling her friend that "now isn't a good time." Portia rang a few times to see if Josie wanted to do anything, but those calls, too, ceased when Josie repeatedly replied that no, she didn't want to do anything.

———

Josie said she was kind of numb, didn't want to do anything, all through the spring. . . . Me, too, maybe forever. I know I cried a lot at first; and I got scared; and I got angry. . . . I didn't know sorrow could be so complicated, so thorough. It wasn't complicated when Steve was killed. He was gone: I was full of sorrow, and made a place in my soul for sorrow. . . . But you, Dr. King, you are different – not my lover, but the world's lover . . . . No, I guess the whole world didn't love you. Whoever pulled the trigger didn't love you. His friends didn't love you. Lots of politicians didn't love you. But I think you loved them . . . us . . . the whole world. That's it. And we counted on you to hold up the light for the whole world so we wouldn't stumble so often. Now you are gone. Just like that. What will happen now that you are gone? Assassinated, they say. Walter Cronkite said so, on the TV. . . . So many things aren't true on the TV. . . . Please don't let this be true, dear God, please don't let this be true. . . . I should probably be worried, now, about the civil rights movement, and about more angry, disillusioned black people getting angrier, white people getting whiter, red-necks getting redder, Congress getting sleepier. I'm not. I'm worried about me, about how I can be a good person without you. . . . I must be wicked to feel this way. . . . You were a minister. Will you hear my confession? Do you hear confessions in Southern churches? I'm worried about me. I envy your wife because she has a big, handsome, still-warm body cradled in her arms. Her tears will not be lost. They will fall on your face, blend with the tears you have shed for us, and they will flow together into the future. But you see, Dr. Martin Luther King, Jr., I am lost. Please help me.

———

In May of 1968, Jeremy informed Josie that he had been invited to conduct a week's seminar in London and would be staying in digs at London University. A fleeting thought passed through Josie's mind about how Jeremy would be spending his evenings, but she didn't ask him to ring her while he was away. The morning Jeremy left for London, Josie changed the sheets on their bed, a chore she normally wouldn't do until Wednesday. Then she bundled up the children and walked to the wine merchants, bought three bottles of her favorite wine and continued on to the tobacconist where she purchased three packs of Marlboros. Josie occasionally smoked, but Jeremy didn't like it and objected to her buying expensive American cigarettes.

"A pack for each bottle, and no one to bitch at me about it. Next stop, ye olde book shoppeeee. Let's see with what we can come up, let's see what we can come up with, let's just go and buy some damn books, American books, maybe trash, maybe not. Who knows? Only the Shadow knows."

The week went by quickly for Josie, and she had good days playing with the children, fixing fun food, and allowing her family to eat in the living room in front of the television. They all got the giggles so badly they could hardly eat when Josie added red and green food coloring to the morning pancakes. They read Dr. Seuss, and Josie told them stories about Misty, and the ranch, and how difficult it was to drown a bat.

"How, horrible!" exclaimed Caitlin, "Why would you want to drown a bat?"

"I didn't," Josie replied, "but Auntie Mattie told me it was something I needed to know. She hated bats, said they might get tangled in your hair. 'Why don't we just climb out the window and go out to the barn,' Auntie

Mattie would say when we were sent to our room for being naughty. That sounded okay to me, so she would lean way out and lower me down. Once she leaned a little too far and fell out on top of me."

That sent the children into raucous giggles, Gareth rolling on the floor, and Caitlin shrieking, "Tell us more, Mummy, tell us more!"

"We would escape to the dark and musty barn. Auntie Mattie would poke a stick into cracks between the rafters to make the bats fly out. And then she would try to hit them with a broom. You can catch them while they're still dazed, you see. And then we would take the bat in a jar or an old tin can to the horse trough and try to drown it."

"Can we drown a bat?" Gareth asked with excitement. "What is a bat anyway, Mummy?"

At night, after the children were settled, Josie would have a leisurely bath, using the entire supply of hot water, then put on her comfiest nighty and settle in to drink, smoke, and read far into the night until the words blurred. On the last day of Jeremy's absence, she hired a sitter, took the bus, and spent hours sitting on the beach at Whitfield, gazing out on the ocean and listening to the birds.

"I've been so closed off," Josie mused as her senses took in the smells, the light, the sounds. "Where have I been? I'm not going back to wherever I've been when Jeremy comes home. I can't."

———

"Why are the children still up!" Jeremy exclaimed as he came through the door. "Why are you lot still up? I'm rather glad you are because I've missed you." Hugging each of them in turn, Jeremy gave them the little gifts he had purchased in London.

"I've missed you, too, Josie; it's been a long week, and I'm exhausted. Why are the children not in bed?"

"I've been letting them stay up a bit later," Josie answered, as she returned Jeremy's hug. "We've been having such a good time!"

"Quite," replied Jeremy, "but off to bed, you two. It's not good to get out of habit, is it?"

"Why isn't it, Jeremy?" Josie asked, but before he had time to reply, the phone rang, and Josie turned away to answer it.

Josie's Bath

Jeremy's right, I suppose, but I don't know how I can do it. How can I take one and leave the other? . . . Jeremy's right, though, Gareth's too young, and both children would be more than I could handle on such a long flight . . . all the travel, the funeral. Gareth would be miserable, and I would be exhausted. I wish Jeremy could come, but I guess I understand. He did take time when his father died. Why can't he do that when my father dies? Too many days to be away, he says. Well, I don't know how many days it will be. How do you judge how many days you'll need when your father dies? There weren't enough days when he was alive to fix what was wrong. How many days will it take now that he's dead. . . . Emma said she'd come. She'll be good with Gareth. She was Clifford's favorite sister . . . a gentle soul, smart to be living way off in the West Country. . . . She can't stand Catherine either, I could tell at Clifford's funeral and the one time she came to Briarwood at Christmas. . . . Suzanne's nice, too, but she couldn't come because of her horses. I always wanted to get up to Yorkshire to ride horses with her over the windy downs. But we never did. Jeremy kept saying we would, but we

165

never did. . . . How will it be to leave my baby, my little boy, my little English boy? Jeremy actually did something this time when Catherine said she would come to help out. I didn't even have to tell him; guess he was trying to make things easy for me. She will come though, if I stay away too long. She'll come and steal my baby, want to send him to boarding school, put him away like she did Jeremy. Gareth will be fine. I'll phone and talk to him. He likes the telephone. I'll phone and tell him bedtime stories, and he'll know I love him. . . . Cait will be fun to travel with. She's so independent and grown-up. She'll get to see home, and Mattie, and everybody. I wonder if she'll remember them. Will I remember them? . . . Mattie never changes. . . . Why did Father have to die so fast, before I could say goodbye? Why couldn't he have just gotten real sick for a long time so I could go and fix things. . . . But he would never help fix them, and I couldn't do it alone. He never once said he loved me that I remember. Maybe I wasn't loveable to him. Maybe I'm not loveable to anyone except probably Mattie. Jeremy says he loves me, but I don't know what he means. I don't think Howard loved me very much, and Mother says she loves me unconditionally, whatever that is. I don't think I like unconditional love. Maybe she means conditioned love; she's conditioned herself to go through the motions, say the words, pat the pats. . . . Does Peter love me? A phone call once in a while, but he never wants to know what's going on for me, only talks about his travels, his work. . . . Bo might love me, but we've been so out of touch. Gareth and Cait love me; I know they do. Now I'm flying away and leaving Gareth behind with Jeremy just like Mayzie Bird leaving Horton to care for her egg.

CHAPTER 10
Many times I've been alone
And many times I've cried
The Beatles: Lennon/McCartney
The Long and Winding Road

Caitlin plugged herself into the earphones and spent most the flight from London listening to music, mouthing the words. Josie slept as much as she could, pushing the past and future from her mind. *I'll take this time out. This won't count. I'll pretend it's a dream, and soon everything will be as it should be. I can't sit here and cry among all these people so I just won't feel anything.*

Shortly before their landing at San Francisco airport, Caitlin began to quiz her mother. She liked to know what adult expectations were all about.

"What if I can't cry at my grandfather's funeral the way Jeremy cried at Clifford's? Am I supposed to cry even though I never met my grandfather?"

"If you feel like crying, Cait, then cry. America doesn't have as many rules about how to behave properly. Just relax and be yourself. Besides, we're not just going to cry; we're going to laugh a lot, play and have fun in the sunshine. Auntie Mattie said she couldn't wait to hug you; Peter and Bo haven't seen you since you were a baby. Think of this trip as an Easter Egg Hunt. Instead of eggs, you'll be collecting family members, people you will love. It'll be exciting for you, Cait."

Caitlin tightened her grip on the arm rest as the huge plane skimmed the surface of San Francisco Bay and settled its huge body on the airport runway. "There,

167

we've landed. It's so bright here. Let's go. Don't forget your sweater, Mummy."

Peter hurried toward Josie and Caitlin as they emerged from customs, offering a rapid-fire apology for almost being late and a quick hug to his sister. "Let's go," he said. "I left the car in front unattended."

"Where is Melanie? I thought she was coming; Mattie said she was coming. Slow down, Peter. We can't keep up. Caitlin can't keep up."

"Melanie didn't come. She's not part of the family, so why should she come?" Peter shot back over his shoulder. "Come on, Josie." Peter hustled the two travelers through the airport and into his rental car, Josie in front and Caitlin in back. He crammed the luggage into the trunk, and pulled out into the busy airport traffic.

"Peter, why are you so hurried and so angry? I haven't seen you for years, and you don't even seem glad to see us. You hardly said hello to Cait, much less to me. What's wrong?"

"What's wrong, Josie, is that Father picked the worst possible time to die. I had to fly back from Africa, leaving my work at a crucial time, and instead of going directly to Gridley, I had to stay over to pick you up today. I don't know why Bo and Mattie couldn't have waited for you. I'm on a very tight schedule, and I can't afford to take on these responsibilities."

"Do people pick the time they're going to die," Caitlin asked, but her question was lost in the noise of early-morning traffic. By the time they had crossed the Bay Bridge and turned north toward Sacramento, she had found refuge in a nap.

"I want to tell you right now, Josie, that I'm not taking Father's place. I'm not going to be responsible for all of you in any way. It just wouldn't work. I'm too busy, and I can't help you all out of all your messes."

"Peter, I don't know what you're talking about. I've never asked Father or you, for that matter, for much of anything. Why are you doing this?"

"I can see it coming," Peter answered. "Mother phoned me last night and crowed about how I was now the family patriarch. 'The patriarch of such a wonderful family' was how she put it. Well, I'm not accepting that position, Josie, and you, Mattie, and Bo will just have to accept it. I've got my own life to live, and I haven't made a mess of mine like you all have."

"What mess, Peter? What mess have I made? Mattie and Bo? What messes have they made? This isn't making any sense."

"What do you mean, it doesn't make sense? Just look at it, Josie, just look at it all. Mattie has a child by some invisible guy who sends money but never shows up to carry out the garbage. Now she's pregnant with his second. Bo's a queer, and you're about as neurotic as anyone can get."

"Mattie's pregnant!" exclaimed Josie. "Why didn't she tell me? I don't know why she didn't tell me!"

"Probably wanted to wait until she could tell you in person. Just found out for sure a few days ago. Why are you asking me, anyway; how should I know why Mattie does what she does. See, it's just like I said. You're expecting me to be in charge of everything, and I'm not going to do it."

"Peter, please calm down, you're scaring me. Caitlin is only dozing in the back seat. Please don't scare her, too. What do you mean Bo is queer?"

"He's a fag, he's gay, whatever you want to call it. He's living with his lover and doesn't even hide the fact very well. Mother told me all about it."

Josie didn't pursue Peter's comment about her being neurotic. It was a well-worn label.

"Peter, we're your family. Whatever happens, we're still family and care about each other, don't we?"

"I never cared much about my family. You were okay until you started acting like a whore. Mother told me about your fling in England. For Christ's sake, Josie, how many men do you need? Let's see, there was Kurt, Howard, Jeremy, the carpenter, and God knows how many others. I'm telling you, as soon as Father is buried, I'm washing my hands of all of this. I don't need a mess in my life."

They spoke little the rest of the journey up the valley to their place of beginning. When Caitlin awoke, they stopped for lunch at a truck stop, and Peter halfheartedly tried to engage Caitlin in conversation about the airplane
ride, her friends, whether she liked school and her brother, but talk dwindled to nothing when Caitlin answered him only with a short yes or no. Peter explained the arrangements to Josie, and told her Mattie had reserved adjoining motel rooms for herself, David, Josie, Caitlin, and Bo.

"Where will you be?" Josie asked. "Aren't we all going to stay together?"

"Together? I'm going to have more togetherness than I want. I'm staying at the house with Marge. Father made me co-executor, and we have things to discuss. You're all to come there after the funeral, and we'll go over the will."

"But I wanted us all to go out to the ranch together, just see it together," Josie pleaded.

"It's not there any more," Peter responded. "It's all gone. Didn't you know Father sold it to housing developers? Some of the most fertile soil in the world, and he sold it for tract homes. Remember when he and Marge went to China? The ranch paid for that trip, and I

170

expect that most of what's left will go to Marge. I don't expect we'll get much of anything."

Peter made the trip as short as possible by taking the Zamora cut-off route, as his father had often done. Josie hated the Zamora route. She never understood why her father chose to take winding, narrow, county roads through this part of the valley. She remembered how she would slide off her place in the back seat and cringe, fetal-like, on the floor of the car, waiting helplessly for the inevitable to happen. An old, board-sided farm truck would appear seemingly from nowhere like a mysterious phantom lumbering along the dusty, deserted road, and the father thing would begin.

"Damned Okies! Why can't they learn to drive," the father would yell, pounding on the horn and veering back and forth over the line trying to pass. "There ought to be a law!" the father would continue, hunched forward over the steering wheel, knuckles white, shoulders tight, as Josie tried to swallow her car sickness.

Because Josie had always spent this part of those journeys on the car floor, she had never actually seen Zamora, and, as time went by, it had taken on a sinister, dream-like quality, becoming a place she always went toward, never arriving.

"It's Za-mor-a," Josie sang to herself to the tune of Dean Martin's *That's Amore*, trying to fill her mind with something other than memories of her father's tirades. The drone of the engine and the flatness of the landscape began to lull her into a torpor, when another memory began to weave its way into her mind.

Driving in the Buttes, the family . . . another family outing . . . the Sunday family outing that maybe somebody enjoyed. It didn't matter; they did it, the family outing. Her father was driving fast as he always did. The road was twisty, but he straightened it out,

171

laughing at his cleverness, challenging another vehicle to appear around the corner ahead of him.

"The shortest distance between here and there is a straight line," he informed the family, crossing the double yellow line and chuckling. "We'll get there in no time."

For the child on the floor in the back of the car, the throb of the engine began to reverberate in her body and provide the rhythm for her mantra.

"I want a horse, I want a horse, I want a horse."

"Shut that kid up," the father said softly, tensely to the mother.

"Quiet," the mother said, "Quiet, your father is driving. Be quiet."

"I need a horse, I need a horse."

The father increased the speed of the car, and his hands tightened their grip on the steering wheel. "Shut that kid up," the father yelled. "Can't you shut that kid up? I'll put her out of the car if you don't shut her up!"

The mother turned in the front seat and stared down at the child huddled on the floor. The two older children were intensely watching whatever was passing out the side windows and pretending not to hear what they had so many times heard before.

"Do you always have to spoil it for us? Why can't you be good? I'll give you to the gypsies if you don't be still," the mother warned as she jostled the infant Bo on her lap and recited her part of the mantra, playing the role she had accepted. "Do you always have to act up?"

"I have to have a horse," the child sobbed.

The vehicle went faster and faster and then came to a rough, abrupt stop, throwing gravel and stopping within an inch of a steep drop to the right of the driver's side.

172

"Put her out," the father said to the mother or the older children. It was hard to tell because he was staring straight ahead, not moving, like a statue. "Put her out."

It wasn't clear in her memory who put her out. There was no one on the country road. The hills were towering high in the distance. The dust from the disappearing car was settling. The child stood there on the side of the road, not crying, not feeling, not being.

"It was real. I remember," Josie said as she forced herself back to the present.

"What was real?" Peter asked. "What are you talking about?"

"Nothing," Josie replied. "I was just talking to myself. It doesn't matter."

"I think it does matter, Josie. Which self are you talking to?"

"Rosa, I've missed you! Thanks for coming to my father's funeral. I guess it's a pretty big event in my life, having my father die, coming back all the way from England. . . . Rosa, I'm scared. Maybe I won't be able to cry at the funeral. Maybe I'm still that child standing beside the road, not feeling, not being. . . . Or maybe I'm a good girl, even a princess returning to the kingdom, graciously greeting the mourners, soothing their pain at the loss of such a fine man, a man who led the way in this lush valley . . . . Aren't the blossoms pretty, Rosa, look. . . . No other place on earth smells quite like this valley. . . . Or maybe I'm a grown-up woman, a mother with children who need me to make things right for them . . . a woman whose father just died."

"Who do you want to be, Josie?"

"Do I get to decide? Or am I a captive, a little child, captive in this grown-up mother-body?"

Josie glanced toward the mirror that Peter had just adjusted. A sorrowful woman returned her quick

173

glance, and Josie reached for a handkerchief to wipe away the tears.

"Bear up now, Josie," Peter insisted. "Plenty of time for tears."

"Peter, I don't know how to schedule sorrow, but I'll deal with it. Myself. Please slow down and watch the road."

As Peter and Josie moved through the valley to the birth and death place of their father, Bo and Mattie, with David comfortably asleep on Mattie's lap, were arriving at their grandfather's little house on the edge of the farm community that had hosted so many of their family members. The "little house" Grandpa R had moved to didn't seem little at all to Mattie. It was a pleasing, rambling house nestled beside an ancient mulberry tree and next to a thriving walnut orchard. A tired, old dog of no recognizable lineage ambled down the lane to greet them, no barks, but a busy tail announcing his pleasure at a change in his routine.

"Grandpa R always had a watch dog,"

"Right," Bo responded. "They watch the mosquitoes and flies as people come and go at will."

As she approached the house, Mattie smiled to see that both the screen door and the heavy front door were ajar. Grandpa R must have given up his quest to control the mosquitoes, and she thought back to the community's delight when the DDT pesticide was introduced into the valley shortly after the war. She remembered, too, the hours of fun she shared with her siblings playing tag in the hazy miasma. The image of their carefree play rested at the edges of Mattie's awareness as she thought back to the uproar caused by Rachel Carson's disconcerting *Silent Spring* and the ensuing brawl among the chemical industry, research scientists, and government regulators. She remembered reading a government official's vicious attack on Carson: "I thought

174

she was a spinster. What's she worried about genetics for?"

Mattie shuddered and moved toward her brother as she patted the tiny embryo she was nurturing. She tightened her hold on David and edged up next to Bo so their shoulders were touching.

"I had forgotten that nobody in the valley locks doors. Most don't even bother to keep them closed," Bo offered. "Not like that in Washington."

Bo rapped lightly as he eased the door open, and the siblings stepped into their grandfather's home.

"Hello, Will. Is it Rotary today?"

"I'm not Will, Grandpa, I'm Bo."

Mattie quickly acknowledged the resemblance between her brother and her father; it was a resemblance she had always enjoyed, one that offered her comforting ties to both past and future. She wondered if it was the filtered light in the large living room that had confused her grandfather.

"Mattie, where are your pigtails?"

One of the few times her grandfather had ever scolded her was when Mattie got her first haircut. She was in the seventh grade and wanting to look more like the town kids, not so much like a farm kid. She didn't think she needed to ask permission to cut her own hair, but there was a sizeable family ruckus that evening when she returned home from Bette's Hair Parlour. And there were tears in Grandpa R's eyes as he threatened to get a switch and tan her hide.

"I'm growing my hair out again, Grandpa. It's okay. Are you ready to go?"

"Well, I need my hat."

"Here, Grandpa, you hold David and I'll get your hat. Top shelf of the hall closet?"

Mattie was sure there would be a hall closet harboring a 1945 hat that Grandpa carefully saved for special occasions, and she was pleased for an excuse to hand David over to her grandfather. His blessing of her son was a kind of baptismal ritual Mattie had longed for.

"Where's that damned Okie," the old man suddenly yelled, and a cheerful, roundish Hispanic woman appeared in the doorway leading to the kitchen. There was sorrow in her eyes, but the laugh lines permanently embedded in her face drew Mattie instantly toward the woman. She remembered that all transient workers in the valley were "damned Okies" to her grandfather and her father. How caring people divided their world into manageable pieces was an enigma to Mattie; she quickly forgave her grandfather his bigotry but wondered what purpose it served, wondered how it functioned in her own life.

"Hello," Mattie offered. "I'm Mattie, Will's oldest daughter. Please tell me your real name."

"I am Felicite," the woman responded. "I pray for your father and your family today."

"Thank you," Mattie said. "I think you should ask my grandfather to call you Felicite."

"No is importante what he name me," the woman responded. "Your father was good person to me and my family. And I been taking real good care of your grandfather."

"Thank you, then," Mattie said, and the two women reached for one another to share their grief and to lessen the inevitable gap of time and events. Mattie could not imagine when or how or in what manner her father had been good to this woman and her family, but she had an instant awareness that her father's life in this community had been rich and complex, much of its intricacy unavailable to her.

"Mattie, the tomatoes are already up. Come, I'll show you." Grandpa R shouted across the room.

"Here's your hat, Grandpa. We do need to hurry. Let's look at the tomatoes after the . . . when we come home, okay?" Mattie reached for David as she placed the tired hat on the old man's head.

"I'll drive," Bo said, as the family headed out the door and down the dusty, gravel drive." You can point the way, Grandpa."

The old man gave careful and correct directions to the only funeral parlor in town and remarked, as Bo pulled into a designated "family" parking place, "Lots of people at Rotary today, Will."

———

Caitlin and David were both restless and quarrelsome by the time the family arrived back at the motel. Peter had left for San Francisco as soon as they had all spent the obligatory time with Marge, driven Grandpa R back to his home, toured his tomato garden, and made a quick trip to what had been the ranch. Mattie and Josie put the children to bed in Josie's designated room, and Bo said he needed a walk.

"I noticed a liquor store about a half-mile back. I think I'll get a gallon of Gallo, for old times sake. I need to self-medicate, and I expect you do, too. When I get back, we can drink and talk. Okay with you two?"

"Get me a pack of Marlboros, too," Josie requested.

"I'll do it," Bo replied, as he left his sisters to have a private chat.

Caitlin could hear the muffled voices of her mother and her Auntie Mattie as she lay in the strange bed in the motel room. She cried quietly to herself, not because she was in any certain distress, more just winding down from what had been the strangest day she had ever had. The plane was fun for a little while, but the ride seemed to go on forever, and at one point during the flight there had been some turbulence that terrified her, mostly because she had seen so much fear on her mother's face.

Then that man came to the airport, and he was scary, too. Caitlin kept looking at him from behind – at the airport, in the car, at the funeral – seeing only his head and back that weren't very friendly, all stiff and hard looking. And he called her mother a whore, as well. Caitlin wasn't certain what a whore was, but she knew it was a bad woman of some sort, and the child couldn't fathom why her mother's brother would think she was a bad woman. *They don't look alike either*, she thought. *Mummy is so pretty, like a princess, and that Uncle Peter looks all leathery and brown.* She had a brief notion that maybe this Uncle Peter man might be an imposter. It had been a long time since her mother had seen him. Young Caitlin wasn't at all clear on what was real right now.

The funeral certainly didn't seem real, at least the flowers didn't, and the man they said was her grandfather didn't, and where was Mona? Caitlin thought that Mona would be there to snuggle her into her huge, fur-coated bosom and call her "rollin' sugar donut," but she hadn't been there, and nobody wanted to explain anything to her, because it was all very sad for them. Stuffy, too, in that room with all the flowers. A lot like the airplane cabin, only wider. Caitlin looked around to see if the motel room could give her a clue about the States, and about what was real, and what might not be real. It was a strange room to the little English child. The furnishings, the colors, the fabrics were all unfamiliar, and she knew from seeing Uncle Bo's room that it was just the same. Were all bedrooms in America like this? No, she reasoned. She had stayed at inns in England, and she knew this was pretty much the same sort of thing. But in England the rooms were all different from each other, and the curtains and linens were lace and cotton, not this orangey, heavy material.

She felt lonely and mystified, but wasn't about to go out to her mother or Auntie Mattie. She had a child's understanding that her presence would not be especially welcome in the next room, not right now. She remembered her mother sighs of relief when Gareth finally ceased his infant explorations of the world and went down for a nap; she knew that at this moment, she was the bothersome child. She was expected to stay here in bed, in this room, with that little boy, David. She didn't mind that part, actually, having David in the room with her. *He is sweet, kind of like when Gareth was a bit younger.* She thought about Gareth and what he was doing now. In her child's eye view of the world, time was the same, despite locale, so she thought of Gareth in bed in his room back home, in England. She imagined him in his pajamas, having had his bath, and getting his story, and his cup of milk, and then she imagined Jeremy tucking him in and kissing him goodnight. "Jeremy tucks you in nicely," she whispered. And then she cried – almost silently – missing the fathers. She cried for herself and her own lost Daddy, for David, who seemed not to have a father, for her mother and Auntie Mattie, and Uncle Bo, and even Uncle Peter, who had just lost their father, and for Jeremy back home. "Do all the fathers go away?" she queried the unfamiliar room. "I want to go home and see Jeremy," she sobbed into her pillow. "I want to go home." And then she slept.

"Both children are sound asleep," Josie announced to her sister, pausing then to see which part of the day would want their unraveling first.

"Before we get into anything, Josie, I have to phone Raymond. I need to hear his voice for just a minute . . . so sad he never got to meet Father. Would you like

179

to say hello, kind of meet Raymond over the phone? I'd like it if you would. Bo's the only family who's met him."

"Sure, Mattie," Josie answered. "I could really use a diversion just now. Somebody from the outside, somebody in the real world out there."

After the brief but comforting call to Raymond, the sisters plunked down on one of the beds, and Josie gave Mattie a synopsis of the trip up the valley with Peter.

"He actually said he didn't care much about his family?"Mattie sobbed.

"I don't think he really means it. I just wonder if he's going to live his whole life hiding from things he cares about. He did finally cry, once we got out to the ranch. And he did actually hold David for a minute or two. Kind of stiff, but he did it."

Mattie reached for a Kleenex and made an effort to meet Josie's acceptance of things as they are.

"I'm going to miss Father," Mattie offered.

"Well, I'm not sure yet how I feel. Do you remember that time we took a trip in the old green car and Father actually stopped beside the road and put me out?"

"Josie, please let's not talk about that . . . one of the nightmares of my life. Probably Peter's, too. We were so helpless. Why don't we try to remember Father as the person he wanted to be? I guess it's different for each of us. Poor Bo, wanting Father's blessing so badly; Peter feeling just the opposite, Father's blessing a curse, a huge burden. And how about us, Josie? What did we want that we didn't get; or the other way around. What did we get that we didn't want? I'm horrified to think what it must be like for Grandpa R. I wonder if he really knows that his son died? I think so. The worst thing that could happen to me is to have David die before me."

"Me, too, Mattie. I can't even think about that. And I'm missing Gareth so badly. Let's talk about this new baby you're going to have. And Raymond. Let's talk about Raymond. I guess I feel a little better about him now that we've at least talked on the phone. Wonderful voice. And maybe I believe he loves you and is going to get things sorted out. Mattie, you know, I have a really hard time trusting any man. Strange creatures!"

"Yes, and strange what Peter said about Bo. Did he really call him a 'fag?' I hate that word. Do you think it's true? That Bo's homosexual, I mean?"

"I guess it could be. Can't quite imagine."
"Well, Josie, I can't either, but I have so much trouble understanding my own body, I'm not going to take on someone else's. My ob-gyn relates everything to raging hormones, but this new child certainly does a lot more raging than David did. I'm sick every morning, my back aches all the time, and I'm not even showing yet."

"Am I interrupting something?" Bo inquired as he poked his head around the door that had been left open to entice some fresh air into the stuffy little room.

"Just girl talk," Mattie responded as she slowly rose from the bed to look for glasses. "How was your walk? How are you feeling?"

"Walk was fine, but I'm not sure how or what I'm feeling. I have such mixed emotions about Father. I think I spent my entire teen years when I lived with him trying to get everything right so as not to displease him, and I remember that I was frightened the entire time. I mean really frightened."

Josie's ears perked up at Bo's statement. "Frightened of what?"

"Well, I'm not sure. I guess I just never knew who he was. I mean, he was terribly respected in the community, did so many positive things for the county, held so many offices. But I never could connect, never felt comfortable during that whole time. I knew there was another side to him, a side I never understood, a side he

181

never let anyone understand, not even Marge. I think they had an understanding that they would ignore that part. Maybe they had some kind of agreement when Father got dark."

"What kind of understanding?" Mattie asked. "What do you mean?"

"I could feel the tension building up," Bo replied slowly, thinking it through. "Sometimes it would build up for days, sometimes weeks, but I could always feel it. That's what was frightening, I think, the build up, and not knowing what would happen. It was kind of like the movies when scary music announces the gory part you know is coming, but you're not quite sure of the moment. You both remember how Father would blow. It was horrible. Well, he never got to the blow part while I was living with Marge and him because he would disappear before the moment came. That's what I mean by an understanding. Father would just leave in the car, going somewhere, but I never knew where he went, maybe to the office, maybe he just drove around. Once I asked if I could go with him, and he didn't answer, didn't acknowledge I'd even asked. It was like he didn't hear me at all, although I knew he did. At least I think he did. I'm not sure he could hear anyone when he reached that point. We never knew when he'd return. Marge would go to her room, and I would go to mine. Neither of us would come out until he returned, and when he did, it was really scary for me to come out. Again, it was like a horror movie. Slowly opening the door, not knowing what monster would be on the other side. But I loved him, too. That's the part I don't understand. I loved him so much it hurt, and I wanted him to love me. I think he did, but, you see, I never knew for sure."

"I wish we had talked about this before," Josie offered. "I never knew you felt that way. You never said. None of us ever shared what we really felt. Peter just

182

locks it away behind his anger and business, Mattie builds pretty bubbles, and I go out looking for men to fill the empty place. Mother would probably say I'm looking for a good daddy. . . . I don't remember Father ever holding me, not in my whole life. I asked Mother once, and she said he was afraid of girl children, didn't know how to relate to them. Boy, that answer was really helpful. She's something else, she is."

"Let's be fair," Mattie interjected, "we all had good times with Father, too. You know we did."

"Mattie, you always want to wrap things up in pretty packages," Josie snapped.

"Maybe, Josie, but there's no reason for you to get testy right now. I just don't see much point in carrying around a lot of heavy baggage."

"Maybe there is no point, Mattie, but I'm not sure where to stow it away, don't seem to have your stash of pretty wrapping paper."

"Josie, I've got lots of pictures of Father holding you, holding each of us."

"Mostly of you, Mattie. You were special to Father. Little Miss Goodie Two-Shoes."

"Josie, I don't know why you're mad at me. I didn't invent Father. I just tried to get along."

"Okay, Mattie, so we had a father who held us from time to time, even took pictures to record the event, but I just never knew when . . ."

"You just never knew, did you?" Bo interrupted. "Kind of like a volcano. Do you remember the trips we used to take to Shasta and Lassen? Such beautiful, fun places to hike, but at the same time you're aware that they're smoldering deep inside."

Josie and Bo became quiet, lost in their private memories.

"Let's get some sleep," Mattie eventually suggested. "I'm really tired, and I'm feeling the wine.

Shouldn't have had it anyway. I don't think it's very good for the baby. A nice hot bath for me, then bed. Josie, it looks like we're sharing a bed again . . . if you're over your snit."

"I'm trying, Mattie. Really trying."

Mattie's Bath

Nice of Father to leave us all a little money. . . . Marge seemed pleased, too, kind of like the money made up for something. And the special gifts mentioned in the will, how wonderful, how puzzling. The gold locket for Josie made me cry. I wonder if she remembers that terrible Christmas when the locket Father got for her was mixed up and given to cousin Julia. We'll talk about it in the morning. She needs to understand why she got a gold locket. I love it that he gave me his Roswell Pioneers book with stories about Grandmother R's people, the Millers. I want to go there someday, poke around Roswell, New Mexico, and see if I can find my grandmother's spirit hovering about, maybe carrying water to some dry garden. I think that's what she would be doing. . . . I guess Peter and Bo liked getting Father's guns; they spent a lot of time with him learning to bring home ducks and pheasants for dinner. We didn't need those birds for dinner, but I guess hunting is something I just won't ever understand. I'll ask Raymond. I don't think he hunts things. I'm not sure. . . . Strange to be having another of his babies when I know so little about him. Well, I know I love him, and that's enough. I hope it's enough.

"I don't want to go through Zamora," Josie announced as she crammed Caitlin's pajamas into her

184

suitcase. "Let's stay on the highway and stop by the Milk Farm or the Nut Tree for lunch. Mother never took the Zamora way. She always loved stopping at the Nut Tree and buying all those overpriced things. I always knew what people were getting for Christmas   another walnut salad bowl."

"Okay," Bo agreed. "It'll take longer, but I'm in no hurry. I'd rather stop at the Milk Farm, though, and I think Caitlin would like that better, wouldn't you, Cait? There's a big cow on the roof jumping over the moon."

"I'm sorry, Uncle Bo, but I don't quite know what you're talking about. I was hoping we could see Alice's Restaurant in the States, but I'd like to see a cow jump over the moon, too. . . . Gareth likes that nursery rhyme. 'Diddle, diddle, fiddle,' Gareth says it like that."

"What's your favorite?" Bo asked as he checked the room for items that might have been missed.

"I like 'Sing a song of six-pack, pocket full of rhyme,'" Caitlin chanted, jumping on the bed and trying to get David's attention.

"It's the Milk Farm, then, and I think we're ready to go. Mattie, Josie, are you ready?"

"I have to wet first," Mattie announced heading for the bathroom. "I'll meet you at the car."

"Mattie, dogs wet, people pee," Josie corrected.

The early morning sunlight soon put the funeral, though not their loss, in the past, and the siblings were all looking forward to sharing their own individual tales of adventure. The Milk Farm lunch stop was fun and brought back good memories of the many times the family had broken journeys at this now rather dilapidated cafeteria. Josie had a hot-roast-beef sandwich with mashed potatoes and gravy and explained to Caitlin that this is what she always had at the Milk Farm.

"It was the only thing I could be sure of on those trips," she explained. "Kind of a security blanket. If I had a hot-roast-beef sandwich with mashed potatoes and gravy, I would get home safely."

"Mine was meatloaf," Bo added, "and strawberry Jello."

"Well, eat up," Mattie said. "What we're having tonight in Berkeley is left-over left-overs."

By the time Bo dropped the sisters and their offspring off at the Russell Street cottage, left-overs sounded tasty to the weary travelers. Mattie hurriedly unlocked the heavy front door to her home.

"What a lovely cottage," Josie exclaimed as she walked in carrying David and an armload of gear that had been scattered about the car. Caitlin was clutching Mattie's hand, and the two were tiptoeing into the living room. Mattie had told Caitlin the fairies came out when she was away, and if they were very, very quiet, they might just see one.

"No fairies today. Maybe next time. But here's Nemesis; he's a bit magical in his own silly way. One day soon I'll tell you the story, Caitlin, of how Nemesis protected me from a nasty ogre. If you have any ogres bothering you, Nemesis will help you. He'd probably like to sleep on your bed, sort of a guardian, I think."

"Where is my bed?" Caitlin asked, her eyes rapidly searching the little cottage. "This looks quite like an English cottage, Auntie Mattie. I like it here."

"I fixed up David's room for the two of you. Do you think you can share with David? Maybe help look after him? He still wakes up sometimes at night. I know he'd feel good if you were right there next to him."

"Oh, super!" Caitlin squealed, jumping up and down. "I know how to take care of him. I took care of Gareth quite a bit for Mummy. I bet I can find our room. May I go upstairs?"

"Of course you may, Cait. I'll be up in a few minutes. You and I can bathe David and get him ready for bed. He'll need a little supper, but mostly sleep, I think."

Caitlin's enthusiasm for adventure was momentarily checked as she looked up the narrow stairs and contemplated unknown territory.

"Doesn't David have a Daddy?" she asked as she turned back toward Mattie.

"He does, indeed, Caitlin. And he's eager to meet you. He'll be here late in the summer, in this very house. We're going to get married this summer."

Caitlin took in the new information with little hesitation, started up the stairs, and then paused for one more question to her aunt, "I don't remember very many stories like that, Auntie Mattie. Are there many stories where you have a baby and then get married?"

Mattie glanced at her sister for some guidance in answering a six-year-old's questions about the proper order of things, but when Josie responded with only an amused smile, Mattie said, "True, Caitlin, not many stories like that. But sometimes we just write our own stories. Maybe you and I can write some stories together while you're home."

Caitlin had disappeared into the upstairs hallway, probably not too concerned about writing stories with Auntie Mattie, not too concerned that Mattie had referred to this place, this little cottage, as Caitlin's home.

"I thought you and I could share my bed, Josie. It'll be like old times. I didn't know how long you'd be here, so I didn't do too much rearranging. Do you think we can manage?"

"Of course, Mattie. It's palatial compared to our little Channing Way apartment, but we had some fun there, didn't we? Everything will be fine. 'Coping' is my middle name. And, Mattie, I don't know how long we'll be staying. Is that a problem?"

"Problem?" Mattie squealed. "Just stay forever. I've been so lonely, Josie. Raymond tries so hard to be a good long-distance father, husband, lover, friend. . . . Emily and Frank have become good friends, and Brenda, of course. But, Josie, I've just been really lonely. It's that simple. And I've got a lot of stuff to ask you about, medical stuff I mean. These doctors I see for my pregnancy there are four of them in one office, all male doctors – and I'm not sure I understand what they're telling me. They say I'm too old for more children. I'm not old, Josie. What does "old" mean?" Mother was 36 when Bo was born, and she isn't old yet, still stirring things up in Kansas City, I guess. . . . These doctors say I should have a hysterectomy after our next baby is born."

"That's vicious!" Josie barked. "Can't you find a female doctor, someone who isn't quite so willing to snip away body parts, someone who would understand how you feel?"

"But I'm not sure how I feel, Josie. I need to be healthy for David and this new baby. . . . I haven't even talked to Raymond about this. And that's another problem. He wants us to move to Florida."

The words that might describe how Mattie felt about the dilemmas she faced didn't emerge, and the sisters sat in a peaceful silence for a few minutes, each enjoying the notion that whatever challenges were in store for them, they could, at least for a while, face them together. It was Josie who finally broke the silence.

"Mattie, while Caitlin and I are here, let's get out, walk on campus, maybe up in the hills, maybe even into the mountains. You need exercise, and I need a break, some kind of a break. And I need Caitlin to see her real home. That's how I feel, you know. I try so hard in England, but this is really home for me."

"Wonderful, Josie! And let's go see *Hair* when it opens in San Francisco. Maybe Bo will go with us. He said he was seeing old friends, but he'd come back by, not hurrying off the way Peter did."

Late that night when the sisters finally settled into Mattie's big, luxurious bed, Josie struggled to remember an F. Scott Fitzgerald quote: *The worst things: To be in bed and sleep not . . . to want for one who comes not . . . to try to please and please not.* "I think I got that right," she mumbled as she drifted into a restless sleep.

Kneeling on the hardwood floor of a sunlit, cavernous room, the woman is frantically wrapping something in mounds of white, gauzy fabric. The woman's back is blocking the view, and Josie can't tell who she is or what is the object of her hurried care. Josie senses the woman's terror and cautiously eases forward to discover a small, white coffin, open, in front of the woman. Startled by a staccato ringing that intrudes malevolently into the empty room, the woman's frenzied hands quicken to their task. She must get the child wrapped and into the coffin before the soldiers break down the door. It is the only way the boy will be safe. The ringing is insistent now, and the woman glances quickly toward the door, her eyes meeting Josie's, recognizing herself, acknowledging her defeat. Another, louder ring proclaims the woman's failure, and Josie opens her eyes as her senses register that she is in Mattie's bed, the bath water is running, and the bedside phone is ringing.

"Hello, hello, who is this?"

"It's your mommy, Honey. How are you?"

"I don't know. . . . I was asleep. What time is it?"

"Eight o'clock, aren't you up yet?" Nora replied.

"It's only six here, Mother, surely you know that."

"Oh, dear, I forgot. You don't sound so good. Is anything wrong?"

"I was having a bad dream," Josie answered. As if they were emerging from a different body, Josie's tear-stained words now gushed toward her mother as she described the disturbing visions of her nightmare.

"That's just your subconscious trying to deal with your guilt," Nora began. "Your inner child is frightened, and your inner parent is trying to take care of her."

"What do you mean *just* my subconscious. Is that something so unimportant I should have it amputated?"

"Now, Sweetheart, just consider. You must feel some guilt about leaving Gareth behind, and you're putting your face on him."

"Maybe I didn't describe things well. The woman's face was mine."

"Well, guilt has a way of doing that."

"Instead of guilt, couldn't I just be feeling sorrow, maybe grief, maybe despair? Why are you calling, Mother? Do you want to talk to Mattie? She's in the bath, I think. She has to work today. I'll tell her you're on the phone."

"No, Dear, I'm sure your sister's just fine. I really called to talk to you. How is my rollin' sugar donut? Is she still asleep? How was the funeral?"

"Yes, Caitlin is still asleep unless the phone woke her up. The funeral was a funeral — wretched organ music, stiff flowers, you know. Is that what you're asking? Do you want to know about the flowers, or what?"

"I understand you might be feeling a little irritable, but wasn't that nice what your father did for Gareth?"

Josie sat straight up in bed, totally awake now. "What did he do for Gareth? What are you talking about?"

"Well, maybe I wasn't supposed to tell you. I can't seem to remember what Peter said. I forget a lot of things at my age."

"Stop playing games, Mother. And where does Peter come into all this?" Josie asked as she reached over to the night stand on her side of the bed and groped for the last cigarette she knew was in the pack.

"Well, Peter was nice enough to call me last night just to let me know how it all went. He knew I would be anxious about my dear ones coming to terms with their loss. We had a nice talk, and he told me your father left some money for Gareth's college education."

"That wasn't in the will! We all read the will, and that wasn't in it!"

"Well, I think Peter said something about your father arranging this sometime ago, not making it part of the will. Your father felt guilty about not putting you through school and wanted to make it up to you. Isn't that nice, Dear? Peter said it was something about a fund for school at Cambridge."

"Nice?" Josie shouted. "Nice? What do you mean, nice? Why didn't Peter tell me? Why didn't father tell me? Did Jeremy know about this? What about Caitlin? What about *her* college education? Cambridge? What if Gareth doesn't live in England? Doesn't want to go to Cambridge?"

"Now, don't get upset, Dear. You know how your father was. He was raised to believe that the boys' educations mattered more, although we know better, don't we? But I suppose that's why he made Jeremy the trustee. Your father was probably afraid you'd go off the deep end and do something foolish with the money. That's just who your father was, and we need to give him unconditional love."

Josie sat cross-legged on the bed, focusing on the shaking hand holding the cigarette.

"I'm sure when you're feeling better you'll see things in a different light, Honey. Losing a parent kicks off all kinds of insecurities. The grieving process takes time. First, you'll go through denial, then . . ."

"Mother, why did you call? Did you want to hurt me?"

"I can't hurt you, Dear. You must understand that you're the only one who can hurt you. You must learn not to give away your power. I was hoping that you could reach a closure with your father, and I'm sorry you didn't. But I have some good news that might be helpful to you. Bertram and I are coming out there to the ITAA Annual Conference. We'll be able to see you if you're still there, and Bertram said he would find time to have a session or two with you. Isn't that nice? Bertram feels connected to you because he had some of the same issues when he was growing up. And maybe we can all go dancing again. . . . Oh, I have to go now, Dear. Bertram wants his breakfast, and you know how these men are."

"You've certainly made my day, Mother," Josie uttered as she hung up the phone.

"You woke me up, Mummy, and you woke David up, too. Why do you have to talk on the phone so early? Who was that on the phone? Was that Jeremy? Did Jeremy and Gareth ring up? Why didn't you let me talk?"

"Come on, Cait, don't be so petulant. That wasn't Jeremy and Gareth. It was Grandma, and I didn't wake you up, she did."

"I'm not being petalant, I'm not a flower. I'm hungry, and why didn't you let me talk to Mona?"

"You didn't want to talk to Grandma this morning, Cait, trust me. Come on, let's get David and go find some breakfast."

CHAPTER 11

Remember when the wine was better than ever again
Tom Paxton
"Outward Bound"

Death again crashed into Mattie's life that summer, again entering her home through the television tube, depositing pockets of grief in every inch of her living space and lingering forever in the fibers of her heart. Mattie had bathed and fed David, told him nursery rhymes, and tucked him into bed. She and Raymond had talked on the phone and had agreed to share their long-distance evening by watching coverage of the California primary, Raymond in Florida, Mattie at home in Berkeley. Josie and Caitlin were taking in a Disney movie and a restaurant meal, a special treat for Caitlin who was seeking more and more information about this bright, sunny land called "the States."

Alone in her cozy cottage, quietly urging Robert Kennedy to fill some of the voids in her world, Mattie heard the "Sock it to 'em" theme pouring from the ballroom of Hollywood's Ambassador Hotel; she admired the power and grace of Mrs. Robert Kennedy's walk; she heard the shots; and then she remembered she needed to clean up David's toys. She cleaned and recleaned, paying special attention to a tiny mirror she used to show David his smiling face. Maybe she remembered Raymond's call that night; maybe she remembered carrying the TV to the trash heap. Maybe she slept for a few hours; yes, she had slept; she remembered waking up to a dream in which she was pleading with deaf gods.

She certainly could remember that the same TV had invaded her home only a few months earlier with the news of Martin Luther King, Jr.'s assassination. She marched then with David to the nearest church and wept.

193

Mattie didn't go to church, but Martin Luther King, Jr. did so she found his spirit there for tears and farewells. And then in May, when the telephone brought news of her father's death, Mattie wept and dutifully made preparations for the sorrowful family gathering. But on this night, Mattie ran out of tears.

Caitlin's worried, early-morning questions about the missing BBC dragged Mattie listlessly into the next day, and she struggled to explain to her niece that the box that used to tower over the bookcase was not called a BBC.

"It's called a TV. And it's gone."

"But where is it, Auntie Mattie?"

"Caitlin," Mattie sighed, "all the stories on the TV were ugly, so I threw it away. You can do that. You don't have to listen to stories that are ugly, you can just throw them away."

Over the next few weeks, Josie managed to convince Mattie that her swallowed grief would soon poison her son and her unborn child, her home, and her family. Some mirth found its way back into the cottage as Josie helped Mattie develop an appropriate "I'm seeing a therapist" walk, and Mattie eventually found that a psychiatrist's office was a good place to cry. She finally wept for Robert Kennedy, for his family, for her country, for herself, for her family, for her shame, for her sins, for whatever might need the moisture of her tears.

Caitlin's contribution to the household was a pleasing blend of questions followed by long periods of silence. Neither her mother nor her aunt was particularly aware that Caitlin was studying — studying this new place, studying its people, their music, their habits and customs, their language, their particular roles in the scheme of things. She was especially thinking about being a woman; she might as well plan for it ahead of time, she conjectured, and now she had a few models to watch that

194

were quite a bit different from her mother and her mother's friends in England. She had always known that Josie was not exactly similar to the other mums in England, but she hadn't understood that Josie's differences were related to her American heritage. Now she was fascinated to see other females who weren't at all like British women and girls — Auntie Mattie, for one, Brenda Darcy, so beautiful in her tall, black body, even that remote Mrs. Feldman that Mattie worked for. Caitlin studied them closely, like an entomologist observing a rare insect.

"Pardon me, Auntie Mattie, are those really truly Indian shoes you wear, or is Mummy only kidding? Can I try them on? Joan Baez wears a headband on her forehead like that, too. Can I try yours? Can we listen to her music again? I can sing some of it for you if you like."

And remarkably, Caitlin could indeed sing Joan Baez, and Peter, Paul and Mary, Pete Seeger, and, of course, her favorite, Arlo Guthrie. Her talent for mimicry was uncanny, and Mattie often marveled that young Caitlin lost her
shyness completely when she worked her little voice around some very big singers. Mattie assured herself that disposing of the TV had been a wise, thoughtful decision, not an act of despair.

"Now we have beautiful music instead of hot, angry noise." Mattie paused for a moment to consider that she might actually be depriving her niece by getting rid of the TV. She had seen a charming program at Brenda's, something new called *Sesame Street,* and she wondered if it would help Caitlin in her quest to adapt to life in the States. And, of course, there was the election. After the Chicago riots had torn open the flesh of the Democratic party, and after Robert Kennedy's death, Mattie had simply wanted to tune out. She was sure her country wouldn't actually elect Richard Nixon to the presidency,

195

but with George Wallace running, and with Hubert Humphrey attempting to get the Democrats to the polls, she was anxious that her bubble of certainty might burst. When she allowed the November '68 election into her mind, Mattie paced and wrung her hands in despair.

"It just couldn't happen," she mumbled.

Caitlin was quick to absorb her aunt's moods and often tried to divert Mattie from despair by offering a song or a new series of questions. Mattie made a perfect audience. Never patronizing, always gentle and encouraging, but not gushy like Josie couldn't help but be, Auntie Mattie listened as a grown-up might listen to another grown-up. Caitlin soon learned to do the washing up and call it "doing the dishes." She experimented with make-up and curlers, even minor sewing projects, all the while giving forth in song the messages that Mattie loved to hear, messages of peace, equality among the sexes and the races, support for victims of war—all the wars, soldiers and civilians alike.

As the niece and aunt began to forge a chatty and relaxed bond, complete with occasional giggles and silliness, Josie was beginning to seem, in Caitlin's eyes, like a terribly misunderstood movie-star heroine. Josie struggled valiantly to be a good mother to her daughter, but little Cait was not oblivious to the pain around her mother's eyes. There had been many nights when Mattie was downstairs on the phone with Raymond and Josie, thinking Caitlin asleep, had let go her grief for her distant baby-boy child, in quaking sobs that Caitlin's quiet tears accompanied from the darkness of the room she shared with David. Who was the villain, Caitlin wondered. Not Jeremy, she was sure, and not herself or her brother. Who was that man in black in her mother's fairy tale? Caitlin began to entertain notions that the injustices of life were random and illogical, and this, more than anything, was what frightened her the most. From Caitlin's vista,

196

her mother was beautiful and tragic, the two qualities joining hands to paint a disturbing picture of the world of women. She didn't want to be beautiful, she decided, not in that way. She wanted to be more like Auntie Mattie, gracious and strong, quiet and thoughtful. Her mother's beauty was petal-soft, and exposed, whereas Mattie was lovely like an oak, an oak whose occasional bruises would be absorbed and mended by time.

Josie was grateful that her daughter had taken so well to Mattie, believing she might otherwise drown in worry and indecision. Her early-morning phone calls to England resulted in little but tears of frustration. Jeremy tried to get Gareth to talk on the telephone to "mummy and Cait," but the child's telephone conversations were as fragmented as the adults' conversations were fruitless. Josie was edgy and frequently unavailable to Caitlin, hoping Mattie's presence made up for her "absence," an absence that was terrifying to Josie as she looked back on her own childhood, her own mother. Mattie seemed to see Caitlin's needs clearly, and both sisters resolved to encourage the young girl down a path strewn with tools for her journey into womanhood – stories, poems, paintings, and songs by women who were care-givers like Mattie, fighters like Josie, with causes past and present.

Caitlin's own causes frequently brought her to the bookshelf where Mattie's *Atlas of the World* was prominently displayed. She noticed that the worn pages about Vietnam, Thailand, Cambodia, and other places she had never heard of were marked by light pencil notes, but it was the British Isles she sought to locate. She would study the colorful pages, wondering how England could be so small when it was so important to her, wondering how far away it really was. Her investigations frequently nudged her to the dining table where she could find a whole basket of pens and pencils, notepads, envelopes, stamps. Mattie was quick to discover that scraps of drawings and scribbles on envelopes Caitlin left on the table were "letters" to her family in England. Caitlin asked Mattie not to clean that part of the table, and the stack grew into a formidable pile of protected treasures.

"Caitlin," Mattie called, "I got you a present. Come see. It's magic!"

The child quickly removed gift wrap from the present and found a long, narrow box disguising the magic Mattie had promised.

"What is it, Auntie Mattie? I need to know what it is. I don't understand this picture."

"Caitlin, I got you a tape-recorder, just like the one Howard used when he read you stories and sent them to England. Now you are old enough to send a letter to Gareth and Jeremy, just by talking into the machine. When theyget the tape you send, they will send their voices back to you."

————

Hello, Gareth. Mummy just told me we are going to stay in America for now. I miss you so much already. I worry no one will sing you your bedtime songs properly. Don't be frightened. Mummy said last night that we are all underneath the same moon. So if you feel sad, just look up. I love you, Sweetie. This is Caitlin talking.

————

Hello, Jeremy. We've moved into Mattie's house in Berkeley. It's a cozy place, with a fire, and pretty doors and those little windows that make a big window, rather like a fairy-tale cottage. It's a bit small for all of us though. I expect we won't be able to stay for very long. Whenever I ask Mum about what we're going to do, she gets annoyed with me and goes all cold. I expect she doesn't have any answers for me, actually, and just doesn't want me to be frightened. I've met some other children my age, only I learned they don't like to be called children at all. They mainly ride chopper-style bikes and stand about at the 7-11 shop. That's a bit odd, too, the 7-11s. They're these shops that sell little bits of everything and more dear than regular shops. They 're almost like our sweet shops, but they all look the same, and there are loads of them. They seem to be everywhere in America, from what I can see. Some of the kids want to be slick. No, I don't mean oily! Slick is American for being great, but rather snobby about it. I don't quite understand it yet, but it isn't exactly friendly. . . . Oh, do you know what they call a lorry over here? A truck. And they have a lot of them, as well. Great big huge ones, with piles of whole trees on them. Log trucks, they're called. I asked Auntie Mattie about it, and she said they're cutting down a lot of the trees in the mountains. Then they sell them for lots of bucks. That's American for dollars, like quid is for pound, you know. I didn't know there were so many trees in any one place — not oaks or birches, or chestnuts, but these really tall pines and other trees like that. Like giant Christmas trees. It seems a bit horrible when you see those giant lorries with all those huge dead trees on them. It makes me think of the carts with horses pulling. You know, in the plague, with all the dead people. I saw drawings of that in one of your books back home. . . . I feel really quite queer here, Jeremy. Mum says that everybody will like me because I'm partly English, but I think they all will laugh, and that nobody will understand me. That's why I have begun to read out loud to myself in an American voice. I think things will go better for me in school if I don't sound quite so different when I get there. I practice all the time, really, and it helps if I read something American so it doesn't seem so silly. I like this one book Mona gave me. It's called *Are You My Mother?* . . . One boy across the road from

Mattie's is really very rude to me. He has come over by Mattie's garden several times to speak with me, but he always says something that makes me feel sorry I ever came here at all. But there's another boy whose name is James Darcy, and he's really nice to me. He took me to the university campus this week, and we went up in a really high tower where you can see everything. You can even see the Pacific Ocean. Auntie Mattie says "pacific" means "peaceful," and I think she's right. It's a very big ocean, Jeremy, and it even has it's own golden gate that lets the ocean into Berkeley where we live now. . . . Are you still going to be my father, as well as Gareth's? I would really like to know a bit more about our future. Can you tell me anything? I try to be calm and brave, like Agnes in David Copperfield, when she has to wait for David to come to his senses and see that all he must do is love her and everything will go all right for him. I love you, Jeremy. You will always be my father in my heart. Goodbye now. I have to reverse this tape so I can send it to you. Mummy made the envelope for me, with the proper stamps and everything.

Josie's Bath

What did he mean? It's so hard to understand Jeremy sometimes, and the connection wasn't very good. Maybe I didn't make myself clear when I told him I was staying. Maybe he thought I meant just for a while longer. He said it would be best, and he and Gareth would be fine. . . . Are fine, actually, is what he said. It didn't take Catherine long to move in. I knew she'd do that, using Cait's room, putting Cait's stuff in the attic. How could Jeremy do that when he knows how I feel? . . . Well the two of them can just have a good old time together after I get Gareth. Jeremy didn't seem to hear me about that. Said we'd

200

discuss things later, said the line was too bad and it wasn't a good time for him. Well, lah-di-dah, we'll see about that. See how he feels when I come to get my son. Then if Jeremy wants his family, he can come over here. He can get a teaching job here, and things will be better. He'll be like the old Jeremy, like before we went to England. It's Catherine's fault and that damned country that just closes in on you and makes you small. "One pill makes you smaller, and one pill makes you tall," and the pills that Catherine gives you, don't do any good at all. That's what England does, makes you small and choked. . . . Jeremy was so much fun before. It's the weather, too. It freezes up your heart and soul. Jeremy will come here, I know he will. Why wouldn't he? He'd love it. . . . "We'll sing in the sunshine and laugh everyday, we'll sing in the sunshine" now that Catherine's away. I'll go over and get Gareth, and Jeremy can stay and sell the house and apply for jobs here. I hope he can get one at Berkeley. I don't want to leave Berkeley ever again. It might take him a while, but that won't matter. Absence makes the heart grow fonder and all that rubbish. . . I know Jeremy's missing us, he just doesn't know how to say it. Catherine was probably listening, too, and Jeremy gets so uptight when she's around. Can't blame him, can you? That's probably why he sounded so cold, and the connection really was bad. . . . I'll phone him tomorrow.

———

By late summer, David added "dada" to his vocabulary and attended the wedding of his parents in his little cottage home on Russell Street in Berkeley. By most accounts, the event was pleasant and unremarkable. Mattie's second pregnancy was becoming obvious, and she made an attempt to stay out of the many snapshots that documented the event. The photos she later selected as keepsakes, however, revealed her preoccupations: Raymond holding David, Raymond holding Caitlin, Raymond holding Lucia Darcy, Raymond hugging Josie, Raymond conferring with Frank about lunar landing modules, Raymond commiserating with Willy about the coming election, Raymond drying a tear from James Darcy's eyes.

"I was going to marry Mattie," James had announced, and Raymond quickly invited the young man into the tiny, backyard garden where he managed to soothe the wounds of a broken heart.

There was no snapshot of Raymond and Bo, but Mattie's little brother called in the early afternoon to congratulate the groom, expressing sorrow at not being able to return to the West Coast for the wedding. And there was no snapshot of Nora. Josie had convinced Mattie that it would be just as well to give Nora a call in a day or two, tell her the deed was done, and tell her "whatever she wanted to hear." The sisters would also call Peter, if they could find him, and they would move into the autumn months with a ring on Mattie's finger and a second child in her belly.

The newlyweds slipped away late in the afternoon to spend their honeymoon night just up the street at the Claremont. Josie had suggested the Alta Mira in Sausalito, but Mattie explained she'd feel more secure closer to home, closer to David.

"Raymond told me you already took him to the Claremont, Mattie," Josie admonished as they were discussing the plans. "You already deflowered our secret place, but I guess it's okay. It's a bit late for a honeymoon though, don't you think? What are you going to do, play cards?"

Raymond overhead Josie's comment and assured his sister-in-law that they would think of some way to pass away the time. Josie and Caitlin continued to entertain the wedding guests with family stories, food, wine, and music. Caitlin agreed to sing "Lemon Tree" just for Frank Feldman, who she decided must be another uncle, one of the best. Josie and Willie enjoyed dancing the watusi; Brenda and Emily helped watch over David; everyone helped with clean-up, and soon "goodnight" was all that was left to say.

Mattie's Bath

What a good day. What a wonderful husband . . . so much fun to unpack his clothes, sniff at the sweaters for his very special scent. . . . I just wish he could stay now, forever and ever. Lord, this is hard, knowing he will leave so soon. I hope he won't mind making love around this lump in my belly. Who are you, anyway, little lump? I knew who David was the instant he began, but you are a puzzle to me. . . . I'll bet you're a girl. That's really frightening. I don't know anything about raising a girl child, so much confusion about where girl-children fit into the world. . . . Raymond will help; he'll be home soon, I know he will. . . . Raymond, I just don't understand, exactly, who you are. I unpacked your carry-on case, and what do I find for airplane reading? *Desert Solitaire.* Well, you surprised me with Shakespeare, and I guess I'm delighted to invite Edward Abbey into our lives. Who could be better? But where does that mind of yours take you? You can't talk about anything but a lunar landing. Well, not true, you talk a lot about David and me, but mostly your mind is on Saturn rockets and Apollo flights. So how does Edward Abbey fit in here?

It would be nearly a year before Mattie discovered how Raymond's growing list of cultural heroes fit into her life, but it was not a colorless year. Early in October, three weeks before the national election, Wally Schirra, Donn Eisele, and Walter Cunningham became the first astronauts to ride with Apollo around the earth. Apollo 7 was launched from Cape Kennedy on October 11, 1968. An hour and twenty minutes after it left the pad, an unimaginable power failure plunged the Houston Mission Control Center into semidarkness, and the flight controllers stared helplessly at their black screens for two minutes, with dull emergency lights casting an eerie glow. While the brief power outage caused the Houston staff a number of rapid heart beats, it did not foretell an abnormal flight, and the 36,000-pound spacecraft made 163 orbits around its home planet during a period of ten days, twenty hours, nine minutes. On October 22, the service propulsion de-orbit burn took place, and ninety seconds later the command module separated from the service module to begin reentry into earth's atmosphere. Splashdown was about 230 miles south of Bermuda, where helicopters from the carrier *USS Essex* made a successful recovery of the tired astronauts and their chariot.

Bo's congratulation call to Raymond was the first to reach the excited engineer, who said he would be in Washington in a couple of weeks and was eager to have a glass of beer with Bo and tell some tall tales about this particular flight. "A major success," he said. "But there were some tense moments, one right after splashdown when the spacecraft fell silent."

"News coverage was puzzling," Bo responded. "What happened?"

"Choppy waves had capsized the capsule, and the antennas were under water, so there was no signal. That's a big ocean, Bo, but finally the capsule flopped over as it was supposed to do, and *Essex* picked up the signals."

When Raymond did get to Washington and had the promised celebration drink with Bo, the brothers-in-law drove up to Baltimore, wandered around the inner harbor for a while, and finally settled comfortably into a quiet booth of a neighborhood bar. Bo was now working as a full-time policy specialist for Medicare, and the men spent a few minutes discussing the impact of a Republican administration on the national health-care program.

"Raymond, you do know better than to talk to Mattie about the election, don't you? I don't know why Nixon's victory is such a personal affront to her, but it's as if she were responsible for the whole thing, says she didn't do any campaign work, and that's what went wrong."

Raymond chuckled and assured Bo that Mattie's primary focus was on getting David to say something into the telephone to his father.

"I don't know. She's pretty upset about a lot of things," Bo said. "Benjamin Spock's court case has her pretty wound up. You know, his *Baby and Child Care* is her Bible for raising David. I guess she bought that book when Caitlin was born, Josie took it to England, and now it's back. And good old Spock gets himself convicted for abetting draft evaders. He led that Vietnam war protest last year in Washington, you remember?"

"Bo, you know Mattie is my guide to the other world. I don't remember the protest march because I was buried in lunar-module problems, but Mattie keeps me up-to-date on things that matter to her. John Steinbeck's death, for instance. It's like she lost someone in her own family. I'm reading Steinbeck now. Mattie said to start with *Cannery Row*, just kind of ease into meeting her family. He wasn't really related to you, was he?"

"No," Bo laughed, "but she and Josie have a way of adopting their favorite people right into your living room, something Grandpa R started, I think. He'd read someone to us, Aldo Leopold, for instance, and then show us pictures, tell stories, and pretty soon you felt these people were relatives, about to arrive for dinner. Nixon's victory is going to fester in her for a long time — not the dinner party she had in mind. . . . What's the new administration going to mean to the Apollo program?"

"You know, Bo, I try to stay out of the congressional funding battles, but it surely doesn't hurt that 7 was such a success. We took the record from Russia's Vostok 5 for the longest manned flight. That seems to make the politicians smile." Raymond signaled for another beer and returned to the conversation with boisterous pride: "We did everything we meant to do! We had to make sure the command and service modules are space worthy. . . . We needed a successful rendezvous with the Saturn 4B booster. And we needed to restart the SPS rocket motor a number of times. We restarted eight times! . . . Still, lots of congressmen are worried about Soviet customs officials who might be there to meet us when we do get to the moon. We will get there, you know."

"And then what, Raymond?" Bo asked.

"Ah, Bo, that's what I'm working on when I'm not focused on Apollo, which isn't very often, I admit. I'm so ignorant about what human beings do, so busy at the Cape these last few years. I didn't even know about the civil rights movement until I came to Huntsville to bail you out of jail. Can you believe that? Probably not, somebody tuned-in the way you are. But it happens, maybe because I had so little family . . . don't know. . . . I've been staring at the stars for a lot of years. Now I want to look around this planet of ours, maybe even get acquainted with what Mattie calls my soul."

"Mattie's a good guide if you're going soul-hunting," Bo laughed. "She told me you had some good stories — insider stories — about this last launch. She made Shirra sound like a maverick cowboy up there in space."

Raymond's mischievous grin quickly transformed itself into an inviting deep-throated laugh as he thought back over some of the incidents of the Apollo 7 flight. "Bo, you know Shirra had flown Gemini and Mercury missions. It was pretty well understood that 7 would be his last flight, so he was intense about it, determined to concentrate on operations and engineering . . . and, you know, he had a bad cold, probably felt miserable. He made a big fuss about any experiments that were suggested. When he learned that TV cameras were going on board, he had a fit and tried to stop the installation."

"Why such an aversion to TV?" Bo asked.

"Well, just one more piece of equipment to go wrong, I guess. He lost that argument, but once he was in command of the craft, he just refused instructions from the ground if they didn't suit him. On one pass when Slayton told him to flip on the TV, he barked back that the equipment wasn't ready, the crew hadn't eaten yet, and he wasn't willing to foul up the schedule. And the first time they fired the service module engine, he yelled "Yabadabadoo" — not quite what the PR people had in mind, I guess. Right to the end, he kept it up. Houston insisted the crew follow mission rules and splashdown with their helmets on, but Wally refused. The doctors had suggested there could be some ear damage, so he told the crew to hold their noses, close their mouths, and try to blow through their Eustachian tubes to keep the pressure in their middle ears. You can't hold your nose with a helmet on, so the crew splashed down looking like a bunch of kids going swimming for the first time."

The seventeen years that separated Raymond and Bo appeared to dissolve at a rate related to the frequency of beer being served by a plump and cheerful waitress. By late afternoon, Bo suggested a walk and offered Raymond the couch in his apartment if he could stay over for the night.

"Sure," Raymond said. "I can catch an early flight, I think. Let's go home and call Mattie and Josie. But you make the call, Bo. I never know what I'm going to get if Josie answers. Not sure I'm a member of the family yet. . . . She's pretty direct. Just wants to know if I'm through playing with my space toys. . . . What was that guy's name? Leopold something? Let's find a bookstore; maybe I can make peace with Josie if I invite some of your grandfather's friends to dinner."

"Aldo Leopold," Bo answered. "Yes, it might work with Josie. We'll look for *Sand County Almanac*."

By the time the men found a bookstore and finished browsing, Raymond's shopping bag revealed a serious hunger to "catch-up on a little reading" and secure a place in the sisters' shared vision of what a hero looks like. With Bo's assistance, Raymond found *Sand County Almanac* and tossed in Thoreau's *Walden* and *On the Duty of Civil Disobedience*.

"That should keep me out of trouble for a while," Raymond laughed, but Bo added *The Bounty Trilogy* for relaxation, and finally reached for a copy of William O. Douglas's biography of John Muir, *Muir of the Mountains*.

"This is written for children," Bo explained, "but you could kill two birds with one stone. Douglas and Muir are both family heroes."

"Great! I'd like to start with a children's book. I feel very much like a child, so much to learn about. What about Greek mythology, Bo, shouldn't I try to know more about what Mattie's always talking about?"

"I'd let it go for now, Raymond. Mattie likes to tell those stories in her own way. You'd never catch up because she's always changing the interpretation to suit the situation."

Their call to Berkeley was one of the happier events in the Russell Street household. Josie reported she would soon see an attorney about getting Gareth across the vast ocean that seemed to be solidifying into a heavy wall of isolation. Her conversation with Bo, and even Raymond, stimulated some energy, and she returned Nemesis to the telephone stand and reached for the Oakland telephone book.

"Robert, this is Josie. Do you remember me? I used to be Josie Townsend, Howard's wife. Do you remember, you handled my divorce?"

"Of course, I remember you, Josie. You're basically unforgettable. What can I do for you? It's been what, three or four years since you left me holding the bag?"

"What do you mean, Robert, holding the bag?"

"Well, Josie, on your instructions, I was attempting to resolve your child-support problems. The next thing I knew you disappeared without a word. No communication at all. I finally got in touch with your sister. Mattie, is it? She told me you married again and moved to the United Kingdom. Do you realize you didn't pay for the work I'd done?"

"I'm so sorry, Robert. You see, things just happened so quickly. I must have forgotten in all the excitement. I guess at the time I thought I wouldn't need the child support from Howard, and it didn't seem to me you were making much headway anyway."

"Josie, I explained to you at the time that it was difficult to enforce child-support orders, and it was next to impossible because Howard left the state. However, it would have been nice if you'd informed me of your whereabouts. . . . Enough of the past. Why are you calling? I'm really busy just now."

"I need some advice, Robert. My son is in England, and I want to bring him here. How do I do that?"

"I don't understand the problem. Why are you here, and why is your son is in England?"

"Well, that's where we lived. That's where Gareth was born. That's where his father lives; he's British. Caitlin and I came over for my father's funeral, and I'm not going back. I just want to bring Gareth over here. I just want to go get him, but I don't know what I need to do. You see, his father said I couldn't have him over here. Jeremy wants me to get a divorce, and he says I can't have Gareth. I know I can get him, I just don't know the legal ins and

outs. That's what I want you to help me with. Will you? I may need the child support from Howard, too, now that I'm on my own, although my father left a little money that will tide me over. Can you fix things for me?"

"Did you register your son as an American citizen born abroad?" Robert asked with resignation. "Does he have an American passport?"

"Not really. I never thought I'd need to do that. I mean, after all, he *is* my son, and I'm an American citizen."

"You know, Josie, you're really naïve. Didn't you think this through when you left him behind?"

"Robert, I'm not naïve. I didn't know I wouldn't be going back when I came over. I didn't decide that until I got here. How was I to know Jeremy would adopt this position? He and his mother have agreed to support me and Caitlin if I don't return to England. But I have to have my son! Don't you understand that? Can't you do something?"

"Not this time, Josie. I'm truly sorry, but you couldn't have made a bigger mess of things. I have to be honest with you. It would cost you more than you could ever afford, and you'd probably lose in the long run. If you'd registered him with the United States Embassy, you might have had a chance, but I doubt it. International child-custody laws are very complex, the case would take years and cost a fortune. As for the situation with your first marriage, I'll see what I can do if you'll clear up your outstanding bill."

As Josie hung up the phone, she failed to find the tears and the anger that she knew must be somewhere inside her numb body. If she located the feelings, she would kill herself. She knew this without question, with her entire being. *I have to handle this. I have to make things right for Caitlin. Caitlin is all I have left, and she needs me.*

———

Josie's early December phone call to Florida left Raymond with little doubt about expectations. "Unless you are actually strapped into one of your spacecrafts and launched into the cosmos, Raymond, be here! Mattie's about to pop, and you are part of her equation."

The birth of their second child was wedged into Mattie and Raymond's lives on the crisp afternoon of December 7, 1968. "Pearl Harbor Day," Mattie mused. "I hope this isn't an omen of some kind, being born when the war began . . . . Raymond, I'm so glad you can hold her on her very first day. Have you seen David yet?"

"Caitlin and David are racing up and down the halls, dodging an army of nurses; Josie's with them."

"Why are you whispering?" Mattie asked, as she smiled at the father-daughter team seated at her bedside.

"I had no idea, Mattie, how this would feel. It's overwhelming, consuming."

Mattie scanned her husband's soul with a casual glance and searched his tear-stained face for more clues about his feelings.

"I'd like to call her Sarah," Mattie announced, "after your sister. Is that okay?"

Mattie's Bath

Now Raymond, you are the logician in this weekend family. Can't you see how the equation works? Of course I want to live with you. I don't want to live in Florida. . . . A+B = California. Oh, I know that's not fair, Raymond. I know. But please try to understand. What is there to understand? . . . I was a hack writer when you met me, but I am getting better; sometimes I am very good. Frank likes my work, says I'm even beginning to understand the science I write about so craftily. But it's more than that, Raymond. I had a piece accepted by *Cry California*, a nice poetic piece on Robinson Jeffers and his sense of place, how important it is to each of us to know where we belong and to care for our place. Please, Raymond, forgive me. It isn't just California, or my work. David and Sarah . . . . I need them to live in California . . . . Josie and Caitlin . . . . They're doing fine . . . but . . . no father. . . . David and Sarah have a father, and I must move to Florida so they can know their father. . . . I'm not sure I can stand this. Raymond, I just need a little time to know that everybody is fine.

––––––

The sisters shared the notion that this might be their last year together in the Berkeley cottage, and with three children in the house, Mattie and Josie made the Christmas season exciting and memorable. They had arranged with a neighbor to have Santa arrive on Christmas Eve, just around dark. Sarah was a wholesome two weeks old; David, a year and a half; and Caitlin just seven, a perfect year to test the child's faith in the magical old man.

"How old were you when you figured out that it was Uncle Howard who played Santa all those years on the ranch?" Mattie asked.

"I never did, Mattie. I was eleven years old before the kids in school teased me into agreeing there was no Santa. But I never really knew how our parents did it all. I remember Father getting pretty serious, making us think we were naughty for being up so late on Christmas Eve, warning us that if Santa arrived, we'd have to hide. And then the doorbell would ring, and Santa would be there — big old bag of toys, the whole thing. 'Ho, Ho, Ho, are the children in their beds?'"

"Do I have to go to bed?" Caitlin complained. Her entry into the kitchen pulled the women out of their reveries and back to the child's persistent questions about Santa Claus.

"It seems to be okay as long as you hide," Josie explained. "That's what I used to do, hide in the woodbox next to the fireplace, worried to death about black-widow spiders, but too frightened to move. Peter always found the good hiding places. Maybe you should find a hiding place, Cait. Take David with you, will you? Mattie, you hide with Sarah. Santa should be here any minute."

Caitlin's eager eyes scanned the festive living room and settled on the coat closet just inside the front door. No spiders there, she was sure, and she could leave the door ajar, certain to see the jolly old elf.

"Since he's coming here on Christmas Eve, how will Santa get to Gareth and Jeremy's on time? I'm not sure how it all works."

Mattie saw the tears beginning to form in Josie's eyes and quickly responded, "He just takes a shortcut . . . drives the reindeer around the other side of the moon. It's easy for him."

213

It was, indeed, the other side of the moon where many in the country were focused on Christmas Eve, 1968. Apollo 8 slipped behind the rim of the moon at 4:49 EST, whereupon its communications channels went silent. Astronauts Frank Borman, James Lovell, and William Anders were traveling upside down and backwards through the black unknown on the night side of the moon. When a stunning array of sunlit peaks emerged through the black carpet below them, William Anders uttered the words that came immediately to him:

"Oh, my God."

At the Cape where NASA staff celebrated mankind's first orbit of the moon, Raymond Robbins lifted a champagne glass to the highly successful mission, to his family, and especially to his newborn daughter whose sweet baby scent seemed to linger in his clothes, softly calling throughout the day and night for his attention.

CHAPTER 12

Love, sister, it's just a kiss away, it's just a kiss away . . .
                    M. Jagger/K. Richards/Rolling Stones
                    "Gimme Shelter"

"Bring shovels, chains, grass, paints, flowers, trees, bull dozer, soil, colorful smiles, laughter and lots of sweat." The announcement in the *Berkeley Barb* in late April 1969 might very well have escaped Mattie and Josie's notice were it not for Caitlin and James Darcy's cheerful plans to help build a park on Sunday.

"Where do you mean?" Josie asked her daughter.

"You know, Mom, on Haste, just up from Telegraph., where that muddy field is. Sometimes you park there 'cause it's free. . . . It's okay, Mom. I go down there lots of times. It's going to be a park now, a people's park. It'll be neat."

Caitlin's excitement was shared that afternoon by several hundred Berkeley people who arrived at "People's Park" to shovel and hoe, plant flowers and vegetables, work, plan, and relax in the sun. When Black Panther leader Bobby Seale arrived the next weekend and announced he would get some Panthers to help out, the expansive moods of springtime ripened into rock music, bon fires, dancing, and the ritualized passing of the weed. Marijuana fumes blended passively into the smoke of the bon fires, and celebrations continued long into the night.

The park continued to grow in vegetation and imagination until the university announced that People's Park would be dismantled during the summer. The university owned the land, and it was time to move ahead with plans to construct a concrete parking facility. Well before the bulldozers arrived, two hundred campus and city police filtered through the park to arrest some street people who considered themselves inhabitants and guardians of the park. By the time construction crews arrived to cyclone-fence the area, marchers were moving down Telegraph Avenue to the somber beat of "Take back the park."

Thus began one of the most controversial confrontations the campus had ever hosted. Attitudes hardened by the war moved from disillusionment to rebellion as bottles and rocks thrown at the police were first met with tear gas, then with firearms. More than thirty demonstrators were wounded. One policeman was stabbed, six others were injured, and one young demonstrator died in a nearby hospital. By the next week, police and the National Guard occupied the campus; helicopters flew low over the city and emitted the same CS gas that was used in Vietnam to flush out jungle guerrillas. The number of arrests grew to nearly eight hundred.

Along with toxic gas, the rhetoric of polarization filled Berkeley's moist, foggy mornings and carried new worries to the Russell Street cottage.

"Josie, I'm not so sure about trying to raise a family here," Mattie announced. "Riots, police, tear gas in the air. . . . Can you believe what that National Guard commander said?"

"Read it to me, Mattie. I'll finish feeding Sarah while you read."

"Well, he says the CS gas is 'an inescapable by-product of combating terrorists, anarchists, and hard-core militants.' And Governor Reagan called the demonstrators a 'professional revolutionary group.'"

"Sounds like a line from one of his movies. It's kind of embarrassing, isn't it, having a movie actor as governor?"

"Well, it can't last long. Did you hear Brenda say Ron Dellums is going to run for Congress? And Willy will probably run for mayor. That's good news."

216

"You really believe in that stuff, don't you Mattie? I guess it helps to believe in something."

Mattie glanced at her sister to see if tears were going to flow again. She didn't want Josie feeding Sarah with tears in her eyes, and most of all, she didn't want Josie to cry any more.

"Who do you think is right about People's Park?" Josie continued.

"Oh, Josie, I think we lost track of right and wrong a long time ago, maybe even before we were born. . . . You're right, though. We need something to believe in. The kids, I guess. Look at David, still asleep. He's such a peaceful child. Dear God, please let him be a peaceful person."

"Well, sure, the kids keep us going, Mattie. . . . But what are they going to believe in?"

After a long pause Mattie suggested "Dignity. How about dignity and grace, Josie? We could try that."

"Sure, okay, Mattie. Kind of like the captain of the *Titanic,* right?"

"Oh, Josie, I just hate it when you're depressed."

"So do I, Mattie, but I'm not sure you're doing any better. You just hide things better than I do."

"I don't think I'm hiding things so much. I'm just trying to figure out what to do. If Raymond ever gets through at the Cape, then what? He says he wouldn't like to live here, in Berkeley — too stressful for the kids. And he says the valley, our beautiful Sacramento Valley, isn't clean and fresh the way it used to be. I guess we can't talk about prime soil anymore, just some warlock's brew from a chemistry lab. It's all pretty discouraging."

"Maybe the next frontier really is the moon. They haven't messed up the moon, yet, have they?"

"Josie, whom do you mean when you say 'they'?"

"All of us, I guess. I guess we're all in this together, trying to make decisions that make sense, but I don't trust very many people. I don't think we're even asking the right questions. You know, questions about what's good for the spirit. . . . Mattie, I think you're right; let's just see if we can develop a new walk. Dignity and grace, you said? How about this?"

Josie had just wiped the rice cereal from Sarah's lips and lifted her from the high chair, handing her to Mattie. The child offered a happy smile to her aunt as Josie drew herself into a tall, straight-backed posture, head held high, shoulders squared.

Mattie began to giggle at the prospect of a new walk in their repertoire, but she glanced quickly at Josie's face and said, "The tears don't add much, Josie. We'll have to work hard on this one."

Late that night Mattie tried to describe the new "dignity" walk to Raymond; and Raymond tried to describe to Mattie the new NASA walk — a walk on the moon.

"If all goes well, Mattie, we'll launch in a few weeks. It could be a big day, a big day for all of us. I'll try to get home for a little while before the launch, maybe get in a TV so you can watch this time."

Mattie quickly confessed that she had already allowed a TV back in the house. She and Josie had purchased a 17-inch color TV so that Caitlin and David could enjoy *Sesame Street.* She didn't mention that she and Josie sometimes sat up late into the night watching old monster movies. They agreed that as long as the kids didn't know about it, they could consider late-night movies their recreational drug.

"How do you finally decide, Raymond? I mean, the actual moment of launch, so many things to consider. Who finally pulls it all together?"

"One of the administrators here made it simple," Raymond laughed. "He said that when the weight of the paperwork equals the weight of the stack, you know, the

218

Saturn V — 2,902 tons! — then it's time to launch." Raymond continued to explain some of the flight considerations. The area designated the Sea of Tranquility was the target, and launch time was carefully chosen so that the lunar module would be landing with the sun low enough to cast good shadows on the moon's surface and give the crew maximum visibility. Apollo 11 would orbit the moon in a clockwise direction so the sun would be behind the module, not in the astronauts' eyes, as they came in to land.

"You make it sound real, Raymond," Josie said. She had taken over the phone so Mattie could bring David to talk to his father.

"I think maybe we've got it right, Josie. Have a little faith. Here's a happy thought for you. Launch is probably the most dangerous moment in the whole operation, but we estimate 99.9 percent reliability.

"How many parts are there in the Apollo stack, Raymond?"

"I'd say about 5.6 million, more or less."

"Raymond, you already know that math is not my strong suit, but I figure if you have 99.9 percent reliability, that leaves about 5,600 things to go wrong . . . . So, who's driving this toy?"

Raymond explained that Neil Armstrong was commander of the flight; Mike Collins was command-module pilot, and Buzz Aldrin was to pilot the lunar module, the *Eagle*. Jim Lovell, Bill Anders, and Fred Haise were the back-up crew.

"Josie, let's call a truce for a few weeks. These 'toys' are pretty important to me, to all of us, I think. Here's a deal we can make. You place some faith in this flight, prove it to me by making me a one-way flight reservation to California sometime around Thanksgiving. Deal? You let me into the family; I'll be there."

July 10, 1967
Cocoa Beach, Florida
My dearest Mattie,

I'm as excited as a kid. I'm excited and nervous and even frightened. But this has become a lucky program, and I'm confident. You know it doesn't seem possible for me to leave a job half done, but if we succeed next week, I will finally be free to live with you for the rest of our lives. I need you to know that being a father, everyday, is frightening for me, and I'm certainly not off to a very good start. I'm not sure I ever thought about what it means to be a good father. Mine just disappeared before I had a chance to watch and learn. But I'm determined.

I've been doing a little reading, and there are several other things that worry me. I want you to know about them so please be patient and wade through this engineer's prose.

a) I know you have the deepest love for the Great Valley where you were born and raised, but I fear that the once-fertile land has become a great chemical soup. You have told me stories about running through the spray behind the DDT truck and your parents' thinking it was all right because the government wouldn't let anyone spray if it was dangerous. Those stories haunt me because I don't believe the government can be trusted to put the peoples' welfare ahead of agribusiness profits. Toxic chemicals are now ubiquitous, and I can't feel good about exposing our children to a continuous diet of herbicides and pesticides in their food and in the air they breathe.

b) There is a finite supply of water on this planet. The valley farmers use subsidized water like there is no tomorrow, consider it their right to have it, but not their responsibility to keep it clean. They have become dependent on massive amounts of cheap, subsidized water, but it is not in the long-term interest of anyone to maintain these systems.

c) I expect a difficult time as mankind struggles to establish a more earth-friendly way of life. I hope we have either some racial memory or some creative imagination that will guide us.

Recommendations: Let us live in the foothills, or mid Sierra, perhaps near Tahoe or Yosemite, above the valley fog and pollution, but below the heavy snows. I intend to grow most of our food. With clean air and water, I think we can focus on the other needs of our children, some of the spiritual things that seem so easy to overlook. I want to take David salmon fishing and help Sarah learn to swim. I want to walk with you in the evening, and I want . . . Mattie, I am full of wants tonight, and I miss you more than words can tell. I can't even think of a Shakespeare line that will tell you how I feel, so I'll just settle for this thought from *Twelfth Night*: "Then westward-ho!"

"Josie, things are going to get better soon. I know they are. I got an a-b-c letter from Raymond." Mattie was making a second pot of coffee while Josie fussed with the difficult task of brushing Sarah's wispy hair and then getting the child into her highchair for breakfast.

"Is an a-b-c letter one of those 'let's get organized' formulas?"

"Sort of," Mattie responded, "but this one's pretty easy to understand. A + B = California."

Josie knew that Raymond's latest letter had delighted Mattie, but she didn't yet want to consider what Raymond's arrival might mean to the cozy let's-work-this-out-together life the sisters had created. Josie gave careful attention to daily routines and seldom stretched her imagination beyond household tasks.

221

"We're having an astronaut's breakfast this morning," she announced as she served David some orange juice followed by steak, scrambled eggs, and toast. "Your dad says it's a tradition for the astronauts to have steak for their pre-launch breakfast."

"Mind if we leave the TV on during breakfast, just this once?" Mattie asked.

It was Walter Cronkite's husky voice and authoritative presence that would lead the nation in its July 16, 1969, early-morning celebration of American technology, foresight, fortitude, and funds. Josie and Mattie had been up since 4:30 a.m., determined to catch every minute of the event, the event Cronkite said would be in all the history books for time evermore. "Everything else that has happened in our time is going to be an asterisk," he declared.

"Well, I'm ready to be an asterisk," Josie commented, as she poured more juice for Caitlin.

"Mommy, I think you mean to say 'astronaut,' don't you?"

"Either way," Josie sighed. "Did you invite James over for the day?"

"Sure, for all the days, until the asterisks get back."

"Caitlin, it's really 'astronauts,' as you said. I was just being a grump. That's short for grown-up, you know."

The mother-daughter vocabulary debate was interrupted by an unusual stillness emanating from the TV, which now revealed a thirty-four-story, gleaming white moonship perched on the eastern edge of the continent. Mattie watched intently for the first flicker of flame at the base of the spacecraft, her heartbeat seeming as powerful as the thundering shock waves that were spreading out across the Florida swamp, sending flocks of startled seabirds into the sky, their raucous calls echoing the announcement: "We have liftoff."

Onlookers at Cape Kennedy reported that the huge moonship appeared to hover just above ground for minutes, but in fact within forty seconds after liftoff, Apollo 11 was traveling faster than the speed of sound, its mighty Saturn V motors slurping up fuel at the rate of thirteen tons per second. It took only two and a half minutes to thrust the craft from its quiet launch pad to a speed of 6,300 mph. Once the empty first-stage rocket dropped into the Atlantic, the second-stage fired and pushed the vehicle on to a speed of 15,000 mph. At a height of sixty miles above the earth, and precisely according to plan, the escape tower and cover were blown off the command module, allowing the astronauts to see out the windows for the first time. At a height of 110 miles, the third stage kicked in and lofted the spacecraft into earth orbit. It had taken twelve minutes to go from motionless on the launch pad to earth orbit and a speed of 17,500 mph.

Two hours and forty-four minutes after liftoff, another burn kicked the craft out of the earth's atmosphere into lunar transfer, and the jubilant astronauts set about the task of joining the command and lunar modules. Collins was the pilot for this maneuver, and he brought the two modules together with little difficulty, finally releasing the Saturn rocket to a lonely solar orbit while the three astronauts continued their journey to the moon.

Apollo 11's flight was recorded in the US Defense Department's log as "Man made object in space No. 4039," but Josie silently renamed the craft "Raymond's Peace Offering." Mattie saw it more as Raymond's private success and her hope that Odysseus might soon return to Penelope. With Caitlin's patient assistance, David was still trying to get his little tongue to deal with the difficult l, f, and t of "liftoff."

It was early afternoon before Caitlin began to lose interest in the repetitious TV coverage of Apollo 11's flight. "Now what, Auntie Mattie? What's going to happen to them now?"

"They have to eat and sleep and check on a lot of things, and then one day soon, maybe a day or two, they will go into lunar orbit. They'll slow down a lot, and then two of the astronauts will get into the lunar module and guide it down to the moon. If everything goes well, they will actually walk on the moon, and then come home. How does that sound, Caitlin?"

"Sounds good. Are we going to watch?"

"Sure, I intend to watch all of it."

"It's the same moon, isn't it?" Caitlin asked.

"The same as what? What do you mean 'the same moon'?"

"I mean, the same moon that Gareth sees. Can Gareth see the man on the moon, too?"

"Of course he can, Cait. Would you like to call him and remind him to turn on his TV so you can both see the man on the moon? Both of you at the same time?"

"Oh, yes, Auntie Mattie. More than anything, I want to call Gareth and tell him to watch the moon."

———

Mattie's Bath

I wonder who did that? Who put a bunch of flowers on President Kennedy's grave at Arlington? Who wrote the note "Mr. President, the Eagle has landed." It was probably family, but it could have been anyone. I could have done that if I had thought of it, if I weren't so self-centered and self-indulgent, worrying all the time about our future, about a future for David and Sarah, Raymond and me, and Josie and

Caitlin, maybe even Gareth one day. . . . Bo was near tears when he told me about the flowers at Arlington. Just like Bo, touched by so many things, and so excited about the moon walk, the return home, the splashdown – only ten seconds behind the flight plan, and only one mile off target. Amazing. . . . And you are amazing, Raymond. You got your man on the moon, and, yes, it is time to "come live with me and be my love.". . . I know this next step for you is a giant step, but now you can take off your shoes and play in the mud. It's a wonderful idea to build a home in the Sierra. We won't actually have a lot of mud, you know, because those mountains were designed by the gods for our pleasure. And for our enlightenment. . . . Do you actually know how to grow our food, Raymond? . . . So much to learn, to make fruit trees grow, and tomatoes, maybe even roses, lots of flowers. . . . How sorry I am we can't grow more children to be strong and healthy in the mountains. . . . Actually, I'm not really sorry; I only regret your disappointment. I don't mind having missing female parts – the doctors were so adamant – but you mind having missing babies, the ones we can never have, and I am sorry for that. But I am eager, now, to have our own growing-up time, you and I together. David and Sarah may forgive us our silliness. . . . Yes, you can name our mountain home "Tranquility Base" if you want to; I was thinking "The Greyhavens" would be nice, but you haven't read *The Lord of the Rings* yet. You will, though, for David and Sarah, for you and me.

———

The architect who designed their home in Garden Valley, California was sensitive to Mattie's request for

225

light and simplicity. She was not the reincarnation of Bernard Maybeck, as Mattie had dreamed, but she knew how to listen to Mattie and liked her dreams. Raymond and the children tried to stay out of the way, and Mattie made only a few modifications to their agreed-upon plan. There would need to be one more room, a kind of all-purpose room that could convert into an extra bedroom "just in case." Raymond had come to understand Mattie's need to be prepared for the unknown, and he agreed that the extra room could house his books and mementos until "just in case" arrived. He imagined that Josie or Caitlin were likely candidates, but Josie had been adamant about staying in the little Berkeley cottage and making things right for herself and Caitlin. They were frequent visitors to the Robbins' mountain home.

"Mattie, have I met all your family yet?" Raymond laughed as he cleared away some of the clutter of a weekend gathering.

"Oh, no, Raymond. Gareth and Jeremy are in England. Peter might still marry and have children. And Mother's brothers are still living, several of Father's people. Grandmother R died when I was a child, but you'll like her. She was born in a covered wagon. Really. Would you like to hear stories about her? She was born in Roswell, New Mexico, well, on the way there, in a covered wagon. And she had a brother who decided to become an Indian. She showed me pictures of Great Uncle Harry, said she missed him terribly. I was thirty years old before I figured out that "becoming an Indian" wasn't something to decide. I'm sure you'll forgive me if I have an Indian in the woodpile."

Mattie had easily forgiven Raymond his long stay at the Cape; she saw his sorrow at missing so much of David's earliest years, and she ached and toiled to make things good for him. Her forgiveness was not as quickly forthcoming when she learned that Raymond had voted for Barry Goldwater in 1964. How could that happen? Mattie tried hard to listen to his explanation, his rationale, but her thoughts quickly blurred as she imagined Grandpa R leading a host of ancestors to her doorstep; they were armed with buckets of literature, and their faces were full of sorrow. Raymond made things better for Mattie, and her army of ancestors, when he said he would not stray, ever again, if it was important to Mattie. It was, and Raymond smiled a lot on election day when Mattie checked and re-checked his intentions before they set out for the fire station to cast their votes.

Raymond took quickly to country living. Many of the pines on their five-acre piece of paradise had to come down because of turpentine beetles, but the Ponderosa pines were quickly replaced by cedars, Douglas firs, and redwoods. "We'll plant a few for Josie and her family," Mattie declared, and Raymond set about the tasks of preparing the soil and delighting Mattie with notions of how the roots would one day stretch out over acres, the mature trees blessing countless generations of creatures. Mattie continued to do some free-lance writing and some editorial work for Frank and Emily, who became frequent weekend visitors, but mostly she threw herself into the pleasures of raising a husband, children, and magnificent tomatoes.

The energy of the power walk that Mattie had found so useful during the '60s found its way into her right index finger when she focused on the big, black "off" button of the television set. She simply refused to engage herself or her family in the tawdry machinations and revelations of the Nixon Watergate scandal. Anyone around her who expressed surprise at the surprising events was met by Mattie's quick, piercing look that left no doubt about its meaning: "Well, what did you expect?"

Mattie's strong heritage of community service and her own peculiar interpretation of its dictates soon drove her to new endeavors. Greenpeace, Nature Conservancy, Sierra Club, and World Wildlife Fund were on a long list of benefactors of her heartfelt contributions and volunteer time. When Raymond pointed out that a) it took a lot of trees to make paper and b) it would be a lot easier on the mailbox if it weren't so crammed with environmental literature, Mattie agreed to narrow her focus. It was an agonizing process because the issues were agonizing, and Mattie eventually asked Raymond to help her decide. She pointed out that Aldo Leopold, John Muir, and David Brower sat right next to Grandpa R in her estimation, so Sierra Club would be a logical choice. She added that her family had always belonged to the Sierra Club, even when it was so dreadfully conservative, so Raymond decided on Sierra Club. Having met her family obligation, Mattie confessed that starving children and endangered species were in her worst nightmares. She pointed out that there was a unique thrust to each of the organizations they were considering. In the end, Raymond and Mattie reduced, by a fraction, the load on their mailbox and lightened some of Mattie's burdens.

"I don't think men realized how easy life would get when they gave women the vote."

"It's so difficult to know what to do," Mattie returned. "Thank you for deciding."

The nightmares that had plagued so much of Mattie's life had been, as far as she was concerned, tucked away in the closet with Black Maria. She slept soundly next to Raymond, who had learned to give her a reassuring nudge before he got up to use the bathroom in the middle of the night.

"Ven nightmares," Raymond whispered.

"What does "ven" mean?" Mattie mumbled.

"Well, when you're a kid playing marbles with the neighborhood guys — my tutor actually bought marbles for me, then made me go out and make friends —

you call out things like 'ven steelies, ven chippies, ven overs'. It just means you can't use your steelies or your chipped marbles, and you can't take your shot over again."

"Sounds great. We shouldn't ever use chippies, should we? I'm going to tell Josie about this spell. Do you think it will work on husbands? She could just call out "ven husbands" anytime she gets tempted by the wrong man. I think the guy she's seeing now is a good man, though."

"Then, in marbles, he's what we called a 'keeper,'"

" Josie said last weekend that you're looking like Dionysus, and I think she's right. You, with your long hair, your nice fuzzy beard, your suntan, your mischievous smile, and those silly clothes you wear in the garden. You come in at night with your hair full of twigs and leaves, like a crown."

"Mattie, Dionysius is a crater on the moon, about twelve miles in diameter. How could I look like that?"

"Not that one, Raymond. I mean the Greek Dionysus."

"When did he live?"

Mattie yawned, propped herself on her pillow, and searched her sleepy thoughts. "He didn't really live anytime. He always lives; he's an idea, a god, the god of wine, and fertility, maybe drama, too. He's pretty reckless and uninhibited, sexy and orgiastic. He's kind of the opposite of Apollo, all disciplined and balanced. We already settled the Apollo thing, didn't we?"

"Ven sleepies, Mattie. I want your body."

———

Josie's Bath

Such fun for Caitlin at Raymond and Mattie's. She loves the mountains, loves having cousins, having a real family. . . . Mattie puttering in the kitchen, Raymond putzing in the garden. Well, I guess it's not putzing. They work hard. . . . I was working hard, too. What went wrong? Robert must be right. I'm naïve. I was so excited when I got the job. My first interview, and I got the job. I thought it was my English accent. Secretary to the Sales Manager sounded pretty good to me. Not much to do except transcribe letters and keep files up to date. . . . The warning signs were there. Why didn't I pick up on those? Well, I did, sort of. I knew it was peculiar that Cynthia went to lunch with the CEO everyday and came back looking kind of frazzled, but she brushed me off when I asked her about it. Said they were working lunches. Working lunches! Right! So it sort of made sense when my boss asked me to lunch. I just thought that was a company policy. How stupid can I be? I'm not eighteen; I'm twenty-eight. How can men get away with that? Do they all do it? God, I don't much like men. Well, I'd like to like them, but they seem to think it's their job to poke it into anything that might produce offspring – continuation of the species and all that. . . .The worst part of the whole thing was those damned letters. I hate transcribing, gives me a headache. But I worked hard, and my work was good. . . . I know he was angry with me. He didn't expect to be turned down. I guess he thought I'd jump at the chance. Divorced woman, out on her own. Cattle fodder. Fair game. No protector. But I didn't imagine he'd do that! I can't believe he did that! Tore up all those letters, fifteen letters that had taken me all morning to do, said to do

230

them again, said they weren't good enough, said I'd better think about my attitude if I wanted to make it in the company. Shit! Dammit! Sonofabitch! I needed that job! . . . And that wasn't enough, was it? The CEO looks at me and says, "This really has nothing to do with me. You'll have to work it out with Ed. You work for him." I shouldn't have thrown those torn letters at him, I know that, but I was so angry. I had to be angry so I wouldn't cry. But I feel so stupid. Why do I feel so stupid? Why do I feel like I did something wrong? Was it my fault? Is there something wrong with "No?" It's not a four-letter word, is it? Did I lead him on like he said? I don't think so. . . . I should've stayed, shouldn't have walked out. . . . Rosa, you would've stayed. You didn't let them push you out I'm such a coward. If everything doesn't go just right, I quit. . . . That's not really true. I tried so hard with Jeremy. I tried hard with Howard, too. What is it with men? . . . Who is that guy Mattie gets so hysterical about? Falwell, I think. Yes, Jerry Falwell – the Moral Majority, right? I'll bet the CEO and my boss – exboss – belong to that group. They act so moral, but there's a nastiness somewhere. How can men talk about morality then go out and screw women every chance they get? I wouldn't screw so I got screwed. They want us to be there for them, take care of them, put up with all their shit, do for them . . . "barefoot and pregnant". . . "don't make waves". . ."be a good girl, Honey!" . . . Who was that guy Howard insisted I read? . . . Oh, yeah, Voltaire. Well, I sort of read him, but about the only thing I remember is when he said "Liberty of thought is the life of the soul." I really liked that. But, I wonder, Rosa, did Voltaire mean that for women, too? . . . None of the men I know seem to have souls. They're so busy telling women what to do, how to

231

behave, what to be. Then they get together and tell nasty stories about their conquests. Even church people do it. "If you don't believe and act like we do, then you're going to hell." Do people in your church act that way, too, Rosa? . . . I wish I knew about your church, Rosa; mine made me feel so nasty. I never wanted to go to Sunday school, but I had to. I don't know why I had to, but Father and Mother made me. The teacher said that anyone who didn't believe in Jesus was going to hell, and I got real scared because I wasn't sure who Jesus was, so I didn't know if I could believe in him. I asked if my dogs and cats and Misty were going to hell because they didn't believe in Jesus. Answer: only people went to heaven and hell, animals just became dust. . . . Then there was all that stuff about the missionaries who went to Africa to try to keep the natives from going to hell. "What if there were natives so far away that the missionaries couldn't find them?" I remember asking that."They will burn in hell," she told me. . . . I didn't mean to cry, just couldn't help it. But it was alright with me when Father said I couldn't go to Sunday School any more because I had tantrums there. . . . I guess I'm still having tantrums. Rosa, do you think I will ever learn how to have the right kind of tantrums? Are there any that matter, that make a difference?

―――――

Josie sat at the window, staring at couples strolling up and down Russell Street, couples holding hands, couples with arms draped over shoulders, couples laughing, some pushing strollers with smiling babies cooing and reaching for the falling autumn leaves. There were others, not couples, but Josie only saw the couples, and she knew she was in trouble. She was familiar with this restless feeling, and yet it frightened her; the intensity

232

frightened her. It was taking control, and she knew she couldn't fight it.

Caitlin was spending the night with the Darcys. She was spending a lot of time with them, and Josie vaguely wondered if that was a good thing or a bad thing. Was she passing off her role as mother to others who were better equipped? She wasn't much fun for Caitlin these days. Listless, bored, tired, not very good for anyone, certainly not good for a young, talented child so curious about the grown-up world. Well, let her be where she's happy, Josie concluded. She glanced through the window one last time, turned, and climbed the stairs to the bedroom. As she stood before the closet, she paused and said aloud to herself, "What am I doing?" Then she added, "Fuckit" and began fingering her meager wardrobe. "Who do I want to be tonight," she asked herself. "Marilyn, are you still in there?"

Josie's Bath

Why did I do that? Why do I always do that? It's never any good, and I know that going in. . . . The sex is no good. How can it be with perfect strangers? Can't feel anything anyway after all the wine. What was this one's name, Cliff, Claude, something like that. Not a bad piano player though. . . . I knew the minute I walked in. I always know the minute I walk in. It's kind of like knowing I'll buy the first pair of shoes I try on. Walk in, sit down, order a drink, look around. That one. And then the game begins. And then the game ends. Always the same. And I always feel the same afterward. . . . Bath water's getting cold. . . . got to get clean. But I don't get really clean. . . . And they never say, "When will I see you again?" Why would they want to see me again? I guess Peter was right. I'm a whore . . . except I don't get

233

paid. It's all free, gratis, on the house. . . . I just want someone to hold me. Just hold me. That's all I want. . . . Doesn't work that way. Can't say, "Come on up to my place, big boy, and just hold me." Nope, got to pay the piper. No such thing as a free lunch, baby.

———

"Sittin' on the dock of the bay," Josie sang as she stood at the end of the Berkeley pier watching the sunrise. She had come-to about 5:00 a.m., glanced over at the man sleeping next to her, slipped quietly out of bed, and pulled on her clothes. She grabbed her shoes and purse, then tiptoed to the hotel room door, remembering part of the late-night conversation, some fuzzy words just before she fell asleep. "Can I see you again?" the man asked. "I get back here every month or so, and I could call you if you give me your number. We could meet here at the hotel, have a few drinks, and . . . you know. . . ."

"I don't know," Josie answered. "What are you suggesting?"

"Well, I told you I'm married, but I travel a lot, and you know, it gets kinda lonely. . . . I just thought. . . ."

"Yeh, okay, we'll see," Josie had muttered.

The gulls were making their raucous morning run at the treasures the receding tide had deposited on the beach as Josie contemplated some muddy deposits of information in her mind, her cousin's suicide the most compelling. Mattie had called the previous afternoon to tell her about cousin Laura, one of the cousins Josie had trouble remembering. Laura was from Father's side of the family, but not one of the cousins who joined the gatherings. Josie smiled for an instant at the notion of a family gathering, but it was a haunted smile that drew without discrimination dark as well as happy memories into the lines of her face. Josie realized she had nearly

234

forgotten about these people's existence, these far-away family people who were supposed to have pretty lives someplace in the suburbs.

Josie could vaguely remember Laura – married to a psychiatrist, living in Marin County, two children. Her husband was heavily into EST. Mattie had explained that Laura was seeing an East Bay psychiatrist – all part of the dance, Josie thought. On her way from an appointment, Laura had stopped her car in the middle of the San Rafael Bridge, and jumped. That was it. Neither the husband nor the psychiatrist had meaningful words to explain things to the children. But none of this seemed strange to Josie.

"They never really know us, do they?" Josie mumbled to herself and to the spirit of her dead cousin. "Not really."

"Did you say something? Were you talking to me?"

Josie wheeled around, startled, to see a middle-aged, short, stocky, gray-bearded man behind her.

"God, you startled me! Are you in the habit of creeping up on people? I thought I was alone!"

"Sorry, I wasn't creeping anywhere. You seemed deep in thought, and then you spoke. I thought maybe you were talking to me."

"No, I was talking to myself. I'm trying to decide whether or not to jump off the San Rafael Bridge. What are you doing here so early?"

"I'm trying to decide whether or not to jump off the Bay Bridge," the man replied, punctuating his statement with a thin smile.

"You're kidding!" Josie shrieked. "Your kidding me!"

"No, actually, I'm not. Were you kidding?"

"No, not really. I probably wouldn't do it, but I was thinking about it."

"I think about it all the time lately when I'm driving into work. It would be so easy it seems. Solve a lot of problems, maybe."

"Where do you work? What are your problems? You don't look down and out. You don't look sick. Do you have a name? My name is Josie." It seemed somehow important to keep him talking. Here was someone as unhappy as she, maybe someone to talk to.

"My name is Abe. Short for Abraham. Abe Erskine. I'm not Jewish. My family was from the Ukraine. I'm not sick, I'm not down and out, as you put it, and I work at the *Examiner* in San Francisco. I live in Berkeley at the top of Russell Street with my wife, Karen, who's an alcoholic. Josie is a nice name, it suits you. What's it short for?"

"Josephine. And I hate that name. Don't you ever call me that. Almost nobody knows that's my real name."

"Is that why you were considering jumping off the bridge?"

"No, silly. My life is a shambles, and I can't seem to get it together. Almost everybody I know goes happily along, but I keep messing up. I keep taking the wrong turn, and I'm just so tired of it. I'm so tired of the struggle. I'm tired of the loneliness. There it is. Aren't you sorry for asking? I'm sorry for dumping all this when you obviously have your own problems."

"Maybe we should have a contest over whose situation is worse. And, you know, I'm curious; from where we are we can see three bridges yet neither of us chose the Golden Gate Bridge. Why is that? Too scary to get washed out into the Pacific? But, you see, we have lots of choices; three bridges. . . . Would you join me for breakfast, and we can lay down the ground rules for our contest, make sure we have chosen the right bridge?"

"Right, unless an earthquake takes out the bridges. . . . I am hungry, and an earthquake just now is the least of my worries. Where are we going? You know, for breakfast? By the way, I live on Russell Street, too. I guess we're sort of neighbors."

It wasn't long before the neighbors became friends, and the bridge debate receded with the tides.

"It is the dawning of the Age of Aquarius," Josie sang along with Caitlin as the two puttered in the kitchen making Sunday morning breakfast.

"Hey, Mom, shall I pick some flowers for the table? Let's fancy things up. And let's use the good dishes and stuff. I'm sure Abe will appreciate it. I mean how often do we get him on Sunday? Sunday isn't usually an Abe day."

"Okay, Cait, we'll make a party of it. We'll call it brunch."

Abe had seemed old to Caitlin when she first met him, old and brooding, but as time went by he somehow got taller, younger, and very funny. He regaled Cait with stories about people he worked with, listened thoughtfully to the child's concerns, and delighted in her curiosity, often calling from his office when Caitlin got home from school. Caitlin loved to get Abe's calls, but she loved him most for rescuing her mother from the dark places where Caitlin couldn't reach her. She sensed that her mother gave much to Abe in return, something like the stability Caitlin treasured on Abe days.

Josie never met Abe's wife, never even saw her. She understood that tenderness and some gnarly sense of responsibility for Karen's alcoholism bound the couple together with a cord that would not be severed. Abe's evening visits could only take place after he had put Karen to bed, and their weekends together were allowed only when Karen was away, often away at another dry-out clinic. Abe and Josie celebrated his buoyant moments of freedom and Josie's comfort, seldom talking about the demons he and Karen shared. Abe had explained that it

237

was his "fault" they couldn't have children. Karen wouldn't consider adopting but confessed to an affair when she became pregnant. She blamed the dark thread of fate on her infidelity when the little boy was stillborn. "It's God's punishment," she announced, opening the first of many bottles of bourbon. She moved into the guest room and never shared Abe's bed again.

Josie shared her bed with Abe, inviting him with considerable dignity and grace, lust and love, care and concern, and she was happy to be in a relationship that made sense to her.

"I'm really not cut out to be a wife," she explained to herself. "How did Marilyn put it? Oh, yeah, 'I have too many fantasies to be a housewife.' It's so much better this way. We love each other, and Cait is happy, too. Nothing much else matters, does it?"

———

Josie was convinced that a new energy in her walk — she called it the Abe bounce — got her the job she wanted at the *Berkeley Barb*, the Bay Area's premier underground paper. She and Abe shared amusing tales about newspapers — right and left — and they occasionally attended neighborhood meetings together, taking part in whatever protests they happened to feel strongly about. Caitlin, too, was expanding her horizons. She and James were trekking further and further afield.

"Hey, Mom, what's LSD? Is it only something you get for your birthday?" Caitlin asked one Sunday afternoon as she and Josie were walking a trail in Tilden Park. Josie paused, bent to pick a piece of miner's lettuce and popped it in her mouth.

"Why do you ask, Cait?"

"Well, me and James have this new friend, her name's Ruth, but you haven't met her yet. She and her dad and a bunch of other people moved in a few weeks ago over on Ashby. They have this great big house and do a lot of funny stuff."

"Caitlin, you should say 'James and I,' not 'me and James,' and what kind of funny stuff? And where does LSD come into it?"

"Well, yesterday was Clive's birthday, that's Ruth's dad, and I was over there for a while, me and James, I mean James and I, and Ruth were there. Clive and the other people were all in the living room smoking those funny cigarettes, you know, those pot things. And Clive was acting really weird, I mean really weird. When I asked Ruthie what was going on, she said her dad always takes LSD on his birthday. So I want to know what it is?"

"Before we get into that, could you tell me a bit more about your new friends – Ruthie and all the others?"

"They're pretty neat, really. There's Kirk, who Ruthie says is living with them to play fantasies. Then there's Clive's girlfriend, Lisa. She doesn't believe in getting married. Ruthie said Lisa thinks getting married is strictive."

"You mean 'restrictive,' Caitlin."

"Okay, Mom, 'restrictive.' But, see, Lisa has a girlfriend who lives there, too, and sometimes she's Clive's girlfriend. Ruthie says they all get to sleep wherever they want to. Clive's kind of like Mona and Bertram. He does, you know, those games things. Ruthie said he helps people who have colic, or something like that."

"Did she maybe say, 'alcoholic' instead of 'colic'? Josie asked.

"Yeh, that's it. Anyway, Ruthie says her dad wrote a book about the games they like to play. Maybe you could buy one of his books, and we could play some of those games."

"Cait, I think I've played pretty much all of them, and they really aren't that much fun. Why don't we go horseback riding instead?"

"Okay, but what about the LSD? Why do people take it and act weird?"

"Cait, LSD is a drug that can make you see and hear strange things. Some people think it expands their minds, sort of like when you imagine stories in your head or like in your dreams. But it's really bad for you, Cait. There was a guy working at the *Barb* who expanded his mind all over the sidewalk."

"How'd he do that?" Caitlin asked dubiously.

"He jumped out the window and went splat."

"Yuk! I'll never take that," Caitlin responded as she danced off down the sunlit trail. "I'll probably just stick to the pot stuff when I'm a grownup."

CHAPTER 13

We're off to see the Wizard
Harold Arlen / Yip Harburg
"The Wizard of Oz" movie

For several years after the Robbins family moved
to the mountains, Caitlin tried to fill the Berkeley cottage
with song and good cheer. Her music was a charm to
Abe, her mother, and to the now-spacious home whose
walls were painted frequently by Josie who would
renovate her life with each stroke of the brush. When
Abe brought Caitlin a used guitar from a shop on
Telegraph Avenue, she thrived in her role as family
troubadour and as part-time daughter to the gentle man
who balanced his commitment to two families with care
and enthusiasm.

There was a quietness in Abe that came from
gratitude, gratitude that Josie and Caitlin gave him an
opportunity to enjoy qualities of richness he had thought
would never be useful in his life. He truly liked women,
and he told Josie and Caitlin they were the stronger sex,
certainly the most appealing and the most cherished. He
spoke of women's accomplishments to Caitlin and
introduced her to women writers, painters, politicians,
and philosophers. His words were treasures, and the child
began to feel a relief she didn't know she needed. And
Abe gave Josie things Caitlin didn't know men could give
to women. Abe was a gentleman, and with her mother in
such loving hands, Caitlin was free to grow up in a
household filled with care.

But there were things going on around her she
didn't understand and didn't care to understand. It was

especially troubling that the American language changed so often. Caitlin was certain Kent State was a place on the map, but now adults around her were using the words to describe an event, a terrible event where people were killed and shouldn't have been. Then there were the words "Jerry Falwell." Caitlin knew Jerry Falwell was a person, a leader of something called the Moral Majority, which had a pleasing ring to it, but when Abe spoke of the Moral Majority, it seemed more like a disease spreading across the country. The "Pentagon Papers" were equally troubling. Caitlin wondered what you had to do to papers to make them leak, and if you knew how to do that, would you be in a lot of trouble. "George McGovern" seemed to Caitlin like good words, maybe like St. George and the dragon because George McGovern was supposed to beat up on that Mr. Nixon who Auntie Mattie said was so demonic. It didn't work though, and now there wasn't much to celebrate, especially when Hugo Black died and made Brenda cry so hard.

There seemed to be a lot of tears outside of her cozy cottage, and for some time Caitlin tried to understand them. Soon, though, she discovered it was much nicer to hear Stevie Wonder sing "You are the sunshine of my life" than to listen to the explanations adults would offer about puzzling dilemmas in the grown-up world. Caitlin remembered the Aesop fables Jeremy used to read to her, and she knew she liked it better in the olden days when there was a moral to each story.

By the time Caitlin was in the fifth grade at Emerson School, she began to explore the art of relative invisibility. Where other children clung to the structure of the classroom, play groups, Brownies and Bluebirds, Caitlin began creating a private world within. She learned to keep her mouth closed and her other sensory organs open, a technique she found handy for being forgotten, unseen, or assumed ignorant by authority figures.

Caitlin knew that her invisibility was not a sure thing. Auntie Mattie, for instance, could see things that other adults didn't see. It was a little spooky to Caitlin when she thought back to Auntie Mattie's presence in the cottage. "Like some sort of good witch," Caitlin thought, "like maybe she would have granted me my greatest wish if I had known what it was." But Caitlin also remembered her Auntie Mattie as a challenge — the supreme grown-up challenge. A person couldn't quite be invisible with an Auntie Mattie around. Not totally. Although Mattie had encouraged Caitlin's explorations, Cait always wondered if she was being tested by her magical aunt. Even today, with Mattie living in the mountains, a part of Caitlin wondered if her aunt could somehow see inside her, know her thoughts and feelings.

Caitlin seldom wanted anyone to know much about her, but she missed the Robbins family, especially the cousins, David and Sarah. Increasingly alone, Caitlin tended to keep company with thoughts of herself as a behind-the-scenes heroine, scaling perilous peaks to break through the clouds to higher ground. In her lively, imaginative world, she might be a girl detective or even an international spy, outsmarting normal folks who hadn't seen her true qualities or, perhaps more realistically, hadn't noticed her at all.

The entire UC campus became Caitlin's territory, and as her range increased with time, she discovered a feeling of security in the distractions of the streets. She could cover large distances in Berkeley and remain anonymous. She watched with her entire being, catalogued and compared, adapting as a transplant with the perfect learning of a child. The Bay Area of the late '60s and early '70s was comparable only to the very hippest parts of London: Chelsea, and Soho perhaps, where Caitlin had rarely been. Those memories of London had some of the colors, the textures that Caitlin encountered in Berkeley, but now there were grey casts to her portrait of England, dulled in memory by the India dyes and body paints of Telegraph Avenue, the oranges and vibrant yellows of the Berkeley hills in the fall, the agate blue of the bay. Visions of English people were soon replaced by corduroy bell-bottomed bodies that reeked of sweat, patchouli, sex, and weed, the smoke brushing past young Caitlin, capturing her fascination and making her a little bit sick to her stomach as she earnestly learned whatever she might, peeking at braless hippies from behind the handlebars of her bicycle. Other, dreamier scents rode the air around her as well and beckoned her to the hills above her town: Eucalyptus and juniper, hot clay earth and live oak sap. Caitlin had moved into a new life entirely; a psychedelic cartoon of characters and countryside that sang to her spirit.

By the time Caitlin reached junior high, she was the tallest in her class. Her peers were preoccupied with parties and slow dancing to Marvin Gaye and The Stylistics, or doing the "hustle" and the "bump" to Kool 'n the Gang. Caitlin loved the music, but she could rest her chin on the head of most boys her age, and she wasn't often invited to those all-important gatherings. Her hair was too wild to feather and layer the way the popular girls wore their hair, and although she achieved the required look in the tight jeans of the day, she was never comfortable in the stretch tops the girls were peeling into and out of, with capped sleeves and scooped necks emphasizing the female torso in a way that embarrassed Caitlin. She much preferred a large, man's shirt, preferably plaid flannel, even though her classmates teased her and called her "the lumberjack" or Smokey Bear. Caitlin didn't object to the nickname, in fact liked it as soon as she changed it to "Smoky" to fit her image of herself as elusive, perhaps nearly invisible. She even introduced herself as Smoky once or twice when she met older men in the park or on campus. Many of the kids she met on the Avenue were called "Moon" or "Star," and Caitlin fancied her elemental moniker gave her some sex appeal. She wasn't certain why she should want such a thing, but she knew she ought to, for whatever reason.

One of the girl's favorite campus haunts was Sproul Plaza. Caitlin could remember the time Jeremy had taken her to Speaker's Corner in London's Hyde Park, where she became fascinated by a funny little man with a rough accent and very few teeth, standing on a produce crate, preaching about the Labor Party. Sproul was a similar attraction. Poets and politicos, born agains and Buddhists delivered their sermons deliciously while Caitlin listened invisibly. Usually they were accompanied by the sound of rich drum music, congas and timbals, providing a cultural background that was just primitive enough to back up any speaker or performer of the day. Caitlin soaked it in like fresh rain. Her life and body were speaking the same language, and as puberty crept toward the girl-child, her senses opened their arms wide.

Males were reacting to her differently, and Caitlin felt the sharp surveillance of their eyes as she walked by clusters of hipsters on the street corners, hipsters smoking dope and hand-rolled cigarettes, pulling off of a bottle in a bag. A bus driver on the College Avenue line tried to come on to her; a couple of high school boys from her neighborhood gave her beer once or twice. Caitlin began to consider being taken for a woman as another kind of being invisible, pleasingly invisible. Wherever she went, she was treated to the form-fitting style of the pop world — Peter Frampton coming alive out of the cheap speakers in every fast-food hut, a bikini-bare Farrah Fawcett beaded in liquid on every 7-11 wall. She could generally play along, wending her way into and around places most kids her age would not go: A Jerry Garcia gig at Keystone Corner, a booth upstairs at Kips with a frat boy and a pitcher of beer, or taking tokes from a joint in the balcony of the Elmwood Theater, watching a

245

double feature of *The Harder They Come* and *The Groove Tube* — films for an older audience.

Caitlin's loneliness increased with her new social forays. She was more isolated from her peers with every adventure she didn't whisper, with each understanding she couldn't fit into the frame of her childhood. In England, she had been "The Yank" despite her perception of herself as British. Here, other kids couldn't seem to get past her accent to know the child behind the voice, uncover the voice inside the child. She had no confidante, and yet she was on fire to know about certain important details. She was trapped in her own curiosity and knew she could never go back.

———

It was on Telegraph Avenue that Caitlin found her backpack — out on the sidewalk, just in front of a souvlaki restaurant, arranged for display on a folded army blanket. Little pots of incense flanked the blanket on either side, giving the space an exotic, third-world market feel that Caitlin found irresistible. A beautiful girl of sixteen or so, suitably arrayed for the time in low-slung velveteen and Mexican silver, sat cross-legged against the wall and braided a feather into her hair. Her nails were dirty, Caitlin noticed, and her fingers were rough with callouses. Her wares were leather and cloth bags of various kinds, cleverly sewn and carefully constructed. What caught Caitlin's eye were the backpacks made out of overalls. She had never seen anything so remade in her life. Her childhood was filled with old things, preserved, while her current world blasted new, disposable realities through television ads and fashion magazines. Here was a different thing altogether.

Caitlin went home that afternoon with a backpack made of wide-wale corduroy. It was burgundy in color, and a pocket from the overalls was stitched to the back and closed with a zipper. On the pocket was a peace-sign patch with the spaces filled in red, white, and blue. The patch was a bonus to Caitlin. If asked about the war, Caitlin could tell you it was in Vietnam and that it was bad because a lot of boys were getting killed. Although further details escaped her, she was aware this small place on the map took up a lot of television time. A peace sign was mainly a popular design to her, right along with the smiling-face emblem that meant "Have a nice day."

It was in the pocket of her new backpack that Caitlin kept the letters and trinkets that made up her internal world — private, secret, rich with treasures collected along the many paths she explored — as her external world expanded beyond her imagining, burdening her with more new words: Spiro Agnew and Watergate, Henry Kissinger, Iran hostages, Jonestown, Three-Mile Island, energy crisis, endangered species.

Abe's death in a terrifying freeway accident, her mother's complete despair, something about a crowd-filled funeral and a grave were buried deep in Caitlin's awareness as she opened her eyes to see a face before her unfurling like a flower in high-speed photography. A sound was coming out of the flower. Was it "Dijereedi?" Caitlin didn't know what to say to the sound. She looked at the face for a moment and then closed her eyes to keep from seeing the blue lines around the mouth and the pimples that appeared to be breathing. With her eyes closed, she could sort out her thoughts a bit better. The face was a person next to her body, wherever that was. The sound was a voice that probably belonged to the face. The voice was asking a question, she could tell by the inflection, and she supposed she should answer it. She wasn't sure what word that sound had been.

"Huh?" she managed to push out of herself without opening her eyes.

Now she could understand the voices. There was more than one. Caitlin could keep her eyes closed and listen, and she might be able to figure out this whole thing.

"Hey, Girl, I'm talkin' to you, Baby. Did you eat it? Man, she's out of it."

Caitlin was practicing spinning silk. She remembered her body was long and tubular, and she was gyrating her hips to make the hula hoop go around. No, wait. She was making figure eights with the blade of her skate, and the air around her held her so she couldn't possibly fall, even if she put her hands out like this . . . and felt the soft comforter underneath her and understood the music she was walking into was a Pink Floyd song welcoming her to the machine.

"Oh, leave her alone, Man," said another voice. "She's just a kid, for fuck's sake. How'd she get in here, anyway? Get her into Pluto's room or something, Man. Let her sleep it off."

"I think she just took another half a hit, Man," the first voice said. "We could be baby-sitting for a while by the looks of things."

"The water is so warm," Caitlin told them. "You guys should try this. It feels great."

The voices must have known what she meant, she reasoned, since they all started to laugh. And she was laughing, too, her hair was staying on the surface, floating like lichen, and the sunlight was breaking into beads as it fell through the canopy of trees above so that warm light moved inside, and she knew with total certainty that everything would be fine always.

"All right, who the hell is this? Where the hell are her clothes?"

248

The woman's sharp voice came into the room like a steel arrow, and Caitlin was running from the Nazi soldier with all her strength. The huge river canyon was underneath her, and she had to tread water really fast to keep herself airborne. She called to her friend Pluto, and he was there, his shiny scales flashing out of the water, and he took his place between her knees. She would ride him high out of here, she laughed. Nobody could catch her now. Her legs were cold, cold and tired from the running. She remembered about riding the huge fish in the sky, in her dream . . . no, not a dream, exactly.

When Caitlin opened her eyes, she discovered she was in semidarkness, with light at her head and feet and the scent of milled cedar filling the dark spaces. She looked around to see where she might be. She was wearing a big suit-coat jacket and her undershirt. No other clothes protected her from the early morning chill. She had blood on her thighs. "Period," she thought. But she'd just had her period a week ago. And this stuff was sticky between her legs. She needed to wash. She reached into a pocket of the jacket to get out a wad of toilet paper that was already stained red. She somehow knew it would be there. The act of wiping brought back her self-consciousness, and she decided to figure out where safety might be. As she investigated her surroundings, Caitlin saw that she was in a cedar tube, part of a new climbing apparatus in the Emerson school playground. She remembered that it was parent-teacher conference day for the whole district. She hadn't told Josie that the high school would be out of session.

"No school for the little ones today. Good thing. I would have really screwed up recess."

249

Josie got a call from Brenda on her lunch hour.

"What is it, Brenda? Is everything okay with Caitlin?"

"Yes and no," Brenda replied. "Did you see Caitlin this morning before you left for work?"

"I slept through the alarm and got up late; she was already gone to school. What is it, Brenda? You are scaring me."

"She's here. And she's not hurt. I don't think she's hurt. But she snuck out of the house last night while you were sleeping, Josie. I think you two have some talking to do."

"I'm coming right now, Brenda. Keep Caitlin there. Please, just keep her there."

The talking Brenda had recommended didn't end until the next morning. Caitlin wondered if she should turn on some more lights in the little cottage or just wait for the sun to come up and spill some of its glow into the dim breakfast room. She could overhear some of her mother's conversation with Mona. It all seemed predictable, and she searched the table top for a writing pad, for something to do while adults decided her fate.

"Grounding her won't exactly work, Mother. I'm not able to be home whenever Caitlin is. I have to work, and there is no one to help me." Josie choked back the tears that insisted on decorating her "no one to help me" statement, tucking images of Abe into her heart and out of her mind.

"Well, what about your friend, the black woman. Can she help you? She was Caitlin's sitter, wasn't she?"

"Brenda is a very dear friend, Mother, with a life of her own. I don't know. I'll see if we can work something out."

"Okay, Dear. You keep in touch. I surely hope little Caitlin doesn't have to play out your script."

250

Dear Gareth,

Here's your weekly letter from your American big sister. I'm in a bunch of trouble these days. Mom would've grounded me, but instead they agreed I can hang out with Brenda for a while. Lucia's going to camp this summer, but James will be here. He'll be leaving for college pretty soon, but I still have years of imprisonment before I can have my adventure. James is fun, though, so it won't be too bad this summer. He said he'll show me parts of San Francisco and some neat places in Oakland where I haven't been yet. He's really straight, you know, but he's still cool. How are you? Please send me a new photo soon. A school one would be okay.

Miss you. Bye for now,
Caitlin

With the passage of a little time, Caitlin remembered a few details about Pluto's pad, vowing never to return to that place, wherever it had been. The summer was fun, and by the time James left for college, Caitlin had learned how to hop on any bus, transfer to BART whenever a station emerged in the cityscape, and eventually arrive in an entirely different universe. She mastered the role of a sightseer, maintaining a notebook in her backpack, occasionally revisiting the museums and galleries where James had taken her, frequently returning to hear her favorite folk musicians in the smaller bistros where she could jazz up on coffee and even sit in on the occasional jam session or open mike. Many of her favorite musicians were as heroes to Caitlin, wandering minstrels right out of fairy tales, the colorful characters who recorded the country's history, retelling the stories for pleasure and just enough coins to buy a meal and move on to new adventures. Caitlin's special kinship with her minstrel friends grew deeper roots when she got a part-time job at a small guitar shop. The job gave her a little money, a stronger sense of independence, and a lot of time to practice her music. The shop owner was disappointed when Caitlin gave notice two weeks before high school graduation.

———

Letters from Caitlin's new universe drifted back to her family over the next ten years. The run-away woman-child didn't feel like a run-away. She tried hard to explain she was running *to* something, not *away*. Her backpack was her treasure chest where thoughts and moods and questions were stored on little scraps of paper, some of them evolving into letters that actually got mailed, some collecting dust from across the country — moss green dust from a commune in Oregon; colorful, sandy dust from the Southwest; heavy, red dust from Montana; olives, browns, and golden-harvest dust from the Midwest.

———

High school graduation day, June, 1979
Dear Mom,
I made it, Mom, and thanks for the new guitar. Now I'm outta here. If only Abe hadn't died. But he did. Where do all the fathers go?
I know you'll be worried, but you need to understand that I'm fine, and I'm excited.
Love, Caitlin
P.S. I really can't handle that Vernon person you've been seeing. Hope you can. It seems to me "faculty wife" never worked for you, but I guess you'll know what's best.

———

Oregon desert, September, 1980
Dear Cousin David,

Don't even think about it. You would hate the commune. And, besides, I'll be moving on soon. There are more rules here than we had in high school, and just as many drugs. Not so much the drugs you smoke or inject into your body, but drugs that invade your mind with slippery messages about how things ought to be, about how you ought to be, but aren't. There's a whole lot of talk about giving up your worldly goods, but that doesn't bother me much. I don't have many worldly goods, just my guitar, and that makes escaping this place a lot easier. I just don't believe that the world outside the commune is so very evil. Got to check that out!

One of Auntie Mattie's letters finally caught up with me, and she told me you were doing real well in school. Good going. I guess you got the family script down pretty well. It's not the only script, but it's a good one. Hang in there! Whenever I see you again, we'll tell each other stories, maybe hide out in the attic and whisper about parents and their funny world. They're probably whispering about ours, wringing their hands and worrying. Mom says your animal drawings are amazing. Maybe you'd do one for me. An eagle. Can you do an eagle? I'll send you my address as soon as I have one.

Love, Caitlin

———

New Mexico, February, 1982
Dear James,

I can't quite imagine you in one of those three-piece suits that men hide in when they become lawyers. But that's okay as long as you are doing what you want to do. I'm doing what I want to do, at least for now. Yes, I'm healthy and safe. No, I'm not doing drugs. No, I'm

253

not hitch-hiking with strangers. That pretty well takes care of your questions. I wish you'd write me more than questions, write me about how you really are and what you are thinking about these days.

Here's something you can write out and paste on your bathroom mirror. "Not all who wander are lost." I got that from a bumper-sticker on the back of a '67 Chevy pick-up truck, the one that got me from Oregon to Colorado. It was really cool how I met this woman named Rhiannon in a little coffee shop in Madras. That's in Oregon, you know, kind of near Antelope. We got to talking, and we left the coffee shop together. Rhiannon's pick-up was filled with stuff like potting soil and hay, so I asked her what she did for a living. She just laughed and said, "Oh, live, I guess." She said she had to make some deliveries in Colorado and finally said I could come along if I would help drive. That was pretty funny because I had never driven a car, so we went out on these dusty, desert roads in Oregon, and I learned to drive the pick-up.

Rhiannon kind of reminded me of Janis Joplin, and she was fun. We listened a lot to The Grateful Dead, and she agreed with me that Sugar Magnolia is really insipid. But the best part about Rhiannon is how she believes she is powerful. She says if you believe you are powerful, then you become powerful. And I think maybe it's true. At night we'd sometimes stop at these campsites, not really campsites, but places Rhiannon knew about, and we'd build a big fire and sing to Loki. Do you know about Loki? I hope I can find you someplace, sometime, and tell you about Loki. Rhiannon says white people talk too much, so at night at these camps she taught me to howl with the coyotes. It's funny, you kind of have to make discordant notes before they howl back at you.

When we got to Boulder and Rhiannon finished delivering whatever she delivers — maybe it was marijuana, but that doesn't matter, I don't use it — she showed me a lot about how to get along in cities. It turns out that big hospitals have cafeterias, usually in the basement. You just line up and get the things you want, and they're really cheap. You can stash some extra muffins and rolls in your coat while you're in the line and nobody seems to care. I guess you would care, but it doesn't really seem like stealing. It's just a way to get along. Rhiannon says it's nothing like the stealing that congressmen do. She actually snuck into a hospital room and had a shower, but I wasn't brave enough. I usually shower at these federal campsites. If you drive in, you have to pay a fee, but if you just walk in, the whole forest is there for the taking. Enjoying, really. I love sleeping under the big trees in these forest places. And the shower water is really warm and nice in the morning. I met some musicians in one of the forests and hung out with them for quite a while after Rhiannon left. I'm going to try to catch up with them in the Midwest. You, too. I'm going to try to catch up with you one day. I hope you are taking really good care and enjoying your mysterious lawyer life.

    Love,

    Caitlin

P.S. How do you like having an actor for president? Since he's called "the Great Communicator," maybe you can learn something from him and send me letters that don't just ask a lot of questions.

P.P.S. There are so many art galleries in Santa Fe, you would think you had gone to heaven. Lots of women artists, too, and some amazing colors. It was raining when I first got there, and I thought some of the artists had just magically made up the colors they use. But they didn't. Those colors are in the sky and in the land and the water. You just breathe them in, and they get right into your dreams and your soul. I'm going back there someday.

255

Kansas, summertime, 1984

Dear Mom,

The sounds of Kansas are coming alive, and the day promises to be hot, humid, and heavy. I've decided not to find Mona while I'm here. I'm not sure why, but I feel like I just stepped into the Twilight Zone. Rod Serling ought to make an appearance anytime now, telling some story about a lonely girl who travels backward in time and ends up here, kind of a *Wizard of Oz* in reverse. Besides, if I go to see Mona, I have to deal with a lot of peculiar words and a lot of people in pastel polyester jogging suits and blow-dried haircuts . . . . Ah, America, land of the free . . . . Okay, I know I'm being snide and judgmental, but this just isn't a good time for me to get stuck, and I don't think my laws of invisibility would be met by a visit with my grandmother. Too many questions, not very many answers.

I'm beginning to like it, though, that I grew up in two different countries. I'm fascinated by the commonality of people and by how fiercely we hold onto our differences, defend them so energetically, and justify our discomfort with anyone else's reality. Two homelands are nice, but sometimes I feel I am living second-hand. I think my generation is further removed from the past than yours and Auntie Mattie's — sort of a motley Zeitgeist with the present rewritten and retooled before you are ever really in it. You probably wonder how I learned "Zeitgeist," and it's probably hard for you to imagine how I am learning anything but survival skills. But, Mom, it turns out that when you travel the way I do, there are hours and hours of time to read. If I can't afford new books, there are always magazines and newspapers, even good novels, left behind in bus stations and museums and hospitals. I'm getting pretty choosy these days. I've been thinking I might like to be a history

256

student, maybe a professor one day. But for now, no Mona, no particular direction. I've been studying the map. Chicago comes after Kansas and before Costa Rica. I think I can hear you saying I have a reckless lack of resolve about the future. That's probably true, Mom, but it's okay for now. I'm beginning to make some plans I'll tell you about in my next letter. Did I ever tell you we all read Kerouac in high school? It was supposed to be the hot retro read of the year, and when I graduated from high school, and you were planning a trip to the Southwest with Vernon, I knew it was time to head out on my own. You know, my whole life up 'til then felt as if I were tied to your adventure, bouncing along behind you, turning corners slightly after you did. I always knew I would forge my own path, and I thought I was magic, invisible upon command. I'd been such a good girl really. Good grades in school, no really big teenage issues, and I always regretted it a bit. I didn't want to rebel, Mom. That seemed so common. Everyone I knew was rebelling, and most of them couldn't tell you why. I wanted to do something less trendy, more original, and truly hip. I just read about how William O. Douglas rode the rails, and I may need to check that out.

I've got to run, Mom. They're closing the museum, and I'm meeting some friends who have a gig tonight on the Plaza. I wonder what you think about Geraldine Ferraro for vice president. I don't think it will happen.

Love you,
Cait

———

Heading South, great weather, 1987

Hi, Mom,

Did you know that there are actually manuals for how to ride the rails in America? I bought one in my junior year at Berkeley High. I carried it in my pack for a whole year, dreaming. So by the time I took off, I really felt ready. And I was, basically. I mean, I was ready in that I knew how and when to board, and de-board, which stations have the friendliest yard dicks, which trains go where, and when they stop along the lines. I even had a complete picture in my head of each type of car, and where to put my body onboard so that it would be warm enough, quiet enough, comfortable and invisible enough. I thought traveling for free on trains that were not meant for people was a great way to hide in the shadows, try on some solitude, go underground like a gopher, only to pop up miles away from my starting point, with no debts incurred, just maybe kind of hungry, lonely, ready to dematerialize and rub elbows with locals. But I wasn't prepared at all for the possibility that I would not be alone. In all of my dreams I was solo and safe. I never thought I might meet up with Quinn. I wasn't prepared at all, really. It isn't at all like Amtrak. Riding inside a boxcar, your floor, walls, and ceiling are so thin and metal, it feels very raw, very grinding. Your body moves involuntarily, and at first you fight it unconsciously, trying to maintain equilibrium, but eventually you give in and go with it. Then it becomes hypnotic and rollicking. It feels like sex when you finally get out of your head and let your body move for you. That's how it was with Quinn. I was streaking across the country on my way to I don't know where. I liked it a lot, the rhythm of the train and the rhythm of the man taking over, my hips and my head swaying and bobbing with the pulse of the train, like

258

you – the little part that's still you – just gets pulled into another place, surrenders to the rhythm, and then pretty soon it isn't you that's doing it, it's the ride!

When I got on the train, I was by myself, and that was how I had imagined it all, getting to know the ride a little on my own – relaxing and drug-like. I felt safe, because the train was going fast enough I knew I was truly by myself. No way could anyone get into my space, as long as the train didn't slow down or stop, so I just let it rock me to sleep. I remember I dreamt about being inside you, Mom, carried in your womb, invisible in a way, and totally dependent upon you, protected.

In Minnesota, the train made a stop, and I got off to pee, feeling like I wanted to walk a little bit, too, maybe get out on the road and hitchhike, but the yard was really stretched out, and I was a long way from the station. It wasn't too safe to walk the length of the yard by myself so when I saw the train starting to move out again, with my car still attached, I gave up on the walk. I had no trouble throwing my guitar and pack up into the boxcar and pulling my butt up to the floor of the car with a running hoist. The adrenalin surged inside me even at that slow speed. I found the whole experience so humbling, and in a way I was really open, for maybe the first time in my life. My emotions were way up on the surface of my character, you know? And I sat with my legs hanging over the floor and above the tracks, feeling the night air rise up inside my chest so that I almost wept. It was then that Quinn cleared his throat from the corner of the car. "Lord a'mighty, an angel!" he said. He made it easy for me, Mom, to share his boxcar, telling me I could call him a black man if I wanted to, easier on everybody, he said. But he was not like any black people I knew in Berkeley. He was part Cherokee, part gypsy, part black, part white. Said he had a whitey ancestor who fought in the Civil War, and when the war was over, just moved his family across the country. I guess they lived in Texas for a while, and everything about whether you're black or white just started getting mixed up. I imagine I should tell you that Quinn's blood didn't get mixed up with mine because my period started right on time after we said goodbye. But it was kind of a delicious notion, mixing his beautiful brown-white skin and his green-black eyes right into my body. Mom, he had a voice a lot like those singers Auntie Mattie used to listen to, you know, the really big tenor voices. But Quinn's voice wasn't all solid like that; he could take his voice off to strange places I have never been before — mellow, gentle, sad places, tough places, hard places, funny places. It was a voice that took you right along with it. I tried to be real small so I could just drift with his notes and blend with his soul. I wondered if I was in love with Quinn. Wasn't sure what that was supposed to feel like. And I liked his odor. He smelled bad, sure, because we don't get a lot of showers, but there was something else, something that pulled me to him so pleasantly. Well, I guess you know all about this man stuff, Mom. I just never knew it would feel so complete, snuggled up next to a man who smelled just right, sounded like God on a holiday. Quinn said I could come along with him when we got to the east coast, but Harlem was pretty hard for me to imagine, and I knew Quinn had family, maybe not family but other musicians, in New York, so I decided to tuck him into my heart and say farewell in Chicago. Before I left, though, Quinn showed me a lot of new chords on the guitar, and he gave me his hat, showed me how to stuff papers in the bottom of it, then toss in some coins and some dollars so I would look successful. And he showed me how to toss my voice into the crowd so people would want to listen to me up close. You can always tell if you're going to have a good day. Right after that Bhopal disaster, and then Chernobyl, people got way down inside themselves, didn't look

260

around, didn't want to hear music on the street corner. They just hurried by. With Bhopal, lots of people were watching the sky as if they could actually see the bad stuff in the air and hide from it. And people don't pay you if they feel sorry for you. They just look away, even if the music is good. But then there are really good days. I call them power days. I've learned how to make people want to hear me, come in right to the front of the crowd and stand around for a long time, smiling, tapping their feet, singing to themselves, and paying me for their good feelings.

Mom, this train is slowing down. I've got to get ready to jump. This should be Howard's town, I hope. Dad's town. I just want to see him, you know? Peek at him maybe, from behind some dusty library shelves, maybe not even let him know who I am. Maybe that would be best of all, because I'm not completely sure who I am, either. I only know I have to see him. And then, I'll go from there.

Missing you, Mom
Caitlin

———

Howard's home, Holidays, 1988
Dear Auntie Mattie,

I don't think I ever told you — actually, I know I never told you — how I used to wonder about your heroes. Never heroines, and I noticed it, and I used to wonder why. But now maybe I'm beginning to understand. It's interesting, this father-daughter thing, for you maybe a mother-daughter thing. I'm seeing stuff now that I know you always saw. The big hole. The father hole. You knew it was there, and so you tried to give me things to fill it up. But you also knew, didn't you, that it wasn't going to fill? It will always be there. Never mind what any of us do to mend it, the stuff we throw in just settles, and there's always going to be one gap or another.

I've been at Howard's now for ten months, and I've shoved about everything I could into our relationship, and somehow it still has a big old hole in it. Some barrier keeps us from truly loving one another, and I can't figure out if it is Howard's, or mine, or if we create it together, and if so, why? How can we want a similar thing and be so futile at getting it? And I thought about you and Mona. Sometimes people want things for each other so badly, they can't even tell if they have it. I don't think I'll ever be great in my father's eyes. The lens he uses to look at me distorts me and I become ugly. Perhaps not ugly, actually, but scarey. I frighten him, I think, and the more he finds to like in me, the more the fear grows.

When I first got here it was just the opposite. I felt like a sleeping princess about to be awakened by a handsome prince. My journey here, my first couple of weeks, all of it so impossibly shrouded in romance, and not just for me. Howard is a die-hard romantic. He cried when I arrived. He drank a toast to us at dinner. He took me to his lectures, and I took his kids to the zoo. We talk well together, and I worked so hard to impress him. I read Proust and Hugo before I even got here, and it worked. I impressed him. But now I'm afraid we are both lying flat on our faces, realizing the end to this story is not about soaring with eagles. It's about shaking hands and agreeing it's probably too late. Too late, but not too bad. I don't live in Howard's eyes, and I don't have to look for myself there. He can love me if he will. He will love me if he can. For his sake, I hope he can. But I've got a few things to take care of now. I'm going to talk with Howard tonight. I know he will be relieved. It's time to pack my backpack once again.

Auntie Mattie, you are so much a part of me. Some part of you is some part of me, and I feel safe. Occasionally when I get frightened by things, I imagine that you have gotten old in my absence. Maybe your body is getting old. Never your spirit. It's part of me, and I love having you along on my adventures.

Love, Cait

———

The nation's capitol, 1990
Dear Gareth,

Thanks for the great photos. Impressive! I'm so proud of you! You look a lot like a blond John Kennedy, so tall and handsome, so impressive in your Cambridge gown. I'm so glad Mom got there for your graduation. She couldn't talk about anything else last time I called her.

I know you have never even met your Uncle Bo, but he is wonderful. I'm staying with him and his partner, Gerald, for a little while in Washington D.C. so I can earn enough money to visit you and Jeremy. The big news here is that I'm a GS-4. That's a label the government gives employees to announce to the world: "No college degree!" It's rather like a scarlet letter. Did you ever read Hawthorne? His prose is pretty gummy by modern American standards — no minimalist here. But it's rich and demanding. It kind of requires the rational mind to focus so the spirit is free to wander. You might like him. What are you reading now that you are so gorgeously decorated in a college gown? What did you think about Mandela finally getting out of jail? Can you imagine being in jail for a quarter of a century? Every time I get to feeling a little lonely or confined by circumstances, I just conjure up images of Nelson Mandela.

Gareth, I'll bring some good books along with me when I leave the States. It'll probably be about a year before I'm ready. Uncle Bo says I can go to college whenever it is important to me, but now he's helping me get organized for my trip. He calls it a journey. I don't know if I'm going "home" to England or not. I just want to see you and Jeremy.

Love you,
Cait

CHAPTER 14

"Where Have All the Flowers Gone?"
Pete Seeger

Mattie's Bath

How irritating you can be, Sarah. I was just telling a little story about how things were rationed during the war – sugar and shoes, tires and gasoline – and you chimed in with "which war?" How clever you are to know the wars didn't stop, they went on and on and on – the Cold War, the Korean War, the Vietnam War, that tidy little "war" in Grenada, and now this wretched Gulf War. But, Sarah, sometimes it's nice to let memories just flow, let them be; they don't always have to be correct. Sometimes the stories are better than history. You don't always have to be perfect though your father says you are. You don't have to carry around a big basket, collecting information to drop into it. You could collect flowers, too; let them wilt as they were meant to do . . . and some seashells . . . . I can't believe I'll be attending your graduation at Stanford. You knew how I felt about Stanford. . . . I wish you'd come home more often . . . don't understand why you're so defiant and independent. You could ride up sometimes with David and Ginger. . . . David, how good of you to find a wife who likes me, doesn't want to fling me out of the teepee. . . . I think she forgives me for loving you first. I worried that Ginger and I would get into some gnarly, primitive dance that would never get untangled. Thank goodness she

265

doesn't see me as an intruder in her tribe, doesn't want to push me out into the snow. And I welcome her. I confess I want her to dote on you, meet your every desire. . . . Don't know how much your mom's wishes fit into your plans, but you should know I'm ready for a grandchild. Do you think you two could get out of the fast lane long enough to get me a grandchild? I don't think Sarah will come through. . . . That's probably best. . . . She and I pecked at each other for so many years. Maybe "mothering" is a disgusting word in her vocabulary. . . . Her career seems all she cares about. . . . But I am counting on you — my first-born beautiful child — to come up with some offspring, you and Ginger. Raymond is building a studio for me, but I know in his heart it is a playroom for grandchildren.

———

Mattie wiped the thick cerulean blue from her brush and replaced the cap on the twisted paint tube as she headed for the kitchen to make coffee. Blue finger prints would be added to the growing paint patterns on the door leading from Raymond's just-in-case room where Mattie spent her early-morning hours. Raymond had adapted graciously to her intrusion into his private corner of the house where soft light now filtered through a young redwood into the couple's quiet, empty nest.

"It's not a syndrome we're going to catch," Raymond had announced when Sarah left for college. "The empty nest isn't a disease. It's a pretty peaceful place."

The couple had, indeed, celebrated their new freedoms when first David and then Sarah departed their mountain home and returned to the Bay Area for college, David dutifully and enthusiastically to Berkeley and Sarah to Stanford, defiant and proud. As time and events pushed

266

the couple into the early '90s, toward the millennium, it was Mattie's painting and her vegetable garden, Raymond's books, his computer, and his rose garden that helped fill the empty spaces created by the their children's departure. "Fruitful" was Mattie's favorite word to describe her life in the mid Sierra, and yet she continued to be a worrier. She didn't understand why work — commuting to work, being at work, bringing work home, talking work, living work, breathing work — had become such a consuming monster in the lives of David and Sarah's generation. She was especially sorrowful about David, who had put his magical artistic skills on hold in order to take a fast-track job that promised, Mattie believed, little but servitude to clocks and calendars.

"Not even time for a proper wedding," she frequently complained to Raymond.

"Now, Mattie," he would respond. "We didn't exactly do things properly ourselves, and it looks like Sarah is going to make up for any of David's oversights. She wants a wedding in my rose garden. I wish she weren't marrying that arrogant jerk."

"Raymond, anyone Sarah marries is going to seem to you an arrogant jerk. You might as well adjust. Besides, Ginger and David say Luis is not so bad. He did seem pretty arrogant, maybe just felt out of place. Arrogance covers a lot of uncertainties. Maybe we'll grow to like him. If we get to see them now and again. Anyway, it will be fun to have a family gathering here. Finally, a proper wedding in this family."

David and Ginger had simply stolen away for a weekend to get married. Ginger, direct and a bit whimsical about her previous, brief, and childless marriage, explained that she had tried out the white satin thing, and it didn't take. When Mattie learned that Yosemite had been the destination for their hurried

267

honeymoon weekend, she softened her grumbling with eager tales of her visits there with Raymond.

As she thought a proper mother-in-law ought to do, Mattie frequently instructed Ginger that she and David must make room in their lives for sunshine and play; they must come up more often, relax, let David have some time to paint again. Ginger took in the information as it was intended, heartfelt and caring, and she assured Mattie that their hectic pace would be short-lived. Ginger's crystal ball was a puzzle to Mattie, who couldn't imagine how the young couple could find a way out of their frantic lifestyle, but she continued to speak encouraging mother-words, assuming her offspring expected some wisdom from her.

Raymond took to Ginger instantly, her presence in the kitchen and in his rose garden soothing some of the loneliness that had crept into his life, like noxious weeds into the garden, when Sarah left for college. Raymond could argue with Ginger, discuss his ideas openly, without fear of worrying Mattie. Mattie did find some of Raymond's ideas troubling, but she was nevertheless pleased that the two conspirators so often found delight in one another's company.

"Help me check out the fences, Ginger," Raymond would suggest, and the two would set out for an evening stroll that seldom approached the fences Raymond had constructed to protect his garden plots from the numerous deer who shared the mid Sierra landscape with the Robbins family. Ginger's rowdy, playful laugh would drift back through the evening air to the redwood deck where Mattie sat contentedly with her first-born, forestalling his Sunday-evening departure and return to Berkeley. The stillness that permeated their home after "the kids" returned to the Bay Area was like a hot wind on the desert, something to be tolerated, never welcomed, although the final steps of the farewell-for-now dance always provided Mattie with some smiles of contentment.

When Raymond and Ginger returned from their stroll, Ginger would pull a deck chair close to Mattie to take in the rosy glow of summer sunsets and to enjoy the father-son conversation that inevitably closed the weekend visits. The young couple's luggage and unnecessary coats were stacked beside the door, car keys jangled in David's hand, and the two men would move to the far edge of the deck, adjusting their Levis and their postures for this particular and hurried version of story time.

"David is the only person I know in our generation who truly likes to hear stories of the olden days," Ginger laughed.

I never know if Raymond is reciting a comedy or a tragedy," Mattie responded. "But, yes, David is hungry to understand his history."

"Why do you call it murder, Dad? Why not assassination?" David asked. The question was loud enough for the women to hear, but never strong enough to invite them into the conversation.

"Looks like a tragedy tonight," Mattie whispered to Ginger, "but, no matter. It's the telling that is important."

"Don't you think 'assassination' has a kind of clinical, remote ring to it, Son? A word you would find in a history book? Something that happened long ago, maybe in a play or a movie, maybe somewhere in a distant land? But to us it was murder, not only murder of our leaders who threatened to unmask greed and ignorance, but murder of our spirit   spirits that had soared in the early '60s. We thought we could accomplish anything we could imagine, some things we hadn't even imagined yet .We had leaders who challenged us with dreams — dreams of racial equality, dreams that drove the human body and the human heart toward the stars."

David stooped to pick up a fallen fir twig and wove it through his fingers as his father paused to allow the glow of remembered moments, good moments, into his voice.

"David, we couldn't wait to get to work in those days. Whether we were in the space program or the Peace Corps, we were convinced that our tasks were important. And maybe they were. We certainly tried to respond to the challenges we recognized. We created Medicare to preserve the dignity of the aged, we acknowledged how poorly minorities and women were treated, and we pushed for new laws and new attitudes about civil rights. And we resisted an unjust war. Your mother will tell you that any war is an unjust war, but I think the important thing is we were learning what Pogo had been telling us: 'The enemy is us.'"

"Maybe, Dad. But what happened? Where did those attitudes go?"

Raymond smiled as he remembered how Mattie had tuned out so much of the world in the early '80s, insisting that the Robbins' family breakfast table would not be a dim and gloomy place.

"Well, David, I confess there were a lot of years when we just disguised our thoughts and our feelings, kind of waiting for the cold-eyed history books to clear things up for the next generation. I'm sorry about that. There was a great blanket of malaise and hopelessness that gripped the nation. We sometimes tried to poke holes in the blanket, but it seemed firmly held in place – by power and greed. We didn't want those tentacles to grip you, too, to grip your hearts, yours and Sarah's, so we kind of hid under the blanket. And then when we peeked out again, there wasn't a lot we could understand. I'll never understand how we can pay sports figures tens of

270

millions, while ordinary people play lotto and search for dreams. . . . I just wanted to take you salmon fishing, David."

"We did a lot of fishing, Dad. We will again."

"I'm not so sure, David. . . . Do you know what's happening on the rivers? Do you know. . . ."

A few of Raymond's words drifted back to the deck as he and David started down the path toward the young couple's car. Mattie and Ginger gathered up the luggage and hurried to catch up with the men who were hurrying to finish their departure rites and to set the stage for the next visit.

"Your mom and I are feeling pretty spunky about Anita Hill challenging the good old boys club, David. They really can't dismiss her the way they'd like to. She's not on trial. He is. Well, maybe we all are."

Mattie heard a few more words – "profoundly unresolved,." "moral implications," "media culture" – as she hugged her daughter-in-law and wished her family safe travel back to Berkeley. She held David tightly, whispering that he must return soon.

Raymond closed the cedar gate behind his departing family and hurried to the deck to greet the evening hours with Mattie. "We need a new word in the dictionary. There is no word in English to describe our adult children. They are destined to forever be 'the kids.'"

"I prefer them as kids," Mattie confessed. "I don't know what their lives will be like in 2000 or 2010 or whatever. So many things are changing. I worry about how they will manage."

"Mattie, let's worry about each other for a while. I need you to worry about this itch in my crotch. And I want to show you some of the new Hubbell images I got yesterday. The pictures are on the nightstand. Come to bed."

"Raymond, if discussing an itch in your crotch or the Hubbell telescope is some new form of foreplay, please let me know 'cause I don't want to miss anything." What Mattie actually missed was her youthful body that had hungered for Raymond's touch. She resented aching joints and body fatigue, low-back pains and muscles that cramped, hot flashes in her face while her fingers felt frozen. She wondered if menopause was a cruel test of character, something she must endure, eventually returning, if she passed the test, to the body she and Raymond had enjoyed for so many years. She nevertheless cherished her place next to Raymond, especially the early-morning hours, waking up beside a warm body that had reflexively wrapped itself around her, slowly getting untangled, wondering which arm draped over her neck was Raymond's, which was hers. Schedules, garden chores, medical appointments, telephone calls, TV news, and unwashed laundry were sluggish arrivals in her day, and she welcomed the brief, morning moment of just being alive — a lizard on a rock with only a few directives: get food, lie in the sun, hide from snakes.

Mattie's painting urge often visited her in the early morning hours. Awake by 4:30 a.m., enjoying a first cup of coffee by 5:00 o'clock, she would survey her invisible list of chores and then frequently slip into Raymond's just-in-case room where she would paint for several hours, encouraging the ghost of Georgia O'Keefe to guide her paint brush as she awaited her drowsy partner's arrival.

"It can't get any better, can it Mattie," Raymond offered, as he presented her with his empty coffee cup. "I like your lizard formula, especially the bit about 'get food.' Are you making breakfast, or shall I?"

"I'll answer the phone. You make breakfast. There's a proper division of labor."

Josie, too, was an early-morning person, and the sisters frequently used the gentle light of the early hours to illuminate matters that were important to them.

"He's not really going to blow up Folsom Dam, is he, Mattie?"

"I don't think so, Josie, but I seriously hope you will think of a better birthday gift for Raymond next year. He couldn't put it down, and I know in his heart of hearts he wants to join the Monkey Wrench Gang. That book's been around for years. Why is he so interested now? I know Raymond wants to wander off with Edward Abbey, 'correcting' mankind's mistakes. . . . It makes him miserable to see that the salmon can't get past the dam. . . . Oh, oh, now he's watching coverage of this wretched war in Iraq. I guess I know who's making breakfast . . . . I know in his mind he's redirecting those 'smart bombs' to the dam — all the dams on all the rivers . . . Never thought I'd be living with a radical . . . an anarchist. . . . Maybe he'll settle down a bit once he gets used to the idea of Sarah getting married. . . . Oh, Lord, I'm getting paint all over this phone, too, the new one, you know, the one I can carry out to the garden and it still works, more or less, no cords or anything. . . . I'll bet Georgia O'Keefe didn't even have a phone. . . . How are you Josie? How is Vernon?"

"It ain't no way to treat a lady," Josie responded and then hurried on to explain that "Vernon is pretty much an asshole. Never thought I'd be living with an asshole. Maybe it's male menopause, Mattie — hot flashes in the brain, that's what it is. He's so determined to be top-dog in everything, squabbling with his colleagues about nonsense and bitching at me about keeping the checkbook in order. It is in order. I just happen to be left-handed. Vernon can't read left-handed writing because he's having hot flashes in his brain."

"Maybe you're being punished for going to England again."

"Maybe. Or maybe I'm being punished for coming back. In any case, there's plenty of punishment around here. . . . You know, I was only gone a week. . . . It was a better visit than last time. I think Gareth and I will find a comfortable place with each other given time. Did I tell you how handsome he is?"

"You did, Josie, yesterday and the day before, but you can tell me again if you want to."

"Are you being condescending, Mattie?"
No, actually, trying to be agreeable, but I think agreeable gets difficult when my back hurts so much. . . . Josie, maybe we need an afternoon at the Claremont. I never thought you and I would be spending our middle years complaining about bad backs and husbands. It's kind of ordinary, isn't it? . . . What do you hear from Caitlin?"

"Guess who she ran into in Washington. James Darcy! You know he's working for Ron Dellums now? Bo knew how to reach him, so James and Caitlin have been playing in the capitol the last couple of weeks."

"You already told me about James, but I love hearing stories about him. . . . Did I ever tell you I had a huge crush on Ron Dellums — so tall and fine and silky. . .
"

"Wait a minute, Mattie. Let me finish telling you about Caitlin. She's on her way to England, you know. Gareth's very excited. But Caitlin sounded kind of down last time I talked with her. Maybe I'll give her a call tonight, give Vernon the phone bill to bitch about. . . . Oh, oh, gotta run, Mattie. Vernon is waking up, and I have to report to the kitchen — not my favorite place — and this probably isn't my favorite day. . . . The Claremont sounds great. . . . Talk soon. Bye, Mattie."

Josie's Bath

Caitlin, oh Caitlin, my dear first born, how I hate you at this moment! For you to destroy my grandchild is more than I can bear! You said you feel "fine" about it. "Fine?" What does that mean? I expect you want me to feel "fine," too. That would make it all better, wouldn't it? We'll just pretend for a while, and after a while, it will all be just fine. Do you believe the reasons you tried so brightly to give me, do you have more when these begin to crumble? "Mother, it's hard for a mixed child to get along in this world. I didn't really love him, just infatuated for a time, didn't want him to be the father of my child, he didn't even know I was pregnant." . . . Caitlin, he was the father of your child, don't you see that? Your loving or not loving, your wanting or not wanting, your telling or not telling has nothing to do with it. . . . This was my child, too, a part of me, and my wants were not heard. . . . Caitlin, you remind me too much of your grandmother. I hear you echoing each other with your "fineness." . . ."Your father wasn't mature enough to be a father," she told me. "There was nothing else I could do." . . . And, you know, Caitlin, it was a fine excuse, she used it twice . . . I want to wash you all off of me, out of my hair, out of my heart, out of my soul. You have broken me into these floating fragments of myself by sharing your "fineness" with me. Where are my grandchildren? Where is the mourning?

———

Dear complicated but committed, brave and messy mommy of mine,

I know you. I know your silences as well as your words. You always work so hard to be there for me, and this time your prime directive was really put to the test, wasn't it? The worst of the silences was the void that occurred right after I phoned and told you I felt fine about the abortion. Oh God, forgive me my trespasses. . . . F-I-N-E: Fucked up-Insecure-Neurotic-Emotional. But you didn't get it, did you Mom? Or actually, you did, but you assumed that I don't get it. You think that I can deny my actions now, but will suffer later, and that I have fooled myself about it, huh? Not so. I am your complicated and messy daughter. I know full well that I will always feel sad and guilty about the abortion. My eyes don't rest the sleep of babes anymore, Mom, I have these very bad dreams now, but I still think it was the best choice I could make at the time. . . . Did you feel it with me, and with Gareth? It was a kind of a ping deep inside, and a primitive wanting that lubricated the way. I need to explain to you somehow, that even though I had to stop it, it was still my pregnancy, and it was special. I said goodbye, and promised the spirit of it that I would try again before I die. James and I will always be friends. We will not be lovers anymore; not parents.

Your daughter,
Caitlin

CHAPTER 15

But the days grow short when you reach September . . .
            Karl Weill/Maxwell Anderson
            "September Song"

The heat that was beginning to build up in the Sacramento Valley had not yet reached the mid Sierra, and by most accounts Sarah's wedding was a grand event. Soft rain and pleasing temperatures early in the week awakened some of the roses in Raymond's garden, and Mattie's young tomato patch awaited the strong rays of summer sun. Josie had insisted that, as the only family member who was an authority on marriage, she would come up a few days early to give a hand with arrangements; Vernon could bring along some term papers he must read before the end of June – June 23, 6:00 p.m., 1992, he said the deadline was. His attention to chronology and calendars and his peculiar obsession with order made Vernon a difficult guest in the casual mountain home, but Mattie was delighted by Josie's presence, and the sisters prepared for Sarah's wedding with the enthusiasm they had shared playing house together as children.

Vernon frequently cornered Raymond to enlighten his host on the place computers would soon have in the lives of "everyday people." When Josie overheard Vernon say he was very sorry Johnny Carson was signing off *The Tonight Show*, she figured the men were on safe ground, although she wondered if Raymond knew who Johnny Carson was. Mattie was nervous when she overheard the men's conversation turn to politics, Jesse Jackson and the Rainbow Coalition, but Luis and Sarah's arrival delivered a welcome interruption. Raymond became quiet and pensive for the rest of the evening while Vernon and Luis engaged in some Stanford

277

vs. Berkeley exchanges and Sarah quizzed her mother on wedding details. When David and Ginger finally arrived close to midnight, Mattie pleaded fatigue and headed for her bedroom.

Mattie's Bath

Good Lord, Sarah, this wedding isn't just about you. It's about you and your family, all of us. It's about you and your whole life, your friends, your groom — the full catastrophe . . . . It doesn't matter that the white roses didn't bloom. They will bloom in their own good time. I have ordered white roses from the florist. No, it's not the same; it's all I can do. . . . Of course your Uncle Peter will be here. I know he's your favorite, the two of you scratching around in the dust of the planet, but Uncle Bo will be here, too. . . Your Auntie Josie has been here all week, working so hard to make things pleasing for you. . . . Please try to see them as other than momentary visitors in your life. They are part of you. You can't just pick and choose the ancestors you find suitable. You can't choose your mother either, Sarah, try as you may. You're stuck with me, just as I was stuck with my invisible mother. And maybe you will find a way to forgive me my trespasses as I try so hard to forgive she who trespassed against me. You could at least try, Sarah. It's really not so hard, but nobody heals who doesn't want to. . . . I can't imagine what walking into the twenty-first century might be like for you, but I do know you will carry us all along with you. You can carry dusty baggage, Sarah, or you can waltz in with handsome luggage, but you can't leave us, any of us, behind. Now, just get used to the idea. . . . I'll iron your petticoat in the morning. . . . You look so beautiful in your wedding gown!

278

What are you doing, Aunt Josie?" Sarah shrieked as she rushed into the kitchen pulling her lavender peignoir tightly around her. "The house smells terrible!"

"I'm cooking breakfast, Sarah, what does it look like?"

"It looks and smells like a disaster. I thought we agreed to keep it simple, have sweet rolls, juice, and coffee. There's flour everywhere, and what is that smell?"

"The flour is because I made tortillas. The smell is chili powder, cumin, and a bunch of other stuff I found in Mattie's spice rack. I decided to make breakfast burritos in honor of Luis. I thought it'd be nice to have something from his home land."

"Well, he comes from Rio, not Tijuana! He doesn't eat that stuff! Are these tortillas? They look like scones. How will we ever get this smell out of here before the wedding?"

"Sarah, the wedding is outside, anyway, and you don't have to eat this if you don't want to. Why don't you go have a long, hot bath, or something."

Peter and Melanie were the first to arrive and push open the cedar gate that gave entrance to the Robbins' home. They were greeted first by David who had offered to cope with car-parking details, and then Josie who had a quick word with her brother about how it was not okay to introduce Melanie simply as a "girlfriend." Was she not his colleague, his friend, his lover, his partner in most of his undertakings? Josie didn't know why they hadn't married; it wasn't important to her, but "girlfriend" wouldn't do.

"She's not just an attachment to you, Peter. There's a whole woman someplace in that attractive body, and you must let her out. Besides, it's silly for a fifty-seven-year-old man to have a girlfriend, unless of course you discovered the fountain of youth in all your trekking."

279

Josie quickly forgave Peter his minor *faux pas* and enjoyed seeing him display his adventurer persona. He had been all over the world, poking and digging in the dust, and if he chose to see himself as Harrison Ford in *Raiders of the Lost Ark*, that was fine with Josie. Not just fine, it was fun having so much glamor wrapped up in one brother. She thought he had taken on the Indiana Jones walk with considerable style. The hat was a bit much, and Josie was certain it would find a home in the back of the closet now that Peter had returned to the Berkeley campus – a distinguished visiting scholar. *Visiting from where*, Josie wondered. *Where is home for Peter?*

Mattie was less pleased with Peter. Time and again she tried to discover how he was – really – but her questions resulted in answers about his work and his travels. Josie reminded her of the "No Visitors" sign that had decorated the door to Peter's childhood room, and Mattie smiled a rather crooked smile, acknowledging her envy that Josie had been invited into Peter's room while she had been banished.

Fierce glances from both Josie and Mattie let everyone know that Bo and Gerald's arrival would not be greeted with anything but grace. Josie thought the two men looked healthy and comfortable, and she and Mattie took every opportunity for conversations with Bo, conversations that were often fragmented by chores and more arrivals, but rich in their appreciation of one another. Mattie was saddened when it struck her that there would be no offspring from Bo, nor from Peter. She wondered what had gone wrong for them, but Josie countered that being childless is not such a dreadful state. Her sorrow over Caitlin's estrangement lingered in the lines around her eyes, and Mattie decided to change the subject. This was not a time for sorrow, they agreed, except for whatever sorrow was festering in Raymond's spirit about the wedding of his daughter.

280

Josie fussed over Raymond a good deal, trying to edge him into a festive mood; she adored the playful Raymond, having long ago forgiven him for being such a slug about taking Mattie into his life. Or was it the other way around? It didn't matter; Josie cherished their place in her life, and she especially enjoyed seeing that Mattie had become more direct in her ways. Mattie gritched if she felt gritchy, snapped at the wine merchant who delivered so late in the morning, and generally let her moods flow as they would. The smart, silver streak that was showing in her hair was more appealing to Josie than it was to Mattie, but Mattie accepted her sister's compliments with genuine pleasure, while most of her spontaneous smiles that morning fell on David who stood so tall next to his father and stood toe-to-toe with his uncles. Peter and David, especially, enjoyed verbal exchanges that were both combative and gentle, each bowing with respect to the other before charging into new territory.

Ginger's pregnancy slowed her down a bit, but her presence in the kitchen was welcome, and her boisterous conversations with Sarah were a blessing, the two young women sharing an intimacy and an understanding of the family that was unique to them. Josie welcomed their naïvete and their wisdom, figuring Sarah would sooner or later forgive her for breakfast and whatever other imagined transgressions might be keeping them at arm's length.

"Sarah, I had an Aunt Tilly in my life, one of Father's sisters. She tormented me, always checking to see if my fingernails were clean. And she embarrassed me because she drank too much and got kind of crazy. She died twenty years ago, but she still haunts me. . . . I'd rather not be your Aunt Tilly, your demon. I'm Josie, and I love you. . . . Let's go open a few presents."

Sarah offered her aunt a tentative hug and led the way toward a stack of gifts in the living room. "Let's just do a few. I want plenty of time to dress."

"I guess there must be a Nut Tree in Kansas City," Josie mumbled as Sarah lifted a large walnut salad bowl from the gift box Nora and Bertram had sent.
"This is pretty, but not too useful on a dig . . . won't fit very well in my backpack. I wonder if Grandma thinks I'm going to be cooking and playing house."

"Be glad she didn't decide to die just before the wedding," Josie offered as Peter and Melanie joined the group.

"Mom's feeling much better," Peter announced. "I talked with her last night. . . . Said she was very sorry to miss the wedding."

"Well, she should be here. This may be the last time we're all together," Josie responded.

"I, for one, am glad she's not here," Sarah announced. "She would somehow manage to be the center of attention, and this is *my* wedding, after all."

It was, indeed, Sarah's wedding, and most irritations were set aside as Raymond led his daughter through the rose garden to become Mrs. Luis Antonio Quieros. When the couple turned from the minister, Sarah paused long enough to know all eyes were on her and plucked a white rose from her bridal bouquet. Before she took the groom's arm for the recessional, Sarah took the few steps that were necessary to present the rose to Mattie.

Mattie's Bath

I got in this tub, wonder if I can get out. Maybe it doesn't matter. "In" may be all that matters. . . . Every woman should have a daughter who gets married at home. Can't become a proper crone without this little dance. Every woman should get a

282

sabbatical after the at-home wedding. . . . How the hell does he think he can waltz into our lives and take away our only daughter to live in South America. It's Persephone in the underworld, alright, and I am Demeter in a rage. . . . He's a taker, for sure. He takes our daughter; he takes her to bed, takes her to task, takes her youth, takes her energy, takes her thoughts and makes them his, takes her off to foreign places to show off his catch, takes her to nasty places to dig in the mud in the name of science. . . . Careful, Mattie, maybe they still burn witches. . . . The gold chain on his fuzzy brown chest made me gag. What is he, a drug-dealer for academia? Well, I smiled and was gracious. Daughter, dear daughter, you knew you could count on that. I hope you don't know what it cost me. Actually, I hope you do know, and I hope you suffer over it. . . . No, Sarah, I don't want you to suffer. I just want to know who you are . . . where you are headed . . . and why. Not so much for a mother to ask. . . . He walked among my flowers, posing and strutting down by the pond, seeing nothing but his own reflection. . . . Okay, take my daughter, but stay out of my garden. . . . Poor dear Raymond, standing there in his tuxedo, giving away his only daughter to the Taker, trying to see her beauty, but, alas, seeing only images of the Taker taking his daughter. Wish I could make it all better for him. Can't. I'll try . . . . How nice Josie came up early; we had a few good secret moments together while Vernon reorganized my kitchen shelves. . . . Josie, this one is not Roy Rogers. Maybe you should have looked a little longer, kissed a few more frogs.

Josie's Bath

I can't do this anymore. I don't actually loathe Vernon, but I wish I could feel something that strong

283

instead of this nothingness. Ten years of his carping has numbed me beyond belief. It's as though I'm wearing ear plugs in all my pores — nothing gets in, nothing gets out. . . . I understand his first wife. She found her release with the bottle and pills. How many women allow themselves to get pushed to that point? And is it truly "allowing?" Do we actually believe we have a choice? Did Marilyn have a choice? I wonder if the fact that they were mostly prominent men made any difference to her right at the end. I wonder if she said to herself, "It's okay I'm killing myself; it's for the good of the country." Maybe she didn't actually kill herself .Maybe somebody prominent gave her a hand, cleaned up her messes for her. . . . Maybe I should have taken after Great Uncle Harry and "decided" to become a lesbian. Maybe after I shave my legs, I should slash my wrists. God, wouldn't that be great! Vernon would have to clean up the mess; it would almost be worth it. . . .Don't think I feel anything about his latest affair . . . can't seem to locate a feeling. Thank the cosmos for the pore plugs! . . . Why do these young, fresh things in his class fall for his bullshit? He does play the part well, with his pipe and leather-elbowed corduroy jacket. I think he became an Eng Lit prof just so he would know what to wear. I guess I can't fault his students. I fell for his bullshit, too, didn't I? Actually, I fell for my own bullshit. That's the real core of the matter. . . . Guess I wanted some order in my life. Well that's what I got — orders. But nothing is ever right for Vernon. This was a terrible trip when it could have been so much fun with the right person. There wasn't anything Vernon didn't go on about. Mattie offered to send yummy sandwiches with us, but Vernon said that's lower class, said we'd stop at the Nut Tree. Oh, boy! . . . He's such an ass. . . . I didn't make it

284

rain, either, so why punish me for the weather on the way home. Nice to have a gentle rain just before summer arrives. . . . And he fussed so much about his belongings . . . couldn't find his toothbrush, angry because somebody moved it. Doesn't know how families function? I know where I'd like to put his stupid toothbrush if he ever finds it. . . . I'm going to turn into a prune if I stay in here much longer, but it's so peaceful to be alone and quiet, a chance to think about the wedding. It might have been a lovely wedding if I hadn't sponged up everybody's feelings. Mattie was a brick, though. Nobody could tell she was crying, standing there so straight in her beautiful garden. . . .The tomatoes! Enough to feed a whole county. Wonder if Mattie still fills her freezer every summer, still cans peaches and pears 'til she drops, still thinks she has to have a lot of food on hand, "just in case." Only she and Raymond living there in that beautiful place, but she's ready for the next wedding, next funeral, whatever she thinks is required of her. . . . Beautiful pines, and the baby redwoods are proper trees now. Raymond's so proud of his work, his efforts, his family. . . . I actually thought he was going to lose it and kill the groom; probably should have. Well, Luis is probably okay, just hard for Raymond to let go of his daughter. . . . God, I miss my kids. Will I ever see Caitlin again? And beautiful Gareth? . . . Okay, Josie, enough wallowing in the bath and in the mind! The "when" is now. The question is "where." I know Mattie would let me stay with her for a while. She always does. I end up on her doorstep every so often right after I take off my ring and throw it in the proverbial fountain. Actually, they're in my underwear drawer. Mustn't forget them. . . . I need to go away somewhere and look for myself. Maybe

I'm in the mountains somewhere just waiting for me to find me. I must be wondering when I'll come.

———

Leaving Vernon was the easiest parting Josie could remember. Vernon made it easier and easier over the few days it took Josie to sort out her personal items. As each drawer was emptied, Vernon washed it, relined it with cedar-scented paper.

"At least there will be some order around here finally. Do you realize how much of a slob you are? What are you going to do with all this junk you've been carting around for so long? You can't take it all; you don't even know where you're going."

"Whatever you don't want, I'll give to Goodwill," Josie answered. "Nobody really knows where they're going, and I'm not a slob. You, Vernon, are just so damned anal. You see me as just another thing to arrange in its place. A place for everything and everything in its place. Do you know how boring that is, Vernon?"

"Well, Cynthia doesn't think I'm boring," Vernon shot at Josie with a smirky grin on his face. "By the way, she's moving in with me the minute you're gone."

"That's fine, Vernon, just fine," Josie replied as she taped up what she hoped was the last box. "I'm sure you both will be very happy. What is her place going to be? Are you going to ask her to put on a little nurses uniform and spoon feed you in your old age? You're fifty years old for Christ's sake, and she's only twenty-two. What is this, male menopause?"

"Well, at least she's young enough to not have all the bad habits you have, Josie. And what are you going to do, find husband number. . . . let's see, what number would that be? I can't seem to remember."

"Maybe the last husband, Vernon. After being married to you, at least I know what not to look for. Do you realize what a great gift you've given me?"

———

Josie's Bath

What a beautiful coast! What a nice place to stay, this Little River Inn. What a great view. . . . Yes, whale, I saw you out there. I saw you flip your big tail at me. Was that a greeting, a message of some kind? I know it wasn't a warning; I know I'm doing the right thing . . . whatever that is. . . Well, husband number three is down the drain with this bath water, and I am free . . . Mattie thought it so strange I asked her to keep my wedding rings, put them in a box somewhere, but that seems right to me. Just box them up and put them in the closet! . . . No, Abe, I don't count you in my list of failures. You are with me everyday. I miss you. I often feel it would be nice to join you, wherever you are. Where are you? Where do we go after we shed these silly bodies? I wish I could be sure I could find you some day when all this busy life stuff is over. . . . Ah, well, for now I'll just hope you are watching over me a bit. You did that so well. Maybe I'll learn to watch over myself. . . . Well, watch out, self! Here I come.

CHAPTER 16

. . . And you say to yourself just what am I doin'
/ On this road I'm walkin', on this trail I'm
turnin' /
On this curve I'm hanging / On this pathway I'm
strolling, in the space I'm taking /
In this air I'm inhaling . . . .
> Bob Dylan
> "Last Thoughts on Woodie Guthrie"

Although Portland's early-morning moisture was
not inviting to Josie's California blood, she took in the
friendly city with pleasure, agreeing with herself to enjoy
her precious cappuccino at an outdoor table where a
tweed-clad, hurried executive was leaving his *Oregonian.*
Josie offered the man a thank-you smile for the seat and
the newspaper, her interest sparked by the man-scent of
moist wool, tobacco, and Ralph Lauren after-shave.
"Careful, Josie, you don't need it," she mumbled to
herself, breathing in the cigar aroma that lingered in the
moist air around her chosen place. She giggled to see that
Princess Di had made it to the front page of the Pacific
West Coast. *Hang in there, Di . . . or, maybe not. Maybe*
you should just leave that country. Leaving isn't so bad .

"I'm leaving on a jet plane," Josie hummed as she skimmed over the political news with only a quick question about how a man called "Bubba" could hope to win the presidency in November. *Might be kind of fun to have some southern humor stirring up the White House. Better than this stiff-starched Mr. Bush, and Mattie will be easier to get along with if we get a Democrat back in charge of things. Of course, Mattie isn't going to be happy unless Jesse Jackson becomes president. . . . Would be nice. If we have to listen to politicians, they sure as hell ought to be eloquent. . . . Wonder if I'm supposed to care about all of that the way Mattie does, and Raymond, Caitlin, and Bo. . . . Wonder when I'll see them again, my family.*

An inside article about a workaholic named Bill Gates and something called Windows was momentarily interesting because of a Justice Department probe — *the government ought to probe itself* — and Josie finished her wake-up read with a thoughtful medical piece on "The Gulf War Syndrome — Real or Imagined." When she finally set aside the front section, her hands hesitated to reach for any more of what was called news. She turned over one of the rumpled sections — the classified ads — and found her eye curiously leading her mind through grey matter that promised jobs and a good life in the Pacific Northwest.

"Historic Hotel, hiring. Apply. . . .

Josie didn't know if it was the word "historic" that captured her attention — she did enjoy the sense of continuity that historic sites offered — or if it was "hotel" — fascinating places that spoke to her of adventure. Maybe just the word "hiring."

I do need to focus a bit. Better pay some attention to how I'm going to go on affording my wanderings. Vernon was being such a pill about the objects, the things, in our lives. Especially the bits and pieces of money.

Josie had a second cappuccino before setting off into some of the most beautiful country she had ever seen. She stopped at Multnomah Falls to stretch her legs and enjoy the mid-morning sunshine. . . . *Well, Abe, what do you think of that? Breathtaking, yes? . . . I guess I'll have to let you go sooner or later. . . . not yet . . .* then resumed her leisurely journey toward Hood River, slightly puzzled by the sensation that a powerful energy source was gently tugging her further and further into the Cascades.

What is it I'm sensing? This is silly. I probably won't get a job, and I probably won't like Hood River. I'm probably just wasting my time. Fifty years old, unemployed, on my own again, and wandering around looking for what? . . . Well, Abe always said that when your very own soul is speaking to you, it's a good idea to listen. Not sure how to do that. . . .

Josie passed the hotel, perched on a high bluff overlooking the Columbia River, and drove on into Hood River to get a feel for the little town. Mt. Hood stood as sentinel over the community, and Josie remembered Howard's fear of earthquakes, wondering what he would think of her living at the base of a volcano.

This feels good. It feels like a community. I think I could be happy here for a while.

By late morning, Josie found her way to the hotel, filled out an application, and told the receptionist that she would be having lunch in the elegant dining room that looked out upon the Columbia River and the Cascades. She enjoyed a tasty salad and a stack of historical information about the hotel, although the literature didn't acquaint her with the important information that the hotel was under new management, again, because of complicated and lengthy bankruptcy

291

procedures. Her last sip of white wine was interrupted by a Mr. Orlick, who sat himself down at Josie's table with no invitation and little ceremony.

"I've read your application, Josie, and I've been watching you. I can offer you the job of catering director, starting work on Friday."

Josie sputtered and wasn't sure if she had actually spit some of her wine at Mr. Orlick.

"Briefest interview I've ever had. You're the general manager?"

"Yep, new here myself. But catering is easy. It's all here in the folder. I can tell you're a great broad, Josie. You'll do just fine. God bless you."

Josie bristled at being called a "great broad" and stiffened at being blessed by God via a sleazy hotel manager, but she offered her hand to the peculiar individual who had entered her adventure with so little grace. *What the hell. What's the worst that can happen?*

"Thank you, Mr. Orlick. I'm sure we will work well together."

That afternoon, Josie found a small, furnished apartment in an old, rundown complex comprised of various-styled houses in various states of disrepair, all hanging on the side of a hill just above the center of town. The rent was cheap and the apartment was available. There was lots of light, and there were drafty floors, mice in the cupboards and Oregon juncos on the pyracantha bushes, fleas in the carpet and azaleas bursting with color. The phone company could install tomorrow.

Josie walked two blocks to the local hardware store, bought a cooking pot and frying pan, wooden spoons, an oven mitt, a turquoise dish drainer — it was the only color they carried — paper plates and a real fork and spoon. She stopped at a neighborhood Safeway on her way home, pleased that her lifelong struggle with food preparation had finally been resolved when she discovered

292

Peg Bracken's *I Hate to Cook Book* shortly after she and Vernon were married. The little paperback that she now referred to as her cooking bible was nestled among the few things she had brought with her, and dinner – alone – in her own apartment was a celebration. Friday's staff meeting in Mr. Orlick's office began with a prayer, moved on to introductions and assignments, and closed with an announcement that payroll checks would be delayed until after the weekend.

Josie's Bath

It's just a sales job, really, I can do this. I thought I would have to know a lot about cooking, but I don't. I won't even have to phone Mattie, and now I can eat whatever I want, whenever I want to. Nobody to criticize me, no man to try to please, except a smarmy Christian who's more lost than I am. I can just take care of myself, do whatever I want, put things wherever I want them in my own place. I've never had my own place, have I? I'm fifty and have never had my own place. The apartment's not much, but I can fix it better. I can paint it and buy little things and make it mine.

———

Josie's formula for being a catering director worked: Smile a lot, listen hard, and make things happen. She quickly learned that it was wise to be on good terms with the volatile chef, and she occasionally joined him at the end of a long work day for Cuervo Gold shooters and conversation. Her hotel responsibilities included supervision of Judy, the banquet manager, and her serving staff. Judy's parents had survived Auschwitz, and she carried with her a combination of sadness and strength to which Josie was drawn. She was honest and outspoken, a welcome addition to the after-hours gatherings. Josie and

Judy were soon spending time together on the riverbank or hunting through junk stores for treasures. Josie started collecting McCoy pottery because it was cheap and because she liked it — not the gaudy pieces, the black-mammy cookie jar or the shiny panther for the top of the TV, but the graceful vases and charming teapots. Judy searched for useful tools she could take home across the river, on the Washington side, where she and her husband were building a house.

Rob had inherited fifty acres bordering the national forest and had spent the summer hauling in building materials on a narrow, dirt road that led to their would-be good life. While the building was going on, the couple had lived in a teepee but had now moved into two finished rooms, bedroom and kitchen. They continued to use an outhouse but were working to complete a pleasing, tiled bathroom with windows on three sides and a skylight. Josie had never heard of building a house room-by-room, but it seemed to work for Judy and Rob. What Josie liked best about visiting in the forest with her new friends were the two llamas Rob had won in a poker game. He let them freely wander the property except for an area far into the forest where he and Judy were cultivating marijuana plants. Judy managed her two lives — frontier housewife and banquet manager at the Columbia Gorge Hotel — with grace and determination. She and Josie soon began arriving at the hotel early enough to share coffee and conversation before Mr. Orlick's prayer, guests, and telephone calls announced the beginning of a work day.

————

"Mattie, I met Danny Kaye. He was a guest last night, looked really ill, and the waitress had never heard of him. She just thought he was old and drunk. . . . And I'm doing a big event for Nike's inner circle. Those

294

people are so young and bright and energetic. All that energy to make shoes? . . . Please come, Mattie. I don't want to hear that the tomatoes or peppers or apples or pears need to be planted or tended or picked or canned. Just come up. You and Raymond."

"You sound so enthusiastic, Josie. That's wonderful! It's not the garden; it's that David and Ginger's baby is due right after Christmas."

"You're not the midwife, are you Mattie? Come just before Christmas. It's a busy time for me, but just a few days would be wonderful. I want to show you everything!"

"Oh, Josie, I worry about Raymond's night vision, and the passes are often icy or closed in winter."

"Mattie, there are airplanes that fly from Sacramento to Portland. I'll meet you in Portland. Ask Raymond about airplanes. He'll remember."

"Are you irritable, Josie?"

"No, excited! Just come."

Josie shuffled her work schedule so she could comfortably show off her hotel, her apartment, her town in the two days Mattie and Raymond would be with her. She made arrangements for the hotel limousine to pick them up at Portland airport, and she reserved the hotel bridal suite and the best window table in the dining room. Shortly before their arrival, Josie met with an elegant, thirty-something woman who had arrived early to make certain arrangements were correct for her employer's dinner meeting. It was Josie's last task of the day, and she was eager to be through with work, eager to relax with Mattie and Raymond.

"Please remember, the senator wants privacy," the woman said. "He's tired and needs to relax."

Josie led her client through the main dining room to a small, freshly remodeled private room that offered elegance and intimacy. There was no view of the river, but Josie and her client agreed the senator had already seen a lot of the Columbia.

"This is perfect," exclaimed the aide. "The senator will be so pleased."

For the next hour, Josie fussed over the staff who were decorating the immense Christmas tree in the lobby, and she kept her excited eyes directed to the hotel entrance, watching for her family. But it was Senator Packwood's limousine that arrived first. She greeted her guest at the doorway and wondered if he had really patted her fanny, or was it just the jostling of holiday crowds. Josie brushed away the question and ushered the senator and his entourage through the main dining room, the senator nodding from side to side as he strolled through the crowded room. When they reached the door to the private dining room, the senator stopped abruptly, stiffly. "This won't do at all." He turned and raced back through the main dining room to the hotel foyer, not bothering to nod at all. Josie shrugged at Judy who was just inside the room, ready to oversee the servers, and hurried away to ask the senator what was not to his satisfaction.

"I must be seen," the senator spit at Josie. "I can't be seen in that small room. I must be out where I can be seen!"

"Senator Packwood," Josie began, "your aide indicated you wanted privacy."

"I never said that!" he sputtered. "I must be seen! You must seat us in the main room."

Josie looked first at the senator's aide who was looking at the floor and then directly into the senator's eyes, stifled the sarcasm on the tip of her tongue, and finally replied, "Senator, I'm afraid the main dining room is completely booked tonight. The holidays are a busy time for us. I'm sure you will be comfortable in the room we have set up for you."

"I'll wait in the lounge while you make proper arrangements. I will speak to the general manager if need be. He'll straighten this out."

The senator dismissed Josie by turning his back and leading his group into the lounge.

"First of all," Josie mumbled, "How the hell does he know the general manager is a 'he'?"

Judy followed Josie into Mr. Orlick's office and soon agreed that the elegant, windowless, private room would be fine for her dinner with Raymond and Mattie.

———

"You look wonderful, Josie. I feel dowdy sitting here next to you."

"You don't look dowdy, Mattie. You look pretty much California casual. It's a look I love, miss it a lot. But things are wonderful for me here."

"But you do seem a little tense, Josie. Is something wrong tonight?"

"No, it's fine now. Just a bit of trouble with the senator who's a guest tonight."

"What senator?" Raymond asked.

"Packwood. You know, 'The Senator from Weyerhauser.'"

"He's here? Now? Tonight? Where?"

"He's in the main dining room, next to the window, at our table," Josie sighed.

It was not a pleasant evening for Josie, but in time she and Mattie would laugh about some of the conversation they overheard:

"You've got the damned nuclear power plant polluting the river upstream on the Washington side; a nuclear power plant polluting the river downstream on the Oregon side; mid way, you've got the Bonneville Dam cluttering up the river. You've got your buddies at Weyerhauser clear-cutting the forests and polluting the streams . And you've got dying salmon runs – entire species destroyed! So what's to be proud of?"

They could both see Raymond pointing his finger at the senator, instructing him, in an ample voice, about his responsibilities, the politician turning bright red – just in time for Christmas.

"Well, the senator wanted to be seen. Maybe he doesn't know Raymond is my guest; maybe I'll still have a job tomorrow. . . . Would you and Raymond prefer to stay at my place? I have a sofa bed. It's not great, but you could manage, I think."

"I'd like that, Josie. I want to see your place. Do you have a cat?"

"Why, Mattie, because old maids always have cats?"

"Josie, you are not old. I am old, and besides old is not a character flaw. Let's collect Raymond and go home."

Holding one giggling sister by each hand, Raymond continued his discourse on political responsibility as the threesome headed for Josie's car.

"Well, Voltaire's prayer was granted again," Raymond laughed.

"Raymond, I don't remember that Voltaire did a lot of praying," Mattie answered, easing herself into the back seat of the car.

"He didn't, Mattie. He said he had only one prayer, and God granted it. 'Oh, Lord, make my enemies ridiculous.'"

Josie stopped laughing long enough to dig her keys from the recesses of her purse. "Home, James," she said, handing the keys to Raymond and climbing into the back seat with Mattie. "Nothing so soothing as a family reunion. Mattie, remember the time. . . ."

———

During the next forty-eight hours, Mattie and Raymond learned that Caitlin had fallen in love with an Englishman and was getting married in the spring; the threesome drank a toast to Bill Clinton who would soon unzip his suitcase in the White House; and the sisters lost Raymond to a local bookstore where he selected his winter reading material.

"He sniffs each book, you know, Josie, loves the smell and feel of books, especially the used ones. It's as if they tell him something about those who have read them before. They're like ancestors, wise ancestors, of course, who have secrets to share."

Abbey in his pocket before we leave. . . . Let's check out that pottery shop across the street."

Mattie's shopping bag was nearly as heavy as Raymond's when the sisters collected Raymond and settled into Josie's car for the drive into Portland. Raymond agreed with the sisters that a flight to Portland now and again might very well be cheaper than telephone calls, but he doubted there was a trade in the offing.

"Listen to this, Mattie. Josie, listen," Raymond said before Josie had even released the emergency brake. "This guy is talking about how modern humans have lost their contact with the natural world . . . about how when we get in positions of power we forget our true responsibilities."

"Who says this, Raymond," Josie interjected. "Sounds like something Mattie would say, but then she'd worry that she sounded whiney."

"No, it's not whiney. It's just true. Let's see, his name is Loren Eiseley. I'm so glad there are used-book stores in the world. Lots of treasures there. Anyway, Josie, just listen to this: 'No wonder, then, that ecologists are regarded as "nostalgic dreamers" when they warn that cash in paper or metal, even in gold itself, or numbers in a bankbook or on a balance sheet are mere symbols and that the real necessities of life, such as pure air and unpoisoned water and uncontaminated soil and an intact protective ozone layer above the earth's surface, will very soon no longer be buyable for all the money in the world.'"

"Josie, I think the difference is that Loren Eiseley says it so eloquently. I *do* often sound whiney, but not today. I've had such a super time. And Raymond, you probably don't remember when I sent you some Eiseley material, way back in '69, I think. You were still at the Cape. Eiseley made a speech about the moon landing. He said we humans have a long way to go in understanding our own small corner of the universe, much less what he called the 'cosmic prison.'"

"I'm into trashy international intrigue these days, kind of a time-out for me, but I suppose Raymond will find some heavy philosophical stuff."

"He's doing natural history these days, loves Stephen Jay Gould, but what do you bet there's another Edward Abbey in his pocket before we leave. . . . Let's check out that pottery shop across the street."

Mattie's shopping bag was nearly as heavy as Raymond's when the sisters collected Raymond and settled into Josie's car for the drive into Portland. Raymond agreed with the sisters that a flight to Portland now and again might very well be cheaper than telephone calls, but he doubted there was a trade in the offing.

"Listen to this, Mattie. Josie, listen," Raymond said before Josie had even released the emergency brake. "This guy is talking about how modern humans have lost their contact with the natural world . . . about how when we get in positions of power we forget our true responsibilities."

300

"Who says this, Raymond," Josie interjected. "Sounds like something Mattie would say, but then she'd worry that she sounded whiney."

"No, it's not whiney. It's just true. Let's see, his name is Loren Eiseley. I'm so glad there are used-book stores in the world. Lots of treasures there. Anyway, Josie, just listen to this: 'No wonder, then, that ecologists are regarded as "nostalgic dreamers" when they warn that cash in paper or metal, even in gold itself, or numbers in a bankbook or on a balance sheet are mere symbols and that the real necessities of life, such as pure air and unpoisoned water and uncontaminated soil and an intact protective ozone layer above the earth's surface, will very soon no longer be buyable for all the money in the world.'"

"Josie, I think the difference is that Loren Eiseley says it so eloquently. I *do* often sound whiney, but not today. I've had such a super time. And Raymond, you probably don't remember when I sent you some Eiseley material, way back in '69, I think. You were still at the Cape. Eiseley made a speech about the moon landing. He said we humans have a long way to go in understanding our own small corner of the universe, much less what he called the 'cosmic prison.'"

"I don't remember Mattie, but that was before I had developed a memory; I just existed in the present tense. That's why I have so much to catch up with."

The threesome were just entering Cascade Locks, and Mattie remembered that the Bonneville Dam would soon appear on the landscape. Hoping to avoid another diatribe about man's follies, Mattie attempted to keep Raymond focused on his books. "Well, Eiseley is a good one to catch up with, Raymond. Please read us some more."

Josie had been looking forward to replaying the Senator Packwood scene but decided Mattie's diversion was a wise one. She hurried past the dam, slowed down at

Multnomah Falls, and then hurried to the Portland airport to deposit her family at the carol-filled terminal.

Raymond's thoughts were buried in a new book called *Ishmael* before the Boeing 737 was airborne and Mattie was being enveloped in the splendor of Mt. Hood, Mt. Adams, and the ragged-topped Mt. St .Helens that watched over her sister's adventures.

"She's fine, isn't she, Raymond?"

"Who?" Raymond mumbled.

"Josie, of course."

"Of course. Here, you need my handkerchief. I never quite understand your tears, Mattie. But I'll give you a kiss for each one, and things will balance out in the end."

———

The long work days of the new year went quickly for Josie, but they were tiring, and she was always pleased to arrive home at her hillside apartment. Sean, the maintenance man, would sometimes drop by and join her in front of the fire for a coffee or a beer. Josie didn't believe half of the tales Sean told, but he was an accomplished storyteller and a welcome relief from the formality of her hotel work, where lunchtime conversations focused on either politics or sex, sometimes indistinguishable. Josie frequently added tidbits from her day to the restful evening conversation, often wondering, though, if politics were a part of Sean's reality. The Pentagon was giving Bill Clinton a hard time over lifting its ban on homosexuals in the military, and Mrs. Bill Clinton couldn't get a toehold in the traditionally male-dominated medical arena where neither reform nor a powerful Democratic female was welcome. Sean did ponder seriously where anyone, President or not, could get a $200 haircut, and neither Sean nor Josie found much interest in "Whitewater-gate."

"Been there, done that," Josie said as she turned to her new friend for an amusing story.

Sean said he was pure Irish, a descendent of Brian Boru, he said. He either knew the legends or made them up, Josie couldn't tell. By late spring, he was telling her about the days he had spent in prison, and he showed her the tatoos he had etched on his arms and legs to pass the time. The prison stories were disturbing to Josie, and she would often tune out and just enjoy the melodic purr of Sean's voice. She would sometimes doze off, but Sean kept talking, more to himself than to Josie. He told her he had spent time with the Weathermen, but Josie knew that story wasn't true. Sean was only thirty-three and would have been a young boy in the '60s.

Sometimes Sean would bring his latest creations — delicate wood carvings and nature sketches — to show Josie. He explained that he loved working with his hands and proudly described a cabin he had built on his father's property shortly after his release from prison. He had lived in it for six months, then moved on to Chicago where he married and later divorced. He was still in love with his ex, he said, but she had remarried and gotten custody of the boy. He wasn't allowed to visit, he said.

"Why can't you visit, Sean?"

"Oh, it's a long story . . . not enough money for a good lawyer."

Sean was tall, over six feet, with long legs and a long, muscular torso. His blue eyes were piercing and prominent, especially when his long, blond hair was pulled back and fastened with a bandana. Working in the heat of summer days, he would often tie the bandana around his head as roofers do; at times he would leave his hair loose, beyond his shoulders, and toss his head as women do. He was fastidious with his hair, would wash it daily and comb it out sitting on the porch spinning his yarns to Josie. He seemed to need a good listener, and

Josie had time to listen, preferring his stories in small doses.

Josie occasionally invited Sean to come along when she was meeting Judy and Rob at a roadhouse across the river on the Washington side. The four of them would dance late into the night, stopping only long enough for Judy, Rob, and Sean to step outside and smoke a joint. Josie would catch her breath and sit down to enjoy a vast array of energetic, country-western gyrations by an equally vast array of body types. She was surprised one evening to observe a Japanese man dancing with one woman after another, never the same, and equally surprised when the man caught her eye and left the dance floor, seating himself across from her.

"Dance?"

"Oh, no thanks," Josie answered, smiling, "I'm kind of worn out. Just want to sit this one out."

"Would you consider to marry me?" Josie thought she heard.

"What did you say?" Josie asked.

He introduced himself as Kim and told Josie he wanted to stay in the United States and needed an American wife. She was a pretty woman; he would love her always and treat her A-OK.

Josie laughed comfortably and asked if he had proposed to all the women he had been dancing with. He looked at her seriously and replied that if he asked enough times, someone would eventually say yes. Thanking him for the compliment, Josie declined the offer, and the man soon excused himself.

"This must be the first time I've turned down a marriage proposal," Josie said when her friends returned to the table. "I must be getting smarter." She noticed a stiffening in Sean, but she ignored him, straining to hear Judy's explanation of why a Japanese businessman was dancing to loud country-western music in a lumberjack's roadhouse.

"He wants a lot more than a wife; he wants our timber." It seemed a bad omen to Judy that much of the timber from the Gifford Pinchot forest was being sold to Japanese interests. She resented the timber industry and went on to relate the abuses she thought Weyerhauser and other timber barons had committed.

Rob added to the conversation by telling a story of a strike a few years earlier when Weyerhaeuser cut workers' pay by $4 an hour and other forest-products companies followed suit. The strike was bitter but short-lived, and Weyerhaeuser profits doubled in just two years. Judy concluded the tale of woe with the information that Weyerhaeuser had released 14 million pounds of toxic chemicals — sulfuric acid, chloroform, formaldehyde, and chlorine — into the air and the water in 1989 and was in constant battle with the EPA, OSHA, and other government agencies.

"Well, for once I'm glad Raymond isn't here," Josie concluded. "We'd be up all night, tracking the ogres and dragons of the world."

"Who's Raymond?" Sean demanded.

"Oh, he's my favorite Don Quixote, Sean, but it's not important right now. I have to work tomorrow, and I need some sleep."

Josie was troubled when she found flowers on her porch the next evening as she arrived home from work.

"Did you leave the flowers?" Josie asked when she found Sean repairing a drain pipe in an adjacent building. It was nothing," Sean replied. "I thought they were pretty so I picked some for you. Thought you might enjoy them after working so hard."

"Where did you get them?" Josie knew landscaping was not a priority item on the owners' budget, and she was certain that these flowers, especially the vibrant pink roses, had not come from the complex.

"I just picked them out of people's yards," Sean replied. "They'll never miss 'em."

"That's not very nice," Josie told him, but she was laughing, too, at the image of tall, angular Sean tiptoeing through neighborhood gardens.

"I'm really tired tonight, Sean. Let's discuss your horticultural obsessions another night. I'm feeling a bit flu-ish. If you have time, would you be good enough to get me some Seven-Up and aspirin from the store?"

She gave him a twenty dollar bill, the smallest she had, and asked him to use his master key to leave the change and purchases on the kitchen counter. Josie went to bed and slept soundly for several hours but was dragged from a haze of fevered dreams by stifled noises coming from someplace in her apartment. *Must be the dog . . . . What dog, Josie? . . . . He was at the foot of the bed. . . . No, that was forty years ago. . . . I would like to have a dog again. . . .* The fear that might have invaded Josie's stupor was ambushed by her awareness that the sounds were all recognizable, friendly sounds, pots and pans being moved about the kitchen.

"Who's there?" she called out in a hoarse voice, reaching for her water glass beside the bed. There was fresh ice in the glass, a red rose beside it.

"Just be a minute," she heard Sean's voice reply.

The throbbing in her temples encouraged Josie to use the requested minute to close her eyes again, suspecting Sean would soon be beside her bed with a tray of food. She had been sweating, and her tatty night gown was crumpled and wet. Her hair was matted, and there was dried drool on one side of her face.

"Let's fluff up those pillows and get some good old chicken soup into you. I made it while you were sleeping. Thought you wouldn't mind if I used the rest of

306

the money. Got some wine, too, but I don't expect you'll want any. You have the Seven-Up, I'll drink the wine."

"Why are you doing this?" she demanded as she eased herself into a sitting position. "I didn't tell you you could come in my house and do whatever you want to. I didn't tell you you could spend my money. That's not fair, Sean, you scared me. What made you think you could do this?"

Sean didn't reply as he picked up the tray from the dresser and set it on Josie's outstretched, sheet-covered legs. He gave Josie a pained, puppy-dog look, grasped the wine from the tray, and left the room and the house, locking the door behind him.

Throughout the next week, Josie realized Sean was avoiding her, and she welcomed the break in her not-always peaceful routine. Her birthday was approaching, and she wanted to carry her contentment into her fifty-first year. She wondered if she had been too hard on Sean, wondered if she should try to smooth his ruffled feathers. "*Better not*," she decided, but it made sense to her to write a quick note thanking him for his thoughtfulness while she was sick. "*That'll be the end of it*," she declared. "*I'll keep my distance from now on.*"

Josie's birthday of 1993 was on a Wednesday, and she had scheduled with Mr. Orlick to have the day off. She hadn't made any plans beyond a pleasing day to herself but had agreed to go out on Tuesday night with Judy and the hotel chef. They shared some pleasing conversation and tequila shooters with lime, more shooters than conversation as the evening wore on, and Josie arrived home very late and very fuzzy in the head. As she climbed into bed, she looked again at the McCoy vase Mattie had sent for her birthday and, smiling, thought how good Mattie was at finding treasures. Thoughts of treasures turned themselves into musical teapots, spirited elves and dwarves, a lurking ogre, even a

307

handsome knight as Josie drifted forward into the day of her birth.

When the outdoor sounds of garbage collectors, neighborhood dogs, and other early-morning folks finally intruded into her mind, Josie lay still, slowly taking stock of how she felt now that she was fifty-one. She drowsily focused on her head to see if she could detect a headache, was pleased to discover there wasn't one. She stretched and mentally examined her body, pleased that it was firm and attractive.

"One year on the far side of fifty," Josie announced, "and I feel pretty good. I guess it's worth getting up for my very own private birthday. . . . Oh my God!. . . .Oh my God! . . .What the hell?"

The sun was filtering through the bedroom curtains and highlighting hundreds of flowers that covered every surface of the room. There were flowers on the dresser, the night stand, the floor, and flowers strewn over the cover of Josie's bed. Every kind of flower imaginable, some that Josie had never seen and couldn't name.

The impact on Josie's pre-coffee mind was intense and fragmented. *This is my birthday? . . . I have to pee so bad it hurts . . . and I have to figure out if I like this attention. First things first, I guess.* Josie eased out of bed, grabbed her dressing gown, and stepping carefully so as not to crush the flowers, left her room and started down the stairs, stairs adorned with rose petals that felt cool under her bare feet, cool and velvety, and pleasant. Josie anxiously took a quick tour of her small space, determined that she was alone, and noticed that the coffee had been made. *Okay, it's coffee I need.. To hell with whoever made it. . . . Sean, of course. . . . I'll have some anyway.* Coffee cup in hand, Josie approached the tiny cubbyhole bathroom and immediately sensed steam in the air, steam and a fragrance so strong as to be heady. She moved straight for the toilet, sat down, relieved herself, and then ventured an inspection of the small space. There were clean towels on the rack, she noticed, and the shower curtain was drawn, and yes, the room was full of fragrant steam. Josie leaned over from where she sat and pulled back the curtain to find that the bathtub was full, but no water was visible. The entire surface was hidden by roses, hundreds of them.

They can't have been there long, they're not damaged by the heat. . . . What should I do?. . . What the hell, no harm in a delicious bath. Josie placed her coffee cup on the rim of the tub and eased herself into the inviting bed of roses. She noticed a few tiny insects scurrying around on some of the roses, probably looking for a way out of the steamy tub.

Josie's Bath

My God, he must have picked every flower in town. Must have done it during the night. It's amazing someone didn't see him and call the police. . . . Why would he do that? Does he think I'll be his girl friend? I think he needs a mother more than a girlfriend. Maybe he wants a mother/girlfriend. . . What do I want? Do I want to be his mother/girlfriend? He frightens me a little, so intense, so . . . I don't know. . . needy. Kind of like he wants to latch on and suck something out, something he needs. If I let him latch on, then what? The attention's nice, but it doesn't feel clean. This bath doesn't feel clean with stolen roses . . . my birth flower, roses, but they're stolen and making me feel dirty. I feel like the flowers must feel with those little bugs scurrying around on them. The roses don't have a choice about the bugs. They didn't have a choice about being stolen and set in hot water to wilt. For that matter, neither did the bugs. . . . Is Sean like a little bug with no choice? Am I like a rose with no choice about a bug invasion. . . . Bug spray, I need bug spray. I must bug spray myself clean, and I must get out of this bath. This is not a good bath. I'll have to shower to get the bugs off, shower and throw the roses away; they're not so pretty now, soggy and turning dark.

———

Josie performed penance by postponing her second cup of coffee until the house was made tidy. When she finally achieved a sense of order, she took her reward out onto the porch and waited for Sean. She knew he was watching for her, knew it and hated it, hated the crawly feeling that moved up her arms and into her chest.

"Happy Birthday," he said with a smile. "I hope you like your present. Took me most of the night. There sure are a lot of dogs around this town."

"Good morning, Sean. That was a sweet thing for you to do, thank you, but I don't feel very good about you filching people's flowers. You could have been arrested."

"Almost was, too. The patrol car came by, and I had to hide in some bushes. Got scratched, see." Sean pushed up his sleeve to show Josie his lacerated arm.

"You should put something on that, Sean, looks a bit nasty."

"Oh, it'll be okay, it's nothing."

Josie took a sip of her coffee and then another sip. A silence feel between the two, and Josie knew it was hers to fill.

"Sean, I appreciate your wanting to give me a present, but I don't like what you did. It's not right to take whatever you want. It's not right for you to come in my house without permission. I thought I made that clear the last time."

310

"Well, I thought you forgave me with the note. You said you were sorry, so I thought it'd be okay."

"Sean, I did forgive you, and I said I was sorry for hurting your feelings. I didn't say you could do it again," Josie countered, becoming aware of a dryness in her mouth despite the coffee. "I don't want you to come in my house again, and I don't want anymore flowers. We can be friends, but only friends. Okay?"

"You acted like you like me. All those times we spent together you were coming on to me, you know? What are you, some kind of tease? Is that it? Do you get off leading a guy on and then squashing him like a bug. Look at all the things I've done for you. Even fixed your car, remember?"

"Sean, I didn't ask you to fix my car, you just did it."

"You didn't complain then, did you?" Sean spit at her. "No, you didn't complain then and when I bought groceries and things."

"I appreciate the help you've given me, but I paid for the groceries, and you never gave back the change, did you?"

"And you never asked for it, did you? I deserved it for being your errand boy. You just wanted to use me, tease me and use me. You don't want to give anything back, do you?"

"What is it you want, Sean? I don't know what you expect."

"I want to fuck your brains out, you bitch," Sean yelled as he rose from his chair, towering over Josie. With a swift blow, he knocked the coffee cup out of her hand and stormed down the steps, quickly disappearing around the side of the house.

Josie's coffee cup had not broken, and she reached down to recover it, then sat for a long while holding the empty cup in both hands. *Is there some truth*

311

to what he said? Did I lead him on like he said? I think I was attracted to him . . . my body was, anyway. Is it a sin for a body to be attracted to another body? Is that one of the secrets we're supposed to hide from the world? . . . That's what Black Mariah was all about, wasn't it? About hiding the body so we don't give ourselves away. Is this fair? All the hiding? . . . God, how could I be so stupid? Haven't I learned anything in all these years? Did I ask for this? "She asked for it," they would say, whoever they are. At the trial, they will say, "She got what she deserved."

Whether or not she deserved it, Josie got more. More flowers left on the porch when she arrived home from work, dead flowers. And dead flowers on her kitchen counter when she awoke in the morning. She installed a safety chain and found it cut one morning. She changed the locks on her doors; she soon found that her car wouldn't start. The battery cables had been disconnected. Her phone would ring at late-night hours, but no one was there when she answered. She disconnected the phone.

When Josie stopped by the police station and asked to speak with someone about a problem, she was ushered into a tiny cubicle of a room where an obese police officer was sitting behind a scarred desk eating a hamburger. Mustard and catsup were dripping from his chin onto his dark tie, and the room stank of cigarettes, stale food, and burnt coffee.

"Want some?" the officer asked, pointing to a Styrofoam cup. "I can git yuh some if yuh want."

"No thanks. May I sit down?" Josie asked moving toward the only other chair in the room.

"Sure, Honey, take a load off. No use standin' when yuh can sit," the officer chuckled as he wiped his mouth on his sleeve and then wadded up the wrapper and tossed it toward a waste basket that was spilling out remains of meals past.

312

"This may be a mistake," Josie mumbled.

"What mistake did yuh make, Missy? What can I do for yuh? What kind of problem can a nice lookin' lady like yuhself have?" he asked and then belched. "'Ex-cuse me!

Josie explained her predicament to the officer who listened but took no notes. When she finished, the officer leaned back in his swivel chair, threatening, Josie thought, to go right over backwards. "Lover's quarrel, huh? Happens that way sometimes. Yuh oughta be more careful with who yuh mess with. Yuh never know."

Josie was embarrassed and began to try to explain that she and Sean weren't lovers when the officer interrupted her in mid sentence.

"Looky here, Lady, as far as I can tell no law's been broken. If'n I hear yuh right, yuh never really saw this Sean guy do what yuh said, now did yuh? Can yuh prove it was him? Maybe yuh got some other boyfriend that ain't so happy with yuh. Could be, yuh know. I 'spect yuh's got more than one dog sniffin' round, pretty lady like yuh are. Did the right thing though, changin' the locks. Guy'll get tired of it soon enough if yuh quit lead'in him on. Yuh gals think it's all a bed a roses 'til it goes sour. Then yuh come cryin' fer help. Just go on home now an' keep the doors locked. Here's my card. Yuh call now if sumpin' real happens. Nice to meet yuh. Maybe see yuh again sometime, never know."

You'll probably see me again when you come to investigate my murder. Would that be real enough?

Josie arrived home feeling grimy and needing a bath. She stopped to check her mailbox and gasped when she felt something wiggle beneath her fingers as she reached for the pile of mostly junk mail. Josie hated snakes almost as much as she hated spiders, and Sean knew her fears. He had told her the legend of St. Patrick driving the snakes from Ireland, and she had told him a

313

childhood story about not answering her mother's "pooo oooo." She had wanted to finish brushing Misty and turn her into the pasture for the night, so Josie ignored the second and even the third pooo oooo. Misty was galloping off — tail high and grand — tossing her head to feel the breeze in her mane when Josie felt a strong, angry hand grasp and pull at her shoulder.

"You come in right this minute, Young Lady," Nora shouted. "I've been calling you for hours, and now I've had to come all this way to get you! Don't you ever mind?" she said, shaking and pulling Josie up the lane toward the house. "You're lucky I didn't get a switch."

Nora was still pulling when Josie stopped dead in her tracks, terrorized by the biggest snake she had ever seen. Mattie and Peter would sometimes catch garter snakes and wiggle them around to scare the city kids when they came to play, but Josie had never seen such a huge snake, and she let out with what she remembered as a primal scream.

"You stay here," Nora ordered, as she hurried off toward the garage. Choked with tears and terror, Josie stood there, unable to move, screaming to her mother not to leave her. When she returned from the terrors of being abandoned forever, of being eaten alive by a monster snake, Josie saw that her mother was beating the snake with Peter's baseball bat; she kept beating the snake from one end of its four feet to the other until pieces of it began flying in all directions. Nora said nothing, but she continued to pulverize the creature with a strength and determination thatmay have been more terrifying to Josie than simple abandonment. Josie suddenly understood, in the manner of children's understanding, that Nora was now beating something other than the snake. The snake was gone in a myriad of pieces, but the beating continued. Nora knew, although Josie didn't, that the creature was merely a harmless kingsnake.

314

Another primal scream, Josie said. *I wonder if they do any good? Is anyone listening?* She tried to reach the apartment's owner at his office in The Dalles, but the receptionist told her that Mr. and Mrs. Lucas were traveling in Europe. Mr. Lucas had instructed her to refer any problems at the complex to Sean, the maintenance man. "We depend on Sean," she said.

———

"Judy, I can't stay there! Can't I stay with you?" Josie pleaded when she found Judy in the employee lounge having a quick dinner before leaving work. "I'll sleep on the floor, it doesn't matter! Maybe I'm just being stupid, but I just can't stay there! I don't know what he'll do next."

Judy didn't think Josie was being stupid. She had never really liked Sean, had expressed her misgivings but had treated him decently when Josie included him in some of their outings.

"That won't work, Josie," Judy explained. "Rob just had a load of sheet rock delivered, and it's everywhere. There isn't any floor to sleep on. Can't you stay here for a few days?"

"The hotel's full. I asked Mr. Orlick, but it's full. What am I going to do?"

"I guess you could use the teepee. There's some junk in it, but I guess we could clear a space. You'd have to get some blankets or a sleeping bag and some clothes. You are working tomorrow, aren't you?"

"Yes, I am," Josie answered, "but I can drive over to your place this afternoon and then leave early in the morning from your place. Why don't we do it now? Will you follow me home to get some things? I don't want to go alone."

"Yah, okay, but let me call Rob first. He can fix up the teepee before we get there, at least get the spiders out. It'll be okay. You need to calm down a bit."

The two women labored up the steep hillside to Josie's place, arriving out of breath at the front door where they discovered blood on the glass pane and the carcass of a rat deposited on the welcome mat. Judy kicked the rat aside and said she would wash off the blood while Josie got whatever she needed.

"Just hurry!" Judy ordered. "I don't feel good about this! Let's just get the hell out of here."

Josie made a mental inventory of basic necessities for camping in a teepee and attempted to strengthen herself by conjuring up images of Indian women readying themselves for seasonal treks, packing a few baskets, hides, and medicinal herbs. She thought, too, of the stories Mattie had told her about Indian ancestors, searching her ancestral memory for a shaman who might guide her through this ordeal.

Rosa, dear powerful Rosa, I need you now. Right now. Please don't be ashamed of me for running away.

What?" said Judy. "What did you say, and who's Rosa."

"Nothing," Josie answered her, "just talking to myself. Let's go."

———

You sit there, Rosa, and be still for a few minutes. Talk to Abe, or something. I don't want to talk about it. If you have to say anything, just let it be words of wisdom about how to make this work. I don't want to talk about my courage or lack of it. You've got enough courage for the two of us, so don't give me any shit right now. I'm tired, and I just want to get organized and go to sleep. You can sit up all night and worry about whatever. I need to sleep. . Judy said to take this pill, said I would

316

sleep like a baby and have great dreams. Yeah, right! . . . Well, okay, I'll just do it. Take the little pill, take the little pill with a little wine. God, Judy, what a great hostess you are – a little pill and a bottle of wine, a glass even. Well, a plastic mug. . . . "Some pills make you bigger, some pills make you small. The pills that Mother gives you don't do anything at all" . . . . Okay, if there's a spider lurking in here, what the hell! Rob did a nice job. There's room to lay my body down, la di dah. "It's the dawning of the age of Aquarius, the age of Aquarius, Aquarius." This is all bullshit. I'm bullshit. I haven't done anything right in my whole life . . . living in a teepee at fifty-one. How splendid! I can just hear it. I can just hear the minister: "She was a unique person, married umpteen million times, deserted her kids, lived in a teepee, and died, bitten by a rare, never-before-seen-by-man arachnid . . . or maybe it was a snake . . . . God, it's quiet . . . except for that scuffling. Must be the llamas. Well, Rosa, we'll just pretend it's the llamas, won't we?. I wish the llamas would come in; I wish the raccoons would come, and we could all curl up together and be safe. We'll just all curl up together and be safe. Somebody will find us someday. . . . Shut up, Rosa, I said I didn't want to talk about it! Shut up! . . . Shut up! . . . "Shut that kid up" the father yelled. . . . "Quiet, Josie, your father is driving! Quiet!" . . . " need a horse! . . . I need a horse." . . . "Do you always have to spoil it for us? Do you always have to act up? Why can't you be good? I'll give you to the gypsies." . . . "I have to have a horse!" . . . "Put her out!". . .

The dust from the disappearing car was settling, and Josie stood there on the side of the road, not crying, not feeling, not being.

"What do you see?" Rosa asked. "Look around, what do you see?"

"Nothing, I don't see anything!"

317

"Look again, look all around. Look over there, what do you see?"

"I see a field, just a field, and the road and the dust and nothing."

"Look closer, look closer, what do you see?"

"I do see something, maybe. Maybe I see something."

"What, what do you see? Look hard! Tell me, what do you see!"

"A shape, it's coming closer. It's moving closer. It's wispy, I can't tell."

"Yes, you must," Rosa told her, "You must! What do you see!"

"Yes, yes, I do see it. It's a horse, and it's coming to me. It's a beautiful horse."

"Yes," Rosa said, "Yes. And now what is it doing?"

"It's coming up to me and snorting, and it wants me to touch it!"

"Yes, and what else? What else can you do besides pet it?"

"I could get on, I could ride it."

"To where, to where could you ride it?"

"Down the road, I guess, down the road."

"Then do it. Get on the horse."

"Yes, I can get on the horse."

"Where are you?"

"I'm riding down the road on the horse, my horse."

"What do you see, look around! Look around now and see!"

"I see a lane, I see white fences, I see a house with a porch all around. I see a barn and I see horses in the fields."

"And what do you do?"

"I ride up the lane, and I tie up my horse, and I go up the steps to my porch and sit down in my wicker chair."

"And how do you feel?"

". . . . I feel . . . . I feel home!"

"Yes, that's right," and Rosa smiled. "You got it"

Lyrics of an American spiritual flowed through Josie's mind and into her dreams as she drifted into a peaceful sleep: "Gonna lay down my burden/Down by the riverside . . .I ain't gonna study war no more."

Josie's Bath

I wonder why I was born. Just an accident? I wonder if each of us has some purpose. I must have a purpose, but it eludes me. Anger has kept me from finding it. Anger, like a blanket over pain, keeping it warm and safe so I wouldn't die. I thought I needed the anger to keep me alive, no other champion, no Roy Rogers to come riding in at the last minute and save me from the bad guys. . . . Who are the bad guys? I've spent my whole life trying to fill the empty space, looking for the other part, my twin. I thought I was Castor, who gentled the horses, but I am Pollux, the fighter, too. The patron deities of seamen and voyagers. . . . And my voyage has brought me here, sitting naked in a hot spring in the forest. Naked and new, letting go of the anger so the pain can wash away. And Rosa, you're here, too. We will share this forest bath and wash away my pain together as you have told me we could do. You said you would hold my hand when I was ready. You have been with me for so many years. I think I can let you rest now, go to your own place of peace . . . . And my purpose? It will find me as I cease to look for it. I expect I have many purposes, and it's not important to know what they are. Little tiny purposes, maybe one each day or week, or . . . I have been searching for the big one, my own special purpose, and it doesn't work that way, does it? What does work? There ought to be a recipe someplace. Let's see. Start with 3 cups of care. Add 2 cups of kindness; a cup of compassion; add a dash of acceptance; a splash of humor; stir with strength and vigor; bake however long it takes; wrap in colorful paper; toss into the universe. That should do it. Sounds so simple. . . . 'Make love, not war,' we used to say. I can do it now that my peace treaty is signed. . . . Another journey? Yes, there will always be another journey. . . . Thank-you, Vernon, for giving me Frost. Actually, Vernon, I think I met Frost in about sixth grade, after Mattie left for college, but thank you anyway for reading him from time to time. How does my favorite go? . . . "Two roads diverged in a yellow wood. And sorry I could not travel both." Yes that's it. Then the part about being a single traveler, looking down both paths, both of them inviting, trying to decide . . . "knowing how way leads onto way. I doubted if I should ever come back" . . . Yes, then he sighs, I can just see him standing there in the early morning – a deep sigh, and then a decision. "I took the one less traveled by, And that has made all the difference." . . . Thank you, Robert Frost. And thank-you, Howard for giving me Ibsen, Stendal, Zola, Flaubert, my precious Madame Bovary. I especially thank you for Caitlin though you gave her without joy. She will be fine now that I have the recipe. My heart string to her will let her know she can put down the baggage she carries with her. . . . And thank-you Jeremy for so much – Gareth, of course, my lovely boy. Your England has captured him, but he will carry with him the best parts of me. You gave me all you could give of yourself, and I will always love you for that. You gave me Thackeray,

Lawrence, the Brontes, and, yes, Dickens. You are, even now, helping Caitlin find her way. You and I will always be together in those places we once ventured, and we are bound in the future by what we still share. . . . And Abe, my dear, wonderful Abe. You never gave me a wedding ring, but you gave me the best. You shared your wisdom and your warmth so generously. We have all traveled roads together. . . . I hope you, too, have gained something from our brief companionship. . . . I think you did. . . . And now it's time we leave these mountains. And where shall we go? The road less traveled by, I suspect.

CHAPTER 17

*. . . And I can't say enough about a lightning
storm/ How they have a way to keep you warm
With the thunder crashin' and the rain
pouring down/Good friends close at hand. . . .*
Peter Blake
"Lightning Storms"

"Will you come, Josie? You're the only one who's not tied down, and I can't do this alone. I have my work, my clients, my men's group. My health isn't all that good, either. I just can't take care of her by myself. She specifically asked for you. She said you're the only one of her kids she wants to have taking care of her."

"Calm down, Bertram. Let me think. I'm not sure what you mean 'not tied down.' It's true I'm living in a teepee that isn't tied down very well, pretty cold and windy this fall, but I am still working, Bertram, and I'm pretty sure I told you Caitlin is still in England. She's married now, and expecting twins in just a few months. I'm planning to leave this area, make some changes, maybe get to know my grandbabies. And, frankly, Bertram, I'm kind of longing to get back to California, back to Berkeley and my beautiful, sunny hills."

"But, Josie, you could still do all those things. Just postpone them for a while. We really need you back here, probably not too long. A few months at the most, just until she's on her feet."

"It's not that simple, Bertram, really. I have an apartment full of stuff. Some of it's important to me – my McCoys, my books, you know, just things."

"Well, you could put it all in storage. I'll pay for it. Then after Nora's better, you can go back and decide what you want to do. You'll only have to be here a few months, like I said. I'll cover your plane fare, too, and

323

you can have the guestroom. We fixed it up so nice with your old bedroom set. That should make you feel at home."

"Thanks a lot, Bertram, that pretty much tips the scales, doesn't it? My old bedroom set. I can hardly wait."

"Then you'll come? We knew we could count on you. You and your mother have always had a special relationship."

"You're right, it has been unique. Yes, I'll come. When did you say the surgery was scheduled?"

"Next Friday, six in the morning, at KU Med Center."

"That doesn't give me much time!"

"You can do it, Josie. I have faith in you."

"Yeh, right. Okay. I'll let you know when I have a flight. Can you pick me up at the airport?"

"Yes, of course, I or one of my clients will be there. I have a tight schedule, but I let some of my clients work off their bills by doing little things I don't have time to do."

"Well, Bertram, I'm not sure how I feel being one of the little things you don't have time for, but I'll get there. Give Mother hugs for me."

"Thank you, Josie. I've never really told you how much I admire your strengths."

———

Rob and Judy agreed to help Josie move her belongings to a storage facility, and the three arrived at Josie's apartment just after 8:00 a.m. Rob reassured Josie that he would handle Sean if need be. Rob didn't have a gun rack in his pickup as so many of the local men did, but Josie knew he had stashed a crow bar beneath the front seat. Josie wondered if she, too, wanted a weapon of some sort in her hand, but instead she grappled in her purse for her keys, just wanting to be done with the chore. She and Judy started up the steps to the apartment as Rob dropped the tailgate of his pickup to get some of the packing boxes he had tossed in.

"This shouldn't take too long," Judy said. "Not with the three of us."

"God, I hope not. This place gives me the willies now. I haven't been back for what? Six weeks? Seems longer somehow."

Josie waited for Rob to catch up before she unlocked the apartment door and slowly peered in.

"My God, Judy! There's nothing here? Where is everything? Oh, my God! What has he done!"

The three friends crept quietly through the empty apartment to the beat of Josie's persistent lament: "There's nothing here! It's all gone. All my things are gone!"

"Have you been sending your rent, Josie? Did the checks clear?" Rob asked. "Do you know if your checks cleared?"

When Josie was finally able to focus on how it could happen that her lifelong collection of books and small treasures were so savagely removed from her life, she answered Rob with the only voice she could find.

"Hell, yes," she screamed. "You think I'm stupid? Of course I paid the rent."

"Try to calm down, Josie. Did your checks clear the bank?"

"Rob, thanks to you and Judy, I've been living in a teepee, having baths in the hot springs, enjoying my life. Balancing my checkbook wasn't a high priority." Tears were finally forming in Josie's eyes.

"My hunch is that Sean got a hold of your checks, tore them to shreds, and had you evicted." Judy offered.

"The man's crazy. He probably sold your things, or took them to the dump," Rob added.

Josie was sobbing now, remembering each of her treasures, especially the albums of Caitlin and Gareth's baby pictures. "Where are they?" she cried.

Judy grabbed Josie with one hand, Rob with the other and forced the threesome out of the apartment and back down the hill. "You need to leave now, Josie. Right now!"

The friends quickly discovered that the crow bar had been taken from beneath the seat of the truck that would soon deliver Josie to the Portland airport. She spent one more night in her mountain hide-away, the night hours filled with thoughts and dreams of loss.

"I'm traveling light," Josie said, as she offered farewell hugs and kisses to her mountain friends.

———

"I'm just going out for a cigarette," Josie whispered to Bertram as they stood by Nora's bed in the ICU. I won't be long, okay?"

"Take your time, Josie, I'll stay with her."

Nora hadn't yet regained consciousness, but the doctor had said everything went well. He had removed a length of Nora's colon and was fairly sure he had gotten "it" all. "It" was the common, comfortable euphemism for cancerous cells, nasty little cells that were difficult for Josie to visualize amidst the confusion of respirators, monitors, and yards of plastic tubing in her mother's throat and arms.

Josie didn't light the cigarette she thought she wanted. The Kansas City air was heavy and moist, already difficult to breathe. And Josie's thoughts were heavy, begging her to be untangled.

"Dehumanizing, dammit! It's all a bit much," she muttered, reverting back to her English accent and wondering when her anger and pain would recede. "It's all a bit much."

326

"Did you say something to me?" came a voice from behind her.

"*Deja vu*," Josie thought as she turned. "Why are people always listening in on my private conversations?" A fleeting image of Abe brightened her spirit as she turned to locate the voice. "Oh, my, you look just like Sean Connery. You have the most magnificent beard I've ever seen!"

"Well, I was thinking the same about you, not your beard, I mean, you don't have a beard, of course, but I was thinking, oh, I'm not saying what I mean."

The man with the gorgeous beard turned and hurriedly walked away.

"Wait! No, wait!" Josie called after him. But he didn't turn. A slight wave of the hand was the only sign he gave that he had heard Josie.

"Oh, well," Josie sighed, as she drew in a deep breath and returned to her mother's bedside.

———

Josie's Bath

Same-ol', same-ol.' Up in the morning, fix breakfast for me and Bertram, tidy up the house, and spend most of the day at the hospital. And Bertram's so strange. What is it Mattie called him? A narcissist? Right. I've got to look that up. Everybody needs a narcissist for a therapist. There might be some good lyrics in that tongue-twister. Wonder why a narcissist therapist never puts anything away? Dirty dishes everywhere, things growing in the fridge. And strange clients, dropping by and calling at all hours. Bertram says they're "in-crisis." Wonder how long a body can stay in-crisis. A whole lifetime? . . . Stop it! They're doing the best they can, and so am I. But, God, I feel so alone. About the only person I talk to is Jack. He's so funny. Really a nice man, too. Like

327

nobody I've ever met. I'm glad he found the nerve to talk to me again. How does he know when I'm going out for a cigarette? He always seems to be there. Doesn't he have work to do? Something to do with hospital construction, he said, running the plumbers, electricians, sheet metal somethings, he said. He seems so solid, somehow, like he's attached to the earth, not hovering two feet off the ground, not in-crisis.

―――――

"Well, I guess that's it then. He must be avoiding me," Josie said to herself as she shrugged her shoulders and set off across the quadrangle toward the hospital entrance. She had won the argument with a host of medical advisors, insisting she hadn't come all the way to Kansas City to keep house for Bertram. Josie had seen the primitive fear in Nora's eyes when the doctor recommended an extended-care facility, and she was certain Nora would recuperate best at home. There would be the occasional aid of a visiting nurse, Bertram, and a constant wave of clients.

As she rode the hospital elevator for the last time, Josie was both relieved by her mother's improving condition and saddened that she would never see Jack again. They had had many days of "getting to know you" stories, and Josie simply acknowledged that Jack was becoming very dear to her. She paused outside her mother's hospital room when she heard muted voices behind the door – laughing, playful voices.

"You're such a dear man to come visit me. Please don't let them put me in a nursing home," Josie heard as she entered the room.

"Well, I'm not in charge of those things, but I think your daughter is determined to take you home. Today, you're going home today."

"What are you doing here?" Josie gasped when she saw Jack sitting next to Nora's bed holding her hand.

"I've been in nonstop meetings for the last three days, and you were never around by the time I got free. I was afraid you were avoiding me."

"This reminds me of a movie," Josie answered. "Cary Grant and Deborah Kerr, I think . . . missed their rendezvous and ruined their lives. How did you find this room?"

"Oh, I kind of know my way around. Should after sixteen years. If this is your mother's last day, maybe you and I should exchange phone numbers so we don't lose each other again."

"Well, that's a unique idea! I wonder why Cary and Debbie didn't think of that?"

———

Josie wore a silk blouse, denim skirt, and Birkenstocks for her wedding. She and Jack met the minimal expenses, and Bertram and Nora were witnesses. Memories of the simple wedding were stored joyfully in Josie's mind along with other grand family events. Josie named 1995 the Year of the Photo: Photos of Gareth celebrating his thirtieth birthday — no family yet, but a fascinating job in a genetics research lab; photos of Caitlin and Ben's handsome twins, a girl and a boy — Zachary and Sophie; a photo of Bo winning an award of excellence for community service; photos of David and Ginger's Jessica celebrating her third birthday at Greyhavens with Grandma Mattie and Grandpa Dancin'. "Raymond" was difficult for the child to say so she used a name that made sense to her.

Jessica's birthday photo and her many scribbled drawings were displayed on Raymond's bulletin board next to snapshots from Sarah and Luis — smiling, suntanned, and dusty. In the center of the display board were stunning images captured from the ends of the universe by the Hubble Space Telescope along with photos of Russian Cosmonaut Valery Polyakov who had returned to earth in March of '95 after spending a record 437days and eighteen hours aboard the space station *Mir*. In June of that year, Raymond would add images of the American shuttle *Atlantis* docking with *Mir*, and by the end of the year, he would add a photo of the Pacific coho salmon, now a candidate for the threatened species list.

The colorful fish image was eventually matted and framed for Raymond by Mattie, who tried to balance her concerns about endangered species with new information about ozone depletion. She frequently lamented that civilization's fast-lane was over-crowded and looking rather like a dead-end alley. Indeed, many of the events of the year were impossible to capture by camera, very difficult to comprehend. The Information Superhighway was chewing up digital bits and bytes at unimaginable speeds, while American drivers were slurping up vehicle fuel at the astonishing rate of 275,446 gallons per minute. The population of the planet was approaching six billion souls, many of them starving. Each year, 20,000 unique species — more than two per hour — would disappear from the planet forever.

"Raymond, listen to this. The paper says that all the people born between 1930 and 2010 — that's our entire family, Raymond! — will see the extinction of nearly half of all the planet's life forms."

"I know, Mattie, and I'm beginning to understand some of your tears. We must simply do what we can, add some amazement and hope and joy to our despair, and press on. Try to live responsibly."

"But Raymond, it's hard to know if we are even doing that. There's so much to understand."

"Mattie, come sit beside me. I'll put on the *Three Tenors* tape and you can "dream a little dream of me.""

330

"Never mind the tape, Raymond. It's your voice that helps me hide from despair."

———

Saturday mornings in Jack and Josie's Kansas City home were savored and protected, the couple lounging in bed with coffee and a newspaper, snuggling, and making love. Josie had insisted that they both give up cigarettes, and Saturday mornings together were part of their reward for having accomplished the difficult task. Saturday was the one day of the week when they could hold at bay the mounting pressures of Jack's job. He would come home on Fridays discouraged and irritable; Sundays brought the realization that a stress-filled Monday was not many hours away. Jack had been relatively happy working with the tools of his trade, but once promoted to management, his frustrations mounted. "Where are the grown-ups at that goddamn place? Can't anyone make a fucking decision?"

At first Jack and Josie would joke about how it couldn't get much worse. But it had gotten worse, and the jokes became thin and half-hearted. The health-care industry — now an industry, not a healing profession — was in serious trouble. The powers-that-be were running scared, especially in the state-run facilities that were dependent on the legislature for funding.

"The politicians are making facilities decisions, the accountants are making medical decisions, and the nurses are worrying about the plumbing," Jack yelled. "The insurance companies are dictating the rules of the game, and HMOs are springing up like dandelions through pavement."

"We've got some dandelions, too, Jack. How about some garden chores this morning?" Josie tried hard to understand and smooth the difficult times for her husband, but he was like a terrier who had mixed it up with a raccoon and had no way to let go. He had admired

331

Hillary Clinton's abortive efforts to address the nation's health-care problems, but he was certain that Mrs. Clinton would be a sacrificial lamb. The massive system was simply out of control, and the costs of medical insurance were skyrocketing. Millions of Americans had no medical insurance, and those who did were complaining about the decline in quality of care.

Josie could remember how her father lowered his voice when he spoke with friends about the merits of a national health-care program. It had seemed a seditious conversation in the '40 and '50s. "I think we've arrived at the Tower of Babel," she concluded. "I just wish you could quit your job."

Jack and Josie spent hours fabricating scenarios of moving to California, settling in near Mattie and Raymond and spending their golden years in the more liveable climate of the Sierra foothills. Josie became obsessed with getting Jack out of his job and getting them both out of the Midwest. She hated the Kansas City weather.

"Is this what we wait all winter for?" Josie would whimper when the temperature and humidity hovered between ninety-eight and one hundred degrees throughout the summer. She did notice that, whatever the temperature, Saturday morning weather was the most agreeable, and she resented giving up the precious time when Nora had a stroke and was placed in an extended-care facility. Jack would reluctantly accompany Josie to the facility, always with some anguish as he remembered Nora's plea, "Don't let them put me in a nursing home."

"Well," he reflected, "you're not in a nursing home, you're in an extended-care facility. The accountants decided that for us. I guess they're in charge of euphemisms, too."

As weeks went by, Jack began to beg off from their weekly pilgrimage to the mother place, and Josie

332

would set out alone, trying not to feel abandoned. She would help Nora into a wheel chair and, if the weather was tolerable, would wheel her outside for a stroll around the small lake adjacent to the complex. Nora loved to watch the ducks and would urge Josie to startle them so she could watch them fly, circling a few times and then returning to the water. Their awkward landings delighted Nora and brought peaceful smiles to her lips. It was during such a moment that Nora reached back to touch Josie's hand and asked her to stop at the little arbor at the far end of the lake. Josie positioned the chair so Nora could watch the ducks and settled beside her on a small wooden bench.

"I need to tell you some things," Nora said, looking intently into Josie's face.

Josie's stomach knotted up, and she looked away into the distance, wondering how much this conversation was going to hurt.

"I know I'm dying. How could I not be? Eighty-five years old, cancer and a stroke. How I wish I could just join the ducks in this lake, feel the water cleanse me, and then drift to the bottom of the lake, rest in the soft ooze. But before I can let go, there are some things I've begun to understand. I want to tell you about them."

Josie adjusted the light blanket on her mother's lap and moved closer in order to hear. Nora's voice was no longer strong, nor was it critical or demeaning or condescending. It was simply soft and thoughtful.

. "When I was a young girl, my father would tell me of wonderful things I would be able to do when I grew up if I worked hard. He was determined that I would attend college and become something. I wondered how I would know when I arrived, when I had become something, but I was eager to find out. Then, as each new child arrived — you know I was the eldest of eight — I took on more and more of my mother's responsibilities. You know my brothers and sisters as delightful uncles and aunts, but to me they became heavy weights on my spirit. My mother would often disappear for hours, leaving me to care for the little ones who were always in need. Years later, when I confronted her about her neglect, she told me she could only survive through her books. She would hide out and read for hours, escaping into her better worlds where life was not so tedious and difficult."

Josie remembered the haunting hours she had spent in London book shops whenever tedium threatened to invade her spirit.

"I did go off to college," Nora continued, "and decided to become a teacher. I would be good at it, I knew, because I had taught seven of my mother's children. I liked teaching, and I began to feel I had become the something my father told me I could be." Josie delighted in the smile that brightened her mother's face, the wispy smile that carried her mother back into times that had been satisfying and challenging.

"The father messages are pretty powerful, aren't they, Mom?"

"Powerful, but not always useful, Josie. . . . Do you know that I actually had to hide the phonics chart, under the world map, in my classroom? We were experimenting with reading methods, discarding the one that worked in favor of new things."

Josie had no trouble remembering the phonics lessons of Dick and Jane, Puff and Spot. "Well, we finally came back around, didn't we? At least Caitlin got Dr. Seuss. What was Father doing while you taught?"

"He worked as a newspaper night editor in San Francisco, a wire service editor. Those were good times, Josie. It wasn't until Grandmother R got sick during the Depression that we moved to the valley. I had to give up teaching and become something else, something I had wanted to escape. Running the ranch was like my childhood all over again, only this time there were cows, chickens, and horses to tend to; ranch hands to cook for; another family to raise. Don't you see, Josie, I never felt I got to be the something my father had promised I could be. I tried hard to bring some glamour into farm life. I loved to give the dinner parties, the Christmas parties, any parties, because I could pretend I was living in a better place just as my mother had pretended with her books."

"The ranch was so beautiful, Mom. I wish you had loved it."

"How could I love it, Josie? I was never there, not in my mind. I never wanted to be there, never! I knew your father wanted me to make it right for all of you. I just couldn't."

Josie allowed her own images of life in England to penetrate the conversation. "It was Gareth's birth that saved me for a while in England," she said.

"Yes, Josie, I understand. Peter's birth disguised my despair for several years, but by the time Mattie came along, despair was bubbling in my spirit again, and I made foolish decisions. I promised myself I would not tell Mattie the lie I thought I had been told. I simply wouldn't let her believe she could grow up and become something, only to be faced with disappointment. I taught Mattie the things she needed to know – cooking, sewing, canning, ironing. I taught her the useful things, but gave her no dreams."

"Well, Mom, she certainly found some dreams along the way. She's fine." Josie knew she didn't want to get into that miserable place where one sibling is compared to the next on some imaginary scale that never made sense. She encouraged her mother to continue.

"When you were born, Josie, I gave you to Mattie. I didn't have any more to give to anyone."

A long silence now separated the two women, each touching, investigating the moments of the olden days that were so much a part of the present.

"When you came to live with me after your father and I divorced, I thought I could make it up to you. I could give you all the things I never had. I had the money, so I bought for you. I didn't realize I was really trying to give myself all those things. It wasn't you I was looking after, was it? I expected you to live my life for me. . . . And you tried in your own way. You tried so hard to be the something I wanted you to be for me, and I kept paying so you would do that."

Josie wondered if the resentments she harbored about her early years would ever dissolve. *Probably not*, she thought. But she had learned to quiet them, tend to them much as she would an orphaned animal, and she reached for her mother's hand to ease them both through the difficult moment.

"Josie, when I die I hope you will find some release from my leash. Please try to forgive me. And Josie, please remember the good about me. You have some of my spirit, some of my good spirit in you. Use that in your life, untainted by the other."

"Mom, Mattie just sent me something you might like to hear. I didn't bring the article, but it said something like this: 'We are all at fault, but we are not to blame.' It's true. We just don't get to pick and choose our handicaps any more than we get to choose eye color. But we do get to make choices . . . . Maybe it takes a lot of generations before we make wise choices. Maybe the wise ones are snugged in right next to the poor ones, difficult for us to recognize. I love you, Mom."

———

It was only a few days before Nora had another massive stoke and was transferred to the hospital ICU. By

336

the time Josie and Jack arrived at the hospital, a tracheotomy had been performed and a tube inserted into Nora's stomach to provide nourishment while other medical procedures took over. Bertram paced outside her room and tried to explain her condition and some of his decisions.

Josie insisted on speaking with the doctor who eventually arrived and ushered the three family members into a small conference room. Josie listened to the doctor and the drone of hateful, hospital noises, trying hard not to taste the bitter blend of anger and sorrow that rumbled someplace between her heart and her voice.

"Don't you know she signed a living will?" Josie asked. "She didn't want any of this! She explained all that to you," she said turning to Bertram, "and to you," turning back to Nora's doctor. "Why have you done this against her wishes?"

The doctor waved the pacing Bertram toward a chair and suggested that Josie should calm down a bit. He would explain the procedures Bertram had consented to.

"But why?" Josie asked again. "She said she didn't want to be kept alive artificially, didn't want any machines."

Josie's simple question, "why," was soon lost is the debris of legalistic verbiage being stirred into the medical soup, none of it tasty and soothing. Josie tuned out and focused on her image of her mother in the small curtained area surrounded by the latest in medical technology. She could hear the sounds of the breathing machine and the monitors, lifesaving machines, perhaps, but to Josie a surrealistic painting about the anguish of not being heard. She tuned back in when the word "terminal" caught her attention and asked the doctor to repeat what he had just said.

"She's not terminal," he said. "I can't say she's terminal, and I can't withhold treatment based simply on

337

the papers she signed. The documents you signed, Bertram, supersede her wishes, and laws determine my procedures."

Josie turned to Bertram, but before she could speak, he lowered his head and said, "I can't lose her, Josie, I just can't. I need her."

Josie slumped back in her chair, diminished by a deep sadness. *She had no Misty to ride in the wind,* Josie mused. She thought of her unconscious attempts to fix her mother's life for her, of repeating the cycle, and of her efforts to avoid passing the inheritance on to Caitlin. *I can let go. . . . I can't take this journey for you, Mother, and you're not asking me to, but I hope you will be on your way soon.*

CHAPTER 18

Sometimes I feel like a motherless child
American spiritual

The little white light reminded Josie of Tinkerbell. It flitted beyond her reach in a sprightly dance, laughing, then spoke to her. The words were musical tones, not really words, but they were clear in meaning and intent, joyful.

"Don't worry about me, Honey. I'm having a wonderful time. Venice is so beautiful."

"Venice?" Josie asked the light. "Mother, how can you be in Venice? You're dead."

The Nora light zoomed high in the mist-filled sky, silhouettes of ancient buildings outlined below.

"No, My Darling, I'm free. I always wanted to see Venice. 'We're called gondolieri, But that's a vagary, It's quite honorary, The trade that we ply.'" The light continued singing snippets from Gilbert and Sullivan while performing a little jig atop St. Mark's Cathedral. 'We're happy as happy can be, tra la – With loving and laughing. . . .'"

Josie woke with a smile on her face and a lightness in her heart.

"Thank you, Mother," she murmured. "I needed that. You have a great time in Venice while we bury you today."

Josie lay in bed recalling the previous day's events. She had arisen early to rinse out and iron Nora's dress before delivering it to the funeral parlor. It was nice, Josie thought, that Bertram had let her choose. He had suggested the red paisley, but Josie picked the pale blue. She knew it was Nora's favorite.

Jack had been at the airport all morning waiting for each flight to land, and each sibling waited with Jack for the next, the group finally making its way to Bertram's just before noon. The men had immediately opened a bottle of Johnnie Walker and retired to the deck. Josie had been at Bertram's throughout the morning, and she met her sister with hugs, suggesting that the kitchen was a good place to hide out while Bertram finished his work with two clients; they were escalating because of Nora's death, he said. The sisters attempted to find refrigerator space for the growing offerings of food that friends and neighbors were delivering. Mattie realized that the various quarts of fresh fruits she had lugged to Kansas City in her carry-on were superfluous.

"I'm feeling a little like Father," Mattie confessed.

"What do you mean? I can't imagine how Father got here."

"No, I guess he would pass on this gathering. But once, after I had a wretched nightmare, he told me about one of his recurring dreams. He was a child, maybe four or five. The family was at a service of some kind — wedding, funeral, baptism. I didn't matter. The occasion changed with each dream, but he always had the same terrifying feeling that he didn't know where he was supposed to stand."

"I understand, Mattie. This is pretty much foreign territory for us. Let me tell you the plan. This afternoon we have a visitation, then a memorial service. Tomorrow morning we'll gather here again . . . ."

———

"The visitation went well," Josie thought to herself, "except for that teeny-bopper who greeted us in the foyer, thinking baby-talk was somehow soothing to adults in mourning. Wish she hadn't been blond; it gives us all a bad name."

340

Most everyone agreed that Nora looked beautiful, and no one mentioned that the stitches holding her lips closed were slightly visible.

"It's just a shell," Josie commented to Jack as they looked down at the body. An image of a hermit crab entered her mind. "Mother's grown out of her shell. I wonder where she is now."

The memorial service was scheduled at Unity on the Plaza immediately after the visitation — a tight schedule, but Peter insisted there was time for a drink before the service. He directed the group to a smart lounge near the church and ordered double martinis all around. "They won't start the ceremony without us," he said.

"I'm not so sure," Mattie mumbled. "Funny how insignificant a person can feel."

"I'm not prepared to take care of your insignificance right now, Mattie," Peter responded.

"Didn't ask you to."

Jack stifled the sibling squabble with a comment to Mattie that "this husband of yours is a pretty good old fart."

"I guess you're right, Jack. It takes one to know one."

Jack and Mattie would become friendly sparring partners over the next few days, but Mattie was, at this moment, silently fussing over Raymond, mentally touching, stroking, and soothing him. The only funeral he had attended was that of his parents and little sister, Sarah. He had gone to memorial services for astronauts killed at the Cape and for Grandpa R, but had declared all other funerals off limits. Now, here he was saying farewell to a mother-in-law he scarcely knew.

Jack turned to Peter and inquired about Melanie.

"Couldn't leave the dig," Peter replied. "We need to finish up."

Josie made a mental note that an ongoing excuse for whatever event you didn't want to attend could be very useful. To Mattie's delight, Bo announced that he and Gerald would be moving to San Francisco in the autumn, Bo still plugging away at healthcare policy issues and Gerald planning to establish a veterinary clinic in the East Bay and to work with the International Bird Rescue operation.

Peter added to the information pot that he and Melanie would be returning again to Berkeley within the year, stirring in Josie an image of a great western migration that would leave her stranded in the Midwest. Jack had agreed they could move to California — someday.

———

Bizarre" was a word Josie overheard several times, spoken quietly among her siblings after the service. Bertram had taken charge of the planning and began by singing "You Are the Love Light of My Life" while facing a portrait of Nora that was propped against a chair. One of her client's had painted it years before — in blues and purples — and it had sat in a closet since it was presented to the couple. Bertram had neglected to dust it off, and Josie noticed a spider crawling around on Nora's mouth. When Bertram invited all the mourners to say something about Nora, there were copious tears and what seemed to Josie like many hours that flowed as one client after the next described the intensity of their love for Nora. The words "generous, gentle, loving, life-saving, like a mother" began to merge into an image of Nora that was pleasing but not entirely familiar to the siblings, rather like the purple portrait that left out so many colors.

Josie wondered if Bo, Mattie, or Peter had planned to speak and had just given up; Mattie hoped that Peter's eyes were closed because he was seeking some solace, not because he was dozing. He sat up with a start

342

when Bertram began playing "Amazing Grace" on his accordion and brought the service to an end by inviting the siblings to join him at the front of the room where clients and friends could file past and give hugs to Nora's children. They lined up next to Bertram in birth order, joined hands, and spent twenty minutes trying to return the intended warmth offered by Bertram and Nora's "other children."

———

Josie was wondering who was most embarrassed, the huggers or the huggees, as she brought herself into the present, nudged Jack, and got out of bed. "Time to get up, Jack. Mattie and Bertram are picking up the ashes at ten. We need to get going."

"Am I still supposed to dig the hole?" Jack asked before he pulled the eiderdown over his head.

"Yep, you are. You offered, remember?"

"Do you remember what made me do that?"

"I guess it's because you're such a sweetheart. Come on, get up, get the shovel. I'll warm up the truck. We need to be there in twenty minutes."

"Why couldn't the guy who dug the hole for the dogwood dig the hole for the ashes?

"He said he's a nursery man, not a gravedigger."

"Well, I guess I'm Jack of all trades. Will you please add "gravedigger" to my resume? . . . You know that story you read me last week?

"*Pride and Prejudice?*"

"Yeah, that one. It was funny."

"Jane Austen isn't really known as a humorist, Jack. What do you mean?"

"Well, it's pretty funny how you never get to know who does the chores in her story, who hitches up the horses to the carriages, who cooks for all those parties, who cleans up afterwards. Things just happen."

"Well, they don't just happen around here. You make them happen, so don't think you can sweet-talk your way out of this chore."

When Jack and Josie arrived at Bertram's, Peter, Bo, and Raymond were on the deck, and Jack hurried to join the men who had reclaimed this comfortable territory where they could quietly toast Nora and move on to football scores and an animated discussion of America's 100th manned space mission. The shuttle *Atlantis* had successfully docked with the Russian space-station *Mir,* and there was a shared sense of pride and well-being among the men who talked quietly about the historic event. Their voices were low and controlled, each rather uncomfortably aware that joyful cheers were probably out of bounds at a burial service.

Josie headed for the kitchen where Mattie was organizing lunch and sipping a glass of white wine. "Oh, great idea, Mattie. Hand me a wine glass. Who else is here?"

"I haven't the faintest idea. I guess it's Bertram's brother who is still in the bathroom, but I'm not sure because we haven't been introduced because Bertram's in the music room with clients — a whole lot of them at once — and I have no idea who that Jamaican is, the one wearing a dashiki and sitting alone in the living room."

"Mattie, you're really upset, aren't you?"

"I guess I am, Josie. I was kind of hoping some part of this death-dance would be understandable to me, maybe even comforting. But I just keep getting confused. I guess I was expecting something like Grandpa R's funeral, and Father's. You know, where you go to a long service, then you go to the graveside, then you go home and figure out what it was all about. . . . Really sorry you couldn't get to Grandpa R's funeral. I think it kind of helps to do the dance, whatever it's about. Did I tell you Raymond and I drove up to see Felicite and her family a

344

few weeks ago? Wonderful time, huge family, lots of grandchildren for her. I don't know how many of them actually live in Grandpa R's old house, seems like a lot, but it was just super that Grandpa R left that house to her. Strange, I guess. Now, there's a story I imagine we'll never get to hear, all about Felicite and Father and Grandpa R. I wish they were here right now; maybe they could help me understand what's going on. But I guess you don't bring ghosts to a burial service, do you? What *do* you do?"

"Okay, Mattie, I understand. Let me help a little. The guy in the sarong — it's not really a dashiki — is an old friend of Mother and Bertram's. He's going to do the service, and then . . ."

"Josie, he's not going to do any service unless you and I find a way to hide the rum. It's only 11:00 a.m., and he's . . ."

"Okay, let's move on. Bertram is in with his clients because he says it's important for them to share their grief. He says it will help them let go."

"Maybe that works, Josie. I don't know. But doesn't it seem a little strange to you that we — her children — are excluded from the 'sharing' and 'letting go?'"

"Maybe. But we're not clients."

"Now, there's something to celebrate!" Mattie snapped, gulping down the rest of her wine and refilling her glass.

Josie began to giggle and soon drew Mattie into her arms and into the tiny circle of humor that inevitably creeps into solemn moments, the humor serving as the little brat-child messenger who may want to announce that the Emperor has no clothes.

"Okay, Josie. I'm better now. But I'm still not sure what to do."

"Just be yourself, Mattie."

345

"Don't think that's going to work. If I were going to just be myself, I'd let go with a major scream, you know, the kind that feels really good, but puts you in the spotlight where you don't want to be. I'd better go find Raymond and hide out for a while."

"I guess you got the ashes?" Josie asked.

"Yes, we did. They're still warm."

"Right. Top up my drink before you go, will you?"

—————

The back yard was overgrown with tall weeds. Bertram said a client had offered to cut them down, but the heavy rain the day before had prevented last-minute garden chores. The hole Jack had just dug already had a few inches of water in it, and rings of mud surrounded the hole and the ceremonial tree.

"I thought we were going to scatter the ashes," Mattie remarked.

"No, I might decide to move someday," Bertram replied. "I would want to take her with me."

The Jamaican minister in colorful attire did give a brief and understandable prayer, his accent helping Mattie focus on the words he spoke. *Words piled upon words,* she mused, *all in nice, sequential order, telling us how to think, how to hide from what we feel. . . . How do I feel? Angry. Lonely. Relieved. Abandoned. Sort of amused. Very, very sad.*

Mattie's inventory of emotions was interrupted when Peter placed the box of ashes in the soggy hole, and Bo took up the shovel and began scooping-up dollops of mud. Bertram interrupted to ask if he might do this last tending-to of Nora and proceeded to shovel in the heavy soil.

"Are you alright, Bertram?" Josie asked. She noticed copious amounts of sweat pouring down his face and neck. "Let someone help you."

"I want to do this. I want to take care of her."

Mattie was staring into the branches of the little dogwood, Raymond beside her; Peter and Bo were still focused on the soggy-soil tasks that Bertram had assumed; and Jack was holding Josie's hand as she watched Bertram clutch his chest and fall to the ground, eyes staring glassily at the overcast sky.

"Shit!" Josie muttered. "I hope you can all change your airline tickets."

———

Mattie's Bath

I can't stand it that you are buried in Kansas City, Mom. I guess I always thought you would come home one day, one day when you had lots of time and we could get acquainted. Maybe it just takes generations to get the mother thing right. . . . I'm doing okay. I will miss you in some peculiar way. I'm hoping I'll make it all the way to the millennium, then maybe I'll come looking for you. Maybe we could flop down in front of a wigwam some place in the cosmos and start the conversations that never were. Yes, that's a good plan. Enjoy your travels, Mom. . . . Kind of nice, I guess, that Bertram has joined you so quickly.

Josie's Bath

It's not going to happen to me. I'm not going to die in Kansas City. I want our ashes scattered in the redwoods or the ocean. But first I've got to get there, have some grow-old time with Jack in my beautiful California. Jack says he understands. Says we can go when he's sixty-two. Don't think he's ever seen a

347

real mountain, never a redwood tree, not even an ocean. So, you old darling, let's go for it!

———

What a good sleep I had." Mattie tightened the belt to her robe and eased into a chair in Josie's kitchen. "Who was that on the phone, Josie?"

"That was Bertram's brother. He's handled everything. We just have to appear; Jack's not digging another hole in the mud!"

Josie turned over a sizzling sausage and began peeling potatoes for what promised to be a hearty breakfast.

"There's so much light in your house, Josie. I love it. And you seem very much at home in this kitchen."

"Jack's a meat-and-potatoes man, Mattie. And I love it. I guess I just spent a lot of years cooking for the wrong man. Got it right this time, though. Got my Roy Rogers. . . . Dale Evans and Roy Rogers in Kansas City. It plays pretty well. No horses, no mountains, no guitars in the background, but it's a pretty good song he sings. Jack says our life together is a "beautiful thang." I *am* going to get him out of the Midwest, though, get him a California accent.

"Where are they, anyway, the men?"

"In the basement I think. Jack is showing Raymond something about a 200-amp box and circuit breakers. I think that's what he said. If there are more words that should go into the description, I have no idea what they are."

"Oh, Lord," Mattie giggled. "I hope he's got some drawings or something. Raymond does everything in his head. You should see the bookcases he built Great plan. A little askew when it was finished. What in the world is that horrible noise and why is it suddenly so grey in here?"

"That sound, Mattie, is a tornado alert. It's grey because God is blessing another funeral with a rainstorm."

"Well, okay. Let me get out some photos of Jessica, one and only granddaughter, queen of the universe."

"Great, Mattie. And as soon as I finish up these potatoes, I'll dig out some pictures of Caitlin's twins. They're amazing. She plans to come home in a couple of years — with twins . . . and a husband!"

Mattie was digging through her luggage for photos of David, Ginger, and Jessica, Sarah and Luis when a sudden, unidentifiable stillness settled into Josie and Jack's house, stillness and darkness, broken finally by raucous laughter and an announcement from the basement.

"We'll have to get some parts."

"Better get your coat, too, Mattie. I think we're eating out this morning. I don't think Raymond's got a handle on circuit breakers yet. Are you sure he's an engineer? Sent rockets to the moon? Well, maybe one of those men can navigate in a tornado. There's a breakfast place just up the street."

Relief at still being alive and delight in their adventure brought tears to the eyes of both men who headed out the front door tangled in a laughter-broken conversation about a dam in California, something Raymond wanted to show to Jack.

"I could really use your help, Jack."

CHAPTER 19

Under the heavens/we journey far,/on roads of life/we're the wanderers, So let love rise,/So let love depart,Let hope have a place in the lover's heart./Hope has a place in a lover's heart.

Roma Ryan lyrics/ Music by Enya
"Hope Has a Place"

"I'd like to play some solitaire when you're through, Josie. What are you doing, anyway?"

"Just browsing the Internet, Jack. I'd like to figure out what's going on with your body. Don't know why you're having so much trouble with your legs and your hands. You know, a person can still play solitaire without a computer. Did you forget how to shuffle? "

"It's just more fun on the screen. Doesn't tire out my hands so much."

" Here, you can have the computer. I'm through for a while, just as soon as this stuff prints."

Jack slid into the warm chair and clicked on the icon of his favorite game while Josie poured over the information she had just printed. Jack was immediately engaged with the mouse, the colorful screen, and the pleasing noises the computer made when he won a solitaire hand. He didn't notice at all that Josie's hands were shaking, her face ashen.

Over 5,000 Americans are diagnosed with Amyotrophic Lateral Sclerosis (ATS) disease each year. There is great variation in the course of the disease frequently called Lou Gehrig's disease. Symptoms usually appear in individuals between the ages of 40 and 70. Survival is, on average, two to five years, although progression varies with each individual. One early symptom is generalized fatigue. Often symptoms begin in the legs, or feet, then

351

travel inward toward the center of the body. With all voluntary muscle action affected, ALS patients in the later stages lose their ability to speak and eventually are totally paralyzed. Through it all, their minds remain unaffected.

Josie's Bath

Jack, how could you? It was so close, our time to softly ease into the last part of our lives together. . . . I should have paid more attention. I knew you were stressed, knew you were losing your energy, but I put it down to the aging we are sharing. You said you must have just pulled a muscle. Why didn't you tell me, didn't you know? Men never know! They depend on us to tell them, and when we do, they poo poo it all, want to tough it out like Superman. . . . Poo poo it. Reminds me of Mother. Mattie, Peter, Bo, and I would stay out in the evening playing kick-the-can until we heard Mother calling "poo ooo." It was poo ooo at first, but after awhile it got to be poooo ooooo and then pooooo ooooooo when we took too long coming. We hardly went beyond the pooooooo ooooooo part because that meant she would send Father after us. Mother never called for us by name. It was never Maaaatie or Joosiiiiiie or Peeeeter, or Booooo. When we got older, I think she tried, but never really got it. Mattie and I were both "Sissy." Wonder if that was what her mother called her, sort of a universal word for "other female?" I stopped correcting her when she got to be about eighty. . . . Jack, you're only fifty-eight. We did finish the house, you know that. When we built the arbor in the back, we knew it was finished. Two long years it took. Two long years of sheet rocking, wiring, roofing. And we did it all ourselves. I remember the picture of me covered in plaster dust. I remember holding the sheet rock with my head while

352

you screwed it to the ceiling. It was so heavy. Remember the time you hitched a rope to me so I wouldn't fall off the roof? Well, Jack, I don't want to fall off this roof. Maybe you better get another long rope, tie it real tight, and hold on. We'll get through this.

The following weeks for Josie and Jack had a surreal cast – thick, gummy, impenetrable, as they gathered information and did the medical rituals leading to diagnosis and prognosis.

"Not sure I can handle another 'osis, Josie. Maybe we just need to decide some things."

"Great, Jack, I've become an expert on deciding things. Here's the plan. . . ."
The decision was swift, easy, and just right; the burdens of selling the house and packing up were shouldered with ease and with immense excitement. Sorrow would just have to wait its turn.

"Come on, Jack, let's go. The van left half an hour ago. What are you doing?"

"Just one last look around, Honey. I'm collecting a few things."

"Everything the van didn't take is in our pick-up, Jack. What are you collecting?"

"Memories, Josie. There's so much of us here, so many things I don't want to forget."

"I know, Sweetheart, I know. But we have the photos, boxes of them. I think we took a picture every time we added a screw. Wasn't it great, Jack? Wasn't it just great?"

"Yeh, Josie, it was, and the next part will be great, too."

"Do you feel up to driving? I'd rather you did until we get out of the city."

Josie and Jack sat quietly for a few minutes in the crowded cab of their 1991 Chevy pickup, Jack behind the wheel and Josie with the map on her lap.

"Hit the road, Jack, and don't come back, come back, come back," Josie sang as she nudged Jack's shoulder. "Let's hit it."

Jack and Josie traveled north on 29 and picked up 80 West. Josie had been quiet for a while staring out the window.

"When are we going to get there, Jack?"

"God, Josie, we've barely started. Get where?"

"Somewhere." There's nothing to see."

"Are you going to complain all the way?"

"Probably," Josie answered. "Probably I am until you find me something to look at."

"Well, Wyoming will be nice."

"Oh, God, Jack, Wyoming is after Nebraska. It'll take forever."

"We have forever, Honey, let's make each day forever."

———

"Wake up, Jack, wake up," Josie insisted as she shook the large lump on the bed that was Jack. "The TV says there's a storm moving in. I think we should try to get ahead of it."

"What time is it, where are we? Why are you up?"

"It's four-thirty, we're in Laramie. Motel 6, remember? I couldn't sleep."

"Four-thirty in the morning?"

"Jack, we need to get through the pass ahead of the storm. Shower, get dressed. I'll drive."

Josie hadn't been driving long when she realized the sun was going to be late in delivering its morning messages of good luck and good cheer. The couple had

354

agreed to skip even their morning coffee, to hurry along and enjoy a late morning breakfast once they had dodged the storm.

"Christ, is that snow?

"I don't know, Josie, it's so dark. Could be a little sleet mixed with the rain."

"Well, it's getting worse, Jack. I can barely see the road," Josie's knuckles were white from her grip on the wheel.

"Just take it easy. Keep your eyes on the line."

"I can barely see the line, Jack. What are we going to do?"

"Just keep going, I guess, not much else we can do. If we stop we'll probably get rear-ended. There's no shoulder, really."

"How do you know there's no shoulder, Jack. I can't see anything!" Josie bellowed as a semi passed and cut in front of them, churning and tossing snow and mud onto the windshield.

"We're going to die, Jack . . . . 'This'll be the day that we die'. . . . Do you remember that song? Caitlin used to sing it. I hope she still sings. I wanted to see her again before I died. And Gareth, I need to see Gareth. You said I'd like Wyoming, Jack, you said so."

"You're getting hysterical. Stop it, settle down. Supposing we did die. There are worse ways, you know. Remember that Abby book, *Desert Solitaire*? Remember the part about being eaten by a bear? Wouldn't you rather die in the mountains of Wyoming than get knifed by a mugger?"

"Okay, okay, you're right. No muggers here. We're in a white out, and we're going to drive off into a canyon, but we're together, an we've had the greatest time."

"Breaker, breaker," squawked a voice from the CB. Josie had suggested they get a cell phone, but Jack insisted they weren't reliable in the mountains and were great accident causers. He had installed an old CB from years ago when he drove a trouble-truck for the electric company.

"Breaker, breaker, red pickup west on 80, y'all copy?"

"That has to be us, Jack. Answer! Answer!"

Jack reached for the hand set and responded. "This is Wire Nut between Laramie and Rawlins. Come back."

"This be Soul Man. You folks look like you're in a shit pile of trouble. Come on back."

"Trouble! Tell him we're going to die, Jack. Tell him to get in touch with my kids."

"Hush, Josie, just drive."

"Hey, Soul Man, trouble's a pretty mild word. We can't see shit. My seat cover is losing it, and she's driving. Come back."

"Hell, you are in trouble. Tell her to tuck in on my trailer. This is my regular run, and I'll get ya through. Tell her to gentle down on the pedal. Don't want y'all up my ass. Come on back."

"Ten Four, Soul Man, give us a safe ride. Come back."

"I'll get ya there, and y'all can buy a cuppa Joe at the truck stop. Come on back."

"Ten four. Wire Nut out."

The knight in shining armor who had guided Josie through her nightmare jumped down from the cab of his truck, stuck out his hand to Jack, and turned to Josie with a bow that required a peculiar shuffling of feet and adjusting of the suspenders that held his Levis.

"That was some job you did, Pretty Lady, and now you can buy me that coffee. Best pie here in 500 miles."

356

Soul Man – Ronnie – was about 5'8", just a little taller than Josie, and she guessed he must be carrying several hundred pounds. His dark, hairy arms were about as big around as his legs, and he walked with what Josie could only call a rooster strut. He and Jack were into tall tales of the road before the pie was delivered to their table, and Josie leaned back in the vinyl-covered booth, hoping the adrenaline flow in her system would soon turn off and allow some space for the lemon meringue. She sat quietly as she imagined "Pretty Lady" ought to, adjusted her brain to what seemed amazingly crude language – from both men – and finally began to enjoy the flow of man-talk.

They're taking care of each other, aren't they? They're huffing and puffing, chewing and spitting – spitting out stories that will bind them together in memory. Well, huffing and puffing aren't really so different than hugging and patting, are they?

When the too-many cups of coffee were finally drunk and the pies were settling into lumpy sensations in the stomachs, the company parted because Soul Man Ronnie said he would be headed south at the next junction.

"Now Pretty Lady, y'all just point that rig o' yours due west. Stop when you get to the Pacific Ocean. You folks don't seem to me much like Ber-zerk-ly people, but there's one thing I've learned in this life: It takes all kinds."

"Pie, pie, me oh my, I like pie," Josie sang as she eased back into the driver's seat and Jack began repeating some of the stories Soul Man had told.

"What was it he said to you, just as he was leaving?" Josie interrupted. "I didn't get it."

"Oh, he was just wishing us good luck."

"I know that, Jack, but I didn't understand a word he said. Something about a shiny blue dot?"

"Not quite, Josie. He said 'keep the shiny side up and the rubber side down, and may the blue dot never shine upon you.' Don't worry about it, Josie. It's a man thing, and it's pretty good advice. Let's go to California, Pretty Lady. Stop at the Pacific Ocean."

———

The north side of the Berkeley campus was nearly unknown territory for Josie, but it didn't matter. The smells were familiar; the eucalyptus and redwood trees were as old friends; the busy bookstores and restaurants inviting, as students and faculty brushed shoulders on their way to bright tomorrows. The house was small by Berkeley standards, but charming and beautifully landscaped with rhododendrons, azaleas, and fuchsias along with their many friends and relations that thrived in the moisture-laden Bay Area. Small-leafed ground covers crept along the walkway, reaching out here and there to explore new territory, to take in the morning sun and produce a pleasing array of tiny blossoms that spoke to Josie of contentment. "I'll take it," Josie said, as soon as the agent stepped onto the tiny sun-lit patio and opened her arms to a vast view of the bay with San Francisco winking in the distance.

The house was a rental and well beyond the terms Josie was comfortable with, but her future had become her present. No more long-range planning, no more worries about having a comfortable retirement nest egg. The nest egg was for now, right now. She was able to negotiate a year-long lease, certain she had a year, perhaps two or three before she would have to become more frugal.

Jack did see the redwoods – all three varieties in the Botanical Gardens above the campus and the graceful coast redwoods in Muir Woods just across the bay. And he saw the grey whales who were making their annual southward migration to Scammons Lagoon. And he saw Yosemite, more breathtaking than he had ever dreamed. And the couple got to Lake Tahoe, threw snow balls at each other and sat for long hours beside the lake, bundled against the cold and exhilarated. By the time Jack's illness dictated that they settle into their nest on the side of the Berkeley hills, the couple had grand tales of adventure to share with family members who dropped by to lend a hand and share good spirit. David frequently came by in the evening, dropping off treats that Ginger and Jessica had concocted. Weekends often brought Mattie and Raymond out of the Sierra and back to Mattie's Athens of the West. Gerald's veterinary clinic was actually within a short drive or a long walk of Josie and Jack's home. Gerald had gracefully eased into family concerns, offering Jack amusing stories about his four-footed clients. Saturdays were especially nice for Josie because many of the men in her family — Bo, Gerald, David, and now Peter — would get together for football games in Memorial Stadium, easily spanning the generation gaps that might have arisen in any other arena, and making a stop at Josie and Jack's for post-game replays. Jack was one of the few men Josie knew who had escaped the football rites of passage, but he eagerly awaited the gatherings, the hot-buttered rum, and tasty treats that Josie stirred up for the occasion.

Jack had good days and bad days. Josie encouraged him to walk about the neighborhood as much as possible, and she stopped preparing healthful dinners that he seldom touched. Back to meat and potatoes, which he loved. She tucked in a few fresh fruits and vegetables and tucked away her anxieties whenever Jack announced he was going for a little walk. She would offer a cheerful farewell as she swept momentary worries out the door along with household dust

"The rain has stopped, Josie. I won't be long. Just a little errand."

But it was clearly not just a little errand. Jack had been gone for nearly two hours, and Josie was reaching for the phone to get help when she caught sight of him working his way toward the front door. He was clumsy and slow, but bright-eyed and smiling. He hugged his coat tightly around him, and Josie hurried to the door with a common blend of irritation and relief.

"Where have you been for so long, Jack?"

"I walked over to Gerald's clinic, Josie. I'm a little tired, but we had fun, and I have a question for you. How would you like a cha-hooa-hooa?"

"Is that something to eat, Jack? It's not like you to try new foods. What's a cha-hooa-hooa?

"You know, one of those little dogs that shivers and barks all the time."

"Oh, you mean 'Chihuahua.' Those aren't really dogs, Jack; they're something else. But in any case, we aren't allowed to have a dog here."

"That's why I got you a cha-hooa-hooa. They don't really count as dogs." Jack reached into the depths of his thick jacket and removed a shivering, nearly hairless creature who snapped at Josie and licked Jack's hands.

"Her name is Angle," Jack said, as he presented the would-be dog to Josie.

"Angle?" What kind of a name is that?"

"I meant to call her 'Angel,' but my hand's not working so well, so I wrote 'Angle' on the adoption form. Gerald said Angle was a good name. You can call her whatever you want. I just wanted to get you a present."

Throughout the spring and summer, days were filled with many presents — blossoms collected from Jack's neighborhood walks, pictures torn from magazines

360

he studied, sometimes a seashell from his treasure collection in the basement.

"I love the gifts you give me now," Josie exclaimed as she rubbed the tiny piece of jade Jack had brought home from Big Sur several months earlier.

"What do you mean, *now?* I've always given you gifts, lots of them."

"Do you remember the chain saw for my birthday and the sander for Christmas?"

"Well, do you remember the duvet cover and pillow shams you gave me for Valentine's Day?

"We had such fun, didn't we, Love?"

"Yes, but I wish I could give you the pictures in my head, Josie."

"What do you mean?"

"You know, the images that stay in your brain, like Half Dome at Yosemite, like you and Angle sorting out territory, like you and me walking around the block, all those pictures that make life so fine."

———

"Brenda, you are more beautiful than ever," Mattie shrieked as she opened Josie's front door to her old friend.

Brenda *was* beautiful. By any measure, her tall, gracious elegance cast a spell about her and captured the attention of all who were in her presence. The spiffy Afro haircut had been replaced years ago by a casual, shoulder-length cut that, though grey with age, defied the signs of ageing. There was, though, a stiffness in her manner, Mattie
noticed, not developed as a barrier to friends, but as a buffer against the bruises that a life in politics inevitably delivers.

Mattie quickly got caught up on family history. Yes, Willy had served on the council and then served as mayor for eight years. By the time James and Lucia were gone from the nest, the couple had investigated other political arenas, but had finally settled into a pleasing, though often hectic, lifestyle, Willy going back into a law practice that thrived under his direction, Brenda serving as a mover and shaker in urban renewal projects.

"It isn't without its stresses, Mattie, but I'm glad to be out of the limelight. You look just as I wanted you to look, kind of a casual earth-mother, California style."

"Well," Mattie said, "plenty of soil under this earth mother's fingernails. Raymond never lets up. One more garden plot, just one more. It's fine and it's fun as long as we have the energy for it."

"I always admired your energy, Mattie. Raymond's a beautiful person, isn't he?"

"Yes, he is. I think we were all blessed by the gods when we did the mating dance. Josie practiced a lot before she got it right. I used to tell her, when we were kids, practice makes perfect."

"You're right, we've been lucky. Willie has mellowed out a bit, more of a guardian now, less a warrior. . . . You know, we frequently run into David and his family. We seem to share restaurant tastes. I always remind him I used to change his diapers. Jessica loves it when he blushes."

"I always thought you would tame Willy a bit, Brenda. I always admired your soul. . . . And where is my precious James?"

Josie joined her friend and her sister with a stack of photos from England, images of Gareth and of Caitlin's family.

When Mattie hesitated over a studio shot of James' daughter, Brenda quickly said, "Yes, Mattie, Matilda is a little on the creamy side. James married a white woman. I don't think he really ever got over his crush on you. I'm glad he didn't. They have their troubles, but they do well together."

Troubles, Josie thought. *I never told Mattie about Caitlin and James, about the baby they never had. I don't know if I have to tell her, or Brenda. . . . No, I don't think so. I think I mourned for each of us. That's enough for now. I hope Caitlin has forgiven herself. I hope she comes home soon.*

———

It didn't matter to Jack what story Raymond read to him. It didn't matter that they never got around to blowing up a dam on the American River. It didn't matter that Raymond's failing eyesight slowed down the story-reading. It mattered only that there was love and laughter in the hours the two men spent together, and there was some relief for Josie whose spirit never sagged but whose body knew the aches and pains of tending to a bed-bound loved one. Jack and Raymond watched *Lonesome Dove* so often they soon had memorized the lines and carried on the dialogue long after the video stopped running. When Raymond brought news that John Glenn would soon make another voyage into space, Jack asked questions and became interested in how space shuttles might work. Raymond described the old, cramped Mercury capsule that had one instrument panel and just thirty-six cubic feet of habitable space and compared it to the 2325-cubic-foot shuttle with its nine workstations. Raymond bought a model-kit of the shuttle, and the two men spent hours together assembling the parts and discussing technical questions. With Jack's dexterity nearly gone and Raymond's eyesight failing, the process was clumsy, slow, and immensely pleasing. They had agreed it would be more fun if they destroyed the instruction sheets, and when the model was finally finished, they agreed it was "a beautiful thang."

Josie finished the sponge bath and struggled to turn Jack to his stomach so she could rub his back and legs with the pleasing skin cream the hospice aide had recommended for bed sores. She had read the questions in his eyes and didn't wait for him to struggle with words that were more and more difficult to utter.

"I don't even want to talk about it, Jack. There's no way I'm going to let you die in a nursing home. People have been dying in their own beds, in their own homes, for thousands of years. Besides, they wouldn't allow Angle to sleep with you. . . . Jack, I know you are worried for me. But I'm fine. There's lots of help from everyone, and Caitlin and Ben will be here soon with the twins. Don't forget, Gareth is coming, too; he'll be a lot of help. So just drop the subject, okay? Here, Angle wants to snug next to you. She hates me, you know. She's a very peculiar gift, Jack."

Josie's Bath

> Angle barked and told me you were gone. You slipped so gently away in the night, leaving me the early morning sun. . . . Another lovely gift, Jack. Thank you. I will miss you. I will miss you so hard! But, Jack, I will be fine because you made me fine. I was always fine in your eyes. Always will be. . . . Jack, please forgive me, but after they come for you, I'm going out on the deck to scream into the cosmos; then I'm going to cry for a lot of days; then, in time, I will find a way to step into the future with you in my heart but not beside me.

Josie dressed slowly, putting on the outfit she knew was Jack's favorite, brushed her hair, and returned to the bedroom to sit with Jack a while longer. Angle was curled up on Jack's chest and with ears back, teeth bared, she growled at Josie.

"Come on, little thing, it's time to let go. We sang a lovely melody, the three of us together, but now the song is over."

As Josie held Jack's hand for the last time and gazed at his peaceful face, she softly sang a few lines from a song she remembered. "Be brave beloved, believe me when I say, we'll dream again and kiss again someday."

There was to be no funeral. Jack and Josie had made the decision to donate their bodies to the University of California at Davis. They were informed that after serving science, their bodies would be cremated and the ashes taken three miles off the coast of San Francisco and committed to the sea. "We can swim with the dolphins forever," Jack had said.

———

"Mom, I'm home!" Caitlin called as she deposited one twin after the other over the threshold of Josie's house.

Springtime had arrived in Berkeley just in time for Gareth's visit and the homecoming for Caitlin and her family. Josie had cleaned and dusted and cooked and fussed throughout the morning, eagerly and often peeking out the kitchen window to watch for the airport taxi. Leaving the front door open to the fresh air and her children, she had raced to the basement for a jar of Mattie's spiced peaches. By the time she emerged from the basement, her family was home.

Angle dealt with the intrusion into her world with proper shivers and barks, finally retreating to the bedroom with twin babies in hot pursuit. A moment of stillness crept into the sunlit hallway as a rich blend of recognition, acceptance, and joy bundled and tangled themselves together before giving way to tears of delight. "Where do we start?" Josie asked.

The twins took charge of determining a starting place by announcing they needed to pee, get a drink, have lunch, pull the dog from under the bed, and find their precious treasures among the stacks of luggage. Ben took charge of many of the children's needs while Caitlin, Gareth, and Josie began to investigate the boundaries of homecoming, the width and depth of sadness about lost years, the height of joy in being united again.

By the end of a delicious evening meal, the dances of hesitation had begun to wear themselves out, and the family settled in for dessert and a long evening of catch-up.

"And your cousin David is eager to get together. His Jessica is so like Mattie was as a girl, at least as I remember her. . . . Bo and Gerald have some theater tickets for you, *Phantom of the Opera*, I think, and Peter says he'll attend "any party in town." And of course, Raymond and Mattie want you to visit them in the mountains. I spent a week with them shortly after Jack's death . . . . How sorry I am you never met Jack. He was my Roy Rogers. I'll tell you about Roy Rogers, and anything else you want to know."

"I'm eager to tell you about my work, Mother," Gareth said, as he reached for a second piece of cake.

Josie hesitated only an instant and then happily responded, "Of course you are, Gareth. You are, after all, Peter's nephew. You will enjoy Peter, I think, and you will understand each other well."

———

Mattie's Bath

What a wonderful gathering – a beautiful tapestry, so many threads. Some so vibrant, some quiet and peaceful, some coarse and strong, some thin and

366

bright. How wonderful to see the cousins getting reacquainted, David and Caitlin, and wonderful to see Jessica meeting one cousin, aunt, uncle after another, weaving them in and out of her mind into something called family. . . . Nice of Ginger to help Caitlin and Ben apartment-hunt. The Bay Area's so unaffordable. . . .They'll manage, just as Josie and I managed. . . Gareth! I finally met Gareth. So like Bo. Better not do that, Mattie. Everyone likes to be himself. Gareth, so beautiful, and so forgiving! . . . I know he must have felt abandoned. So did Caitlin, I suppose, in some way. Certainly Josie did. Sarah? David? Bo? Peter? Me? Probably. For me, maybe just never connected with Mom. Can't be abandoned if you've never connected. . . . Come on, Mattie, you felt abandoned. Right?. . . Right. Maybe we all feel that way. Maybe you have to feel abandoned so you can go find yourself. Josie got that figured out. I know she will accept Gareth's return to England. She knows about journeys that have to be made.

CHAPTER 20

All my relations speak to my soul
Reggie and Kim Harris

It was fate that brought a solution to Caitlin and Ben's frustrating search for housing in the Bay Area. They had been with Josie for several months, having joined her in warm, fuzzy farewells to Gareth and having, each day, set out to search the hills and the flatlands for a place to live. There were no more little apartments or cozy cottages as there had been in Caitlin's childhood; they existed, some of them in the same place, some of them the same structures, but now the costs limited access to an elite few who had somehow successfully launched themselves into the race toward affluence. Caitlin figured that one month's rent for a tiny, cozy, sunlit cottage was twice what Ben might be able to make in two months as a nurseryman with few credentials, no introductions, and a British accent. Mathematics had never been Caitlin's calling, but she could visualize her family walking backwards, blindfolded, into an economic tar pit.

Transportation, too, presented difficulties as Ben set out to find employment, determined to stick with the work he loved. Josie frequently loaned her car and loaned her energy to the many tasks the couple needed to accomplish, but Caitlin hungered for the buses of old, the ones with the friendly drivers who might give a hand to a young mother struggling to get aboard with two children and their gear. The buses now, and the rapid transit system, were perhaps more colorful, even more efficient, but they no longer beckoned to Caitlin about excitement and adventure. They provided transportation; she would need to provide the rest.

369

"Just relax a bit, Cait," Josie would say. "Settle in with me for a while, give yourself time. I got an extension on the lease, so things are fine."

"I *am* settled in with you, Mom. But it's crowded. Ben and I need some privacy, and the twins wake you at night, make you nervous. And I need my own space."

"I understand that, Caitlin. But space rhymes with grace, and you could practice a bit of that."

"I wish you wouldn't correct me so much, Mom. You never spoke to Gareth like that."

Josie wondered if the sorrow in her heart would find its way into her voice when she tried to answer Caitlin. "Cait, I can't undo the past. I do understand that Gareth is not connected to me in the way you are. Gareth has returned to his home, as he must. But you are in *your* home now, connected to me in ways you may one day understand. Until you do, maybe we should just be celebrating our connections, not arguing about them."

These were not truly arguments between mother and daughter; they were shared expressions of fatigue and frustration, and Josie was determined to prevent another rift with her daughter. "We'll find a good path," Josie concluded, and she reached for the phone. "That can't be Mattie. She never calls in the afternoon."

Mattie's directions were simple: "Come quickly. David will pick you up if you don't want to drive."

Josie knew she could follow those directions from her sister; she wasn't so sure she could handle the rest.

"Caitlin, I need to be away for a while, maybe quite a while. And I need to tell you some terrible news."

Mattie's Bath

Never, never, never will I forgive you, Raymond. I'll put this lumpy old body into the tub one more night.

370

Alone. I may even get out of the tub, may even wake up tomorrow. Never, never will I forgive you . . . out in the rain, wiring the greenhouse. Seventy years old, wiring the greenhouse in the rain! In the rain . . . your beautiful old body lying there in a mud puddle. I prayed you weren't dead. I prayed because I love you so much, need you so badly. Never! . . . We danced such a beautiful dance, you and I. I will try to forgive you, I will pretend, but it won't happen. . . . Raymond, I meant to tell you about this thing nibbling away at my stomach. I meant to tell you, and then you wouldn't have been wiring the greenhouse in the rain, lying dead in a mud puddle. . . . Josie, just don't let them put me in one of those terminal homes with nasty green walls. Just bury this body before it's cold. About a year, he said. The cozy, sitting-on-the-right-hand-of-God doctor said, "about a year." What the hell am I going to do with a year? A year without Raymond? I'm ready right now for "happily ever after," and Raymond, you'd damn well better be there waiting for me. You gave me a good life! How about a good death, too? Be there!

———

Josie's Bath

Leaving for Mattie's again after my bath. I always seem to be going back to Mattie's, but this is the last time I expect. I'll stay and take care of her as long as it takes. She'll tell me she can do it on her own, but I won't hear her. We'll bury Raymond, and then I'll just stay for a few days, then a few more, and pretty soon the days will be all gone. She'll want to can everything in sight before she goes, and I'll help her I guess. I don't know what else I can do for her. I'll serve it all when the family comes. . . . I don't want Mattie's Mason jars after she's gone. . . . She'll want to leave the garden just right, and I can help with that, too. She's so worried about how David and Sarah will handle another parent's death. I hope she chooses the late spring or early summer when it isn't raining. I can't bury Mattie in the rain. I'll bundle her up and put her in the bed until the sun comes out; it'll be a Woodrow and Gus thing. . . . How many times have I watched those tapes. I wonder? Jack loved them so, he would mouth the words practically clear through, and I don't really know if he was Gus or Woodrow, a bit of each one I think. So was Raymond. Just like him to be playing with electricity out in the rain. He and Jack would do stupid things like that especially when they were together. Then they'd laugh about their near-death experiences while Mattie and I shook our heads in disgust. They were so alike those two and so much like granddad and his brothers. It's no wonder Mattie and I invited them into our lives. Such good old souls, the old fools! . . . It's better Raymond went first, he wouldn't be able to let Mattie go. Mattie and I can laugh about those times, the things they did! We can look at the pictures, too. Mattie and I take such awful pictures, and we'll have a ceremony and burn them so nobody will ever see them. No, I'll keep the best few, the one's Mattie will say aren't too bad.

———

Accommodating in her death as she had been in her life, Mattie met her sister's wishes. Late in the spring of the millennium, David and Ginger and Mattie's only grandchild, Jessica, drove up from the Berkeley for a weekend visit. Sarah called on Sunday evening as she so often did, and once calls were answered, small gifts were distributed, and the young family was gone, Mattie remembered the old box at the back of her closet.

"Josie, you must remember to get those things to Caitlin."

"What things?" Josie asked.

"Oh, you know, the treasures we collected. They must go to Caitlin."

Mattie pointed to the bedroom closet where several generations of daddy-long-legs were enjoying her neglect, and Josie managed to pull out the tired, old cardboard carton that Mattie was calling a treasure box. She had actually painted tiny flowers on the sides and decorated the top surface with what was meant to be a fairy.

"Oh, Josie, that was before I could draw anything. David used to laugh so at my art, but, you know, now he buys me paints and brushes and canvas and things. He knows I can't paint anymore, but he still brings all the supplies. Maybe we could give those things to Jessica and the twins."

Josie felt a wave of exhaustion as she contemplated the task of finding a suitable home for "those things," and she feared that the contents of the box might simply add weight to the already sorrowful mission. "Let's see what's in the box."

Three of Josie's wedding rings sat comfortably atop a stiff-starched linen table cloth – a gift to Josie from Howard's grandmother that spoke of times past, "when women knew about womanly virtues – how to iron until their backs broke," Josie laughed. 'Did you iron this, Mattie. I know I left it with you in a wrinkled heap when I went to England."

"Only once, Josie. So I could put it away forever. I guess forever is a lot shorter than we imagine."

Josie put the three wedding rings onto her little finger and lifted the old table cloth from the box to reach the next treasure – a ragged leather cat collar. "How long did he live, Mattie?"

"Seventeen years. Nemesis was a scruffy old thing when he finally said goodbye – one spring morning."

"I'm glad he's buried here, Mattie."

"Yes, he loved it here. Never did catch a bluejay, but he gave it his best shot, day after day."

Josie wound the collar around her wrist and reached into the treasure box for what looked like a brand new pair of Levi 501s.

"Are these Raymond's?" she asked.

"Oh, Lord, no. Raymond was never that thin. Well, maybe at the Cape when I first met him. But I fattened him up as soon as I could. So nice to snug next to an ample man."

Josie was eager to hurry past reminiscences of Raymond that had filled so many hours of the past months.

"How we miss him, don't we, Mattie. Please tell me about these Levis."

"Well, of course I miss him. More than I can ever tell. And I miss me, Josie. He took so much of me with him, the part I liked the most. . . . Josie, surely you remember the Levis. Those belonged to Robert. You stole them with a vengeance. I read recently that he had gone to Washington. You know he worked in state government for a lot of years. I saw his name from time to time, saw him on TV one night. But now he's somewhere in the Clinton administration, some kind of an advisor."

When Josie finally remembered who Robert was, she burst into laughter and offered, "Well, I assure you he's not advising Clinton on zipper control. Robert was one of those primitive men driven only by hormones. Just two modes – fuck it or kill it. . . . It would be kind of fun to play dress-up again, wouldn't it, Mattie? Robert was so stunned when we arrived in court looking like Barbie dolls, but, you know, it was his idea to present me as a seductress. Said the judge would understand right away."

"Well, here's just the thing," Mattie giggled as she drew a firm, black satin object from the box.

"Black Mariah! You kept her all these years. How did we ever sit down?"

"I didn't," Mattie responded, "I just perched on edge of chairs, hoping I could get enough air in my lungs to survive whatever the event, found lots of excuses to get up and saunter around. I wore her once to the Curran Theater – three and a half hours, and I can't remember the play."

"Do you remember these, Mattie?"   Josie removed a few tarnished trinkets from the bottom of the box – a little lapel pin that said "War is not healthy for children and other living things" and a hand-carved peace symbol attached to a leather thong.

"Oooh, Josie! James gave me those. When he was only seven. James Darcy, my beautiful little friend. He must be a wonder by now. . . . Don't know why I managed to get black men so thoroughly imbedded in my libido. I probably never told you, Josie, but when Raymond was in Florida so long, I used to invite a few black men into my imaginary bed. Ron Dellums and Jesse Jackson, even Martin Luther King, Jr. I only invited the really important men of our times, and not all of them, certainly not all at once. Do you think that's somehow terrible, Josie?"

"Terrible? How could you ever be terrible, Mattie? You've always had good taste. Besides, we don't get to decide who the imaginary visitors are. They just arrive. Tom Hanks still joins me from time to time, but it's normally Luciano Pavarotti who keeps me warm, Mattie. And I know I often had to boot Sharon Stone out of bed before I could make love with Jack. Besides, we're liberated now. Remember?"

"Liberated" had a soothing sound to Mattie, but as the sisters' laughter blessed the spirit, it nevertheless strained the body, and Mattie was quick to suggest that she and Josie end the evening by reading stories together.

Her suggestion was, in fact, a request that Josie read to her; Mattie's strength was ebbing rapidly, and the sisters had taken to having brief bedtime stories right after Mattie had taken the sedatives that were intended to ease her sleep.

"Mattie, what are these books you keep under the bed?"

"Oh, they're not exactly books, they are more like guardians and guides."

"What do you mean?"

"You know, Father did the same thing, always had some books under the bed that never made it back to the bookshelf. I remember that's where the dictionary could be found, under the bed. And Hemingway, he always kept something of Hemingway's under the bed. And an Atlas, and I remember a Bertram Russell book. Something about happiness. *The Conquest of Happiness*, that's it.

"Well, that's silly, Mattie. What good do these books do collecting dust under the bed? . . . Well, okay, I remember keeping Robert Frost poems beside my bed in Hood River, and the photo album of my kids. It was important to me to have them in just the right order, Frost kind of holding up the album."

Mattie smoothed the sleeve of her white flannel nightgown and brushed away a strand of unruly silver hair. "It doesn't matter, does it Josie, if things are silly? It just feels good to have help at your fingertips."

"Help?" Josie asked. "Let me see what these books are."

Josie got on her hands and knees and stretched hard to gather up the "guardians" Mattie had stored beneath the bed.

"*Emily Post Book of Etiquette?*" Josie shrieked. "You mean Emily Post is a guardian for you?"

"Well, Josie, you remember how mother was always so afraid we wouldn't do things just right? She bought me that book when I went to college. I've never used it, but it's reassuring to have old Emily on my team."

Josie giggled and pulled out another dusty book. "The *Bible?* What is this? Some kind of insurance plan? If all else fails, try religion?"

"Oh, Josie, that one makes me feel bad. Grandmother R gave me that *Bible,* told me I was supposed to keep a family record. You, know, in that center part where you put births, deaths, and things? Guess I haven't been much of a family record-keeper. Maybe she'll forgive me?"

"You told a lot of stories, Mattie. It's all the same. Okay, what about this?"

"*Memories, Dreams, and Reflections.* That's Carl Jung. I paint better after reading him — used to paint, that is. He sort of gives permission for unusual images. You know how sometimes surreal is more real than anything else that's going on?"

"I guess I do, Mattie. Tell me what you'd like to hear tonight."

"Oh, I'd love to hear the Grey Havens chapter at the end of *The Lord of the Rings.* It's so wonderfully bitter-sweet; the best ending of all the books I've read. . . . David loved Tolkien's books so! He asked Raymond to read them over and over; he could recite the scene verbatim where Gandalf fights the nasty balrog. And I love the Grey Havens chapter. Let me see if I can tell it: 'And the ship went out into the High Sea and passed on into the West'. Yes, that's it, Frodo and Bilbo are on

377

board, Elrond and Galadriel, even Gandalf. 'Frodo smelled a sweet fragrance . . . the grey rain-curtain turned all to silver glass and was rolled back, and he beheld white shores and beyond them a far green country under a swift sunrise.' I would love to hear you read that part, Josie."

"Fine. I'll get your pain pills; the book is right here beside your bed. I'll climb in next to you in a minute."

"Oh, I won't need the pills tonight, Josie. Let's just have stories. You can get the cats to sleep with us if you want to."

"Would you like to wear perfume? I'll get some for both of us. We'll pretend we're just home from an important date. Do you remember how we used to . . . . I'll read to you now, Mattie."

CHAPTER 21

. . . And driving down the road I get a feeling
I should have been home yesterday, yesterday . . .
Country roads, take me home/To the place where I
belong . . .

John Denver/ Bill Danoff/Taffy Nivert
"Take Me Home, Country Roads"

Josie planned a family tea party just as Mattie had requested. "Nice of Raymond's roses to bloom so early," Josie offered. "He probably planned it that way."

Ginger, David, and Jessica came up the night before the garden service to give Josie a hand. David had already made two runs into the valley to meet first Sarah and Luis, then Peter and Melanie at the Sacramento airport. Bo and Gerald drove up from Berkeley in the early morning with Caitlin, Ben, and the twins. David and his two uncles made a quick trip to the mortuary for the urn containing Mattie's ashes, and the family finally gathered amidst Raymond's roses.

"What a small container for such a grand person," Caitlin suggested, pleased that no one in the family seemed offended by her assessment of the urn and her aunt as she helped her mother arrange the table for Mattie's final tea party. Josie included some of her sister's spiced peaches in the afternoon tea, offering amusing tales of high tea with her English mother-in-law and allowing ample silences as individual moods bent and swayed with the currents of the moment, a peculiar blend of sorrow and elation that so often accents a family's grief. Bo had prepared a tender eulogy for his big sister, and Josie was relieved she had nothing she wanted to say aloud. David found solace in a poem Caitlin had written, as he did in the hugs that Jessica gave him so frequently. With Melanie holding tightly to his hand, Peter allowed some tears to flow when he offered the notion that the eldest really ought to have gone first, and Ginger and Sarah wept openly until one of Caitlin's children tumbled from Luis's lap and brought the service to a close, the adults hurrying to fetch band-aids and private moments.

Late in the afternoon, David saw that Josie was sitting alone on the redwood deck as the other women tended to supper chores. Alone but not lonely, full of sorrow but not despair, Josie welcomed her nephew's presence, delighting in his tall, handsome body as she delighted in the blend of family traits he had acquired and claimed as his own — a bit of Raymond, a bit of Mattie, a touch of Grandpa R, a hint of Peter, and a whole lot of warm, open David.

"Come sit beside me, David."

Auntie Josie," David said, "I've been wanting to talk to you. Hope you don't mind. Is this a good time? I've been wondering what your plans are now that Mom is dead. . . . You were wonderful to stay with her."

David waited for his tears to subside, took in a big gulp of air, and continued, "You know, Mom and Dad wanted this place to stay in the family. I'm the executor, of course, and Jessica and Sarah's kids, if she ever has any, will inherit this place. So nice Dad got the mortgage paid off before he died. . . . It's really beautiful here, isn't it?. . . . But you see, Josie, Ginger and I can't really leave the Bay Area yet — jobs, Jessica's school, you know, all that — and we were just wondering if there was any chance you would think about staying on here. Caitlin tells me she and her family are having a difficult time with housing, and I was just hoping it might work out for you to live here for a while. Maybe they could stay on at your place in Berkeley. Ginger and Jessica and I could come up on lots of weekends to help out with things. I talked to Sarah; she thinks it's a great idea. She's never around, but

380

I know she'd like to come home for holidays and gatherings from time to time."

Gatherings. . . . That was Mattie's word, and here is Mattie's son asking me about my plans. Do I have any? Am I supposed to have any? Do I want to have any? Most of my plans have taken me on good adventures, but not the adventures I had planned. Funny how that works. Josie was beginning to absorb what David was so gently proposing when Jessica, pigtails flying, came tearing around the corner of the house, followed close behind by Zachary and Sophie.

"Daddy, Daddy," Jessica called. "Mommy, says I can't play in the creek without you. I need to be supervised. You know how to do that, don't you, Dad?" The twins joined in the plea for a "grup," short for grown up, to do a little magic and make the creek available. Jessica had by then attached herself to her father's long legs, twisting forward to throw him a winning smile.

"How much you look like your grandmother, Jessic," Josie said.

"No!" Jessica shrieked. "Grandma Mattie had grey hair!"

"That's almost true. 'Silver' hair is what we called it. You don't get to have silver hair until you have told many, many stories to your children and to their children. Didn't your grandmother tell you lots of stories, Jessica?"

"Well, of course she did. She told me about the elves and fairies in the garden. In the winter they move into the house and live in the dust under my bed . . . and the story about how you fell in the sewer ditch, and she had to wash you all off . . . and about Daddy when he was a baby and got to see the man in the moon. Daddy tells me those stories now . . . and about how you got to have Misty when you were little and you got to ride in the wind. . . . Granaunnie Josie. I want a horse."

381

All the faces of the gathering turned suddenly to Josie as she lifted her eyes and looked out over Raymond's rose garden, Mattie's tomato patch, and the orchard, its branches just setting new fruit — apricots, plums, pears, apples, even the peaches might make it this year — finally resting on Raymond's unfinished greenhouse, still just a shell of a building, undefined except for its sturdy skeleton.

"And you shall have a horse," Josie announced, as she slowly stood and adopted an appropriate fairy-godmother walk, turning in a slow circle and softly tapping each child on the top of the head.

"Raymond's greenhouse will make a fine stable," she said. "Yes, each of you shall have a horse."

"Granaunnie Josie," Jessica shrieked, "Will you help me name my horse?"

"Of course I will, Jessie. Will you help me build a stable?"

The men were hurried off by the children to search Raymond's shop for hammers and nails as Ginger, Sarah, Melanie, and Caitlin joined Josie on the deck to watch the evening creep across the meadow and into the orchard, finally to the rose garden where a soft evening breeze was blending Mattie and Raymond's ashes.

EPILOGUE

Josie awoke to the sun streaming in the bedroom window. She could smell the aroma of coffee and was pleased.

"Sorry, Mattie," Josie said aloud to the empty house, although she knew in her heart the house would never be empty of Mattie's spirit. "I just couldn't deal with that coffee maker of yours. I want my coffee ready and waiting."

Josie thought about how things seemed to come around and around as time went by. Mattie had traded her automatic, electric coffee maker for a pressure pot that in Josie's opinion was primitive, something the cave women would have come up with. Josie liked her own coffee machine, the kind she could set up at night so that in the morning she could enjoy being a princess, with a maid preparing to wait upon her. It was a game Josie had taken to playing now that she was so much alone. If she felt a cold coming on, she would "prepare" for her illness, clean the bedroom, change the sheets, get a pitcher of water, snacks, books. She would finally bathe and put on her prettiest nightie. Only then could she become a pampered princess and climb into the huge bed that Raymond had built – so tall it was necessary to jump up and into it.

Josie had altered that situation, too. The bed was too high for the dogs and cats to join her, so she built steps out of scraps of lumber, using Raymond's tools and Jack's instructions from the part of her mind where he would always live.

Josie threw off the duvet, climbed down off the bed, and padded through the large living room followed by her growing menagerie."Alright you guys, time to go out, go hunting, go fishing, whatever you do," Josie ordered as she pulled open the heavy front door and watched her pets go scurrying. She was pleased to see the deer were in the meadow as she looked out over the land that was beginning to feel like home.

Following her usual morning routine, Josie brushed out her hair, scolded and teased her mirror-image companion about make-up issues, and quickly proceeded to Raymond's den to turn on his computer. As the machine was making its warm-up noises, she got her coffee and returned to check her e-mail. There was a short note from David saying they would be up for the Labor Day weekend to help winterize the horse barn. There was a longer, newsy letter from Caitlin which ended with a comment that they, too, would like to come for the holiday.

"Another gathering," Josie mused. "It goes on."

Josie clicked out of her e-mail program and opened Corel to a fresh document page.

"We won't tell them until it's done, Mattie. Won't they be surprised?"

Josie paused, listening to an answer only she could hear, and then, thoughtfully, slowly began to type:

"Once upon a time there was a storyteller who wrote this story just for you . . . ."

———